Black hearts and white minds?

Carl Gordon **is nothing if not in**

He's a New York Assistant U.S. Attorne... nightmares of his wife's death by lyin... ...ockville, Alabama, to enforce the Civil Rights Act. He arrives unprepared for life in the segregated South, where the Ku Klux Klan controls the town. It's not long before the Klan turns its attention to the outside agitator, him.

Oleatha Geary **wants no part of it.**

She's the tough and tender Black family matriarch who inherits a grand home in an all-white, race-restricted neighborhood called Northwoods. She doesn't want the home, but she's pressured by her adult children to fight Stockville's most powerful white citizens.

Stockville, Alabama, **is about to explode.**

It's the summer of 1964. Stockville is Alabama's fifth-largest city and its powerful white citizens think they've got "their coloreds" under control. Not so fast. Segregation is crumbling. Nonviolent protests have started, and a clandestine group of Malcolm X disciples is planning its revenge against the KKK.

Come decide for yourself...*Black Hearts White Minds.*

THE PRESS PRAISES MITCH MARGO'S
MISSION POSSIBLE PRESS NOVEL

"The early sixties are often thought of as a time of lost innocence. Margo reminds us that the era was anything but innocent in the American south. His novel rings with authenticity and his characters' struggles in the fictional town of Stockville, Alabama foretell the problems we still face today. Stockville is not really so far from Ferguson."

– Bill McClellan, St. Louis Post-Dispatch

"As I read *Black Hearts White Minds*, I was reminded by turns of Harper Lee, Willie Morris, and John Grisham. Like Grisham, Mitch Margo is an attorney; like Morris, he's a former journalist, and like Lee, his writing is evocative with a moral center straight and true. With our new president publicly insulting Civil Rights icon John Lewis and the new administration looking to reverse 50 years of progress, this Civil Rights era page-turner is a must read."

– Richard H. Weiss,
Former Daily Features Editor, St. Louis Post-Dispatch

"*Black Hearts White Minds* dives deep into the Civil Rights movement in the American South at a crucial time: 1964. But Mitch Margo sets his first novel in one Alabama town, allowing him to explore the era on a distinctly human scale through ordinary people and not so ordinary events. The result is a book that feels personal, rather than monumental. Margo, a seasoned lawyer who makes the law and lawyering an important but not overriding element of his story, has a knack for dramatic structure and a sharp eye for contrasting, engaging personalities. And his plot twists manage to be simultaneously startling and entirely credible, no mean feat."

– Eric Mink, Writer, The Huffington Post

"*Black Hearts White Minds* is an engaging tale of the Old South birthing the New South, with complications. Mitch Margo enriches his story of the institutional and personal conflicts during the Civil Rights era with characters whose responses are always felt and are at times surprising."

– Kenneth J. Cooper, Pulitzer Prize Winner

"While a work of fiction, *Black Hearts White Minds* transports readers to a time and place in American history, 1964 small-town Alabama, when the Civil Rights movement was slowly gaining traction, and segregationists, including the Ku Klux Klan, would stop at nothing to trounce the efforts of blacks and whites fighting for justice. Margo has crafted a narrative that is equal parts engrossing, heartbreaking and hopeful, populated with richly drawn, compelling characters, and an overarching essence that captures the enduring nature of the human spirit, no matter the obstacles."

– Ellen Futterman, Editor, St. Louis Jewish Light

ENDORSEMENTS FROM OTHER AUTHORS

"*Black Hearts White Minds* takes us back in time to a small Alabama town during the tumultuous civil rights era of the 1960s. At once magical and poignant and terrifying, the tale unfolds through the eyes of Carl Gordon, an idealistic but naïve East Coast attorney who moves down south with his reluctant son to enforce the Civil Rights Act of 1964 in hostile territory. He will soon learn the meaning of that Yiddish adage: Man plans, and God laughs. You will be enchanted by this powerful story."

– Michael A. Kahn, Award-winning Author,
Rachel Gold Mysteries Series

"Mitch Margo tells a story that combines love, painful history, politics, childhood innocence, prejudice and courage. This novel is filled with surprises at every turn, as well as life's lessons. You will want to read it more than once."

– Lenora Billings-Harris, Author,
The Diversity Advantage: A Guide to Making Diversity Work

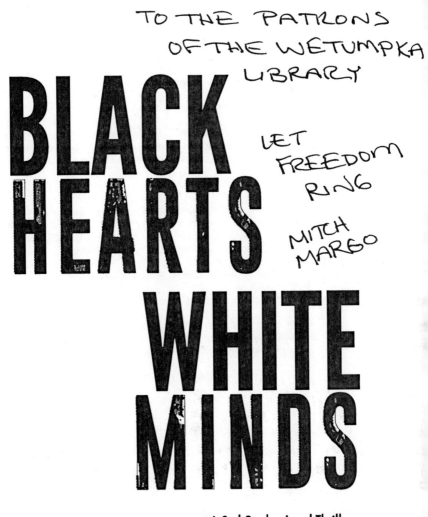

BLACK HEARTS

WHITE MINDS

A Carl Gordon Legal Thriller

The Mission is Possible.

May you thrive and be good in all you are and all you do...

Black Hearts White Minds © 2018 by Mitch Margo

For information address: Mission Possible Press

A division of Absolute Good, PO Box 8039 St. Louis, MO 63156

MissionPossiblePress.com

Cover design: Nick Zelinger, NZGraphics.com

MitchMargo.com

ISBN: 978-0-9861818-4-9

First Edition

Printed in the United States

Publisher's Cataloging-In-Publication Data
(Prepared by The Donohue Group, Inc.)

Names: Margo, Mitch, 1955-
Title: Black hearts white minds / Mitch Margo.
Description: First edition. | St. Louis, MO : Mission Possible Press,
      [2018] | "A Carl Gordon legal thriller."
Identifiers: ISBN 9780986181849 | ISBN 9780986181863 (ebook)
      | ISBN 9780986181870 (audiobook)
Subjects: LCSH: Lawyers--Alabama--Fiction. | African Americans--Alabama--Fiction.
      | Civil rights movements--Alabama--History--20th century--Fiction.
      | Alabama--Race relations--History--20th century--Fiction. | Legal stories,
      American. | LCGFT: Thrillers (Fiction)
Classification: LCC PS3613.A746 B53 2018 (print) | LCC PS3613.A746 (ebook)
      | DDC 813/.6--dc23

BLACK HEARTS HEARTS WHITE MINDS

A Carl Gordon Legal Thriller

MITCH MARGO

MISSION POSSIBLE PRESS

Creating Legacies through Absolute Good Works

Acknowledgments

It's difficult remembering all the people who had a guiding hand in my first novel, a book that had the gestation period of six manatees. But please know that it's with tremendous admiration, appreciation and humility that I acknowledge my friends and family who nurtured me, supported me, and on occasion lied to me (but in a positive and supportive way) on this journey.

Thanks to my son Sam who was the motivation for the original storyline, and who is, not surprisingly, the most important person in my life. To my wife Karen, who, for 24 years put up with my crazy ideas like taking 10 kids to play basketball in Italy, car dancing and writing this book.

Thanks to the Washington University fiction writing workshop teachers and students who so politely read and critiqued all the crap I wrote early on. Thanks to Debra Borden who believed I could write a novel and set the novel writing bar so high.

Thanks to Dick Weiss, my first editor, and the first person who said I should "show" and not "tell" because this isn't journalism, you know. Thanks to the Sugarcreek Book Club that agreed to read the manuscript in its earlier stages and gave me tremendous feedback to make the story better.

Thanks to my mom, Elaine Margo, who loved the story

unconditionally, and did I mention she's my mom? She's also a retired English teacher and I'm so lucky that some of her literary knowledge, grasp of sentence structure and grammar was passed down to me, I think through osmosis. Oh, and you, Spellcheck, I couldn't have done it without you.

Thanks to Julie Miesionczek, a real live NYC independent editor (and tough-love writing coach), who made me focus on the little things that are really the big things. Many thanks to Julie Appel and Mitch Gordon. They are great friends who are selfless and eager to help anyone, but in this case, me. There are many other friends too, who read the manuscript or the review copy and shared their ideas to make *Black Hearts White Minds* so much better: Sari Kushner, Susan Warshaw, Linda Rogers, Carl Lumley, Leslie Greenberg, John and Lili Bruer.

Thanks to the South Shore of Long Island Book Club that agreed to read the manuscript in its later stages, gave me invaluable suggestions to make the story better...and treated me to dinner.

Here's a big thank you to my good friend and erudite advisor, Charles Harris. Thank you, Charles, for spending hours with me and telling me the best story of all—your story of growing up in the segregated south. As you can see, I have used it and abused it, unmercifully.

Finally, thanks to Jo Lena Johnson and her Mission Possible Press for taking my manuscript and turning it into a book. Jo Lena, if your enthusiasm came in a bottle, I'd line up to buy a case.

July, 1964

CHAPTER 1

Carl Gordon peeled himself off the vinyl seat of his Mustang and stood in the motel parking lot, perspiration seeping through his polo shirt and chinos. He arched his back and stretched his legs by pushing against the concrete curb. He tensed his calf muscles. They still had some pop, even though he was nearly 35. The July afternoon Alabama sun bore down on his blond hair, which was closely cropped on the sides with a pompadour on top. He looked back to his 12-year-old son, who was still sitting in the car, biting his lower lip and staring straight ahead.

"Let's go," he said to his son, who had only occasionally spoken since their breakfast in North Carolina. Carl winced as John pulled hard on the chrome door lever of the brand new car, climbed out and slammed the door behind him.

"I wanna go home," John said.

"You've told me that at least five times in every state we've passed through," said Carl.

"Hasn't done any good," said John, glaring at his father and dribbling his basketball so that the New York Knicks autographs his father got him smacked against the sticky asphalt.

"This is going to be home for a while, so get used to it," said Carl. He motioned for John to follow him to the front desk.

"Welcome, travelers. Welcome to the Maker Oak," said the clean-shaven motel clerk, his dark green suspenders clipping worn dungarees that extended over his belly.

"Thanks. We need a room for a few nights," said Carl.

"Where you from?" asked the clerk.

"New York."

"You're a long way from home. Just passing through?"

"We may stay a while," said Carl, ignoring the bead of perspiration tickling its way from the side of his forehead down into his ear.

The clerk nodded, looking them over like a school teacher surveying a transfer student who showed up unannounced.

"You got business here in Stockville?" asked the clerk.

Carl swallowed and straightened his shoulders.

"I work for the government," he answered.

"Good for you," said the clerk. "The name's Purcell Foley. Welcome to Stockville, Alabama, the Family Town of the South. That'll be eight dollars a night for you and your boy, free local calls, no guests after ten and no niggers."

The words flowed from his mouth as easily as the local weather report. He slid a brass key attached to a green plastic medallion onto the counter between them.

"Room 6, two beds, fresh linens," he said.

Carl glanced down at John, who shifted uncomfortably

behind him and gazed out the window.

"Let's do two nights," said Carl, reaching into the pocket of his damp chinos for his wallet. Carl handed the clerk a twenty-dollar bill and picked up the room key, his eyes drawn to the WHITES ONLY neon sign in the window. The clerk removed four dollar bills from a dark green metal box and handed them to Carl. Then he opened a leather-bound guest book to a page held in place by a rubber band and set a ballpoint pen in the center crease.

"Sign right there," said the clerk, pointing to the next available line. "I suppose Stockville's going to be kind of quiet compared to Manhattan Island. But we got our positives. Veranda Lake has the best fishing in central Alabama. Hey, son, do you fish?"

John leaned in closer to his father, pressing his head between Carl's shoulder blades, seeking refuge from his new reality.

"He's shy," Carl lied. "We might try fishing, but he loves basketball."

"This is football country," said the clerk.

John sighed, and Carl felt the disappointed exhale through the back of his shirt.

"Crimson Tide...Auburn, you heard of them up north?" asked the clerk.

"Of course," said Carl. He smiled. Carl could handle sports talk in almost any locale.

"Room 6 is up that way on your right," said the clerk, gesturing to the far end of the parking lot.

Carl backed away from the clerk, nodding his head and smiling. John followed, his basketball pressed against his chest like battle armor. They let the glass door close behind them, and the humidity moved in on them like a New York street gang.

Inside, the clerk rotated the guest book so that it was facing him. He pressed his left forefinger just below where Carl had signed. With his other hand, he picked up the handle of the black desk phone and dialed. It rang once. Then twice.

"Bascomb," said the voice on the other end.

"Sheriff, he just checked in."

❦

Carl sat on the small wood-plank porch in front of Room 6 while John slept, pondering their first day in the deep South. He knew right then he was unprepared. His neck twitched every time that neon sign in the motel office window buzzed. He had lied to the Department of Justice committee that approved his transfer, telling them that his commitment to Civil Rights was sewn deeply into his moral conscience. He made up a story about befriending a Negro teammate while playing for his college baseball team. Carl reached into his pants pocket and drew out a small enameled pill box. He popped a Valium into his mouth and swallowed it without water. He walked into the motel room, stripped down to his underwear and lay motionless on top of the sheets of his bed until the drug kicked in.

On their third day in Stockville, Carl rented a furnished house on a tree-lined cul-de-sac just west of downtown. The two-story stucco house had a 'Bama-red front door and windows on all sides, four bedrooms, a modest kitchen and even had an upstairs sewing room, complete with a female mannequin and a trunk full of colorful fabrics. Carl figured he could make that his office. Carl saw it as a nice house, but all John saw was the basketball hoop in the driveway.

CHAPTER 2

Oleatha Geary stared out her front picture window waiting for three o'clock. That's when three generations of her family gathered for Sunday supper at her modest home. Attendance was mandatory. At 54, the family matriarch maintained much of the elegance she had as a young woman. Carrying an extra 20 pounds with flair, she had a fondness for flower-patterned dresses, most of them made by her own hands on the Singer. Oleatha adjusted her shortly cropped, chemically relaxed hair and beamed at her three children and five grandchildren coming through the front door.

Her firstborn, Micah, was a tough, muscular auto mechanic and part owner of a Sunoco service station. Much taller than the other Gearys, Micah had calloused hands, earned dismantling and reassembling car engines. His neatly trimmed mustache, sprinkled with grey, covered his entire upper lip, nearly hiding a one-inch scar at the corner of his mouth, which he refused to discuss.

Lenore Geary, Oleatha's second child, was 33 years old and beautiful as art. She had Oleatha's curvy outlines, high cheeks, hazel eyes and buttery cinnamon skin.

She had earned a Bachelor's and Master's Degree in Education from Ohio State University. Convincing her parents to let her go North to attend Ohio State over a full scholarship to Spellman took unrivaled logic and steadfast perseverance, strong points for the young woman who was so much like her mother they could hardly stand each other.

Lenore had a teaching job lined up in Ohio, and Stockville firmly embedded in her rearview mirror, when her father suffered a massive stroke two weeks after her college graduation. Within days of the funeral, Oleatha contracted tuberculosis. Lenore moved back home temporarily to cook, clean and nurse Oleatha back to good health.

"You know she did this on purpose," Lenore said to her brothers at the time.

"People don't will themselves into tuberculosis," said Micah.

"I thought you knew Mama," said her other brother Thomas, agreeing with Lenore.

Lenore became a substitute teacher at George Washington Carver High School while she tended to her mother. In less than a year, Oleatha recovered while Lenore was teaching social studies and humanities full-time. She was the most popular teacher in school with both students and faculty.

The youngest son, Thomas, grew to appreciate the formality of being called Thomas rather than Tom. Where Micah was big and powerful, Thomas, age 31, was lean, quick and compact. He earned a scholarship to Hampton Institute in Virginia, where he majored in political science, and returned from Hampton with informed and confident opinions, the charming optimism of his father and a wife named Evie. Thomas was the assistant executive director of the United Negro College Fund, and he started the Stockville chapter of the Southern Christian Leadership Conference.

"Did you hear there's a U.S. Attorney in town?" said Thomas, pulling up the rear.

"I suppose he's going to round up all the white folk and give them a good hand-slapping?" said Micah.

"Not all whites are racists," said Lenore. "I think some of them who you call racist just don't know anything but Jim Crow. They act the way their parents—"

"So it's okay to treat me like shit because your daddy did?" interrupted Micah.

Oleatha glared at him. "Don't use that language in my home. Things are better now than they've ever been," she said.

"That's not what I mean, Micah. It's in their blood. They don't know any other way," said Lenore.

"Last time I checked, their blood was red, just like mine. They need to see a little bit of theirs running in the streets."

"Violence won't get us anywhere," chimed in Thomas.

"Only when you've got white boys by the balls will their black hearts and white minds follow," said Micah.

"Oh, hush up, Micah," said Oleatha. It worried her how much rage Micah carried around.

"Let's have a peaceful sit-in," said Micah, mimicking Gandhi with his hands cupped together and his head bowed. "Let's all just sit down in the mayor's office. We'll bring a picnic and magically segregation will disappear and everyone will love thy neighbor."

"It's not magic. It's nonviolent," said Thomas.

"Little man, you need to read brother Malcolm. Just like you, he says we should listen to great white Americans. Like George Washington. There was nothing nonviolent about him. Thirteen crappy little colonies took it to the British Empire," said Micah.

"And you need to listen to Dr. King. Violence just creates more violence," said Thomas, shaking his head.

Micah rolled his eyes. "Ah yes, your hero. The 'I have a dreamer.' We have 22 million Afro-Americans. If we don't hang together, then we will certainly hang separately."

"You two stop it now," said Oleatha, handing Thomas the oven mitts. "Thomas, take the vegetables off the stove and turn off the burner. Micah, fill the water glasses." With less command and more sweetness, she pointed at her daughters-in-law, Evie and Roslyn, to fetch the three pies off the front porch.

"And Lenore, honey, sharpen the knife for the pot roast."

"Mama, the knife is still sharp from when I sharpened it last Sunday," said Lenore.

"Here's the sharpening steel," said Oleatha, one hand on her hip, the other pushing the instrument right through Lenore's comfort zone.

Lenore took it, turning away so her mother wouldn't see her pursed lips and narrowed eyes. As she ran the knife gently over the round sharpener, pretending to hone its already switch-blade sharpness, Oleatha, wiping her hands on her yellow embroidered apron, spoke again.

"Old Mrs. Paterson asked me about you this morning at church."

"What about me?" asked Lenore, who hadn't been to church since last whenever.

"Just if you're seeing anyone."

"What did you tell her?"

"I told her you were taking gentlemen callers."

"Mama, you didn't."

"Yes, I did."

"It's *my* business."

"Edwin Paterson is a good man with 50 acres. He's been walking in high cotton since Napoleon was in knee pants," said Oleatha.

"That's one acre per year. The man's 50 years old," said Lenore.

"Forty-eight. And honey, 33 ain't no spring chicken," said Oleatha, looking from one of her children to the next.

"Make nice, Mama," said Thomas.

"I don't know how many more good years God has left for me," said Oleatha. "I guess I'll just have to concentrate all my love and affection on the beautiful grandchildren I do have, not one of them by my only daughter, who—"

"That's a good idea," said Lenore, setting the knife on the oval chrome and glass kitchen table and figuring this fight was a draw.

"So Mama, when's dinner?" interrupted Thomas, a diversionary tactic from the dining room.

"In a little bit," said his mother, bending down to check the oven and stirring the pot of simmering okra, tomatoes and corn.

"I've always wondered, Mama," said Micah. "What's a little bit? Is it five minutes? Is it an hour?" Micah bit the bottom edge of his mustache to keep from smirking.

"I think it's twice as long as *directly*," chimed in Thomas. "Like when Mama says, 'I'll be there *directly*.' Thomas glanced at Micah, who flashed his eyebrows and smiled.

"Are you boys making fun of me?" asked Oleatha.

"No, Mama. But check back in a little bit," said Micah, as he ducked behind his younger brother, feigning fear of his mother. Thomas laughed.

"And hey, Mama, when you say you're going to see someone *by and by*, is that more or less time than *directly* and a *little bit*?" he asked, winking at Lenore.

Lenore just shook her head, filled her cheeks with air and continued folding the white cotton napkins next to each dinner plate. Her brothers were always able to poke fun at Mama and make her smile, but when Lenore tried it, it invariably led to hurt feelings and tears, followed by apologies, usually from Lenore. So instead of taking part in the Geary family banter, Lenore rearranged the square satin pillows on the velvet living room couch. Next she wound the mahogany clock that sat on the fireplace mantle and straightened the shade on the floor lamp beside the radio. It was her way to maintain invisibility.

Just then, Harry burst into the kitchen, inadvertently slamming the backdoor into the polished pine countertop.

"Grandma, I'm hungry. When's dinner?"

"Directly," said his father.

"In a little bit," chimed in his Aunt Lenore.

"By and by," said his Uncle Micah.

The most loquacious and precocious of the grandchildren, Harry stood staring, looking perplexed.

"Talking to Grandma now," Harry announced. "What are we having?"

"Pot roast," said Oleatha.

"I don't like pot roast. What else we got?" asked Harry.

Oleatha put her arm around Harry's shoulder, squatted a bit and looked him sweetly eye to eye.

"Honey," she said. "You know at your Grandma's home, you always have a choice."

Harry smiled in agreement.

"You can take it or leave it," she said.

Then as she not-so-gently pushed Harry back out the kitchen door, she said, "We'll call y'all in for dinner in two shakes of a lamb's tail."

Oleatha turned to her children, who were together standing shoulder to shoulder between the pocket doors separating the dining room from the parlor. They had been holding back chuckles, knowing from experience the answer Harry was going to get before he got it. Oleatha eyed the three of them like a sergeant doing dress inspection of her most favored troops and said, "Don't y'all be standing around useless as teats on a bull moose."

❦

Oleatha was tired by six o'clock, sitting at her kitchen table eyeing the stack of clean dishes yet to be loaded into the cupboard for next Sunday. The second and third generations of Gearys had left her home, and the loneliness of early widowhood returned. Oleatha stared at the varicose veins on the backs of her hands and at the shriveling on her fingertips which took longer and longer to disappear after washing the dishes. She reached across the table to the last wedge of lemon meringue pie and slid the plate to within fork's reach when the phone rang. *One of the grandchildren must have forgotten a notebook or baseball glove,* she thought. Oleatha picked up the receiver and spoke.

"Hello."

"May I speak with Oleatha Geary, please," said the female voice on the other end of the telephone call.

"Speaking," said Oleatha.

"Are you the wife of Lester Geary?" asked the voice.

"Widow."

"Excuse me, yes, I'm sorry," said the voice. "Your husband used to work at the Tatum Foundry?"

"Night shift manager."

"Please hold for Attorney Barry Beckley."

Oleatha removed her clip-on earring and held the receiver to her ear. She had never received a call from an attorney before and it was Sunday night. She got nervous that maybe something bad had happened to one of her children or grandchildren. She closed her eyes and prayed while she waited. Then she thought it might be news on the death of her great Aunt Velma in Albany. She waited some more. Her breathing became labored and she concentrated on pushing air in and out of her lungs. She considered hanging up when a male voice came on the line.

"Mrs. Geary?"

"Yes."

"My name is Barry Beckley of Beckley & Callahan. Ma'am, I am the executor of the estate of Theodore Tatum."

"God rest his soul," said Oleatha.

"Yes, Mr. Tatum passed last Thursday."

"I read it in the *Times-Gazette.* Who are you again?" asked Oleatha.

"I'm the executor. I'm in charge of his financial affairs

now that he's gone," said Mr. Beckley.

"Lester didn't owe Mr. Tatum any money, did he?" asked Oleatha.

"Nothing like that," he said, a small chuckle in his raspy voice. "But Mr. Tatum's will instructs me to contact all his beneficiaries and invite them to the reading of his will."

"Beneficiary?"

"Yes. Mr. Tatum left you something."

"Me?"

"It relates to your late husband, but since he's deceased, yes, you get the bequest."

"Bequest?"

"Like a gift. Sorry, I'll make it plain," said Beckley.

"What kind of gift?" asked Oleatha, as she nervously broke off a piece of the pie's crust and placed it into her mouth.

"I'm not at liberty to say. The reading of the will is at our office, 201 E. Washington Street, Wednesday at 3 p.m."

"Are you serious?"

"Yes ma'am."

"Can I bring my son or daughter?"

"Absolutely."

"This ain't no trick, is it?" asked Oleatha.

"No ma'am. If your son or daughter has a question, have them call me. Attorney Barry Beckley, Stockville, 325-8987."

"One moment, let me write that down," said Oleatha, her hand shaking and her voice cracking just a bit. "Thank you, sir."

"See you Wednesday then?" said Mr. Beckley.

"I guess so," said Oleatha, still suspicious.

Oleatha pressed down the button on the top of her table

phone long enough to get a new dial tone when she released it. She dialed Thomas's phone number at home.

CHAPTER 3

Jimmy Cooper, a handsome man with green eyes and a square chin wore his slightly receding hairline well. He kept his waistline from cascading over his belt buckle by playing touch football twice a week, and limiting his beer drinking to two glasses of Budweiser after the games. Jimmy had been Stockville's most decorated star high school athlete and played two years of football at Cumberland Junior College near Waverley before he blew out his knee.

"I love God, family and this magnificent shoe store," Jimmy said to his cadre of steady customers. "The Juniper Tree has the largest selection of children's shoes in Alabama and we sell only high quality shoes, and none of those new tennis shoes, which have no arch support. They'll ruin a child's feet."

Jimmy's confident smile and boyish dimples lent to his southern charm and his self-assurance that he knew every shoe he had in stock at all times. His favorite part of selling was making the kids laugh.

"How'd your foot get so pretty?" he asked Samantha, his

nine-year-old customer.

Jimmy slid the white patent leather size four on Samantha's foot.

"You must have inherited your mommy's pretty feet," said Jimmy, looking up at Samantha's mom with a smile and a wink. "Take a little stroll darling. How do those feel?"

Samantha looked at her feet in the tilted floor mirror.

"Mommy, aren't they beautiful?"

"Samantha is her cousin's flower girl next weekend," said Ginny Anderson, whose mother had bought all Ginny's shoes at the Juniper Tree when she was a girl.

Samantha gushed and twirled around twice, her shoulder length blond hair swinging like a square dance. She scurried back to where Jimmy was straddling the bench and gave him a big hug.

"I love them," said Samantha.

"They're lovely," said Ginny.

"Can I wear them home, mommy?" asked Samantha.

"Too fancy for a weekday," said Ginny.

Jimmy winked again at Ginny, knowing that those white patent leathers were sure to make their maiden voyage at the weekend wedding. He loosened the tiny buckle of the Mary Janes, a style that had been part of the inventory since 1904, when Jimmy's grandfather bought a license to sell them while at the World's Fair in St. Louis. Jimmy removed the shoes, wrapped them in their pink tissue paper and placed them toe-to-heel back in the cardboard box.

"On your account, Ginny?"

"That's great, thanks."

Ginny and Samantha left the store hand-in-hand and Jimmy watched them stroll down the sidewalk. He turned back into the shop, noted it was five minutes to noon, locked the door and began ambling down Deacon Street. *Another perfect day in my paradise*, he thought. The midday sun was hazy behind low clouds, making his clothes feel tight and sticky.

Jimmy had been eating lunch at Woolworth's every working day for the past seven years. He sat at his regular spot in the back booth with Paul Owens, the editor and publisher of the *Stockville Times-Gazette*. Owens had a youthful excitement which still lingered under his 50-year-old surface. A pot belly had snuck in where sit-ups previously governed. His slacks were belted below his belly, which meant they sat half-way down his backside, making him look like he had no behind at all.

"What's tomorrow's news?" Jimmy asked, sliding his six-foot frame onto the green, laminated bench seat.

"If I tell you, you won't buy the paper," said Owens.

"I've been a subscriber for 30 years," Jimmy said with a laugh.

"Front page has a story about Governor Wallace throwing his support to Goldwater."

"Never thought I'd see the day that a Republican would get any help here," Jimmy said.

Jimmy respected Owens, a respect that had to be earned by anyone who wasn't Stockville born and bred. Owens attended the right church, his wife belonged to the right clubs and their children were brought up to be righteous. The puffiness under Owens's eyes and his plasticized cheeks could be traced to his fondness for Southern Comfort, straight up and often, and the Lucky Strikes which burned between his teeth. In his down moments, which lately came more frequently, Owens thought bourbon and cigarettes were his only dependable friends.

"Tomorrow we're running a big picture on page one of Ellie Baxton, the Spanhower High School homecoming queen who has enrolled at Ole Miss."

"She's a looker."

"Pictures of pretty girls sell papers," said Owens, who, if nothing else, was certainly a pragmatist.

"You've got a great paper," said Jimmy.

"You say that because your picture has been in it so many times," said Owens. He raised his arms, outstretched above his shoulders, like a ringmaster directing a crowd into his circus tent. "October 26, 1947," he announced. "Headline. 'Spanhower High Star Scores Three Touchdowns in State Championship.' Isn't that right?" he asked Jimmy.

"Long time ago, who remembers?" Jimmy replied. It only took him a moment to add, "Four touchdowns."

Both men chortled. They'd had this exchange at least twice a year for the past decade. When Jimmy took over the Juniper Tree the *Times-Gazette* ran a two-part feature on the store, calling it "the best children's shoe store in the South," an accolade occasioned in part by the *quid pro quo* of a weekly full-page ad the Juniper Tree purchased every Thursday. The story had included two large pictures of Jimmy, one with his father and grandfather in front of the store in 1935, and the other of Jimmy, his wife Patty and sons Jimmy Jr. and Oren standing in front of their four-pillared home in the Northwoods neighborhood, Stockville's exclusive enclave.

It was a residential community of born-wells and married-wells, conceived during Reconstruction by Confederate ex-patriots seeking to regain their social superiority. Some called themselves visionaries; cynics thought the more accurate moniker might be *re-visionaries*. The neighborhood tolerated the arrival of a recently self-made man, as long as his wallet was full and his background Anglo. The Northwoods men heralded themselves a cut above the rest of white Stockville. They were bankers, doctors, entrepreneurs, as were their sons and grandsons. The truly bright attended Harvard, Yale, and Dartmouth, or at least Vanderbilt, as did the reasonably bright son-legacies, their resumes vitamin-enriched with trust funds or campus landscaped quadrangles named for their grandfathers. The academically less-endowed attended University of Alabama, and made up for their lack of a high functioning neo-cortex by joining the best fraternities.

The Northwoods women played bridge at *the Club* while Negro maids in white uniforms supervised their husbands' heirs. The maids were bussed into and out of the neighborhood, with public transportation allowed access to Northwoods twice a day, once in the morning to drop them off, and once in the late afternoon to usher them out. The residents felt there was no other reason for a bus to soil the park-like, pristine streets and cul-de-sacs.

By 1964 there were 98 homes in Northwoods, one built on every available acre lot. The homes were sturdy brick, colonial or Tudor in style, and kept immaculately uncluttered most of the time. Edith Spinz, aging widow and the daughter of Stockville's first state congressman, was the self-appointed, honorary mayor of Northwoods. She was its den mother, its guardian of all things perfect and proper.

Spinz, dependably attired in a summertime tangerine pleated skirt, hemmed exactly two inches below her knee, and a white cotton blouse closed at the neck by a cloisonné broach, drove around the neighborhood in her '62 Cadillac, stopping to remind those who needed reminding that their pampas grass should be trimmed or that parking the family Buick in the driveway instead of the garage was collectively frowned upon. Always wearing one of her colorful scarves which held her hair-sprayed bouffant in perfect harmony, she believed it her God-given obligation to straighten off-kilter Negro lawn jockeys, much the same as Florence Nightingale's mission was delivering medicine to the infirm. In Northwoods, arriving home and finding a Spinz note, always inside a pink envelope and quietly referred to as a *Spinz-ter*, tacked to your front door was like having your house quarantined for smallpox.

Even the Cooper and Owens families were Spinz-ter victims on occasion, guilty of high crimes like *failure to remove duck droppings* or harboring glass doors that were *improperly Windexed*. Most of the Northwoods men, including Jimmy Cooper and Paul Owens, viewed Spinz-ters as women's problems, like yeast infections and stomach cramps.

"Got a Spinz-ter just the other day," said Jimmy. "Seems we've developed a crack in the driveway which exceeds Edith's 16-inch acceptable crack allowance."

"She's our acceptable crack allowance," said Owens.

"That's why you're in the newspaper business," responded Jimmy.

Jimmy ordered a BLT on toast, heavy mayo, French fries and a Coke. It arrived with Owens's egg salad three-decker sandwich, chips, apple pie and lemonade. The two men talked politics, the weather, kids and wives, but as usual the conversation drifted to sports by mid-sandwich.

"Bama's going to win it all this year," said Jimmy.

"Auburn will beat them just like last year," said Owens, a '34 grad.

"Nobody's going to stop Namath."

"What's with that? The Tide go to Pennsylvania to find a quarterback?"

"He's special," said Jimmy, wiping mayo from the corner of his lips.

"Loud-mouthed Yankee is what he is. DOA in this year's game."

"Wouldn't want to make a wager, would you?"

"Ten bucks," said Owens, reaching into his pants pocket, drawing out a ten dollar bill and smacking it down on the table.

"Deal," said Jimmy.

Jimmy finished his lunch and pulled his napkin from his shirt collar, checking that his thin, striped tie made it unscathed.

"Be there tonight?" he asked.

"Not really my thing."

"Okay, see you tomorrow," said Jimmy.

Jimmy put a dollar down on the table and headed for the exit.

Back at the Juniper Tree, Jimmy made four more sales that afternoon. It was rare that a customer left empty handed, due to Jimmy's adept salesmanship and the fact that the Juniper Tree was the only children's shoe store in town. As the clock approached 7 p.m. he tallied the day's take and smiled. He had sold seven pairs of boy's shoes, four of them to the Sanders family, and five pairs of girl's shoes. *Thank God for summer weddings*, Jimmy thought.

Closing up for the night, Jimmy walked his aisles of shoes with purpose and grace, like a bride to the altar, smiling at the symmetry and beauty of his kingdom. He emptied the brass cash register, and placed the day's receipts into the stockroom safe. Then he stopped at the back room closet, pulled out his keys and unlocked the door. He returned to the checkout counter holding a large, white rectangular cardboard box in both hands, steady and proud, like a soldier carrying a wreath to the grave of his fallen general. He placed the box on the counter and gently lifted the top off to make sure he had everything he needed. He looked inside and smiled, appreciating the meticulous attention to detail of his faithful wife.

"What a sweetheart," he said aloud, though he was alone.

Jimmy gazed into space for a few moments. He closed his eyes, bowed his head and mouthed a small prayer, thanking the Lord for his two healthy sons, his shoe store and his good fortune. He breathed in the aroma of tanned leather and cardboard, as intoxicating to him as garlic and cumin to a chef. Jimmy's attention settled back on the open box. His white robe was immaculately pressed and folded. The hood was perfect, with just a hint of starch to keep it neat and erect. The embroidered red circle with the white star prominently displayed on the front of the robe made his pulse quicken.

He glanced at the meeting agenda he'd prepared between customers:

1. Pledge of Allegiance.
2. Old Business.
3. State Fair entries.
4. Voter Registration.
5. Kicking the ass of the goddam New Yorker back where he came from.
6. Niggers who need a message.

CHAPTER 4

Carl arrived back at the Maiden Lane house with bags of food, a tool box and a giant pea-green attic fan strapped in the trunk of his quickly depreciating car. While John shot baskets outside alone, Carl had gone grocery shopping and stopped at a road-side flea market. It took Carl and John 30 minutes to lug the vintage, 60-pound fan up the stairs and shimmy it into the now screen-less window of their second-floor sleeping porch. Looking at the four-foot square behemoth teetering in the window frame, and knowing his father's dubious mechanical history, John was sure of one thing: he would not walk outside underneath it.

"Who wants to do the honors?" asked Carl.

He was holding the heavy-duty electric plug proudly in his left hand, gesturing to the outlet on the wall with his right. His affectation reminded John of the smiling models at the annual New York car show they used to attend together.

"Sir, wouldn't you look handsome behind the wheel of this new Chevrolet?"

Unlike the pretty models, however, Carl had perspired completely through his short-sleeved shirt and khakis. He had a habit of speaking as if he were lecturing to a jury, even when John was the only person in the room.

"Not me," said John. "That thing looks like it came out of the laboratory in *The Bride of Frankenstein.*"

"As you wish, then," said Carl, reaching his arms in front of him, channeling Boris Karloff. Carl rambled toward the wall, arms locked straight out in front of him, grunting, "I am no monster!"

Carl jammed the slightly fraying two-pronged plug into the wall socket. Nothing. Then a low rumbling. Then the motor inside the fan made a guttural noise like a Bowery bum awakening from a whiskey sleep. John recoiled. The blade started to turn. Slowly at first, and then faster and faster and faster and faster.

It was only then that John discovered that an attic fan didn't blow air into the house like a normal fan. Instead, it pulled the stale air from inside, out. The inside air was replaced by fresh outside air being sucked in from the open windows on the other side of the house.

In 15 seconds the fan had reached a spectacular speed, raucous and chugging. First the morning newspaper that had been lying open on the kitchen table came flip-flopping, page by page, up the stairs and right at him. Then some legal papers from Carl's desk down the hall streamed by and were sucked right against the cage surrounding the gargantuan propeller. Carl delighted. John shuddered.

"Good thing we don't have any pets," yelled Carl, as several Dixie cups danced their way along the floor and jumped into the fan.

John pleaded, "Turn that thing off!" but Carl was dancing with his hands in the air like a football referee signaling a touchdown.

"I'm going to turn it up to max," Carl yelled. "Here, take this rope and tie yourself to the dresser."

Carl handed John the rope they used to haul the fan upstairs. John's eyes panicked.

"I'm only kidding. It can't suck you in. I'll turn it down to medium."

Carl turned the rusty dial, the wind settled down a bit and the pages of Carl's reports and the Dixie cups fell to the floor. On medium, there was a nice breeze and the knowledge that if they could get used to the noise, a good night's sleep lay ahead.

Having sweat through his clothes for the third time in three days, Carl pulled up a red-cushioned wicker chair, placing its back three feet from the fan, his legs splayed, so that the breeze circulating around the house passed right over him. In the moments that followed, Carl allowed himself the indulgence of his recollections.

❧

Carl had graduated near the top of his class from Abraham Lincoln High School in Brooklyn and City College of New York, but he was in a different league at Columbia Law School. He readied himself to contend with the Yale and Princeton stiffs but the student he found himself most inclined to avoid was neither of those. There were 260 men and 11 women in the 1949 first year class, and Carl quickly learned that only Beth Schoenwald of Montclair, New Jersey, turned heads. It seemed to him that Beth might be the first law student in history to experience the equivalent of a fraternity rush for a law student study group. In Contracts class she was shy and modest, but delivered a bolt of Socratic lightning when appropriate. At the student orientation luncheon she introduced herself as an introvert with good social skills. Carl spent the entire fall semester dedicated to steering clear of Beth Schoenwald. *Too risky*, he thought.

Six weeks into the spring semester, Carl was hunkered-down at the library, neck-deep into *Prosser on Torts*. As he tried to focus, a familiar scent of jasmine, rose and spicy vanilla floated along the blond oak tables and over his stack of law books: Schoenwald. He continued reading, keeping his head down, soldiering on. But in the next few minutes he read the same page three times and absorbed none of it. He sighed and placed his bookmark back in its spot halfway through the chapter entitled "Infliction of Emotional Distress." *A bad omen*, he thought. He spoke anyway.

"What's that you're wearing?" he asked in a library whisper.

Beth looked up and around her stack of books. A hint of lipstick glossed her smile and, with her sandy hair tied back in a ponytail, she looked the part of a big-time college cheerleader. Carl was smart enough to know this woman would not take that as a compliment.

"Is that a usual conversation starter for you?" Beth whispered back.

"No. Most of the time I say, 'Hey lady, you smell good,' but you seemed more classy than I'm used to." Carl was suddenly aware of his Brooklyn accent.

"I am," she said, and returned to her text book.

"It's Chanel. Right?"

Beth looked up again, this time without a smile or any readable expression on her alabaster face. Her arms and neck appeared translucent in the illuminated green glass of the table lampshades.

"How do you know that?" she asked.

"I worked summers in the perfume department at Macy's."

"Pretty impressive," said Beth, setting her pen down on top of her class notes.

"Thank you," said Carl.

"Why are you here?" she asked.

"I want to be a lawyer. Why are you here?"

"I mean tonight. Why aren't you at the mixer?"

"Valentine's Day? It's never been my favorite," said Carl, allowing his voice to rise to a level where it might annoy a nearby law student.

"Too bad. I think it's special," said Beth.

"Shhhh," said the student.

"Why's that?" asked Carl, shooting the other student a look that said, 'mind your own business.'

"I'll make you a deal. If you invite me to have coffee with you now, I'll tell you a secret."

Carl thought for a moment, trying to assess all possible outcomes.

"Would you like to have coffee?" he asked.

"What a great idea. Yes I would."

Carl and Beth closed their law books with the precision of synchronized swimmers. Carl shuttled his things into an ostentatious black briefcase, a best-he-could-do graduation gift from his Uncle Preston; Beth slipped her books into a beige canvas satchel, its Dior label discretely sewn into the shoulder strap. Together they strolled past the library's turnstiles, and once outside a slice of the Manhattan moon edged out from behind a shadowed cloud and lit a path to the coffee shop on Amsterdam Avenue.

"What's the secret?" asked Carl.

"I'm not wearing any perfume."

❦

Carl's sturdy chin dropped and his neck reflex snapped him back into the Alabama evening. He knew that a sweat-free sleep certainly couldn't hurt John's morale, but it wasn't going to make Stockville that much more appealing either. He decided John needed a plan. After dinner, Carl suggested John make a list of the good things about their new home. After sitting in front of a notepad for ten minutes, John had one item on the list, a good basketball hoop in the driveway. On the other hand, he had written down 16 dreadful things about living there.

God awful hot, was number four.

No friends, was number three.

Missing Shirley, was number two.

No mother, was number one.

John shook his head, crossed his arms on the table and then lowered his face into his arms so his father wouldn't see him crying. John knew he couldn't have his mother back and Shirley was probably working for another family by now. He also knew he couldn't do anything about the heat. It was obvious that new friends weren't going to find him. He decided that if nobody stopped by while he was outside playing tonight, then tomorrow when his dad went to work, he was going out on his own.

That night when John fell asleep, Carl unfolded John's tear-stained list. He rubbed his eyes and willed himself not to cry. He reached behind the stack of coffee cups in the painted cabinet, grabbed the small bottle he had placed there, and popped a Valium into his mouth. Then he picked up the receiver of the kitchen wall phone and dialed Shirley's phone number.

CHAPTER 5

Men in white robes began bursting out onto Main Street in the grey dusk of downtown Stockville, like popcorn cooking over an open fry pan. As the colors of the Alabama daytime receded to shades and shadows, the white men in white robes exited Buick sedans, Chevy pickups and delivery vans. They popped out of taverns and storefronts on foot. Main Street was a chess board of white pieces moving in patterns down the street between the rows of two story brick buildings. They greeted each other with confident handshakes and laughter. As if being drawn by magnets, their pace quickened so that the cotton flapping against cotton of their robes sounded like hooked fish slapping against the floor of a boat. They were all heading to the meeting of the White Citizens' Council.

The Stockville White Citizens' Council headquarters was relocated in 1962 to a two story brick building, a former furniture warehouse, necessitated by an increase in membership in reaction to the burgeoning Civil Rights movement. The warehouse provided enough space for both the weekly board of directors meetings and the monthly full membership gatherings of the 16th Battalion of the Imperial Knights of the Ku Klux Klan. By day, Stockville's Klansmen blended seamlessly into the country landscape. Some were farmers, some worked construction and some were veterinarians, day laborers and successful businessmen. They were fathers and grandfathers, devout husbands and active church members. All folds of white Stockville's geographic and socio-economic fabric were welcomed and represented.

But for the white cotton robes with pointed headgear donned by all the members, a passerby might have easily mistaken the Klan meetings for an Elks Club convention or Stockville Chamber of Commerce reception. In this, the regularly scheduled monthly meeting of the faithful, there was no need for anonymity, so the members wore their hoods, absent the facemasks which were often employed in the late night burning of Negro homes or churches or when extracting revenge for Negro civil disobedience. The white cotton robes were tied around the waist, some with a green rope and others with gold. A few of the members, distinguished by great feats of segregation, had earned shiny green sashes that they draped over their right shoulders, rejoined at their opposite hip. Embroidered into their robes, covering their hearts, was a large white X inside a red circle, the size of a softball. Centered on the X was a small black diamond and inside it, a bright red drop of blood.

The main meeting room offered a showroom's worth of space adorned with brown wood folding chairs set up for the usual crowd. With the "Negro Problem" on the rise in

Stockville, the July meeting overflowed with more than 100 robed men, congregating in groups, smoking cigarettes and making small talk. At precisely 9 p.m., the Grand Cyclops, he alone dressed in a radiant scarlet robe and hood, entered the room and took his seat with the other Klan leaders at the raised dais. One of them stepped up to the podium, tapped the microphone to make sure it was working and called the meeting to order.

"Attention everyone...attention. Please find a place," said the organization's secretary, a heavy-set man with bushy eyebrows and a round, clean-shaven face. When the membership had assembled, still standing, he led the traditional opening statement and all members joined in.

I pledge allegiance to the flag of the United States of America. And to the Republic, for which it stands, one nation, under God, indivisible, with liberty and justice for all white men.

"White power," yelled one man in the back right corner, as enthusiastic as if they had just finished singing the Star Spangled Banner at a baseball game and he was yelling, "play ball!"

"White power," answered the rest.

The secretary guided the membership through the more mundane agenda items.

"Congratulations to member Frank Salter, whose daughter earned a blue ribbon at the Alabama State Fair for having raised an award-winning heifer. Best of luck to member Sean McDonnell's son Jacob, who is headed to the University of Oklahoma on a full academic scholarship."

The secretary then asked for an update from the Voter Registration Committee. Ezra Turner, one of the other men on the dais stood up and switched places with the secretary. Turner, a tall, lean man with a full head of jet-black hair, was considered the finest lawyer in Stockville, both in courtroom presentation and political connections.

"I am happy to report that in the last quarter the Alabama Sovereignty Commission has successfully prevented the voter registration of 17 Stockville Negroes."

Turner waited for the smattering of applause to subside.

"The newly legislated literacy requirement for Negroes has been extremely effective in keeping uninformed citizens off the voting rolls. I am confident that the test will pass constitutional scrutiny and will keep our great State of Alabama safe and pure for years to come."

More applause.

"Are there any questions?" asked Turner, tipping his hand from his forehead to the eager crowd. The group was silent. "I'll turn the microphone over to the head of our Public Safety Committee."

Up stepped Sheriff Peter Bascomb in his scarlet, silk robe.

"As you know, there have been many nigger problems in Birmingham, Montgomery and Mobile. So far I think our niggers still know what's best for them. Most are happy with the way things are. I've been getting reports that outside agitators are targeting Stockville. You probably heard that Washington sent an assistant U.S. Attorney here. A young pissant, name of Carl Gordon. If he's smart, he'll get the hell out of Alabama and run his Yankee ass back to New York."

"He don't know shit about Stockville," yelled a man in the third row.

"We're going to be vigilant," continued Bascomb, "to let those integrationists and subversives know there ain't no place for them in Stockville."

Alger Stock, whose great-grandfather founded the city, stood up.

"I heard that Martin Luther Coon is coming here next week."

"I got no report on that. I do know that the *Times-Gazette* is preparing to run an article that proves that for the last ten years King has been closely advised and controlled by communists."

"He's asking for a stringing up," yelled one of the Klansmen.

"Last item I got to report is we're keeping an eye on two niggers here in town. I got a complaint that one of them has been shooting his mouth off a little too much and was seen being friendly with one of our girls. The other one has been trying to organize our niggers to join the protesting," said the sheriff.

"Send a message," screamed a member from the back.

"Loud and clear," said another.

The secretary stepped back up to the podium. Sheriff Bascomb turned and saluted his fellow Klan leaders on the dais. Then he walked down the two steps on the side of the raised platform and out the front door of the building to return to the sheriff's department.

The last man to address the crowd was Jimmy Cooper, the chairman of the Stockville chapter of the Alabama Commission to Preserve the Peace. A Governor Wallace creation, it had subpoena power and a mandate to keep the southern way of living intact. It also used its legislative authority to circumvent both law enforcement and the courts.

"I just have two items tonight," said Cooper. "Our dear friend Ted Drummond who couldn't be here tonight sends his thanks. He came to our committee last month with irrigation difficulties when his well went dry and he didn't have access to the river on the other side of Melba Nickens' farm. Well, good news. The Nigra Nickens has agreed to sell her acreage to Ted. Many thanks to Don Logan at The Central Alabama Seed Company for letting the Nigra Nickens know that he couldn't guarantee there would be enough seed for her next year or whether he'd be able to extend her credit. I believe that helped her make the right decision."

Cooper pointed to Don Logan.

"Stand up and be recognized, Don," said Cooper.

Logan stood up to a vigorous round of applause.

"White power," yelled a man in the front row.

"I hear she's moving to Chicago," said Cooper, biting his upper lip to keep his smug smile to a minimum. "After the formal part of our meeting, we've got refreshments courtesy of Framingham General Store. There's checkers and cards on the tables in the back. If there's anything on your mind, come on up and visit with me. One last item," said Cooper.

Cooper raised his hands over his head and made a gesture for everyone to quiet down. When he had their attention, he continued.

"My lovely wife, Patty, has asked me to remind all of you that the 2nd Annual Stockville Cotillion is set for October 22nd. Last year we raised almost $4,000 with all proceeds going to support the Central Alabama Children's Fight Against Cancer. This group does amazing medical research and treatment of children with cancer, and also helps families cope with the expenses of caring for their sick children. Same as last year, I'm going to kick off the fundraising right here, right now, with a pledge of $250."

The crowd applauded.

"So please help. Buy tickets to the event. Make donations. I hope to see all of you at the Cotillion. Thank you and good night."

CHAPTER 6

Oleatha, Thomas and Lenore arrived at the law office of Beckley & Callahan precisely at 3 p.m. They had actually arrived 20 minutes early and sat on a bench in the shade until they were on time. If it was up to Oleatha, they'd have left her house hours earlier for the 12-minute drive.

Thomas opened the wooden door next to the brass wall plaque inscribed with the law firm name. Oleatha entered first, immediately noticing the six identical dark red leather-like chairs in the waiting room, perfectly aligned with nailhead, faux elegance. Lenore followed close behind, walking slowly, allowing her eyes to adjust from the bright Alabama sunshine. Thomas approached the frosted sliding window and as he did a hand from behind it slid it open.

"Good afternoon," said a young brunette woman.

"Oleatha Geary is here to see Mr. Beckley," said Thomas. "I'm her son Thomas. This is my sister Lenore."

"He's expecting you. Please have a seat and I'll let him know you're here," she said.

Thomas was guarded at the pleasant and respectful

greeting, his defense mechanism learned from a lifetime of societal bait and switch. Oleatha had dressed like she was going to church on Easter. She wore a white and gray woven hat with a small black strip of lace falling half-way down her forehead. Her dress was red, green and white, a tulip pattern that was fitted above her waist and flowing below. Oleatha sat down and sank comfortably into one of the chairs, arranged in a rectangle around a glass coffee table. Lenore sat across from her mother, suspicious as much about the unusual meeting as she was that her mother invited her to attend.

Thomas remained standing and skeptical. He surveyed the four walls covered with original oil paintings, each one depicting a different Alabama Civil War battle, identified by the small silver plaque centered at the bottom of each matching rococo frame. There was the Battle of Athens, Battle of Day's Gap, Battle of Decatur, Battle of Fort Blakely, Battle of Mobile Bay, Battle of Selma and the Battle of Spanish Fort. From his American history course at Hampton, Thomas knew that his home state had the dubious distinction of being the only southern state where every Civil War battle of consequence was won by the Union Army. He smiled.

Moving down the row of paintings Thomas wondered about the attorney he was about to meet. What white businessman in Alabama would prominently display these paintings, each one depicting retreating confederate battalions, advancing Union troops, confederate flags burning as grey-suited Confederate soldiers ran for their lives, bloodied, some with missing limbs. *This is going to be interesting*, Thomas thought.

Just then Barry Beckley burst through the door.

"You must be Thomas Geary," he said, offering his handshake. Thomas and Beckley shook hands comfortably and Beckley offered Thomas a genuine smile rarely exchanged in Stockville between people of different races.

"This is my sister, Lenore," said Thomas.

Beckley smiled and nodded his head. Lenore put her left hand up to her chest and offered her right for a handshake. Beckley was already moving away and didn't notice.

"And this must be Oleatha," said Beckley, taking Oleatha's right hand in his right hand and then placing his left hand on top, an act of unusual congeniality between a white man and a Negro woman. Beckley's hand, like the rest of him, was rounded and thick. "Please follow me," he said.

Beckley led them back to a conference room where he pulled out a chair next to him for Oleatha, who instead sat down at the far end of the table and crossed her arms. She looked uncomfortably at Lenore who was noticing the water rings on the wood table and the eight chairs surrounding it. Five of the chairs had matching blue upholstery, two were black leather and one had a green and gold weave on the chair that sat tilted back like a rollercoaster car going up the track. A handwritten note taped from one arm rest to the other proclaimed, "Don't even think about sitting here."

Barry Beckley was large. His light blue button-down oxford cloth shirt had to be at least a 3XL, and still pulled in all directions under the pressure of his just sitting down. His tie, loosened around his burly neck and reaching only to the bottom of his well-insulated rib cage, indicated egg salad for lunch. He wore brown loafers and no socks, a necessity, thought Oleatha, for someone unable to touch, or even see, his toes. Oleatha looked at the critically injured chair and thought it must be a Barry Beckley victim. Thomas sat down next, to the right of his mother. Lenore sat on her left. Beckley spoke first.

"I asked you here a little early," he said, and Thomas immediately crossed his arms. *Another example of separate and unequal*, thought Thomas. Beckley, extra-large in perception as well as total volume, picked up on the body language.

"Let me explain," he said. "Ted Tatum and I were close friends as well as lawyer and client. As you can see from looking around the office, we're not your fancy corporate law firm, but Ted wasn't your normal titan of industry either."

Lenore unfolded her arms and now was genuinely intrigued. Oleatha put her white-gloved hands on the table and remained steadfast.

"Ted never married and had no family. He told me 20 years ago that he was sure he'd live to age 82, and he died last Thursday on his 82nd birthday. There was no sign of foul play or suicide. He even died like he said he would."

"Lester always spoke fondly of Mr. Tatum. I didn't know he was laid up," said Oleatha.

"Ted kept to himself most of the time. He was always specific to me about what he wanted done with his money," said Beckley. "Much of it is going to charity as you'll see in a few minutes. I just wanted to be available to answer any questions you might have before I bring in the other beneficiaries."

Thomas smiled at his mother and shrugged his shoulders.

"And you can't tell us exactly why we're here?" said Thomas.

"That's right. The fact that you're a beneficiary should

give you some idea. It's all good," said Beckley.

"I don't count chickens before they hatch," said Oleatha.

Any other questions?" asked Beckley.

"No," said Thomas.

"Nope," said Oleatha. Lenore shook her head.

"I'll be right back," said Beckley, as he pushed himself out of his chair and left the conference room.

Thomas took his mother's hand and cleared his throat. "This should be interesting," he said.

"I can't wait," said Lenore.

When Beckley returned he had three others with him and made introductions.

"This is Lenore Geary, Thomas Geary and their mother Oleatha Geary. Please meet Pricilla Wentworth, executive director of the Central Alabama Audubon Society, Mr. Nathanial Vincent, president of the Alabama Children's Aid Association and Mrs. Edith Spinz, President of the Northwoods Neighborhood Association."

The guests nodded their heads at each other, but handshakes were not exchanged.

"Pleased to meet you," said Mrs. Wentworth to the Gearys. She was a tall woman, dressed impeccably with matching red shoes and scarf tied smartly around the neck of her dress, an outfit you might expect to see at a southern evening function, rather than an afternoon meeting at a storefront law office.

"Good afternoon," said Mr. Vincent, tipping his straw fedora before placing it on a gold hook at the top of the corner coat rack. He wore an older-styled, but well-preserved, brown pinstripe suit, with a stiff-collared white shirt and a 1930s artsy tie.

Spinz sat down without a greeting. Everyone found a seat

around the table, as Beckley nervously shuffled documents in front of him.

"Thank you all for coming today on such short notice, but this was exactly how Ted Tatum instructed me, as executor of his estate, to settle his affairs after his death," said Beckley. "I see no reason to wait, so I'll begin by reading the Last Will and Testament of Theodore R. Tatum."

Beckley stood up and unfurled the blue-foldered, legal-length will by untying the red ribbon around it and giving his hand a flip. He looked like a burly town crier about to announce the king's arrival.

"I, Theodore R. Tatum, being of sound mind...spent it all, thank you very much."

Beckley laughed and looked around the room, where all the others sat stone-faced.

"Sorry, that was a little joke of mine," he said. He started again. "I, Theodore R. Tatum, being of sound mind and body, do hereby declare this will to be my last will and testament. I wish that my assets be divided as follows."

Beckley again looked up and around the table. All eyes stared at him.

"My greatest pleasure in later life has been the restoration of the antebellum plantation called Clarkson Hill, which I purchased in 1951 but which has gone unused during my lifetime. It is now restored to its pre-Civil War beauty, and I desire that it be used by the community as a park and museum. I am therefore donating Clarkson Hill to the Central Alabama Audubon Society, with the following caveat."

All attention in the room turned to Mrs. Wentworth, who coughed politely into her hand and moved closer into the table, turning her head slightly to the left so as to hear what was coming with her good ear.

"This gift is contingent on the Audubon Society continuing its policies of non-discrimination. At no time shall there be any rules or regulations limiting the use or enjoyment of Clarkson Hill by all people regardless of race, religion or any other distinguishing feature or factor. If Pricilla Wentworth is still the society's executive director at the time of my death, I want to say 'well done Mrs. Wentworth, keep up the good work and thank you.'"

Beckley looked up from the will at Mrs. Wentworth, who pulled a white handkerchief from her dress sleeve and demurely tapped it on the bridge of her nose. Beckley continued.

"As some of you who are sitting in this room know, I was abandoned by my father when I was six years old and left in an orphanage. I wouldn't change that for anything, because the hard-scrabble times made me who I am, but at the same time I wouldn't wish that childhood on my worst enemy. The rest, residue and remainder of my property I leave to the Alabama Children's Aid Association so that the organization can continue the good work it does for unfortunate children. This is probably as good a time as any to tell them that the anonymous annual $100,000 donations have been coming from me for the past 22 years. So I guess the bad news is you won't be getting those anymore."

"I never knew," said Mr. Vincent, looking around the table with a huge smile.

"Just so you know," said Beckley. "I estimate Mr. Tatum's estate to be worth about $7 million."

"Oh my God. The board of directors...what a glorious

day," said Mr. Vincent.

Thomas and Oleatha looked at each other again, feeling the wonderment of the situation, but still not knowing why they were included in this meeting.

"There's more," said Beckley. He continued reading.

"For the past 37 years I have lived at 55 Watkins Road in the Northwoods neighborhood on Stockville's west side. It's a lovely area but not without certain problems and neighbors who can be closed-minded."

Beckley hesitated and looked up. A short huff was heard coming out of the nose of Mrs. Spinz, and her back arched just a little more than usual.

Beckley continued reading. "Although modest, I believe my home to be a perfect symbol of the American dream, that anybody in this great country can achieve success."

"Modest?" Interrupted Mrs. Spinz. "His home is one of *our* best."

"Let me continue reading," said Beckley, a smile gently curling up around his upper lip.

"One great American who I had the pleasure to befriend was Lester Geary. He was the hardest working and most entertaining man I have ever known."

Thomas moved his chair closer to the table, he unfolded his arms from in front of his chest and placed his left hand on top of his mother's right. Oleatha dabbed the corners of her mouth with the tissue she had nervously balled up in her left hand.

Beckley read on. "Lester told me incredible stories and kept me laughing so much that I purposely stayed at the company late into the evening when Lester ran the late shift. Lester was the best shift foreman ever at the foundry.

Unfortunately he died too young, leaving a family that I regret I never got to know, except through Lester's stories. I hereby gift and bequeath my residence at 55 Watkins Road to Lester's wife, Oleatha Geary, and I want her to know that her late husband was as good a man as our creator has ever made."

Oleatha sat motionless at the end of the table, her mouth open and her eyes unfocused. She wasn't at all sure what just happened. Thomas chuckled. Then he laughed out loud.

"Mama," he said.

Oleatha turned toward him and shrugged her shoulders.

"Mama, you own a home in Northwoods."

Lenore quickly cupped her hand over her mouth and bit her lip to hide her astonishment.

"Don't be silly, Thomas," said Oleatha. She turned the other way and looked at Beckley.

Beckley nodded his head affirmatively. "Yes, Mrs. Geary, your son's right. You now own Mr. Tatum's home and property. Well, you will when you sign the paperwork."

Beckley paged through the pile of documents on the table in front of him, pulled out a folder and asked Mrs. Wentworth to pass the deed for the house to Oleatha.

"Wait one minute," protested Mrs. Spinz, bolting to her feet on her side of the table. "She can't own that house. There are no Negroes allowed in *my* neighborhood. Give me that deed," she said, lunging in a most unladylike way across the table, but unable to reach it.

Mrs. Wentworth handed the deed to Thomas, who put it safely inside his jacket pocket.

"No you don't," said Spinz directly to Oleatha. "We've got a restrictive covenant since 1902. No niggers. This is not going to happen."

"Please settle down. There's more," said Beckley.

Spinz stopped talking but didn't sit back down. She swayed nervously from foot to foot and in her light pink blouse over a darker pink skirt she looked like a buoy bobbing up and down in the harbor.

Beckley continued.

"Finally, I asked Mr. Beckley to invite the president of the Northwoods' Neighborhood Association today, because they will claim that Negroes cannot own property or live in Northwoods because of an antiquated and unconstitutional race restriction in the Northwoods' trust indentures. Therefore, as incentive to change the neighborhood's racist ways, I further bequeath to the Northwoods' Neighborhood Association the sum of $100,000 if, and only if, within 30 days of this date, the residents vote to remove the hateful and illegal restriction."

"That's a bunch of hooey," said Mrs. Spinz, her ears flinching and her eyes blinking as she grew angrier. She banged her fist on the table, which made everyone jump back in their seats. "If you think you're moving into Northwoods, with that lawn jockey of a son sitting next to you, well you... you...have another think coming," spurted Mrs. Spinz.

"Do I need to call the police?" asked Beckley.

"No counselor you don't. I'm leaving."

Spinz glowered at Oleatha, who was clutching the neckline of her dress and holding her large brown purse in front of her for protection. Spinz knocked into Mrs. Wentworth as she raged toward the conference room door. When she slipped slightly, her Jackie Kennedy pink circle hat flew off her head onto the floor, where she accidentally stepped on it with her white sensible shoe. She didn't bother to pick it up, and when she pulled open the door, she turned back to the group and glared at Oleatha.

"We'll see you in court," she said.

CHAPTER 7

Carl believed in romantic celebrations and on his and Beth's first Valentine's Day anniversary, their second year in law school, Carl bought her a heart-shaped pizza with meatball slices in the shape of an arrow and vowed to make all her Valentine's Days special. Their second anniversary Beth woke up to see Carl dressed as Cupid, wearing a red satin sash and a ring of leaves in his hair, a cardboard fig leaf and nothing else. They laughed and made love all morning, missing their classes. Their third anniversary, six months into their marriage, he made her wait all day wondering if he had anything planned and then arrived, riding in a velvet-lined, horse-drawn carriage, champagne flutes balanced on the tips of his fingers.

"Dear lady, will ye join me for a frolic 'round Central Park?" he asked, as he bowed and almost fell out. Beth was too stunned to do anything but laugh.

Beth had graduated from both high school and NYU as the salutatorian of her class. Carl was certain that she had calculated exactly what it would take for her to rank second to avoid the valedictorian spotlight. Years later Beth cringed any time Carl articulated that theory, but if she was clever at manufacturing her class rank, she displayed brilliance in timing the birth of their son. Conceived in September of their third year in law school, John Matthew was born on May 22, 1952, ten days after classes ended and two weeks before Beth began her clerkship for Judge Charles Edward Clark in the 2nd Circuit Court of Appeals. Judge Clark appreciated Beth's hard work, great research skills and edgy writing style. She clerked at the court until April, 1961, when Beth first noticed there was something wrong with her.

At the beginning, she thought she was just getting clumsy when she dropped her pencil or knocked a glass of milk off the kitchen counter. When her entire left side went numb one morning she called Dr. Nathan Gilbert and underwent some tests. Dr. Gilbert telephoned a few days later.

"I'd like you and Carl to come in," he said.

"Just tell me," said Beth.

"Why don't I stop by later?"

"Please."

"It's not good, but you should see a specialist before we jump to any conclusions."

The diagnosis, confirmed by two neurologists, was that Beth had ALS.

For a few months Beth walked slowly with a cane and then transitioned into a wheelchair. As the motor neurons in her brain and spinal cord shut down, her legs went limp and lost their athletic shape. Her arms dangled, lifeless, like the roots growing down from a banyan tree. Beth's speech slurred and then disappeared entirely when her tongue refused to take directions from her brain. John sat with her, reading to her and showing her his latest basketball moves, which included dribbling on the blond oak floors, a practice his parents had previously banned.

On Valentine's Day 1964, 14 years to the day they officially met, Carl sat on the edge of their bed looking down. The only part of Beth's body she could still control were her eyes, which followed Carl as he settled in a spot where he thought she could easily see him. He squeezed her hand and wiped the persistent drool leaching out of her stationary lips. He brushed her long brown hair away from her face, like sweeping his fingers over the strings of a harp.

"I love you," he said.

Carl picked up the fluffy heart-shaped pillow that he had embroidered with the words *Love Potion Number 9*, his gift to her on their 9th Valentine's Day. He pictured their summer strolls at Jones Beach. He smiled, remembering the splendid debates he lost to her.

"You're magnificent," he said. He imagined a blink of recognition. There was an occasional, random muscle twitch, but other than that, nothing.

"Remember when we brought John home from the hospital? Your father drove and he refused to go more than 15 miles an hour? 'Precious cargo!' he said."

Carl used the white lace edging of the pillow to wipe his eyes.

"I know what you're thinking. How is this idiot husband of mine going to manage his job, the apartment, and Lord knows he's going to screw up our son."

Carl laughed nervously, moved in, and kissed Beth gently on her forehead.

"I promise you, Beth. I can do this. I'm going to be the guy you think I am," he said.

Carl shifted his weight and instinctively held the pillow to his chest. He looked over to Beth's nightstand. The silver-framed 8"x10" of them on their wedding day was a road map unfinished. Vows unfulfilled. Carl clasped his hands together to stop them from shaking. He took a deep breath and placed the pillow over Beth's nose and mouth. He held it there and whispered goodbye. Beth was pronounced dead a few hours later by Dr. Gilbert.

❦

Shirley Wallace's devout Christianity, evidenced in both stature and conviction, sometimes clashed with her sense of fair play. She navigated through difficult decisions, erring on the side of pragmatism over theology. Her skin was the color of French roast coffee, and her face was long and glassy. She wore her dark hair pressed and curled like her favorite singer, Mary Wilson of The Supremes. Though she had her high school diploma, Shirley didn't mind cleaning white families' New York City apartments. Other Negroes who migrated north worked in textile mills, furniture factories and for clothing manufacturers. Even the women. Shirley made enough money to save a few dollars each month and was happy to be in New York City, ecstatic to be anywhere out of the South.

Hired as a once-a-week housekeeper for the Gordons in 1960, before Beth's illness, Shirley cleaned other apartments in their building at the time. She agreed to move into the Gordon's apartment six months before Beth died.

"Good salary. And I don't have to pay rent," she told her roommate when she moved out of their Long Island City two-bedroom.

Shirley was fearless and spirited, and believed she could do the job of any two white women. Living with the Gordons, she could still clean the other apartments in the building when Beth didn't need her to run errands or help her navigate the bathroom or kitchen. Shirley also went to night school. At age 43, she was only 14 credits shy of a degree at Pace College of Nursing.

When Carl read her John's list of dreadful things about Alabama, and she heard that missing her was second and that "no mother" was number one, her voice cracked and she took a deep breath. In the week since Carl and John left for Alabama she couldn't get thoughts of John out of her mind.

"Just a month," Carl had said. "John asks about you every day."

"Not fair, Mr. G. You're playing to my weakness."

"He says my cooking isn't like yours, he misses talking to you. Your hugs are better."

Shirley was delighted to hear that John missed her too.

"I'll think about it," said Shirley.

"You'll have a chance to visit your father in Birmingham."

"Bombingham," she corrected him.

"You could help him with the arthritis in his shoulder," said Carl.

One of Carl's best attributes was that he remembered. *He must be a damn good lawyer*, Shirley thought.

"You are so charming, Mr. Gordon," said Shirley.

"Just a month," Carl promised again. "Just help us get acclimated."

"Ain't nothing good going to come from this," she said.

"It'll be a vacation for you more than anything," Carl said.

"You've been doing a lot of hiking and putt-putt golf so far?" Shirley asked.

"Not exactly."

"That doesn't sound like a vacation."

"Maybe vacation is too strong a word. What would you call it?" asked Carl.

"Stupid."

"Come on, Shirley."

"Crazy."

"Okay, crazy. Same salary as in New York."

To drive the persuasion home, Carl returned to his obvious strong suit.

"I can't tell you how happy this would make John. If you could be with him when I'm working. Your evenings would be completely open. Weekends too."

"I'll think about it," Shirley said again.

"So you'll consider it?"

"You make it sound so good," said Shirley. "I'll get back to you."

Shirley thumbed the phone lever off. She looked around the crowded third-story walk-up she shared temporarily with three women friends. School was out until September and several of the white families for whom she cleaned were away on summer vacations.

This would be a chance to see John again. Visit her father. Good pay. *Why not*, she thought.

Three days later there she was in her blue pleated skirt and white blouse, sitting in the third row of the Trailways bus. There was no denying it. Damn if Alabama wasn't coming up the roadway by morning.

Shirley broke out in a rash outside of Philadelphia and suffered a shortness of breath by the time the bus passed through D.C. At dusk, she felt the grind of metal on metal as the bus driver down-shifted and slowed. The bus bucked just a little as they left Route 33 and entered the peripheries of downtown Greensboro.

"We're stopping in Greensboro for 15 minutes," announced the driver. "We've got a few people to drop off here and we're scheduled to pick up a few more."

Shirley decided her best strategy was to sit still, read her Bible and mind her own business.

Sit like I don't exist, she thought. She remembered that much.

As the bus pulled into the station, Shirley stared down at her lap. She recollected the first rule of being Negro in the South—avoid eye contact with white people. Head bowed. Subservient. Obedient. Like a well-trained dog. Shirley clasped her hands together and willed her fingers to stop their nervous twitching. Sweat formed on her forehead and shifting slightly, she felt her skirt sticking to her thighs. The warm air felt close and slept in. It was as if there was a familiar odor hanging from the tree branches, wedging the entire town tightly in 1950.

My God, I'm back, thought Shirley. Her heart pumped at twice its normal rate. Her face lit on fire, her lips numb from biting her teeth, adding to her uneasiness. To calm herself she read from Isaiah.

"Those who hope in the Lord will renew their strength. They will soar on wings like eagles; they will run and not grow weary, they will walk and not be faint."

Shirley's private moment was interrupted.

"Ma'am...excuse me ma'am?"

Shirley looked up to see the bus driver, a tall, balding man with eyeglasses struggling to stay put on his forehead.

"I'm sorry, was I reading too loud?" Shirley asked.

"No ma'am. We're in Greensboro."

"Yes I know."

The bus driver swallowed hard and his jaw clenched. He looked like a marine sergeant dispatched to relay tragic news to a fallen soldier's parents.

"You'll have to move to the back of the bus."

🌿

CHAPTER 8

Carl held the steering wheel with a death grip, as his new Mustang seemed to have a mind of its own. The owner's manual described the inaugural 1965 Ford as an aerodynamically designed sports car to be driven at high speeds on paved roads. On Stockville's country gravel and dirt, the steering wheel fought against his every turn, bucking and rocking side-to-side like the Tilt-A-Whirl at Coney Island. Carl fought back, weaving right and left to avoid the deeper gullies and honking the car's horn to scatter wayward chickens. Carl drove three miles out of town, far removed from civilization, even as he now lived it. He passed fields of dark soil, dotted with row after perfect row of small corn stalks that reminded him of headstones at Arlington Cemetery. He drove past bevel-sided shanties, with small children playing marbles in the bottomland dirt out front. He wasn't even sure he was heading in the right direction or had enough gas to get there and back.

In another half mile he reached a wide open cotton field and at the far end spied a small brick building with a church spire at the top. He steered the Mustang toward the front of the building. Above the door in wooden letters painted gold was an inscription: *First Thankful Baptist Church of Stockville.*

When moving, the Mustang provided some breeze in the thick Alabama summer air, but now that the car was parked, the late afternoon weighed on him like a hot air balloon. The pants of his blue cotton suit grabbed the backs of his legs. In spite of the heat, he re-buttoned the top collar button of his white dress shirt and tightened the knot of his forest green and yellow striped tie up to his neck. He put his suit coat back on out of respect and to make a good impression.

Out of the car and bending down to the side-view mirror, Carl slipped his black comb from his back pocket and plastered his windblown hair back in place. He walked up the stairs of the church and knocked on the door. No answer. He knocked again. No answer again. Grabbing the oversized silver door knob, he turned it to the left and pulled the door open.

Inside, eight rows of dark-lacquered wooden benches flanked a center aisle. At the front of the church was the pulpit, two feet high with a wooden podium, painted white, surrounded by two hardback chairs. On the wall behind the podium hung a large wrought iron cross, painted black, and a handcrafted sign reminding the parishioners to *Walk with Jesus.* A single ceiling fan twisted in the rafters high above.

In the far corner, Carl spotted a middle-aged man, hunched on all fours, hammering nails into a replacement slat of pine. Carl cleared his throat, both to dislodge a mouthful of dust and to announce his arrival.

"Excuse me sir, I'm looking for Pastor Williams," Carl said.

The man, dressed in a white undershirt and overalls, first looked up, then slowly rose to his knees and pushed himself up the side wall. He stood there, wobbling a little, catching his breath and checking Carl out for what seemed like an uncomfortably long time, without saying anything. Then, peering out from over his bifocals, he said, "That would be me."

Carl approached, thinking he might be met halfway, but the pastor remained where he was. Pastor Williams held out his hand and Carl watched as his own hand disappeared inside the pastor's enormous grip. Pastor Williams, a ring of grey hair circling his otherwise bald head, had deep creases on his forehead and clear brown eyes, shining like buttons on a new overcoat. Big shoulders topped his six-foot frame.

"I serve the Lord in many different ways," he said. "I repair warped souls and warped floor boards too. Are you lost?"

"No, I'm a Christian," Carl replied.

"Son, I mean what brings you to my church?"

Carl blushed and sweat returned to his brow.

"Oh. I'm Carl Gordon, Assistant U.S. Attorney."

"Are you?" said Pastor Williams.

"Yes sir."

"Where are you from?"

"New York."

"Are you?" he said again. "What brings you to Stockville?"

"The Justice Department. On orders of President Lyndon Baines Johnson, I'm here to monitor and enforce the Civil Rights Act."

"Are you?" he said a third time, nodding his large head, and treating Carl as if he was a mischievous child caught in a flimsy lie.

"At least you're smiling while mocking me," an emboldened Carl said.

"Am I?"

"Mocking me?"

"No, smiling," said the pastor, the skin wrinkling around his eyes as a bigger smile crept up the corners of his mouth. "How long have you been in town, son?"

"Five days," said Carl.

"Congratulations, you're still alive," he said, a big smile taking over his face. "Come on back."

The comment made Carl flinch and his gait unsteady. He brushed a flood of perspiration from the spot just behind his left ear.

Pastor Williams waved for Carl to follow him into the church's small rectory. Without saying anything, the pastor picked up the receiver of the phone sitting on his desk and dialed. Carl watched.

"Thomas. It's Pastor Williams. Can you come out to the church?"

The pastor gestured to Carl to sit down on one of the four metallic chairs which sat around a rectangular lacquered wood table.

"Yes. Right now," said the pastor into the phone. "There's someone here I think you should meet." He hung up the phone and turned back to Carl. "I took the liberty of asking Thomas Geary to join us. He'll be here in 10 minutes. How old are you?"

"Thomas Geary is the second name on my list of people

to contact, after yours. I'm 35, why?" asked Carl.

"Just wondering. I think Thomas is about your age. I guess you know he's the head of the Stockville chapter of the Southern Christian Leadership Conference."

"Yes sir," said Carl.

Pastor Williams poured two glasses of sweet iced tea and placed them on the table. He asked Carl about his background, his family, the Justice Department and New York City. When Carl asked the pastor about himself, the pastor adeptly ignored the question and continued exploring Carl. A few minutes later the men heard a car pull up outside and Pastor Williams opened the rectory door to let Thomas Geary in.

"Thomas, meet Carl Gordon, United States Attorney General," said the pastor.

Carl and Thomas exchanged handshakes.

"Assistant U.S. Attorney," said Carl. "Robert Kennedy might not like it if I take his title."

Thomas poured himself a glass of tea and hung his suit jacket over the back of a chair. The suit had a silky sheen woven into the fabric and Carl made a note to ask what kind of suit it was, since it appeared to be wrinkle-free compared to Carl's one-hundred percent cotton monstrosity. Thomas loosened his narrow red tie which was clipped to his white shirt half way down his chest. His full head of dark black hair had been recently trimmed close to his scalp. Thomas had a relaxed and confident demeanor. He looked friendly, a look Carl realized was missing from everyone else he had met in Stockville.

"Thomas, I heard a rumor that your mama might be moving," said Pastor Williams.

"It's true. It's crazy. Old Mr. Tatum left her his house when he died because Pops was one of his favorite employees."

"The Geary family moving to Northwoods?"

"Mama says she doesn't want it. Lenore and I think she should take it. Micah thinks it's a white supremacist plot. At the reading of the will, the president of the Northwoods neighborhood association said they'd keep Mama out. They have a race restriction."

"They can't do that," said Carl.

"What?" asked the pastor.

"Keep her out. Race restrictions in neighborhood indentures are unconstitutional."

"Wish I had a nickel for every unconstitutional action of the Klan," said Thomas. "Enough about the Gearys, we've got sit-ins to plan. We have training sessions almost every morning. Would you like to observe?"

"Absolutely. Don't people have to work?" asked Carl.

"Most of our volunteers are college students. Some have part-time jobs but they're out of school for the summer."

"I'd like to learn first-hand. Most of what I know, I've just read about," said Carl, sensing his heart beat slowing down to normal. He felt comfortable admitting his lack of experience, at least to Thomas.

"I think what's most important long-term is voter registration," said Thomas.

"What's the percentage of Negroes in this county?" asked Carl.

"We're 57 percent. But we make up six percent of the voters," said Thomas.

"How—"

"Literacy tests," interrupted Thomas.

"I couldn't pass, could I?" asked Carl.

"I don't know. Can you name all 67 of Alabama's county judges and the year each was appointed to the bench?"

"No."

"Can you tell me the year Mississippi was admitted to the Union?"

"No."

"And how many bubbles are there in a bar of soap?"

"Seriously?"

"All real questions on the application," said Thomas, putting his hands in his pockets and shrugging his shoulders.

Carl's nostrils flared. Thomas's expression remained stoic and unchanged. He had Carl's attention. Thomas explained his idea to boycott any store that would only sell to Negroes on certain days at certain times, or not at all. Thomas mentioned a voter's rights march in August.

Pastor Williams mostly listened intently and politely, all the time shaking his head in seeming affirmation. Carl took notes. In all, Thomas mentioned 14 action plans, non-violent demonstrations, and boycotts. Carl offered the National Guard to make Stockville's whites-only public schools open their doors to Negro school children, even though he had no authority to make such an order. Carl said he could back up Thomas's boycotts with the might of the United States federal government, if necessary, even though Carl wasn't sure he could deliver on that promise either.

The pastor often sat back in his rocking chair and looked up at the ceiling when he was thinking. The late afternoon sun bounced off his forehead and highlighted his ashen temples. He stroked a day's growth of white beard with his right hand and rocked back and forth some more. Then, for the first time in an hour, Pastor Williams spoke.

"I think you should go," he said to Carl.

"I'm not due back in town until 8 p.m."

"I mean go back to New York," said the pastor.

Thomas looked away. He had seen this before. The pastor was clearly going off script.

"I think I can help here," said Carl.

"Son, have you ever seen a lynching?" asked the pastor.

Of course he hasn't, thought Thomas.

"No sir," said Carl.

"Can your federal government guarantee me that when we take on this crusade I'm not going to find one of my brothers hanging from a tree?"

"I can tell you that the Department of Justice will use all of its resources to punish anyone who breaks the law," Carl said.

Thomas could see Carl falling into the pastor's trap, but he was unable to rescue him from the pastor's warnings.

"Or you, hanging from a tree?" asked the pastor.

Carl flinched. His pragmatic side knew there was danger in accepting the Stockville assignment, but he'd never heard someone actually say it.

"Time to go," said Thomas, trying to stop the conversation before it scared away Carl. He grabbed his jacket and handed Carl his jacket too, indicating the end of the meeting for Carl as well. "I need to get home to Evie and the kids," he said.

Thomas and Carl both thanked the pastor and left the church together. Once outside, their conversation turned personal.

"How many children do you have?" asked Carl.

"Three. Harry is 12. Denise, eight and Cara six. How about you?"

"Just one. John, also 12."

"A wife?" asked Thomas.

"Beth passed away five months ago after a long illness."

"I'm sorry," said Thomas.

"Thanks. Maybe we can get our boys together sometime," said Carl.

"Your New York is showing," said Thomas.

"My accent?" asked Carl, "I hope that's not a—"

"No, not that. This is Alabama. Harry has never played with a white child."

"Huh. Any chance we might break that color barrier?" asked Carl.

"I'd like that," said Thomas, placing his brown felt fedora back on his head. Thomas handed Carl his business card from the United Negro College Fund, writing his home phone number on the back. Carl didn't have a local business card yet, but gave Thomas a card from his New York office, also writing his Stockville phone number on the back. Talking to Thomas was like winning the lottery, thought Carl.

"You can usually find Harry and me at the Carver High School playground after dinner," said Thomas.

"I'd like to talk to you more about SCLC's plans," said Carl.

"Anytime. I hope Pastor Williams didn't scare you off."

"Interesting character."

"He's a great man with a history, but every time I talk to him I leave thinking he's up to something."

Carl and Thomas shook hands again, this time matching palm to palm perfectly.

Carl wasn't the same after Beth died. He was rarely home, and he forgot John's 12th birthday. He found fault with just about everything his son did.

"Stop bouncing that damn ball."

"Can't you figure it out yourself?"

"Leave me alone. I'm busy."

John responded to his father's impatience by withdrawing. He rarely spoke. Shirley continued living at the apartment out of loyalty and a developing affection for John. She noticed John's personality changing and, four months out, realized that although she loved the boy, her shoulder to cry on was no permanent solution. She called Eugene Maylor, a minister and Carl's high school classmate who had presided over Beth's funeral. Pastor Gene had visited Carl a few days after Beth's memorial service and Carl told him, "You can go to hell and take Jesus with you."

The pastor, who was the varsity football team's middle linebacker in high school and checked in at 6'4" and 250 pounds, could have decked Carl right then, but divinity school had taught him to turn the other shoulder pad. Instead, he cringed, hesitated, opened his mouth with every intention of telling Carl to "shove it where the sun don't shine," but backed off instead. He was back, knocking at the apartment's front door, sure that weeks later, Carl would have calmed down. Carl opened the door.

"You again?" said Carl.

Pastor Gene, dressed in a heavy black overcoat, filled the entire opening like a highway billboard set on its side. He ducked his head so as not to hit it on the doorway casement and walked past Carl to the center of the living room, as if this was his home, not Carl's.

"Fine, thanks for asking," said the pastor.

"What do you want?" asked Carl.

Pastor Gene turned his back to Carl, slipped his massive hands out of their black leather gloves and placed the gloves on the edge of a mahogany end table next to the couch. He unwound a grey woolen scarf from around his neck, and pulled it inside one of the sleeves of his coat which he set down on the couch's arm. He turned, and glared down at Carl.

"I don't know why the good Lord chose to take Beth," said the pastor.

Carl was shaken. *That was me, not your good Lord,* he thought.

"If you were to ask me what you did to deserve this terrible fate, I wouldn't know. My guess is that you didn't do anything," said Pastor Gene. "Let me ask you this—back in high school, when you aced chemistry, did you look up to God and say, 'Dear God, what did I do to deserve such a good grade?'"

"Your point is?"

"When you got your dream job in the U.S. Attorney's Office, did you ask God why you were deserving of such good fortune?"

"I worked hard for that."

"And when John was born, I bet you didn't ask, 'Oh Lord, what have I done to deserve this beautiful, healthy son.' What I'm trying to say is, I'm not sure you're asking the right questions."

"Anger is the answer to all the questions I have right now, Gene."

"Sad *is* hard," said Pastor Gene. "But you have to embrace it."

"Just flush the dead turtle down the toilet?"

"No, it's more than that," said the pastor.

"It's settled, leave me alone."

Carl walked down the hallway to the apartment's front door and opened it, indicating that their conversation was over. Pastor Gene didn't move and his facial expression remained impassive. He wasn't giving up that easily this time.

"You need to get to a place where, when you think about Beth, there isn't the soul-shaking pain. Try looking for melancholy instead," said Pastor Gene.

"Got a road map, padre?"

"God."

"All your roads lead back to Him."

"Look, maybe you're not the luckiest man in the world like you thought, but you're still lucky. You've got John and he's a living, breathing, growing reminder of Beth."

"Yes, constantly," said Carl, who hesitated and looked away as he wiped a tear with his sleeve. "And you think that's good?"

Carl crossed the room. Gene just stared at him, a silhouette, with the sun full tilt behind Carl. Gene was acutely aware that his brow was popping with beads of sweat. Though massive in stature, with a full, erudite black beard, Pastor Gene was still unsure of his skills as one of God's consolers. Carl sensed the insecurity and made another move across the room for the front door, but like a bishop on a chess board, Gene moved quickly and blocked Carl's path, towering over him like Moses on Mount Sinai.

"I don't give a shit if you're dead set on ruining your own life, but John's too?" he asked.

Carl steadied himself on the dining room chair. Then he sat down, wavering hands covering his face. He stayed like that for a long time, and the pastor didn't budge. Carl didn't dare shed his burden. But finally, he looked up at the pastor, his upper lip trembling and staccato breathing holding back a stream of tears. Carl stood up, fought off a moment of dizziness and walked back to John's bedroom, navigating the narrow hallway, his eyesight hindered by tears rolling down his cheeks. John stood in his doorway, pretending not to have heard the whole thing. Carl opened his arms, unsure whether John would retreat or respond. John took one look at his father and started crying too. Carl stooped down to one knee and John ran into his arms. They hugged the way they hadn't since John was much younger.

"I'm so sorry," said Carl. "I promise you, I'm back. Things are going to be better. *We* are going to be better."

"I miss her so much," said John, his wet cheek resting on his father's shoulder and his long, spindly arms wrapped tightly around Carl's neck.

"Me too," said Carl.

"What are we going to do?" asked John.

"I'll think of something," said Carl.

The next day Carl walked into the office of his division head and asked if the job he saw posted for an Assistant U.S. Attorney to monitor the just-passed Civil Rights Act had been filled. Told it was still open, he made a phone call and arranged an immediate interview. He got the job on the spot, no other attorney in the office having any interest.

Full of renewed optimism, Carl arrived home and told John he had accepted a transfer to Stockville, Alabama.

"We are starting a new life together," said Carl.

"You can't do this," said John.

"It's going to be great."

"Our first game is next week."

John was the starting center on the Douglaston Pistols summer basketball travel team. He was a natural. At 12 years old, he was the tallest kid in the sixth grade and remarkably coordinated for an early bloomer.

"Look at this as an adventure," said Carl.

"I'll live with the Alexanders," said John.

"Living down south will be a cultural awakening."

John looked squarely into his father's eyes, so as not to be misunderstood.

"I hate you," he screamed.

John ran to his room, slamming the door behind him and shattering the plastic mini-basketball hoop attached to the top of the door.

"We leave next Friday," Carl shouted back.

🌿

CHAPTER 9

John struggled with Alabama's matching weather report numbers. At 3 p.m. both the heat and the humidity hit 93. Even so, he hopped on his banana seat bike and took off in search of friends. His closely cropped blond hair, flattened by the rush of wind from the bike's forward movement, felt comfortable and reminiscent of happier days. His bike tires felt low on pressure and were just sinking ever so slightly into the heat of the asphalt road. There was an aroma of bacon, then oatmeal, then freshly baked bread as he sped past the houses that flanked Maiden Lane. As he pedaled, his knee high socks flopped down in a bunch around his ankles, looking like he had Slinkies sitting on top of his sneakers.

For the first time since arriving he felt a sense of optimism that he might turn this bike ride into an adventure, or at least something to build on. He peddled steadily on the shoulder of the flat, black road. In his Crimson Tide red and white striped t-shirt, light blue gym shorts and Converse high-tops, he blended into the streetscape as he rode. He turned right on Penrose Avenue and then left on Main Street, peddling with enthusiasm. John popped a wheelie just for good measure and then gently set his front wheel back on the ground.

Reaching downtown Stockville, John spotted water fountains in a bricked area off to his right. Hitting the brakes hard, he lowered his kick-stand and walked over to get a drink. As he bent over the fountain and flipped the lever, the water reached his tongue and a loud male voice interrupted.

"Boy, don't you be drinking from there."

John turned around. The sun shone from behind the voice, creating a faceless, giant silhouette. John squinted and put his hand up to his eyes. All he could see was the bright outline of a straw hat, big shoulders and shoes the size of Kentucky.

"Can't you read boy?" asked the man.

"Yes sir, I can," John said.

"Then read," said the man, pointing over John's head.

John looked up at the water fountains. Above the one to his left was a small sign that read, "Whites." Above his fountain was a smaller sign that read, "Coloreds."

"You drink from that one over there."

"Yes sir."

"Where are you from anyway? Visiting?"

"No sir. New."

"From where?"

"New York."

"Damn, son. You better learn the rules."

"Yes sir."

"Go on then, drink," said the man, who now seemed more demanding than suggesting.

John sidestepped slowly over to the other fountain. He pushed that lever even though he wasn't thirsty anymore. He took a longer than normal drink of water that tasted exactly the same as the other fountain, then he just let the water hit his lips for a while, wasting time and silently praying that when he was done the man would be gone. He was. John's prior excitement tempered, he straddled his bike, wondering what other mistakes he might make in this strange place.

"Nice bike."

John turned and saw a tall boy sporting a buzz cut and a face full of freckles astride a blue three-speed racing bike. The boy was dressed in a plain white t-shirt and blue chinos that had been cut off at the knees. He had black suspenders clipped onto the tops of the shortened pants.

"Thanks," said John.

"You play basketball?" asked the boy, pointing to the Spalding ball still nestled in the bike's rat trap.

"All the time," John said, tilting his head slightly to the sky, smiling and mustering all the courage he could to answer in a friendly but not desperate way.

"My name's Rudy," said the boy.

"I'm John Gordon."

John and Rudy struck up what passed for conversation between boys. They were the same age. Rudy told John about a schoolyard just west of Atkinson Road and Palmetto Street where Rudy played basketball almost every day. Rudy knew right away that John was new to town.

"You look different," he said.

"I put on this shirt to look the same," said John.

"Maybe it's the way you talk," said Rudy.

John asked Rudy for his phone number so that they could arrange to play. Rudy said his family didn't have a phone. They agreed to meet the next morning at the schoolyard.

"Welcome to Alabama," said Rudy, as he sped away down the street where his mother was waiting.

"See you tomorrow at 10," John yelled back.

When John arrived back at the house on Maiden Lane, he set his bike against the side of the porch out back and stopped dead in his tracks. The aroma wafting out of the kitchen window was familiar and delicious. He grabbed his basketball and ran up the stairs two at a time. He swung open the screen door to find Shirley cooking his favorite fried chicken.

"Hey, handsome!" said Shirley, dressed in a green gingham dress with her white cotton apron around her neck and tied behind her back.

"Shirley!" screamed John. "How did you get here?"

"Same way I left 15 years ago. On the bus," she said, putting down her tongs and spreading her arms to hug him.

John ran to her and hugged her tightly around her waist. He pressed his face into her apron and breathed in her familiar scent of roses and lime, enhanced with beer-battered fried chicken. She breathed in a 100 percent 12-year-old boy in need of a bath.

"Are you living with us?" asked John.

"I'm here for about a month, helping you and your dad get used to living in the South," she said.

"That's fantastic. How did you find us?"

"Your dad found me. You know how convincing he can be. He invited me here and knowing I'd get to see you again, I just couldn't say no."

"That's so great. Will you shoot baskets with me?" asked

John, picking up the ball he dropped in order to hug Shirley.

"I sure will. How about after dinner, sugar? I've got chicken on the stove and corn in the kettle. Your dad should be home soon."

Shirley gave John another hug and John noticed she wasn't smiling as big as usual.

"What's the matter?" he asked.

"Nothing sweetheart. Just feeling uneasy. Fish out of water thing," said Shirley, taking a Kleenex out of her apron pocket and wiping her nose.

"What does that mean?" asked John.

She was quiet for a moment, considering how to answer. "I've spent the past 15 years trying to forget places like Stockville. The boundaries, unwritten rules, distinctions that seem ridiculous now, but they're serious, deadly serious here," said Shirley.

"I just got yelled at for drinking out of the wrong water fountain," said John.

"I remember my mama pulling me off the sidewalk when a white person walked by. I never asked why, it just was," said Shirley.

"It doesn't seem fair," said John.

"I was just food shopping and four white women walked right in front of me to pay before the clerk paid me any mind. Then when I pulled out my money, the clerk held it up to the light, rubbed it to make sure it wasn't counterfeit."

"I don't get it," said John.

"It hurts, honey."

"Dad's going to change it."

Shirley put her arm around John's shoulder and let out a deep sigh.

"I'm rooting for him, baby. How about some lemonade?"

🌳

Carl turned the corner from 75th Street onto Central Park West, and ducked under the forest green canopy cascading out from the elegant front door of a French Second Empire, pre-war apartment building. He gave a familiar wave to the doorman, who stopped polishing the brass handle on the inside of the glass front door to open it for him.

"Good afternoon, Mr. Gordon," said the doorman.

"Hello Clyde," said Carl.

"I'll buzz Miss Harlowe and tell her you're on your way up."

Emily Harlowe had been an intern at the law firm of Cadwalader, Wickersham & Taft during the summer of 1951, along with Carl and seven other rising third-year law students. She was *order of the coif* at NYU. Emily interned in the real estate department, Carl in litigation. Carl, Beth, Emily and her husband Walter took full advantage of the perks that came with being courted by New York's oldest and most successful law firm. The two couples sat behind the Yankee dugout watching DiMaggio, Berra and Rizzuto lead the team to 98 wins. They saw *South Pacific* and *The King and I* from the firm's 10th row center orchestra seats. They spent a long weekend at a partner's summer home on Martha's Vineyard.

In return, Cadwalader got neither Carl nor Emily. Carl took the job with the U.S. Attorney's office and Emily decided the law was boring and stifling her creativity, as was her husband. She divorced Walter and moved to Paris, where she wrote the first of her four highly successful crime novels. She moved back to Manhattan as the toast of the New York literati in 1957. The money rained down like tickertape.

Emily was tall and lean, at home in the clingiest designer dresses or a pair of slacks and a white blouse. She always showed enough cleavage to command attention, but not enough to label her promiscuous. Her blond hair, occasioned with red highlights, was shoulder length and her penchant for diamond stud earrings added sparkle to her light grey eyes. For Emily, flirtation was an art form, mastered by osmosis, she claimed, at the Follies Bergere. She was at the top of her game at book signings, where women were awed by her star quality, and every man came away believing he was, at that moment, the most important person in her world. Emily traveled often, touting her books and their multiple translations into other languages.

Emily opened her apartment door wearing a black lace negligée and high heels. She pulled Carl in by the stem of the Hermes tie she had bought him on her last Paris trip, pressed her lips to Carl's and gave him the lustful French kiss he found irresistible. She wrapped her smooth arms around him and brushed one of her freshly shaven legs against his pants. Carl kissed her neck which smelled of red roses and mint. Carl was resolute in his decision to call off their relationship, but he supposed it could wait a couple of hours. He placed his hands on the small of her back and she pressed her pelvis against his.

"Your belt buckle is so cold," she said, looking demurely into his eyes. "I can fix that."

She unfastened Carl's belt and slid it briskly out of its belt loops. She tossed it on the floor, hooked her finger into one of the empty front loops, and drew Carl to the bedroom, where flickering amaretto candles filled the room with soft light and intoxicating aromas. She poured two martinis from a readied stainless steel shaker and handed a long-stemmed glass to Carl. He watched as the gin slid down her throat in one well-choreographed tip of her glass.

Carl kicked off his loafers. Emily loosened his tie and slipped it over his head. She playfully pushed him onto the bed, the two of them spread across Emily's goose down comforter. They kissed again. She unbuttoned Carl's shirt and pulled its shirt tails out of his pants with two short, meaningful tugs. Carl's fingertips tracked the contour of her breasts. He kissed them, sliding down the strap of her negligée, which was as pliable as its occupant. Emily unfastened Carl's pants, lowered the zipper and put her hands inside. She looked into his eyes.

"Something wrong?" she asked.

"Keep trying," he said.

She did, but her clever fingers and tongue produced no results. Carl couldn't muster the tumescence that had been automatic in the skillful company of Emily Harlowe.

"What's the matter?" She searched his face for a clue.

"I don't know."

"Is it me?" asked Emily in a rare display of insecurity. Her hands tightened and she breathed in through her nose.

"No. It's definitely me."

"We can try again later," she said, moving back up the bed and pressing her red lips against his.

"We should talk," said Carl, their lips still touching.

"Sure, baby," said Emily, smiling slyly. "Let's talk about your powerful hands on my body."

"I'm having second thoughts," he said.

Emily pulled away. "What?" she asked. Her sensual tone vanished.

"I think I need some separate time," he said.

Emily got up off the bed and wrapped herself in the silk kimono which was draped over her art deco chaise lounge. She pulled the robe's ruby red belt tightly around her waist and closed the top edges around her neck, like the petals of a tulip closing for the night.

"Are you breaking up with me?" she asked.

Carl couldn't shake the thought that Emily was the anti-Beth, a temporary replacement part for his broken heart. For Carl it was a moment of unusual, Valium-free, clarity.

"How long does a fling last?" he asked.

"Is that what you think we are? A fling?" demanded Emily.

"Affair?" said Carl, half as a response and half as a question.

"What about *relationship*?" she asked. "What about our plans?"

"There can't be an *our*, if there isn't an *us*," he said.

"When did you decide this?" she asked.

"I'm moving to Alabama."

Emily started laughing.

"With a banjo on your knee?"

Carl thought for a moment.

"Actually, I think that guy was *from* Alabama and going to Louisiana."

Emily glowered at him and her face reddened. She tilted her head and nervously rubbed her earring between her thumb and forefinger.

"This is a joke, right? Like the time you flew from Chicago to New York and told me you billed the time change."

"No joke. I'm taking John and we're starting over," he said.

"When are you leaving?"

"Friday."

Emily reared back and her whole body tensed, like a trapped rattlesnake.

"What about the past eight months?" she wanted to know.

"It was great. We needed it."

"We? Maybe you *needed* it? What was I, your Beth substitute? Now I'm supposed to walk away so you can find the real deal again?"

"That's not it at all. I need to get away."

"No. You need to get out, now," Emily shouted. She picked up one of Carl's shoes and threw it at him. Carl caught the shoe in midflight, making her even angrier.

"What kind of asshole are you?" Emily said.

Carl pulled up his pants and tucked one of the tails of his shirt back in. He slipped one foot into the previously flying loafer and jammed his foot back into the other one.

"Why don't we talk about this," he said.

"Get the fuck out my apartment," she said, pointing to the front door.

Carl left the bedroom with Emily stalking behind him. In one horizontal sweep, he bent down and picked his belt up off the floor without breaking stride. He opened the apartment door, his sport coat and belt in his arms, his hair disheveled. He took one step into the hallway, paused, and then turned back to Emily.

"What?" she said.

"I forgot my tie."

Emily slammed the door in his face.

CHAPTER 10

Shirley wore a light grey maid's dress and white apron while she prepared peanut-butter and jelly sandwiches, cut up carrot sticks and put three peaches together with a handful of napkins into a covered wicker basket she found in a closet. She placed the basket, a green cotton blanket and a large bag of potato chips onto the back seat of the Mustang. A few minutes later, Carl locked the house behind him, and he, John and Shirley walked out the kitchen door to the car, where John, excited about a new adventure, jumped into the backseat, landing squarely on the bag of chips, crushing it flat and making a large crunching sound. He stared up at his father, who was bending at the waist, looking right back at him. John took an uncertain breath and pressed his lips against each other, waiting. Shirley was silent at the passenger-side door.

"Good thinking," Carl said, giving his fist a little pump in front of his chest. "Now we have twice as many potato chips!"

John smiled and arched his body up, gently sliding the bag over to the other side of the backseat. Shirley laughed.

Carl winked at John, got into the driver's seat and the three
of them set off for a park Carl had overheard mentioned at a
local café.

Lewis Garrison State Park, a sprawling, heavily wooded
area southwest of Stockville, was officially designated as an
Alabama State Park in 1926 by an act of the state legislature.
It was named after Lewis P. Garrison, a Confederate
brigadier general, whose middling Civil War record included
successfully assisting the retreat of other Confederate
generals' beaten troops at the Battles of Shiloh and Perryville.
On the plus side, he was a native son of Stockville, or at least
that part of Central Alabama that became Stockville years
later.

When Carl, John and Shirley arrived, they set off in
search of a perfect picnic spot. They didn't know that the
615-acre Park was divided almost perfectly down the middle
by Garrison Creek, the natural demarcation separating the
west side of the Park for white Stockville from the east side
for colored Stockville. The Park had no segregation signs.
The creek itself, a rushing, bending river in winter, spring
and fall, was calm and subtle in the summer, and a popular
place for white Stockville to cool off from Memorial Day
until late September. Coloreds were allowed in the water on
Wednesday evenings and Saturdays.

On this weekday morning the park was empty, and the
trio was drawn to the park's centerpiece, a 150-year-old
Oak tree, situated on the western bank of the river where
the two trailheads met, creating a figure-eight design for the
seven mile hiking loop. Shirley and Carl laid out the blanket
beneath the majestic antebellum tree that had survived both
the War and the tornado of '27 to become, with its strong

and angular branches, the Klan's tree of choice for hanging Negroes.

Since 1882, 38 Negro men and two women had been lynched from its branches. So many, that by the early 1930s, the tree took on the moniker *Maker Oak*, because it was the place so many Negroes met their Maker. The inventory of lynchings was documented, open and notorious, often publicized in the *Times-Gazette*, and was, on occasion, the cause for a Sunday afternoon celebratory Klan family gathering.

Bertram Richmond was murdered for making eye contact with a white woman, a violation of the Alabama law called *Associating with a White Woman*. Other Negroes were lynched for the crime of success, like Billy Hatchins, who found himself in the unfortunate position of being a talented blacksmith at a time when the Stockville Mayor's brother-in-law was in the same trade. Other Negro crimes punishable by death included being uppity or insolent.

Not one of the 40 Stockville lynchings had ever been seriously investigated by the Frost County Sheriff's Department. Not even the death of 15-year-old William Benson. Benson, a slightly built, gregarious teen, was visiting Stockville from his home in Connecticut in the summer of 1954. Unfamiliar with Jim Crow and the southern way of life, Billy asked Sally Slone, a 22-year-old shopkeeper, for directions to a public bathroom and winked at her when he said thank you and goodbye. Three nights later, at 2 a.m., Sally's father, brother, and three other hooded white men arrived at the house where Benson was staying with his cousins, and pronounced him under arrest for rape, although none of them was a sheriff's deputy or involved in law enforcement. With heavy duty rope they tied Benson's feet together, attaching the other end to the rear bumper of a Ford pickup and dragged him a half-mile until he was nearly dead. Then they lynched him on the Maker Oak, leaving his body naked, castrated and hanging as a warning to all the town's Negroes.

William's Connecticut grandfather, a prominent businessman in the railroad industry, applied significant political pressure to take the investigation out of the hands of the Frost County Sheriff's Department and get the FBI involved. In response, Mr. Benson received the following letter:

July 15, 1954
Dear Mr. Benson:

The facts in this case indicate a state offense of kidnapping and murder but there is no indication to date of a violation of the Federal Kidnapping Statute or the Federal Civil Rights Statute inasmuch as the action was taken against a private citizen by a group of citizens. There has been no allegation made that the victim has been subjected to the deprivation of any right or privilege which is secured and protected by the Constitution and the laws of the United States which would come within the provisions of Section 241, Title 18, United States Code. It should be noted that recently in Washington, D.C., a group of white boys from the State of Mississippi were beaten and knifed by Negro youths and this Bureau did not conduct an investigation into that matter upon the instructions of the Criminal Division.

J. Edgar Hoover, Director, FBI

Eventually Sheriff Bascomb questioned Kyle and Barry Slone. No charges were filed, no indictments sought and the investigation itself died a slow death when the father and son claimed the same alibi—on the night in question they were visiting Kyle's sister in Tuscaloosa. That was good enough for Sheriff Bascomb. Case closed.

As they ate their sandwiches, fruit and tiny chips, Carl, John and Shirley saw only two other people. One, a young, blond woman with a baby stroller, approached on the dirt path, but immediately turned in the other direction as soon as she saw them. The second, a slender Negro man in overalls, sat on an upside-down white bucket, fishing from the other side of the riverbank.

"This park's kinda neat," said John, who traveled with his basketball under his arm even when there was no game on the schedule.

"I think maybe I'm coming down with something," said Shirley. "I feel achy and a little bit nauseous." She scratched the back of her neck, which prickled with hairs standing on their ends.

"Me too," said Carl. He looked up through the oak's branches. The slight wind rustled the leaves but even on a bright summer day, the effect was eerie. "Let's finish up and go home." Something just didn't feel right about this place.

John slammed the brakes and skidded his bike sideways to a stop at the playground of the Robert T. Spanhower High School, 15 minutes earlier than he and Rudy had agreed. He flipped down his kick-stand with the practiced aplomb of a dancer, and parked his bike next to the court at the rear of the school. He looked around. He was alone. The two blacktop basketball courts, each the official length and width, and already hot under his hi-tops, may have been the nicest outdoor courts John had ever seen. The orange rims were tight and netted. The key and foul line were white and precisely painted. The backboards, he noticed, were shaped like half-moons rather than the large rectangle he was used to seeing up North. John wiped his brow with the sleeve of his t-shirt and tugged at his floppy socks. The back of the school complex also had four tennis courts, a football field with wooden bleachers on both sides and a manicured, sprinklered baseball diamond.

This is sports heaven, he thought.

John grabbed his ball from the rat-trap on his bike seat and dribbled toward the nearest hoop, a few right-handed, then some left-handed. Starting in close to the basket, John took a short jump-shot from the right side. Good. Then one from the left. Nothing but net. Not too many kids his age could shoot a jump shot and he was accurate only from close in. Another short jumper missed. Some more left-handed dribbles. Another shot, good.

A few minutes later he heard a buzzing sound echoing off the brick wall of the school and reverberating around the playground. A low buzz at first, then as the noise grew louder he stopped shooting and turned in the direction of the hum. It was a familiar sound that both calmed John's nervousness and excited his competitive spirit. No doubt about it, Topps rotary engines, maybe five of them or more.

John leveraged the ball under his arm and faced the corner of the school, waiting for the increasing sound of baseball cards slapping against the spokes of moving bicycle wheels. Rudy led the way, shooting around the corner at top speed. Like a flock of geese behind him flying in a "V", six more guys on bikes came screeching around the corner too, jamming on their brakes and burning rubber. The boys dumped their bikes near John's, some using kickstands and others just letting them fall over on their pedals.

"Heyah John," said Rudy, proud to be the only one who knew the new kid. "This is Ray, Ben, Jimmy, Jack, Hack and Mickey... ya'll say howdy to John from New York."

Following a barrage of "heys" and "y'alls" and "dangs" and other forms of the English language John was learning, all the boys took turns shooting four basketballs for the eight of them. They were *shooting around*—a universal pregame ritual that has no formal name and needs no instructions among basketball players. To John's delight, *shooting around* transcended geography.

A guy shoots, but it has to be from a sufficient distance. Layups don't count. If the shot is made, he gets to shoot again, with one of the rebounders catching the ball as it falls through the net and passing it back to the successful shooter. If he misses, one of the players without a ball rebounds and makes his way to where he wants to shoot, first passing the ball to the guy who just missed. That guy shoots a layup and then passes the ball out to the new shooter.

While the seven Stockville kids concentrated on making their shots, John concentrated on them. He could never be sure until a game began, but at least pre-game, he thought he could more than hold his own with this group.

"Let's play," said Ray, after the boys had warmed up for all of four minutes.

John was again comfortable with what he recognized was another universal boy attribute, that non-competitive *shooting around* can't hold a candle to the real thing. Rudy divided the teams. John was teamed with Ray, Jack and Hack, who were identical twins. Rudy, Ben, Jimmy and Mickey played skins, peeling off their shirts.

"Make it, take it," said Rudy in a voice indicating he was the main man of this blacktop. John had no idea what that meant, but didn't want to look stupid, so he just stood there and watched as Rudy proceeded to shoot a high arching shot from the foul line that went in without touching the rim.

"Swish," John said, and all seven of the Stockville boys looked at him like maybe he had grown wings and a beak.

"Must be a Yankee thing," said Mickey.

Rudy, Ben, Jimmy and Mickey took positions around the perimeter of the key while John, Ray, Jack and Hack adopted their defensive spots between their opponent and the basket. Rudy tossed the ball to Mickey and the game began.

Thirty seconds in, it was easy to see that Rudy was the best player of the southern lot. He was tall, maybe 5'5", and slender. *Long*, in Alabama-speak. His faded blue gym shorts were too big for his skinny legs. His clothes and his game were surely hand-me-downs from an older brother. Instead of a t-shirt he wore a ribbed undershirt that actually looked like the uniforms worn by professionals, except that it had several small brown stains on the front and no number. Identical twins named Jackson and Henry, nicknamed Jack and Hack, wore identical big grins and crew-cuts that made their ears look too big for their heads. John kept that observation to himself. He remembered what his dad told him about new games and new players. *Let the game come to you. No quick mistakes. No long shots. Just feel your way for a while.*

The twins were serviceable. You could count on them to immediately dribble the ball when it was thrown to them and then look around to pass to a teammate. That was just fine with John and Ray.

Ben, Mickey and Jimmy were all pretty good. Rudy was excellent. Slowly, John turned his game up a notch and then another. He grabbed a couple of rebounds and scored a few buckets. He made sure he fed the ball to his teammates a lot, because he wanted to fit in more than win. The boys played for an hour, switching teams each time a team won by scoring 11 points.

"Anybody thirsty?" asked Ray.

"Let's go to Hudson's for pop," said Jimmy.

"You coming?" Hack asked John.

"Sure. What's pop?"

"C'mon," said Rudy.

John looked completely lost.

"Coca-Cola?" said Rudy.

"Oh, you mean soda," said John.

"Yeah, soda pop," said Mickey.

The boys hopped on their bikes and roared toward town.

Rudy pulled his three-speed up beside John as they peddled on the smooth, recently paved road.

"We got a team in the Police Boys Club called the Jacks. Jimmy plays and so does Ray, Mickey, Jack and Hack. We could sure use a player like you. Would you wanna?"

"Yeah," said John, trying not to sound too desperate, while his insides were pumping adrenalin.

"Jimmy's dad is the coach and we're practicing at the

Christian Brothers Church gym tomorrow at 6:30 p.m. Just show up. Mack Stinson quit last week and Coach said we need to pick up two new players. Jimmy said he'll tell his dad the good news tonight."

"I'll be there."

John popped another wheelie and pumped his fist.

The boys bought pop and candy bars at Hudson's, congregated around the fountain in the middle of town and figured out what other words were *spoke different* up North. The Stockville seven were hysterical when John called his Converse All-Stars *sneakers.*

"You sneak around in them?" Rudy asked.

"We call 'em tennies," Hack said.

"If you lose one, are you left with fives?"

Everyone stopped, creating a moment of truth for John's adolescent boy future. His comment was either funny or stupid. It would take a few dreadful seconds to see which.

"Good one," said Rudy.

John exhaled.

If it was okay with Rudy, it was okay with everyone else. John was in. He looked around at his new basketball pals. He couldn't wait to tell his dad and Shirley that he'd met a great group of new friends who were also basketball players.

❧

CHAPTER 11

John rode his bike so hard his feet fell off the pedals and he almost crashed twice. Right on Main, left on Addison, right on Kingdom Way. He weaved his way through Stockville's rush hour traffic, which was less congested than a typical midnight on East 83rd. He spun his bike to an acrobatic stop at the open side door of Christian Brothers Church. An olive green metal folding chair held the gym door open for a large fan on a pedestal that blew some outside air onto the steamy basketball court. John gave a tug to his lucky sweat socks, a gift from college All-American Barry Kramer when Carl got an invitation last winter to visit the New York University locker room before a game. The two skinny purple stripes at the top of the socks reached above John's knees, but one hard sprint up or down the court and the socks flopped around his ankles, a look he preferred anyway. John also wore his blue and orange Pistols jersey, hoping to send the message that he'd already played on an organized team.

When he entered the gym, John saw Rudy shooting baskets with Ray and two other boys. As John took stock of the two unfamiliar kids, he bent down to tie his white canvas high-tops tighter. When he put his basketball on the floor, it slowly rolled toward the west bleachers. Observation one, the gym floor wasn't level. John scooped up his ball and ran over to where the other boys were shooting.

"Howdy, John," Rudy said.

"Hi," John said.

"This here's John," Rudy said to the other two boys.

John watched the other two look him over like he was a science fair experiment. Rudy had built him up so much to the other players that they were nervous about losing their playing time to him.

"I'm Billy Jenkins," said the taller one.

"I'm Frank Simonetti," said the other.

John shook their hands and they all shot baskets together. In spite of the indoor temperature of 84 degrees, John felt no heat. This was the day he'd been waiting for. His shots were falling and the other boys were noticing.

"I told you," said Rudy to Frank, glancing over his shoulder at John. John always felt at home on a basketball court. Right now, finally, Stockville was starting to feel a little like home, too.

A few minutes later Jimmy arrived with his dad, who had a silver whistle at the end of a red cord around his neck, dangling to his belt. He set down the army green canvas bag that he'd carried on his shoulder and four more basketballs tumbled out. Jimmy Sr., wearing a red t-shirt with Stockville Jacks emblazoned across the front in big white letters, looked like a University of Alabama football star. John liked him immediately.

Little Jimmy bolted toward John and grabbed the top

strap of his Pistols' jersey, dragging him back toward his father. Rudy followed close behind.

"Dad. This is the guy. Wait till you see him play," said Jimmy.

John's face flushed, but he tried to remain calm and polite. The younger Jimmy spoke again.

"John Gordon, this is my dad, Coach Cooper."

John offered his handshake the way his father taught him, firm grip and steady. John got nothing in return. Just a cold stare.

"Dad. This is our new power forward," said Jimmy.

"Gordon?" asked the coach.

"Yes sir, John Gordon."

"From New York?"

"Yes sir."

"Sorry you came all this way, but we don't have any spots on this team," said Cooper.

Rudy interrupted. "When Mack Stinson quit you sa—"

"I didn't ask your opinion," Cooper snipped at Rudy.

"Daddy, this guy's as good as Rudy," the younger Jimmy said.

"Real sorry. But there are no spots on this team," said his father.

Rudy and Jimmy looked at each other, having no idea what went wrong. John was still absorbing what the coach was saying and when he did, he felt the same stabbing pain in his stomach he had at his mother's memorial service.

"Son, John, whatever your name is, you go on home so the Jacks can get some practicing done," said Coach Cooper.

Cooper turned his back and walked away. He blew his whistle for the players to assemble at the center circle of the court. The basketball under John's left arm fell to the floor. He looked over to Rudy, who gave a confused look and a shrug that said there was nothing he could do.

John's knees buckled slightly and he felt like he might faint. He closed his eyes to stop the spinning. He scooped up his basketball and ran for the door. His eyes welled and when he wiped them with his sleeve, he smashed into the metal folding chair that was holding the door open, cutting a nasty slit just below his left knee. The door to the gym slammed behind him. John bounded onto his bike and hurled his basketball into a nearby dumpster. He peddled furiously. He swerved two or three times off the road's shoulder and back close enough to passing cars that they swerved and honked their horns at him as they sped by. John's vision blurred. He couldn't stop crying. He started coughing and heaving. His body was unable to get enough oxygen into his lungs. All that time he was completely oblivious to the stream of blood running down his sweaty left leg, turning his sock a queasy pink. He crossed two streets without looking both ways. He just knew he had to get out of Stockville. Whatever it took.

Back at Maiden Lane, John ditched his bike in the hydrangea bush next to the front steps, climbed them two at a time and ran back to the kitchen where his dad was fixing dinner because Shirley had gone to visit her dad in Birmingham.

"I wanna go home," John sobbed.

"What happened?" asked Carl.

"I hate it here! Why did you make me come? Mom never would have made me come here," he screamed.

In the five months since Beth's death, John had only invoked her name like this once before. At the mention of

Beth, Carl felt his muscles tightening around his spinal cord from his waist to his neck.

"Can we talk?" asked Carl.

"I hate you," John screamed, and sprinted up the stairs to his room, slammed the door and screamed again, "I wanna go home!"

Carl cringed at the slam and the scream. His mouth dried up and his tongue felt like a big ball of cotton. Waves of guilt made him dizzy. He reached into the kitchen cabinet and grabbed the bottle of pills. He sucked two of them down with a last gulp of beer left in the can of Budweiser. He sat down to calm himself before making the trip upstairs to confront John, but John screamed again from his bedroom. Carl stood up and rushed past the strip steaks he was seasoning. He ran to the front hallway and up the stairs. The pine floor boards, saturated by the Alabama humidity, cried out for leniency when anyone, even a small child, walked across them. So when 6'1", 200-pound Carl jogged across them he created a cacophony of squeaks and moans. Carl took a right at the top of the stairs, following the rosewood banister around to just outside John's room. With the floor announcing his arrival before he even got to the door, John yelled, "Go away!"

"Can't we just talk for a minute?"

"No. I want to go home."

Whatever went wrong, Carl wanted so badly to fix it. That's what Carl was, a lawyer, a professional problem solver. He knew he couldn't make it better by saying they'd leave Stockville for New York. He had been so hopeful when John met those boys at the playground.

"Just let me come in and we can talk about it," he said.

Carl waited outside the door, which had a big poster of

Yankee sluggers Mickey Mantle and Elston Howard pasted to it. John could hear him breathing outside.

"Go away," John said.

"I can't go away."

"Go AWAY," John said again.

"I can't."

"Why not?"

"I'm stuck."

"What do you mean?"

"I thought it would be cool to see if my foot fit in between the spindles that hold up the banister."

"So?"

"So it did. But now I can't get it out."

After a few moments Carl could hear John picking himself up off the bed. John reached for the doorknob and turned it. He gently pulled open the door. Sure enough, there was Carl, balancing on his left foot, with his right foot slightly elevated and definitely caught between the spindles.

"Can you give me a hand?" Carl asked.

John reached over the railing.

"Be careful," said Carl.

The admonition startled John. He stared. Still angry.

"Can you untie my shoe? That might do it," said Carl.

Once again John bent over the railing and this time untied his Dad's clumsy Oxford, but it wouldn't budge, like it was glued to Carl's foot. The harder John pulled, the more it battled to stay on. John gave it one last heave-ho, and the two-pound black leather, cap-toed size 12 went flying across the staircase, hit the opposite wall and careened off the hallway table, narrowly missing Beth's favorite glass vase, before landing with a thud in the vestibule.

Carl and John looked at each other with great relief.

Carl then slid his foot out from the spindles just a little too easily. John looked at him suspiciously.

"I was stuck, really," Carl said.

"Yeah. Right."

"Really."

"Let's try it with your head next time," said John. He turned to go back in his room and Carl smiled one of those infectious smiles that women jurors couldn't resist. John plopped himself down on his bed and put his head in his hands. Carl sat down next to him.

"He wouldn't let me try out."

"Who wouldn't," asked Carl.

"The coach. Rudy and Ray and me and two other kids were shooting baskets. Then Jimmy and his dad arrived."

"What happened then?"

"Ray and Rudy took me to meet him. Jimmy's father. He's the coach. I went to shake his hand and told him my name, just like you taught me. He said they had enough players and I should leave. He wouldn't even let me show him what I can do."

"Who's the coach?" asked Carl.

"Jimmy's dad."

"What's Jimmy's last name?" asked Carl.

"Cooper, I think," answered John.

Carl hesitated.

"Owns a shoe store?"

"I don't know," said John.

"Maybe you can show him what kind of player you are anyway."

"He said I can't play on their team."

"How about another team?"

"Every good player in town is on the Jacks."

"Every one?"

"Yes, every one."

"That can't be true."

"Why not?"

"Well, first, because you're not on the Jacks."

John fought back a smile. That comment made him angry and happy at the same time, which was definitely premeditated by a father/lawyer. John, however, wasn't ready to stop being disappointed. Carl put his arm around John's shoulders, which John would have to admit, felt really good.

"I think there are other 12-year-old basketball players in Stockville."

"What do you know?"

"Sometimes I know a little. Let's take a ride," Carl said.

Then he gave John a wily grin and a wink. John knew that when his dad gave a wily grin and a wink, he usually had some plan up his sleeve.

"First let's clean up that knee," Carl said.

Carl grabbed a wet towel from the bathroom and dabbed all around the gash. John cringed twice from the anticipation of pain, although it didn't hurt at all. Carl went back to the bathroom and returned with a box of large Band-Aids from the medicine cabinet. He peeled off the plastic on the back of one of them and placed it around the cut, which had finally stopped bleeding.

Carl stared at the Band-Aid. His nostrils flared and he let out a deep sigh from his pursed lips.

"You want to know why we're here?" he asked.

Before John could answer, Carl continued.

"I'll tell you why we're here. See this bandage I just put on your leg. Here's the box it came in. Do you see what it says about these bandages?"

John held the box delicately, like he might a baby chick. He looked at the front, the top and the side and still had no idea where his father was going with this.

"It says they're strong and absorbent," said John.

"Yeah it says that. It also says right here that the box contains ten bandages that are *flesh colored.*"

"Right."

"Whose flesh are they talking about?" said Carl in his annoyed voice.

"Mine?"

"Yeah, yours *and* mine, but not Shirley's. And not any other Negro people. What kind of presumptuous bullcrap is that?"

Carl hardly ever used curse words. John swallowed and shifted nervously back a few inches.

"Johnson and Johnson. A big company and they're either oblivious to anything other than the white world, or they're just racist."

John locked eyes with his father. His mouth quivered slightly. He'd known since age six, you don't interrupt Dad in closing argument.

"Why don't they just make these things out of clear plastic? Then it would be whatever skin color you are!"

"I'm going to write them a letter," said John, nodding his head and answering with the poker faced sarcasm he had inherited from his father.

"Damn straight," said Carl.

He put his arm back around John and led him down the stairs. Carl slipped his shoe back on, tied the laces and moved the steaks back to the refrigerator. The two of them stepped more confidently now down the kitchen steps and out to the car.

"On the way to wherever we're going, can we stop at that church so I can fish my basketball out of the dumpster?"

"You threw your ball in a dumpster?"

"Yeah."

"Did you make it on your first shot?"

"Can we just go get it?"

"Absolutely. Where we're going, you'll need it."

❧

John started tearing up again when he heard the basketballs bouncing inside the church gym. Carl put the car into park and gave John a reassuring look and a helpful boost up the side of the dumpster. The dumpster hadn't been emptied in a few days and John had to wade through rotten banana peels, rancid chicken bones and boxes of brown goop Carl couldn't identify. The stink reminded Carl of Manhattan during the garbage strike of '59. He had to cover his mouth with his sleeve to keep from vomiting. He looked over the top rim to see that John wasn't just smelling it, he was sloshing through the crud. John held his nose with the fingers of his left hand and rolled the basketball up his foot, ankle and leg with his right. Once the ball was back in his arms, he sprinted back to the corner where Carl helped him climb out. John wiped an unidentified liquid off the word Spalding with a rag they had in the car and then Carl tossed the rag into the dumpster, like a soldier tossing a grenade. They got back in the car, making sure all the windows were open.

"How do you like my 4-40 air-conditioning?"

"What's that?"

"That's four open windows at 40 miles per hour."

John still wasn't in the mood for humor. Not that the comment would have been funny any time.

"Where are we going?" John asked.

"You'll see."

"Gimme something," said John.

"New adventure."

"That's it?"

"That's all I know."

They rode for 15 minutes. Carl noticed the flat pavement on the streets gradually deteriorating to gravel roads, pocked with dips and mounds. Stop signs were bent or missing altogether. The cars and trucks in driveways and parked along the streets were older. The homes, smaller. Carl's mouth was so dry that he couldn't swallow away the queasy lump that had lodged in his throat. Carl pulled the car to the curb in front of an Armory-looking brick building with a sign out front proclaiming it "George Washington Carver High School." Several of the bricks on the front façade were missing and the granite front steps were uneven and cracked. Carl removed the key from the ignition and together they walked around back.

Carl immediately noticed grass growing up between cracks in the pavement. The sports fields were burned brown by the hot summer sun. They saw a handful of Negro boys playing basketball on the uneven court that looked like a sprained ankle waiting to happen. The rims were straight, but without any nets. The backboards were wood, warped and discolored. They shook when a basketball hit them and looked like a strong push on the pole holding it all up would bring the entire rim and backboard crashing to the ground.

"What is this place?" asked John.

"It's London after the blitzkrieg," said Carl.

John gave him a confused look.

"Sorry. This is the Negro high school."

Carl remembered John's description of the Spanhower High playground where he met the white kids.

"Separate but equal," Carl said, loud enough for John to hear.

"Equal to what?"

Carl pulled some air into his lungs. He had never seen a school this run down. He noticed the playground, where chains dangling from a crossbar were all that remained of a 1940's swing set.

"The two high schools. Spanhower for Whites. Carver for Negroes. It's supposed to be equal."

"There's nothing equal about this place," John said.

"I can't believe it," mumbled Carl, trying to manage his outrage and regain his composure.

"How do they get away with this?"

"Intimidation, violence, control of the police and the legal system."

"It's not fair."

"It's not just illegal, it's immoral," said Carl, trying not to let John see that he was getting this picture for the first time, right along with John.

"What's immoral mean?" asked John.

"It means beyond all decency. Inhuman," said Carl, still in a daze.

"What are you going to do?"

Carl snapped back to the moment and avoided the question.

"Right now I'm going to introduce you to some basketball players."

John and Carl walked up to the court where five Negro boys, who all looked about the same age as John, were shooting baskets. Two Negro men were standing on the side. John was surprised when his father addressed one of the men by name.

"Mr. Geary, I'd like to introduce you to my son, John."

"Pleased to meet you," said John. He held out his hand and got the handshake he was expecting earlier in the evening.

"The pleasure is mine," said Thomas Geary, shaking John's hand with a firm grip out in front of a genuine smile.

"Let me introduce you. Carl and John Gordon, meet Benjamin Elsberry."

"Bennie," he said.

"Bennie's daughter Nina and my Cara are best friends," said Thomas.

Bennie Elsberry's pants were pressed and without any of the wrinkles you'd expect on an Alabama summer evening. In spite of the heat, he looked relaxed in his dress shirt and solid blue tie snugly fastened at his neck and spit-polished oxblood loafers.

Carl extended his hand and noticed that Bennie had a gold ring on his right pinky and soft hands.

"Pleased to meet you," said Bennie.

"John, meet Mr. Elsberry," said Carl.

John switched his basketball from his right hand to his left and wiped his still-sticky right hand down the front of his shorts. Bennie reluctantly shook hands, his hesitancy born of germs rather than custom.

"Good evening," said Bennie, his brown eyes wandering over John's head, showing his uneasiness at the respect being shown to him by this unknown white man and boy.

"Carl is an Assistant U.S. Attorney from New York. He just arrived. He's helping the cause," said Thomas.

Bennie looked younger than his 32 years. His skin was a deep brown and his thick eyebrows revealed a clever intensity. He had a small scar which ran from just below his right ear, down his jaw and circling down his neck, like a fishhook had been pressed into his skin. That scar didn't come naturally and Carl was sure it harbored a terrifying story, but you wouldn't know it from Bennie, who was highly articulate and ruggedly handsome.

A self-made man, Bennie had little time or respect for the white people who were born on third base and thought they hit a home run. He realized that his success was the product of his hard work, but also the help of others. Always affable, he walked the line between confident and pretentious, both attributes that made whites nervous. He was proud of his financial successes, especially in light of his modest beginnings.

"Do you think it would be possible for John to play ball with your son and his friends?" Carl asked Thomas.

John always hated it when his father set up introductions for him. This time he'd make an exception if it got him in the game.

"Harry," Thomas yelled out. "This is John. Find a spot for

him in your game."

Harry, skinny and short, looked up, stopping in his tracks when he noticed the white man and boy at the Carver playground. John ran over to the others. The six boys stood there, not exactly sure what came next. Victor, a miniature version of his father Micah, nervously dribbled the ball he was holding, watching its path from his hand to the pavement and back. Another boy wiped his sweating hands on his baggy shorts, unsure if his mother's admonition never to talk to a white person until that person spoke to you held true for white kids too, or just adults. John held his basketball tightly to his chest, as if it had special powers to break through ice. He stood silently and straightened his back. He had never felt so much like an outsider. The only times he'd played with Negroes in New York, *they* were in the minority. There was only one Negro player on the Pistols.

"I'm Harry Geary," said Harry, and it was like a group of foreigners discovering they spoke the same language. "This is Doug, Wesley, Victor and Kenny."

Harry was much smaller than John, but what he lacked in height he made up for in speed and quickness. He was a take-charge kid. He split the boys into two teams and said, *play ball.* John was teamed with Harry and Wesley. Harry handled the ball as well as any player John had ever seen. On defense his hands darted in and out, crowding his opponent and daring him to try and dribble past him. He was the kind of player a radio announcer might describe as flashy. He had dark, smooth skin like his dad, and his long arms flew in all directions when he ran. His body and his mouth were in perpetual motion.

"Get the ball to the big man," Harry yelled, referring to

John. In fact, Harry didn't stop talking the entire game.

"Give and go," he chattered. "Backdoor. Take him to the hoop."

Wesley, John's other teammate, didn't say one word. He wasn't the player that Harry was, but he was wide and could set a mean pick. He occupied a lot of room under the basket. When their team scored, Harry was jubilant, Wesley was silent and John was cautious.

It became obvious quickly that Harry, maybe unknowingly, had stacked the teams in his favor. He could play with the best, Wesley was good, and John was the perfect complement, hitting some outside shots and making some great passes to Harry, who never stopped moving while he never stopped talking. He reminded John of Bob Cousy of the Boston Celtics.

While the boys played, Carl, Thomas and Bennie talked in the shade of the school building.

"Bennie grew up on a farm about 15 miles outside of Stockville. His daddy was a sharecropper."

"I'm not sure what that is," admitted Carl.

"My father rented 105 of Earl Fisher's 500 acres. No written contract. It's rare for any money to change hands in sharecropping," said Bennie.

"How's that?" asked Carl.

"In the spring my father bought seed and fertilizer on credit at an unspecified interest rate from Fisher, who had purchased it for a third of the cost he sold it to my father. Fisher then rented my father his tractor and other tools, again at unspecified prices. When daddy harvested the cotton and corn, he was required to give it to Fisher to take to market, and we received half the price of the goods sold.

Each October Fisher presented my father with a one-page accounting that my father couldn't read."

"Why not?" asked Carl.

"My father was illiterate," said Bennie, his face calm as if he were just reporting the mundane local news. "In a good year my father earned enough to pay Fisher the rent on our two-room clapboard house, pay him back for the seed and use of the tractor and grow enough food to feed us. We might have had a few dollars left over, except Fisher kept it for expenses like the Central Alabama real estate renter's tax," said Bennie.

"Alabama has a renter's tax?" asked Carl.

"No," said Bennie.

"What was—"

"In a bad year, my father had to borrow money from Fisher to get through the winter. Then the best he could hope for was getting a little bit closer to even," said Bennie.

"When you got older, did you put a stop to the cheating and get your money back?" asked Carl.

Thomas laughed and shook his head. He smiled, but wondered how the federal government could have sent someone so uninformed and naïve.

"By the time I was 11, I knew we were getting swindled. I showed my father the numbers and he told me to keep out of it. He said he knew what was going on, but if he rocked the boat, Fisher would evict us and make sure no other white farmer would make us a sharecropping deal."

"You don't look like a farmer," said Carl, who swallowed hard as his eyes tightened around the injustice.

"November 13, 1944," said Bennie.

"What's that?" asked Thomas.

"That was a Monday. I was 12, a rural boy's purgatory between childhood and farmer. I was sitting on a big rock after school when I spotted a cream-colored Cadillac convertible coming up the dirt road to the house. Behind the steering wheel, Alfred Chestnut smiled wider than the whitewall tires. The inside of the car was all soft burgundy leather and it had body stripes running the full length of the car, including the rear wheel covers," said Bennie.

Carl and Thomas both leaned in a little closer.

"Mr. Chestnut turned the ignition key and the steady hum of the engine dropped as cleanly as the country sunset. He flipped a lever and the car door seemed to open itself. And then out he stepped, in a three-piece herringbone suit. His shoes were so shiny, it was like the Red Sea of Central Alabama dirt parted to let him through," said Bennie.

Thomas's attention was diverted for a moment as he kicked the errant basketball back toward the kids' game. Bennie continued.

"As he walked past me staring up at him, I could see the pomade in his relaxed, wavy hair reflecting sunshine just like the polished hood of his car. I said, 'Excuse me sir. But, what do you do?'" Bennie smiled to Carl and Thomas like he did that day 20 years earlier.

"He said, 'My name is Alfred Chestnut and I am the Central Alabama Regional Director of Sales for the Farm Sentinel Life Insurance Company.' I remember that word for word," said Bennie. "He told me how every day he drove to see his customers all around Alabama and how he collected $4 a month from lots of people, including my parents, so that if something happened to my father his company would pay my mother $5,000 to take care of me and my brothers. He told me that of the $4 dollars, he got to keep 40 cents. From that day on, I knew I was not going to be a farmer."

"Bennie is one of only 17 gold-level insurance agents for the Rural Insurance Cooperative out of Topeka, Kansas," said Thomas.

"Fantastic story," said Carl. "Congratulations."

"I'm a lucky man," said Bennie.

They heard a holler from the court as one of the boys landed a particularly smooth shot. "I saw in the *Times-Gazette* that there's a basketball tournament," said Carl.

"What tournament?" Bennie asked.

"Police Boys Club, 12 and under," said Carl.

"No Coloreds allowed," said Bennie.

"It's a new day," said Carl.

"It's an old Police Boys Club," said Thomas.

"If you'll help me put together a team, I'll get it in the tournament," said Carl, trying hard to be the self-assured assistant U.S. attorney he hadn't felt like since he arrived in Stockville.

"Really?" asked Thomas.

"Why does everyone here say that to me? Really."

"You don't recognize skepticism?" said Thomas.

"I'm a lawyer, I majored in skepticism."

"Wait 'til you meet it here," said Bennie.

"Can we give it a try?" asked Carl.

"Do you have the National Guard?" asked Thomas.

"I think so. If necessary."

"If he's game, Harry can play."

Thomas and Carl looked at Bennie.

"You'll be sorry," he said, shaking his head.

Together they walked to where the boys were panting and sweating, and between games, contemplating the water fountain that hadn't worked since 1961.

"Boys, this is Mr. Gordon. He's John's dad and he has a question for you," said Thomas.

"How would you boys like to form a team and play in the Police Boys Club State Tournament?" Carl asked.

"No disrespect sir," said Harry. "That's a Whites-only league."

"Not anymore," said Carl. "If you want to play, we can get you in."

"Do you want to play?" Thomas asked Harry.

"Sure," he said, "but I don't want any trouble."

"Victor?"

"Yes sir."

"Y'all better watch out for us," said Harry.

"John?"

"Oh yeah!" said John, his eyes wide and a smile taking over his face.

Thomas addressed the other three boys.

"You go ask your folks. Tell them I'm coming to talk to them in person."

Ken, Wesley and Doug took off in different directions to seek permission.

"You sure you can do this, Mister?" Harry asked Carl.

"Even if it takes a federal court order."

Neither Harry nor John knew what that was, but it sounded great. John and Harry shook hands for the first time. Then John and Victor. Thomas and Carl shook hands again too. Thomas picked up Harry and tucked him under his arm like a loaf of bread. He gave him a big kiss on the top of his sweaty head and said, "Son, we're going to make some Stockville history."

Once they were back in the Mustang headed home, John turned to his father.

"Can you really get a team into the state tournament?" he asked.

"I have no idea," said Carl.

❧

CHAPTER 12

Micah Geary barely graduated from high school and skipped college altogether, but Oleatha always thought he was the brightest of her three children. Micah studied history on his own terms, reading who he wanted to read, like Frederick Douglass, W.E.B. Du Bois and Booker T. Washington. He mail-ordered early poems by Phillis Wheatley and Jupiter Hammon and credited Hammon's *An Evening Thought: Salvation by Christ with Penitential Cries* as a life-changing piece of work.

Micah took his first engine apart at age 11 and even though it was a boat engine, he knew from that moment on that his future was under the hood of a car. He opened the H&M Sunoco Service Station on Biddle Street 13 years ago when he was 22. Hands down, Micah was the best auto mechanic in Stockville.

A quiet man, bordering on gloomy, Micah didn't boast, but as Thomas liked to say, "it ain't bragging if you've done it, and my older brother is the Micah-angelo of auto repair."

Micah hated the whites in Stockville, who wouldn't

live near him, eat a meal with him or shake his hand, but enthusiastically ignored his race when faced with a broken alternator. He hated himself for putting up with it, but he did it for the sake of his family.

When Micah barely graduated from Carver High, he was all set to enlist in the Navy as a mechanic when the job at the Sunoco station was offered, with the opportunity to buy in later. Micah couldn't resist and called off his scheduled physical at the recruitment office in Birmingham.

Micah strolled the three blocks from his service station to Thomas's office at the United Negro College Fund. He needed to turn sideways to get his shoulders cleanly through the office door, and stood for a moment as the oscillating electric fan made its way back in his direction and blew air on his forehead. Thomas looked up, blinked his eyes and jerked his head back, surprised to see his brother looming in the doorway. Micah wasn't one for social calls.

"You have an appointment?" Thomas asked.

"I need an appointment?"

"I'm a busy man," Thomas joked.

Micah looked around the fastidiously clean office, at the in-box, the out-box, the to-do list on the desk's right corner, the perfectly aligned stack of paper and the newly ribboned typewriter. Micah entertained the thought of *inadvertently* smearing grease on one of his brother's files and watching him cringe. Instead, he walked past the desk to Thomas's photo gallery on the wall.

"Look at this," he said. "My little brother with Dr. Martin Luther King, Jr. Where was this taken?"

"Last summer at the Student Nonviolent Coordinating

Committee training session," said Thomas.

Micah continued on.

"Thomas Geary and Medgar Evers?"

"May he rest in peace. Winter. 1962 in Birmingham," said Thomas.

"I didn't know you were this big," said Micah.

"I am the Central Alabama Regional Assistant Director of the Southern Christian Leadership Conference. You know what they say, the longer the title, the less important the person."

"You're too modest. Just be careful."

"I will," said Thomas.

"Can we talk?" asked Micah.

"Let me check my appointment book," said Thomas, straining to hold back a laugh at his brother's expense. Thomas flipped three pages back in his appointment book, then three pages forward in mock investigation.

"You're in luck. Ralph Abernathy just cancelled. Have a seat."

Micah sat down in the chair, air rushing out from all sides of the seat cushion under the strain of his 220 pounds. He leaned back and flexed his massive biceps by locking his hands behind his neck. Thomas slipped forward on his chair behind the desk and leaned in. He nodded.

"Item number one. This house in Northwoods is the stupidest thing I've ever heard," said Micah.

"The Lord works in mysterious ways."

"Or Mr. Tatum had a sadistic sense of humor. They'll never let her move in."

"It's symbolic."

"They'll kill her first."

"I don't think she even wants the home," said Thomas.

"The news is already spreading. I think she's in danger."

"I don't know what to do about it."

"Item number two. What's it going to take for you to realize that you're being played by the white man?" said Micah.

"Don't beat around the bush. Tell me what you really think."

"You really think you're going to change anything around here?"

"I think we're going in the right direction, but I must admit, your suggestion last week at dinner of having the white boys by their balls is an interesting alternative. Maybe even an attractive one," said Thomas. "But I don't think it solves a problem, it just creates a different problem."

As Thomas spoke, Micah stretched his arms above his head, clasping his hands together.

Thomas looked at Micah's flexed biceps and shoulders and thought Micah might just be the strongest man in Frost County. He smiled, remembering how Micah used to entertain the entire Geary family doing curls with his son Victor hanging from his outstretched fists.

"You didn't just come here to debate the advantages of non-violent civil disobedience," said Thomas, loosening his tie and unbuttoning the collar button on his white cotton shirt.

"Item three. Don't know about this basketball thing," said Micah, shaking his head.

"What thing?" Thomas responded.

"The kids' tournament? What do you know of this Carl Gordon guy?"

"Not much," said Thomas.

"He's white," said Micah.

"Yes, I know that much."

"That just means trouble," said Micah.

"We've had trouble our whole lives, what's a little mo—"

"We're talking about our kids," Micah interrupted.

"I know. And I know it's just basketball, but it's bigger than that. We can sit-in at Woolworth's and March on Washington, you can promote your revolution, but what does that really mean to our kids? I don't know that they grasp any of that," said Thomas.

"Basketball?" said Micah.

"Think about what it will mean to Victor and Harry to play against white teams in a tournament that has never allowed Negroes. They'll be the trailblazers. That they'll remember."

"Jimmy Cooper is dangerous," said Micah.

"A big bully, yes," said Thomas.

"Stockville is a better place for Harry if he has a father," said Micah.

There was a pause while the men stared at each other. Two sides of the same coin.

"I think it's the right time."

"It's just a basketball tournament. You can't let that go?" asked Micah.

"Jackie Robinson was just a baseball player," said Thomas.

"In Brooklyn."

"So Stockville gets dragged kicking and screaming into the 20th century, 20 years later. Seems normal to me."

"This guy Gordon?" said Micah.

"Carl?"

"Carl Gordon."

"What about him?"

"You're going to trust a white man?" asked Micah.

"I think so. He seems sincere and tough. His kid's a good player."

"So he stirs up the shit and then high-tails it back up North?"

"I think he's here for a while," said Thomas. "This basketball tournament is not something he got sent here for. It just happened," said Thomas.

"I'm not agreeing to anything until I talk to him."

"That's fair."

"Does he have a phone number?" asked Micah.

"I can do better."

"How?"

"Tonight's our anniversary party."

"We'll be there."

"So will he," said Thomas, leaning back in his chair.

"You invited him?"

"I didn't think he'd just show up."

"You invited...You invited a white New Yorker?" asked Micah.

"He'll be easy for you to find," said Thomas, biting his lip to keep from smiling.

"You continue to amaze me."

"Thank you," said Thomas.

"That was me being polite, not complimentary," said Micah. "You have this idea that if you just bring everyone together they'll all get along. That we just have to look for the good in each other."

"How awful," said Thomas, mocking his brother's cynicism.

"How naïve. Some people just don't want to get along."

"See you tonight, big brother."

Micah shook his head in exasperation. He turned to leave. On his way out the door he dragged his forearm across a file cabinet, leaving an oily black streak.

"This place is a mess," he said.

❦

Carl practiced several different poses in the full-length mirror. Each one worse than the last.

"Do you think I should wear a tie?" he asked John.

"Too hot," John said, glancing up from the bed where he was reading his Superman comic.

"How about the belt?"

"Yes."

"No, what color?"

"Blue."

"Black or brown?" Carl asked.

"Black to match your shoes."

"My shoes are brown."

"Change them to match your belt," said John, this time not taking his eyes off his comic.

"Is a short-sleeved shirt okay?" Carl continued.

"Dad, are you okay?"

"I just want to fit in or at least make a good impression," Carl said.

Carl had chosen a pair of lightweight grey gabardine pants, finely tapered at the bottom, and a white button-down shirt.

"You look good. Nobody will see the mustard stain," said John.

"Where?" Carl asked, twisting his upper torso clockwise and his hips counterclockwise to sneak a look at his own backside.

"Gotcha!" said John, smiling at his father's contortions.

Carl took a deep breath to reduce his nausea.

"Shirley's due back from Birmingham later tonight. You'll be all right here by yourself until then?" Carl asked.

"Fine, Dad."

"Then I guess I'm on my way," said Carl, closing the closet door, brushing his hair back and feigning a confident Fred Astaire down the stairs. Carl grabbed the bouquet of daisies he picked from the garden and stored in the refrigerator and headed out the front door to the Mustang.

Mile 3, Route 7 might pass for directions in New York, but in Stockville it was a home address. Carl headed east toward Stockville proper and the Grove, the Negro neighborhood. Navigating the uneven cobblestone streets kept him alert if not jostled, and it occurred to him that this was his first party since before Beth's diagnosis. Three years. At that realization, his heart beat faster, flaming his already acute anxiety.

Carl was consumed by the differences between white Stockville and Colored Stockville. They were stark and in-your-face. The roads were smooth and paved in white Stockville. In the Negro sections it was strictly gravel or dirt. In white Stockville, large, manicured fescue lawns delivered asphalt driveways from the street to side-yard attached garages. New homes were vinyl-sided in shades of beige or red brick over stone foundations. Roofs were uniform, dark grey slate or orange clay tiles in the more affluent neighborhoods like Northwoods, light grey asbestos shingles in working class white Stockville.

As he drove into the Grove, Carl again watched the changing streetscapes. Broken curbs. Potholes. Missing street signs. The few parked cars—a blue Pontiac, a white Buick—tended toward mid-to-late 50s models. With the sun starting its descent to the western skyline, elderly women in white aprons sat in wood-framed chairs sipping sweet tea and lemonade. Carl had all his car windows down and he heard pieces of conversation, intermittent laughing and the admonishment of several Negro children racing around a front yard. The houses were shotgun styled or white framed bungalows, most with rough-hewn front porches. Of simple design and materials, most houses were well-cared for, at least from the point where maintenance changed from the city's responsibility to the resident's. Carl fumbled for Thomas Geary's directions, written on the back of a U.S. Government envelope. B.B. King's music flowed into the driver's side window and out the other side. Carl pulled over to the side of the road, where he was reasonably certain he had arrived at the Geary home.

Carl stepped up to the front threshold of the white-shingled home, standing outside on poured concrete steps, his body frozen despite an 80-degree evening. He felt as though he was staring into one of John's elementary school shoebox dioramas. Grabbing at a sharp pain in his stomach, he felt lightheaded and nauseous, like he did after his first few drags on a cigarette back in high school.

In a few moments, the partygoers inside noticed Carl and all conversation stopped. A stunned guest lifted the needle of the Victrola and the Shirelles stopped singing "Soldier Boy." Carl tried to breathe, but there was no air on his side of the screen door. Thirty pairs of brown eyes stared down his blue ones. *I picked the right clothing, wrong skin color,* Carl thought. He was sinking in the silent, social quicksand. The daisies slipped from his hand and fell to the stoop, providing a brief distraction. He thought about turning around and slinking back to his car when Thomas Geary walked in from the kitchen and saw him.

"Someone get this man a beer," he said, and, like a freshly wound jewelry box, the party started up again.

The living room had the scent of lavender candles and the bacon rollups which were being passed around. Carl mingled as best he could. At first there wasn't much common ground. Law school, no. Big city childhood, no. Thomas walked Carl around the room, making brief introductions, before excusing himself to the backyard grill, abandoning Carl in a choppy sea of unfamiliar black faces.

Carl looked toward the back of the room and saw a large man dressed in a grey button down short-sleeved shirt coming toward him. The man's biceps filled the entire sleeve opening and the front of his shirt fit tightly on his 6'2" sculpted frame. His forehead was creased and he had a moustache that was full and menacing. He looked like he might walk right over Carl like he was a warehouse floor mat. Carl stepped aside and avoided eye contact, hoping the man would continue walking past him, but Micah stopped right in front of Carl and stared down at him six inches from Carl's nose. Micah's mouth was clenched and stressed. It was Carl who broke the silence.

"I'm Carl Gordon," he said, offering his handshake.

"I know who you are," said Micah, crossing his muscled forearms atop his chest. "What I want to know is what you're doing."

Carl took a step back, his spine bumping into a wooden curio cabinet, preventing any further retreat.

"I'm here—"

"I know about the civil rights crap. I want to know why you're trying to get our kids killed," said Micah, leaning in, his eyes staring directly into Carl's.

"I don't know what you—"

"Basketball. You don't know shit from shine-ola about this place, do you?" asked Micah.

"It's just a—"

"Just a way to integrate?"

"Well, yeah," stammered Carl.

"In New York City you think that all Negroes want to integrate. Then it's 'Negro problem solved.'"

"Well—" said Carl.

"I don't need help and I don't want any shit from the white man," said Micah, his voice on the rise and attracting the attention of some of the guests.

"I thought we were talking about kids' basketball," said Carl, taking a deep breath and holding it, like a man about to be pushed and held under water.

"My son Victor...he's all excited about playing in the PBC state tournament."

"That's a bad thing?" asked Carl.

"Well we'll see, won't we? If you pull this off, I'll be at the games and I'm warning you. If Victor gets hurt, I'm holding you responsible," said Micah, making a fist in front of Carl's face. Several other guests turned to see the commotion.

Carl stammered and as his adrenaline surged he felt light-headed, but he just couldn't back down.

"If he has the best experience of his life, do I get the

credit?" he asked.

"Oh, go to hell," said Micah, walking away past a handful of guests, their mouths wide open.

Carl took a deep staccato breath and thought it would be best if he left the party. He went looking for Thomas, but on his way across the room he saw a huddle of laughing guests including Bennie Elsberry.

Bennie was even more sharply put-together at the party than at the playground, with a cream-colored suit, dark blue shirt and beige tie with red and black Egyptian hieroglyphics vertically aligned from the knot at the top to the bottom point. Carl approached and Bennie smiled in warm recognition.

"So, Mr. Gord—"

"Carl."

"So, Carl, I see you've met Thomas' brother Micah."

"Yes," said Carl. He tried to temper the fear in his voice.

"He's not a bad guy," said Bennie. "A bit tightly wound."

"I'll note that," said Carl, swallowing some beer from a cup Thomas had handed him.

"Are you married?" asked Bennie.

Carl had successfully navigated that stroppy channel in the past with evasive references to life's little setbacks, but in a panicked moment left over from his Micah confrontation, he described Beth's illness in detail.

"Sorry to hear about your loss," said Bennie, nodding sympathetically. Bennie's graceful demeanor showed in his calm voice and a soothing tilt of his head. As a life insurance salesman, he was experienced in tragedy, and he always delivered insurance checks to his grieving customers in person.

Talking about Beth made Carl's brow twitch, and his eyes

scream for an intervention. He felt the room shrink again and his larynx tighten. Bennie turned the painful moment into a more comfortable business opportunity.

"I suppose a misfortune like that makes you think about providing for your son," said Bennie.

"I should, but I haven't," replied Carl. "That's your line of work, right?"

"I'm with the Rural Insurance Cooperative, out of Topeka, Kansas. If you're interested, maybe I can show you our products some time."

"I'd like that."

"I have a card."

Bennie reached inside the breast pocket of his jacket and withdrew one of his business cards. Carl noticed the hand-sewn silk maroon lining of Bennie's suit and his initials "BAE" embroidered in white script.

Carl retrieved one of his Assistant U.S. Attorney business cards on which he had written his new address and phone number in Stockville. He handed it to Bennie.

"Please call me," said Carl.

"I'd be delighted," said Bennie, wondering if he was talking to his first white client.

Bennie introduced his wife, Annell, who had turned to join the conversation. Carl immediately noticed her delicate eyes, the color of light brown sugar, and her calming smile.

As much as Bennie exuded energy, Annell brought ease and relaxation into the party mix. She asked about John, and Carl listened to stories about their daughters. Carl smiled when he realized that parenting was the universal solvent of awkward chit chat. Talking to Bennie and Annell made Carl comfortable. His neck and shoulder muscles released. They chatted about family, showed photos and then moved to music. Carl liked the Supremes. Bennie pantomimed playing the harmonica when he told Carl that he and Annell saw Bob Dylan play a concert in Birmingham.

Carl glanced over Bennie's shoulder. On the wall above the fireplace hung a large painting of a wooden storefront in turquoise with white-trimmed windows and doors. It was striking for its stormy sky, and a sliver of sunshine casting shadows down from the palm trees and electricity poles and wires. A bright red car drew Carl's attention to the center of the painting where four Negro figures were headed into the building, perhaps for lunch. Carl moved closer to admire the work. He couldn't make out the signature at the bottom.

"Harold Newton," said Bennie.

"What?" asked Carl, his attention drawn away from the painting and back to Bennie.

"The artist," said Bennie.

"It's beautiful," said Carl. "Is he local?"

"He and other Negro artists sell their paintings out of their cars near Fort Pierce, Florida."

Carl sat down on the couch, still staring at the painting. He reached for a handful of peanuts sprinkled with salt and cayenne and without looking, he tossed them in his mouth and began chewing. By the second chew his tongue and palate were burning. Spitting them out would be certain social suicide, so he swallowed them between gasps and wheezes and tried to make believe he was cool with the whole experience, smiling at Bennie. Bennie laughed and offered a glass of water that he poured from a pitcher perched atop the coffee table for just such emergencies.

"I'm alright," Carl said, through stifled coughs and

intermediate wheezing. Tears formed in his eyes and Bennie reached out and grabbed Carl's hand just before he rubbed his eyes with the fingers that had just been holding the peanuts. That mistake would have resulted in temporary blindness and a trip to the emergency room. Carl took two gulps of beer, three deep breaths and rested on the back cushion of the paisley couch. He swiped his handkerchief across his damp forehead and began breathing normally again. Regaining his social sea-legs, he leaned back onto the armrest of the couch and bumped into a rum and Coke.

"Are you blending right in?"

Carl followed the hand around the cocktail up her arm to a beautiful young woman dressed in a white cotton sleeveless dress.

"Actually feeling a little pale," Carl said.

She smiled. Carl smiled back.

"I'm Lenore, Thomas's sister."

"Carl."

"I know who you are."

"That's good, because I've spent most of tonight wondering."

Lenore brushed her bangs away from her finely manicured eyebrows. Her cheeks had been dusted with a hint of pink, and her smooth skin, lit up by a ray of sunlight sneaking through the window shades, highlighted her long neck.

"You're the handsome stranger who knows nothing about Alabama," she said.

"Have I been complimented or insulted?"

"Suit yourself." Lenore smiled again, her lips parting slightly, revealing a playful mystery of perfectly aligned white teeth.

"Why don't you teach me?" he suggested.

"How to be insulted?"

"No. About Alabama."

"How much time have you got?"

"How late do these parties go?" Carl asked.

"I think you could pick it up in 30 years."

"Again. Complimented or insulted?" he asked.

"Definitely complimented," she said.

Carl was sure it was his serve, but before he could speak, she did.

"Are you here to save us?" she asked.

"I think that's the pastor's job," said Carl.

"Funny. Then what's your job?"

"I'm going to make sure the Civil Rights Act is enforced." Lenore laughed at him.

"If I say *Brown vs. The Board of Education*, what do you say?" she asked.

"I say Supreme Court decision that found separate but equal to be inherently unconstitutional."

"Year?"

"1954."

"And today it's...?"

"1964."

"So in 10 years we've gotten where?"

"Nowhere," Carl said, recalling everything he had seen of separate and unequal. "Congratulations Mr. Gordon. You have completed your first lesson on Alabama."

Carl hadn't been out-maneuvered like that since before Beth got sick. It was strangely delightful for a man who believed that if you marry a woman smarter than you, you're smarter than her. Carl slid into his uneasy expression and laughed.

"Who are you?" he asked.

"I told you. Thomas's sister."

"Is there a Mr. Thomas's sister?"

"You mean a husband?"

"Yes."

"He's out there," she said.

"In the kitchen?"

"No, out *there*."

Lenore waved her smooth right arm, pointing to the space between the backyard and the rest of the universe. Carl followed her elegant gesture but quickly came back to the moment, transfixed on her shapely figure, tightly wrapped in a white leather belt with a silver buckle. Thomas arrived.

"You've met my sister?"

"I was just leaving," said Lenore. "I don't want to monopolize the Assistant U.S. Attorney's time."

"No, you're fine," Carl said, immediately realizing that his comment might be misunderstood. "I mean, I'm fine."

"Mr. Gordon. I'm sure at least one of us is fine. Do you need a refill on your beer?" she asked.

"Sure," he said, offering his glass.

"Then please help yourself," she said, as she pushed open the swinging door that led to the kitchen, pirouetted on her high heels and disappeared into a cluster of women gathered on the back porch.

❦

CHAPTER 13

Oleatha set the balls of yarn, one pink and the other white, on the couch cushion to her left, each attached by a single strand to the lime-green aluminum knitting needles sitting in her lap. She turned on *As the World Turns* and inspected her previous day's work, eight inches of what would be the front panel of a Christmas cardigan for her granddaughter, Cara. Oleatha compared her work to the pictures in the knitting magazine. Her snowflake pattern on the front was a perfect match. The instructions listed mother of pearl buttons, but with Oleatha living on Lester's Air Corps pension, Cara's sweater would get plastic buttons instead. Satisfied with her creation thus far, Oleatha's dexterous fingers went to work. At full bore, her fingers moved over the needles like Little Richard's flew over the piano keys in *Good Golly Miss Molly*.

About 15 minutes into her knitting and her soap opera, there was a hard knock on the front door. Oleatha put down her knitting to see a large sheriff's deputy on the other side of the screen. She nervously primped her hair and untied and removed her sapphire colored apron from around her waist.

"May I help you?" she asked, without opening the door.

"Are you Oleatha Geary?" he asked.

"I am."

"I have these papers for you," he said.

Oleatha opened the screen door and the sheriff's deputy handed her some official looking papers, folded in thirds.

"What are these?" she asked, but the man had already turned and was walking away without responding to her question.

Oleatha shut the door and looked at the stack of papers. On the top of the cover page it said *Subpoena* in large black letters. Without reading any more, she called a family meeting.

Lenore, Micah and Thomas arrived together at 7:30 p.m. Oleatha had laid out the documents on the kitchen table. There was the subpoena, something called a Petition for Declaratory Judgment and a Court Order signed by a judge.

"I can't make heads or tails of this," said Oleatha.

"It's simple. It's the white man keeping you out," said Micah.

"Is that your best legal opinion?" asked Thomas, who rolled his eyes and took the legal documents off the table.

"I'm sure you can do better," said Micah.

The Petition listed the Northwoods Neighborhood Association as the plaintiff and Oleatha Geary as the defendant. At the top it said, "Twenty-First Judicial Circuit, Frost County, State of Alabama."

"It says here that you, Mom, are causing the neighborhood 'immediate harm,'" said Thomas, reading from the petition.

"I haven't even been over there yet," said Oleatha.

"It says they *demand* a hearing on July 30th at 1 p.m.," said Thomas.

"That's only 12 days from now," said Oleatha.

"We need a lawyer," said Thomas.

"I called one," said Lenore.

"I can't afford a lawyer," said Oleatha.

"Oh, no," said Micah to Lenore.

"He'll be here any minute," said Lenore.

"Not him," said Micah.

"You have a better idea?" said Lenore.

"I can call the NAACP in Birmingham," said Thomas.

"Can they get a lawyer here in five minutes?" asked Lenore.

"No," said Thomas.

"I can," said Lenore, smiling. "An Assistant U.S. Attorney lawyer."

On almost perfect cue, there was a knock on the front door. Oleatha stood up from the couch to let Carl in.

"I thought only doctors made house calls," said Micah, in a tone designed to lay his claim as the alpha male in the room.

"Make nice, Micah. The man's here to help us," said Lenore.

"Hi, Lenore. Hello, Mrs. Geary," said Carl, offering his hand.

Carl looked nervously at Micah.

"Ever seen one of these?" asked Micah, taking the papers out of Thomas's hand and pushing them toward Carl.

Carl thought this was no time to take on Micah Geary in a battle of machismo, which he could never win, or words, which he thought he could. He paged through the petition and the neighborhood trust indentures that were attached to the petition as Exhibit A.

"Once or twice...a week," said Carl, glancing from Oleatha to Lenore to Micah.

Carl quickly reviewed the documents, flipping the pages like a croupier dealing black jack. He shook his head a couple of times. In less than a minute he folded the pages back to the way they were when he started. He purposely looked first at Micah, enjoying his decidedly superior position when it came to understanding court procedure.

"What are we up against?" asked Thomas.

"In a nutshell, Northwoods says that in 1902 the owners of the land agreed that no Negroes could own land there or live there, forever. So, since your mother is now in possession of the deed to 55 Watkins, that ownership is no good and the deed should be disregarded. They have asked the court for an immediate ruling on Monday because if Mrs. Geary moves in, they claim, the neighborhood will never recover."

"What a pile of shit," said Micah.

"Watch your language," said Oleatha.

"I agree with Micah," said Carl.

"We fight fire with fire," said Micah.

"You mean in the courtroom, I hope," said Thomas.

"Can we win?" asked Lenore.

"We should win. But I don't know about the judges here in Frost County," said Carl.

"We need to more than win. We need to destroy them," said Micah.

Thomas scowled at him. "In the courtroom," he said.

"Hold it right there," said Oleatha. "Y'all are going off

half-cocked and ain't nobody asked me what I want."

All the attention refocused on Oleatha, standing now, in a position of authority. She straightened the white lace neckline of her pale pink dress, its recurring pattern of green-stemmed calla lilies lined up perfectly at the seams.

"I don't want to live there. I'm fine right here. I think we put the house up for sale to the highest white bidder."

"You can't do that," said Thomas.

"Mr. Gordon. Who owns the home?"

"You do," said Carl.

"Can I sell it if I want?"

"Of course."

"I don't need another house, but I sure could use the money," said Oleatha, a gleam of light shining down on her straight nose.

"Mama, it's the principle," said Thomas.

"I can't eat principle, child," said Oleatha.

"I'm with Thomas on this, Mama. You can't sell," said Micah.

"Listen to y'all," said Oleatha. "All high and mighty. You all want to fight the fight. It's your fight, but it's my house. My grandfather was born a slave in Frost County. And look at me. I own two houses!"

Everyone couldn't help but smile at Oleatha's zesty proclamation.

"Dearest children, you're the first Colored generation completely removed from slavery. I think you lack historical context," said Oleatha, scrutinizing each one of her offspring.

"Where'd that come from?" said Lenore, surprised by her mother's vocabulary.

Oleatha took the comment as arrogant and patronizing

in front of Carl and let Lenore know it with a subtle nostril flare in her direction. Meanwhile, Carl thought he might have a solution, but was hesitant to get into the middle of a Geary family fight. Finally, he couldn't resist.

"May I make a suggestion?" he asked.

"Please," said Lenore.

"Do you have to?" said Micah.

"I'd like to hear it," said Oleatha, "and I'm the only one who counts."

"The Neighborhood Association is seeking what lawyers call an extraordinary remedy. They want the court to enter an order that prevents you from moving in. This case is going to move quickly. Even if there's an appeal, the whole thing could be finished in a month," said Carl.

"So," said Oleatha.

"So, hold off on your idea of selling it for a while. Keep that quiet. If the court rules in your favor, which it should, I bet the good folks of Northwoods would pay double, maybe triple the price to keep you out."

Carl wasn't sure how the Geary family would take his last comment. Thomas took him off the hook.

"Mama. We fight the fight *and* you get your money," said Thomas.

"Win, win?" said Lenore, hoping her mother would say yes.

"Do I need to go to the courthouse?" asked Oleatha.

"Your lawyer does," said Carl.

"I don't have one," said Oleatha.

"You do now," said Carl, smiling at Lenore. "I can at least get you through the hearing and then we'll see."

"How much?" asked Micah.

"How much what?" asked Carl.

"How much money?" said Micah, suspicion oozing out of his question like hot tar under pressure.

Carl pondered the question for a few uncomfortable moments.

"I'd like a minute alone with my client please," he said, taking Oleatha's hand and gently pulling her toward the kitchen. They sat down across from each other at the table.

Lenore, Thomas, and Micah stood together and waited, unable to hear what they were saying. Micah paced from wall to wall like a caged lion. Thomas wrote notes in the small pad he kept in his pocket. Lenore stared at Carl as if she was trying to memorize everything about him to recite later, like a poem. At the kitchen table Carl drew a legal pad of paper and a pen from inside his briefcase. He asked some questions and wrote down Oleatha's answers. Oleatha laughed twice in response to something Carl said, and at one point reached over and touched his hand. In five minutes Oleatha and Carl returned to the living room. Carl spoke to the family.

"You're all certainly welcome to attend the hearing Monday if you like, but in the meantime I need to be going. I've got some preparing to do," said Carl, as he picked up the legal documents that he had set on the arm of the couch and stuffed them in his briefcase. He quickly shook hands with Thomas. He did the same, diffidently, with Micah. Before departing, with his blue eyes firmly latched on to Lenore's beauty, Carl moved closer and kissed her on her cheek.

Lenore recoiled, blinked her eyes twice as her face flushed with embarrassment. Then she smiled at Carl. Micah's hands instinctively curled up into two large fists.

It wasn't often that the Geary family was gathered

without at least one of them talking, but there they stood, in shock, each expecting someone else to say something. Carl broke the silence.

"I'll let myself out," he said, and exited through the front door.

All eyes turned back to Oleatha.

"Well, Mama?" Thomas said.

Oleatha looked lovingly at each of her children.

"I think some things should stay between a client and her attorney."

CHAPTER 14

Shirley knew it was frivolous. She had pledged to put every cent she saved toward her nursing degree, but a new dress to wear to her niece's wedding in Montgomery was enticing. Something that would let all her relatives know that her flight to New York had been the right move. *Something simple and elegant. Maybe chiffon with lace and a scoop neck. Fitted at the waist and full and flowing down from my hips to my knees*, she thought.

As a girl in Birmingham, Shirley had heard of Adderson's Dress Shop, and noticed there was an Adderson's in downtown Stockville, with a sign in the window that said, *The Women's Shop for Special Occasions.*

There's no harm in looking great, Shirley thought.

From the sidewalk, Shirley studied the dresses in the window. Her arms and legs ached like they did when someone described a particularly gruesome crime scene. She knew she wasn't sick, because that feeling had come and gone several times since her arrival in Stockville. She sucked in a mouthful of fresh outside air, expanding her chest to its fullest and opened the glass door. Her eyes adjusted to the inside lighting of the well-stocked dress shop, as a small bell that was hung above the front door rang, announcing her arrival. Shirley's back stiffened at the ring and she immediately noticed the aroma of starch and Primitif, a popular cheap perfume sold in New York department stores.

Shirley's eyes gazed up and down the aisles and she noted for the first time that all the mannequins were manufactured to look like white women, both in skin tone and facial features. *The small, flat behinds are a dead give-away*, she thought, and it took all her self-control to keep from laughing aloud at her private joke. Shirley thought about the Negro dress shops she'd patronized. Even in those shops the dresses were displayed on white-lady mannequins. She wondered if there *were* any Negro mannequins. She'd never seen any, not even up North.

Two salesgirls looked up, saw Shirley, and then continued folding blouses. Shirley took a deep breath and another step in. She cleared her throat and stood up straight, like she did at the playing of the national anthem. Shirley moved her purse closer to her chest and noticed to her far left was a pale yellow summer dress in a style Elizabeth Taylor wore in a picture in *Look* magazine. She took a small, hesitant step to examine more closely a blue dress in the window and to avoid eye contact, not that anyone appeared to have any interest in her.

The blue dress is too bright but the yellow one is perfect, she thought. It was silk taffeta, with a slight sheen, like the reflection of honeysuckle off a still lake. She checked the price before falling too deeply in love. $29. She curled her lower lip over her teeth and bit down softly at the expensive price.

She looked for the size, half hoping it would be too big or too small, given the steep investment. It was an eight, her size. *Divine intervention*, she thought. She looked in the direction of the two salesgirls, hoping one of them would notice she needed assistance and directions to the fitting room.

The salesgirl who was folding continued folding. The other one, a chubby consignment in a green pleated skirt and white blouse, held the receiver of the phone to her ear, looking everywhere but at Shirley, and apparently not talking to anyone on the other end.

As Shirley checked the quality of the stitching on the hem of the yellow dress, she heard the entrance bell ring again and spotted a thirtyish white woman enter the store. The folding salesgirl stopped folding and the phoning salesgirl put down the receiver. They rushed the new customer, like wolves on fresh white meat.

"Can I help you?" said the folding salesgirl.

"Yes, what can we do for you," said the phoning one, racing down the store's far aisle. Shirley pretended not to notice. She'd chalk it up to the southern way of life, ignore it and carry on.

Finally, a middle-aged, matronly woman who was the source of the perfume, and carried herself like the manager, emerged from behind the cash register and acknowledged Shirley's presence.

"Do you need help," she said.

"Good morning. I'd like to try on this dress."

"What size are you?" she asked.

"I'm an eight," answered Shirley, her hand resting delicately on the mannequin's shoulder.

"I'm sorry, we don't have that dress in an eight."

"This one right here is an eight," said Shirley.

Reaching for the sleeve of the dress on the mannequin, Shirley showed her the tag.

"I'm sorry, I can't sell the window display," she said. "How would women know what we have?"

"Can you show me the others like this? Maybe I can try a ten, or a different color."

"I'm afraid this is our last one."

Shirley remained stoic and nodded to be polite. She spoke slowly and clearly.

"If you only have one dress and it's in the window and you can't sell it, then it's obviously not serving the purpose of informing window-shopping women what dresses they can buy," said Shirley.

The manager folded her hands over her chest and focused her eyes on the wall behind Shirley. Shirley remembered that there was no point in challenging a white woman. It didn't work that way.

"What about this rack of dresses over here," asked Shirley, pointing to the far end of the store. When Shirley looked at the manager eye-to-eye, the manager's attitude changed from false and affected to arrogant.

"These dresses are expensive. Have you tried Sadie's on Locket Street?" she asked.

Shirley's muscles tensed and her adrenalin surged, but she willed herself back to composure and she opened her purse. She pulled out three ten dollar bills to prove her seriousness and ability to pay.

"I really like this one and I don't see why we can't take it from the window, especially since it's your last one."

The manager refused the offer.

"Perhaps there is some business we might be able to do," the manager said, her bulbous nose rising slightly higher and her chin pointing at Shirley. "Would you happen to know any nigger bitches looking for domestic work?" she asked.

Shirley and the manager locked stares, neither one willing to look away.

"Ma'am, I don't know any nigger bitches," said Shirley.

Without hesitation the store manager raised her right arm, open-handed, and slapped Shirley hard across her left cheek, stinging her face and causing her to drop the money.

"Don't you ever speak disrespectfully to me," the woman said. "Get out."

Shirley didn't know if it was 45 years of pent-up rage or ethnic pride instilled by her mother and cultivated on the streets of New York. Or sheer stupidity. She did not flinch. Shirley stared back hard and angry. She remembered how much of her youth was spent avoiding eye contact with whites, looking down in demonstrations of inferiority. Those days were over. She was nobody's nigger bitch.

Shirley let fly with her open left hand, cracking against the woman's overly-rouged cheek, coming away with a stinging, pancake-powdered palm. The woman grabbed the side of her face, screamed and fell, grabbing at and toppling the yellow-dressed mannequin on top of her. Blood flowed from the right nostril of her swelling nose.

"I'll call the police," shouted the chubby salesgirl.

Shirley ran for the door, pulling it open and ringing the bell again. Before she fully closed the door behind her she remembered her $30 was still on the floor. She knew she needed to get out fast, but she couldn't afford to leave a month's rent behind. She shoved the door back open, ringing the bell again, this time violently. The manager was still on the floor, holding her face and swabbing her bloody nose with the yellow dress. At the return of the crazed Negro woman, the two salesgirls ran screaming into the back room, the white shopper close behind.

"Don't hurt me," cried the manager.

Shirley reached down quickly, snagging her nylon stocking on the leg of a table displaying Fall sweaters, and slipping on the polished terrazzo floor. She grabbed the bills and scurried back to her feet, looking down at the cowering manager, who was now fully employing the mannequin as a shield. Shirley stuffed her money back into her purse.

"Honey, that dress would've looked ten times better on me," she said.

Then she ran.

※

Carl grabbed the receiver of the kitchen wall phone, looked at Thomas Geary's business card, and dialed the number of his office. Carl explained the events of the day as they had been described to him by Shirley and listened carefully to Thomas's advice and opinions. Thomas related a similar story, where a Negro visitor to Stockville, a male, bloodied the lip of a white bartender, who served him kerosene instead of bourbon at the back door of a restaurant. Almost poisoned, the man just wanted his money back.

"He was detained by the sheriff," said Thomas, "and never heard from again."

Thomas said he would make arrangements and call back when everything was ready.

"Please hurry," said Carl. "I'll have Shirley ready."

Preparing dinner that night fell to Carl, as it was too dangerous for Shirley to leave the second floor and risk being seen from the street. Since arriving in Alabama, much to his surprise, Carl found that he enjoyed cooking. Never one to accept circumstances without supplying a rationale, Carl spent considerable time pondering his fascination with meal preparation. He came up with two equally plausible explanations. First, he thought, he liked cooking because when he was prosecuting, his cases lasted for months, sometimes years, before resolution. Preparing dinner, start to finish, took an hour, maybe two.

Second, Carl spent most of his days answering questions and telling people what to do. The police wanted to know where to store the evidence. The lawyer representing the target of the investigation wanted to know when the indictment might be handed down. All day long, Carl supplied the answers. With dinner it was completely different. Carl reached for one of the cookbooks on the shelf, and the book told him what to do. How spectacularly mechanical and perfect, he thought.

On this particular afternoon, Carl had stopped at the butcher shop and purchased enough chopped beef to make four large hamburgers. There was one hamburger for him and one for Shirley, who always seemed uncomfortable when Carl cooked dinner. Also, there was one for John, and one for posterity, which used to mean Carl, but lately meant John, and an imminent growth spurt. Carl was mixing the meat with some salt, pepper and A-1 steak sauce, unquestioningly following the directions in the *Better Homes and Gardens Cook Book*, which Carl bought for 10 cents at a Stockville garage sale. He was drawn to it by its red and white checked cover and the promise that all the recipes were from the magazine's *tasting test kitchen*.

In a robin's egg blue apron he had found hanging on the wall in the stairway to the basement, Carl took a handful of chopped meat and began molding it into what he believed to be the most perfect hamburger patty south of the Mason-Dixon. He cupped the ball of meat in his left hand and gently pressed it into his right hand, pushing it and squeezing it, like a potter about to turn a blob of clay into an object d'art. As he was forming the last of his prized patties, there was a knock on the front door. A knock Carl had been expecting earlier. Carl washed his hands at the porcelain kitchen sink with warm water and Palmolive and headed for the front door. Through the frosted glass Carl could see the silhouette of a man in a large-brimmed hat, his hands placed on his hips. He opened the door. Sheriff Bascomb, in full, authoritative uniform, and wearing a stern face, stood on the porch.

"Nice getup," said the sheriff.

Carl untied the apron and pulled it over his head.

"Good afternoon, Sheriff."

"I'm looking for Shirley Wallace."

"Social call?" asked Carl.

"Official business."

"What's the charge?"

"Why do you need to know?"

"Just making conversation between two guys in the same industry," Carl said.

"Is she here?"

"Have you got a warrant?"

"No. Just want to ask her some questions."

"She isn't here."

"And if I had a warrant?"

"Why should we speculate?" said Carl. He took a deep breath, moderately surprised at his flippant response to local law enforcement.

"My daddy used to say Yankees are like hemorrhoids. Pain in the butt when they come down and always a relief when they go back up," said the sheriff.

"Huh. That's clever, Sheriff. My mother used to say that laundry is the only thing that should be separated by color," Carl responded.

"Your Mama needs to mind her own business. When do you think I should come back?"

"I hear Stockville's beautiful in October."

"I'll be back this evening with a warrant."

"I'll call you the minute she shows up," said Carl.

"I'd appreciate that. Tell me counselor, have you Feds got a related crime to Alabama's law against harboring a fugitive?"

"Sure do. 18 U.S.C. Section 1071. Talk about coincidence, Sheriff, I just read that section about an hour ago."

Carl opened his copy of the Code of Federal Regulations that all U.S. Attorneys were required to keep handy, and that he had left on the window ledge on purpose. He had dog-eared the proper section.

"Good day Mr. Gor—"

"It says, Sheriff, that in order to be harboring a fugitive, there must first have been a warrant issued by a judge. Otherwise there's no fugitive to be harboring."

"Back in no time," said the sheriff.

"Looking forward to it," said Carl, a wry smile pursing his lips.

"By the way, where were you between four and six?" asked the sheriff.

Carl hesitated, thought for a moment, and made direct eye contact with Sheriff Bascomb.

"Kindergarten," he said.

Sheriff Bascomb shook his head and muttered "asshole" under his breath as he turned and walked down the front stairs, shifting his gun belt, undoubtedly for Carl's benefit. Carl saw John Wayne do that in *The Man Who Shot Liberty Valance*, but he resisted the temptation to call out, "I'll be waiting right here, pilgrim."

When Carl was sure the sheriff was gone he closed the front door and climbed the stairs to where Shirley was sitting on her bed, crying.

"Remember back in April when you told the assistant to the U.S. Attorney that I was out on an assignment, when I was really in my bedroom having a breakdown?" Carl asked Shirley.

"Yes," she said.

"Well, I just lied to the county sheriff. We're even." Carl put his arm around Shirley, and called out across the second floor hallway for John.

"Yeah, Dad," he answered from his room.

"Can you come here a minute? I need your help."

Carl met John in the hallway. Shirley sat on the bed. She stared straight ahead and remained still as the early evening. She was dressed in a navy blue cotton dress and a hat that had a geometric print pressed into Wedgewood blue fabric. Her left arm sat atop her packed suitcase. With her right hand she clutched her Bible. Shirley could hear Carl and John moving things around inside the house, climbing up and down the stairs and carrying something out to the attached garage through the covered breezeway. About 20 minutes later, Carl came back upstairs and sat on the bed next to Shirley.

"This is all my fault," he said.

"I slapped her," said Shirley, looking down at her knees that were shaking. Carl cupped Shirley's hand in both of his. She looked up and met Carl's eyes with her own.

"I can be a terribly selfish bastard," he said. "I never should have asked you to come here."

"I made—"

"No, I made a lot of mistakes. You covered for me at work and at home. You're the only reason John still talks to me."

"That's a beautiful boy you've got," said Shirley, dabbing her eyes with a handkerchief she fetched from her purse.

"They're here," yelled John as he ran up the stairs.

"It's time," Carl whispered.

Shirley stood up from the bed, no longer crying, but her unsteady gait and deep breathing revealed her anxiety. She looked at John.

"Young man, you promise me you'll mind your dad. Now come over here and give me a hug."

John ran to Shirley and threw his arms around her midsection, squeezing her tightly around her waist. After a few moments John extended his right arm toward Carl.

"Dad, we need you here. Three-way hug," he said.

Carl put one arm around his son and the other around Shirley. They stood there until Carl said, "We need to get moving."

Carl grabbed Shirley's valise. John held her hand and the three of them walked down the stairs together toward the back door where the Drake's Dairy truck was backing up to the breezeway door.

"Everybody ready?" asked Carl. There were assenting nods all around.

🌿

Carl and John exited 30 minutes later, walking out the back door, their faces illuminated by the brilliant sun hovering on the western Alabama horizon. Once in the garage, Carl slid behind the wheel and John climbed in the back. Carl backed the car out of the garage and the driveway, shifted into drive and headed for town.

"Where are we going?" John asked.

"Ice cream?"

"Definitely," John said.

"I also thought we'd go fishing," Carl said.

"At night? Wait a minute. You don't know how to fish, day or night."

"Think big catch," Carl said.

"You know a place?" said John.

"I hear there's a good ice cream shop near the Greyhound bus station."

"I've been to Hudson's," said John.

"We'll go there if we can't find this place."

Traveling east, with darkness setting in, Carl glimpsed at his rearview mirror and saw lights flashing from a car about 100 yards back.

"I think we got a nibble," Carl said.

John looked over his shoulder, out the car's back window. In a few moments they heard the sheriff's squad car siren and saw the flashing lights. Carl immediately steered the Mustang over to the right side shoulder of the road and shut down the engine.

"What's going on?" asked John.

"Not to worry. It's just the sheriff."

Carl put his hands high on the steering wheel and watched in his mirror as the sheriff opened his door and came strolling toward them, a flashlight in his right hand.

"Evening, Sheriff," Carl said out the open window when Bascomb was still a few feet behind.

"Mr. Gordon. Headed to the bus station?"

"No sir, we're looking to buy some ice cream."

"I got a warrant and I'm going to have to take Shirley in. Assault and battery. Please step out of the car lady," he said.

The sheriff pointed his flashlight past Carl to the front passenger seat. Resting firmly in the seat was the top half of the sewing mannequin from the house, with one of Shirley's best Sunday hats atop a black-haired Halloween wig.

"Not so funny, counselor. Where is she?" Bascomb shifted his weight from his left to his right and put his hands on his service revolver.

"What time is it?"

"It's about 9:15," the sheriff said.

"My best guess is northern Kentucky, maybe Tennessee by now."

"You're lucky I've got a good sense of humor or I'd drag you in instead," said Bascomb, whose cheeks rose slightly, revealing some enjoyment of the prank.

"Thank you sir and no disrespect meant. I'm just here to

do my job. A Mr. Johnson sent me and gave me this badge." Carl reached into his jacket pocket and handed the sheriff his gold U.S. Attorney's badge with its silver bald eagle emblazoned on the crest. Carl stroked the day's growth of beard on his chin, feeling confident for the first time in weeks. The sheriff took a quick look, then closed the leather billfold and tossed it back into the car. "I don't think he'd be too pleased if something happened to me or my boy. Why don't we work together?" asked Carl.

"You have no idea what you're up against."

"You may be right, but it doesn't mean I have to be up against you."

"I don't think we'll ever be on the same side," said the sheriff.

"I'll keep trying," said Carl. "Is there anything else?"

"Yeah, your left tail-light is out."

"I don't think so, this is a new car," said Carl.

As the sheriff walked back to his car he nonchalantly drew his nightstick from his waistband and in one smooth move of his left arm, he smashed the Mustang's tail-light, sending shards of red glass flying in all directions.

"I'm pretty sure," he said.

❧

CHAPTER 15

John and Carl arrived at the Police Boys Club of Alabama on Pinewood Street in downtown Stockville when it opened at 9 a.m. The PBC's venerable history dated back to 1943 when it'd been established in support of young boys with fathers oversees, fighting Germans or Japanese. It had quickly become the sponsor of kids' sports tournaments. Whites only. Carl presented his completed entry form, a team roster and the $10 entry fee. Had Thomas and Harry Geary arrived with exactly the same documents they would have been told that the entry deadline had passed, or they didn't accept cash payments, only money orders, or only cash if they arrived with money orders. The middle-aged brunette behind the desk might have just bluntly told them the truth—they don't take Negro teams. For this job, at least, John and Carl were supremely qualified.

"I'd like to enter a team in the 12-and-under basketball tournament," Carl said to the husky woman behind the oak desk. She looked up and gave them a toothy smile that said good morning all over it. She had a small, button nose that made her hazel eyes look as big as the fresh-water cultured pearls around her neck.

"Team name?"

Carl looked at John, realizing that in their alacrity they had neglected to discuss a name for the team.

"Greyhounds," said John.

"Greyhounds?" she repeated.

"The kids picked it," said Carl, trying to sound like he was in charge and he knew the name all along.

"Roster?"

Carl handed her the roster.

"Coach's name?"

Carl and John shared another brief and anxious moment.

"John Gordon and Harry Geary, g-e-a-r-y," Carl said.

John held back a smile. Sure, why not, he thought, all the time keeping a straight face.

Miss PBC continued unfazed, not realizing the two coaches were 12 years old and were listed as players on the roster.

"Address for correspondence?" she asked.

"620 Maiden Lane," said Carl.

"I just love the Crepe Myrtles in that neighborhood," she said. "Entry fee?"

Carl handed her the $10 bill, which she slid into the desk drawer. She pulled out a pad and pencil and handed Carl a handwritten receipt. She also handed Carl a flyer about the local play-in tournament and the PBC Official Rule Book, which John immediately grabbed and started reading.

"That's it then," said Miss PBC, looking up and giving them her sincere, southern congratulations. "Good luck in the tournament. I hope you win."

Miss PBC told Carl he'd receive a schedule in the mail once the entry deadline had passed. Carl thanked her and he and John, who had burrowed into the rule book, walked out the door and into the street.

"Greyhounds? Good name," Carl said. "Greyhounds are fast and sleek and they'll bite you if you mess with them."

"We chose it because we're grey-hounds."

"So."

"Grey. Like us. Like what you get when you mix black and white."

"I like that even better," Carl said.

According to the flyer, the first two rounds of the Central Alabama qualifying tournament would be held at the Stockville Recreation Center on Saturday, August 1st, beginning at 9:30 a.m. with the elimination games three weeks later. Carl wrapped his arm around John's shoulder and told him how proud he was of the way he was handling the move to Stockville. John looked up at his father.

"I'm proud of you, too."

John put his arm around Carl's waist and they walked together triumphantly down the block to the car.

"Registering was easy," John said, bouncing his basketball as they walked.

"For now."

"Why?"

"At some point the PBC is going to realize it just registered its first Negro team. Then, who knows..."

When they got back in the Mustang, John continued reading the PBC rule book. Within minutes he had it all figured out.

"The 12-and-under state tournament starts with

regional elimination tournaments that are broken into four-team pods," he explained. "Every team in each pod plays the other three, with the two top teams moving on to the state tournament. The bottom two teams are out, but can try to qualify by winning a statewide *losers' bracket* tournament of those teams that didn't qualify in their home regional."

"That sounds hard," Carl said.

"Nearly impossible, I think. Only the winner of that tournament goes to the state tournament, which, according to this booklet, probably means winning six games in a row."

The PBC Rulebook was eight pages of small type. It covered everything from proper attire, to coach's demeanor, to expanding the roster by one player after the regional tournament, to how to decide the winner when teams ended pod play with the same record. John explained it as they rode home in the car.

"If there is a two-way tie, the winner of the game between the two teams is the winner," said John.

"That's easy," Carl said.

"Here's the complicated one. If there is a three-way tie, the two teams that advance are determined by the point differentials among the three tied teams."

"Huh?"

"If there's a three-way tie, that means three teams finished with two wins and one loss and the other team finished with no wins and three losses."

"So far so good."

"So in head-to-head competition, each of the tied teams won a game and lost a game to the other two."

"Did I mention I majored in English?"

"Concentrate, Dad."

John pulled out a pencil from the car's glove compartment and sketched out the possibilities on the back of the tournament rule book.

"Let's say team A beat team B by 5 points and lost to team C by 10 points," said John.

"Good."

"Their point differential is minus 5."

"Five, plus negative 10 equals negative 5. I'm having horrendous flashbacks of seventh grade, but I've got it," said Carl.

"Team B is minus 5 from the five-point loss to team A, but let's say they beat Team C by 12 points. Team B's point differential is plus 7. Minus 5 for their loss and plus 12 for their win. That leaves team C."

"I'm lost."

John took a deep breath, trying to be patient with his arithmetic-challenged father.

"Team C. They beat Team A by 10, but lost to Team B by 12. So they are minus 2."

"Not good."

"It's good enough."

"Huh?"

"Well, Team B comes in first place with a point differential of plus 7. Team C comes in second place with a point differential of minus 2 and Team A comes in third place with a point differential of minus 5. Teams B and C move on to the State Tournament. Team A goes home."

"How do you know this stuff?" Carl asked.

"You may be my dad, but Mom was my mom."

"Have I ever told you the burden I carry being the

dumbest one in the family?"

"Don't feel bad," said John.

"You know what I think?"

"What?"

"Just win all three and we won't have to worry about math."

"Exactly. Seriously, Dad. What if we arrive and they won't let us play."

"I may not be algebraically valuable, but I've taken care of that."

Having entered the Greyhounds in the tournament, Carl and John continued their drive to Carver High School for the team's first practice.

"Hey, Dad. What happened with Shirley?"

"She crossed a line and I was afraid her life was in danger."

"Where'd she go?"

"She's safely back in New York. I shouldn't have talked her into coming here."

John leaned back in the Mustang's bucket seat, his basketball sitting comfortably between his knees.

"Hey, Dad. With the Greyhounds-"

"Yeah?"

"Aren't we crossing a line?"

Oleatha sat reading the newspaper on the couch in her living room. An early morning Alabama breeze moved through the screen door in her kitchen, past her slippered feet and out the open front door. Thomas knocked on the door frame out of habit, and pushed open the screen door before there was any response from inside, knowing it wouldn't be locked.

"Morning baby," said Oleatha, her hair coated in chemicals and her sunflower-patterned housecoat tied at the waist.

"Hi Mama," Thomas responded.

He was handsome in his brown, summer weight wool suit. His hair was short and brushed. His face was clean shaven. He looked every bit the part of a young civil rights activist, calculated to avoid offending anyone, especially the white southern population that already felt threatened. Micah openly resented that part of Thomas and the movement, and told him so every occasion he got. Micah argued it was phony and ineffectual, even cowardly.

Thomas walked over to Oleatha, bent at the waist and gave her a kiss on her cheek.

"That stuff in your hair smells awful," he said.

"Don't let your mouth overrun your tail," said Oleatha.

"Like rotten eggs," he continued.

"Anything else? Have I put on a few pounds? Maybe the house isn't Spic and Span enough?"

Thomas backed off. Although his first reaction to his mother's morning attire was to laugh, he resisted. He knew from 31 years of experience that something was bothering her. Oleatha was never one to hide her feelings.

"Sorry, Mama. You look fantastic. Evie said you were looking for me."

"Want coffee?"

"No thanks. I'm kind of in a hurry this morning."

"You're always in a hurry."

"Is that what you want to talk to me about?"

Oleatha crossed her arms on her chest, his mother's

signal that their chat was going to be more than a quick morning chat.

"No. I want you to stop," she said.

Thomas looked confused. He sat down on the pine rocking chair across from his mother and crossed his legs, one pant leg over the other, revealing his brown, cotton hi-rise socks and excellently polished shoes. The last time his mother looked at him like that and said she wanted him to stop, it turned out she wanted him to stop hanging around a group of undesirable boys in 10th grade. He studied his mother, like a biologist looking at an amoeba under a microscope.

"Stop what?" he asked.

"Do you always have to be out front?" she asked.

"What are we talking about?"

Oleatha walked over to the stove and refilled her blue porcelain cup.

"Coffee?" she asked again.

"No."

"Things don't change overnight," she said.

Thomas tried to stay calm. Wading through his mother's conversational Morse code to find out what was really on her mind was like playing chess. He had to think both offense and defense at the same time.

"Still your move, Mama. What's up?"

"It takes time to change the way white folks think," she said.

Now Thomas understood. He ran his hand around his prominent chin and down to his neck.

"I get it," he said. "Don't you think 100 years is long enough?"

"Things are better now than they've ever been," she said.

"That doesn't make them good or right. Aren't you tired of going to the back door? Walking with your head down?"

"Can't you slow it down a little?"

"Dr. King said it, Mama. *Slow* has always meant *no.*"

Realizing that expressing concern wasn't going to get her what she wanted, Oleatha tried another tactic.

"I think you're just a selfish, foolish man," she said.

"Selfish?"

Thomas lifted himself out of the rocker and walked right past his mother into the kitchen. He opened the wooden cupboard above the counter and reached far into the back for the coffee mug he was looking for, the one he bought from SNCC in Memphis. The one that read, "Come let us build a new world together."

"I think I'll take you up on that cup of coffee, black," he said.

"Don't you even think about Evie and the kids?"

"Mama, that's all I think about. I think about my wife having to wait at the grocery store to see if the white man will *allow* her to buy food for her family. I think about Harry having to sit in the back of the movie theater, reading outdated text books with yellowed pages and entire chapters ripped out by prior white students. I wonder how I'm going to explain to Cara that she has to give way to every white person on the sidewalk, without destroying her self-esteem. I think about it all the time."

"What do you know?" asked Oleatha. "You're just a child yourself."

"I'm a man, Mama, and I know plenty. Let me tell you what I know. I know when we were kids, the reason you told us to take a drink of water at the house before we went downtown was so you could avoid the degrading scene of your children drinking from the *Colored* fountain."

"Oh hush."

"I know you brought clothes home from Dalton's Department Store and told us that it was *easier* than going to the store together. Remember, Mama? Don't you think we knew it was because if we went there, Dalton's wouldn't let us try on the clothes, while all the white kids did?"

"That's not a big deal," said Oleatha.

"I think all the time about the father I had and the kind of father I want to be."

Oleatha suspected where Thomas was going with this conversation and tried to head it off at the pass.

"Don't you say anything bad about your father," she said.

"Why not? I was there to see dad kowtowing to that bastard Gerald Hudson to get a decent cut of meat at the butcher shop."

"He did that for you, and watch your language."

"I remember him acting like he was stupid in front of white people because that's what white people wanted. Stupid, shuffling, lazy Negroes. That was my father too," he said.

"How dare you," shouted Oleatha.

Thomas had come this far before but always found his way out by remaining calm. Today, as Oleatha's volume increased, so did his. His eyes blinked and his fists clenched.

"Let's talk about what we don't talk about," he said.

Oleatha threw her arms up in the air. "Stop!" she said.

"Not this time. You wanted to talk. We're going to talk. My father did nothing after the attack. No complaint. No charges. No eye for an eye. No tooth for a tooth. The sheriff didn't sweep it under the rug. You did," said Thomas.

Oleatha scowled at her son, the rational one. She had heard this kind of impudence on occasion from Micah, but never from Thomas, and this topic was off limits.

"Stop it. I don't want to hear another word," she said.

"It's who we are. Why can't we talk about it?"

"There was nothing your father could do."

"Not true."

"You want us all dead?"

"No, Mama, I want us all to be proud of who we are."

"He had plenty to be proud of and don't you forget it," said Oleatha, her voice three octaves above normal.

"Everyone says I'm just like him, but I'm not. I'm non-violent, but that doesn't make me a coward."

"We did the best we could!"

Oleatha collapsed back on the couch, her hands covering her face. She started sobbing and coughing and gasping for air. Thomas stood for a moment, his heart pounding, then shook his head and sat down next to her, putting his arm around her.

"Mama, I'm sorry. Sometimes I can be a real idiot."

"No. You're beautiful. You're all beautiful," said Oleatha, wiping her nose. "We didn't do half bad," she said, no vitriol left in her tone.

"I'm part of something big, Mama. This is the right time. The right way."

"Medgar Evers was shot dead in his front yard."

"The Freedom Riders were courageous."

"Four little girls blown up in their church basement."

"The Birmingham sit-ins last year changed Jim Crow."

Oleatha walked to the living room couch, picked up a

folded newspaper that was sitting on the coffee table and handed it to Thomas.

"What's this?" he asked.

"This is why I'm so upset. Those three missing boys in Mississippi? They were found a few days ago, murdered by the Klan and buried in one shallow grave. James Chaney. Mangled, tortured and beaten to a pulp of raw meat."

Thomas had heard the news, but hadn't seen the horrible discovery in print or the picture. He glanced at the headline of the Meridian, Mississippi, *Star*.

The Nigger Was Found on Top

Thomas sighed deeply and looked up at his mother.

"You shouldn't read this stuff," said Thomas.

"Maybe *you* should," she whispered. Oleatha started crying again. "I'm just so scared. These people will stop at nothing," she said, wiping her tears away with her kerchief.

Thomas walked to his mother and put his arms around her again.

"We're all on the line. We're leaders in this community. Everybody's talking about you inheriting the house in Northwoods."

"I told you I don't want it."

"The kids playing in the state basketball tournament?"

"Don't do that."

"We have to. It's the right time. What's that saying you have about how a person has to be who he is?" he asked.

Oleatha looked into Thomas's eyes and managed a small smile.

"To thine own self be true?" she said.

"That's the one."

Thomas smiled at his mother and wiped a tear off her cheek with his finger.

"I guess if it's in the Bible, it has to be right," said Oleatha.

"That's right," said Thomas. "Pretty sure that's from the Old Testament, the book of Hamlet." Thomas smiled. "I'll be careful, Mama. I promise."

❦

Lenore was becoming Carl's dusk before dark, when long shadows replaced the day's colors. She filled Carl's mind like a rushing black river in the moonlight. With John asleep, Carl laid down on a blanket in the backyard staring up at a thousand stars, trying to conjure a plan to see Lenore again. Carl knew it would take careful preparation to create a chance meeting. Especially so, he was realizing, in the Jim Crow South where the entire social order was set up to prevent the mingling of races. Carl didn't know where Lenore lived. He had a phone number but thought calling to ask her out was too awkward. At the party he overheard that she was teaching summer school at Carver. Carl quickly decided he needed a meeting with the Carver principal to discuss student activism or teacher involvement in the upcoming voting rights march on Stockville. He wondered at what time of day he was most likely to run into Lenore.

Carl decided to try for tomorrow at noon. Then he had a chance to see her leaving a morning class or arriving for an afternoon session, or getting lunch in the school cafeteria. He knew from the pastor that the principal's name was Jackson Talbot. The next morning he got the school phone number from the Stockville phone book and dialed the number.

"Carver High School."

"May I speak with Mr. Talbot please?"

"Who shall I say is calling?"

"This is Carl Gordon from the U.S. Attorney's Office."

"Hi, Mr. U.S. Attorney. It's Lenore Geary."

Oh God. Now what? He wasn't prepared for this. *Hold it together big boy*, he thought. *Don't blow this. You're 35 years old. Act it.*

"Hi, Lenore. I didn't expect you to answer."

"Who did you expect?"

"I didn't expect anyone..."

"Then why waste your time calling?"

Carl was completely bewildered.

"Can we start again?" he asked.

"Sure," said Lenore. "Hello, Carver High."

"Hi Lenore."

"I'm sorry, Miss Geary is at lunch. Would you like to talk to Mr. Talbot?"

"No thank you."

"You wouldn't?"

"No. I'd like to leave a message for Miss Geary."

"Okay. I have a pen and paper."

"Please tell Miss Geary that I think she's beautiful but it's her wit and charm that really drive me crazy."

From the other end of the phone there was nothing. Complete silence.

"Did you get that?" Carl asked.

She hung up.

❦

CHAPTER 16

John learned quickly that what he called going to the movies, the kids in Stockville called going to the picture show. For Stockville kids, the picture show meant Saturday afternoons at the Hill Theater. Located downtown, the "Hill" was an elegant brick building with spires on either side of the façade, topped off with sandstone sculptures of harp-playing angels. The name "HILL" rose above the façade in striking yellow neon on all three sides above the marquee, which listed the current movie name and show times. The marquee itself, back-lit in white, had tall black letters announcing its current movie, *From Russia With Love*. The box office was tucked under the marquee overhang, centered on the building with three glass doors on either side.

Mrs. Hill sat propped up high in the box office taking money and dispensing tickets. She reminded John of the carnival fortune-teller machine. She took his money, pushed a button, waved her hand over the stainless steel countertop and a blue ticket came shooting out of a small slit, like magic.

From Russia With Love was the second James Bond 007

spy movie. John had seen *Dr. No* in New York when he was 11. Even though Carl said he was too young, John had snuck into the Orpheum on 62nd with his friend Kyle.

"It was so cool," John told Rudy, when they met in front of the Hill at 12:30 and waited in line for the one o'clock show. John looked at the others in line. Most were kids ages 12 to 15. There were small groups of girls his age, cooing over the poster of Sean Connery behind the glass window display attached to the side of the building.

John thought maybe Stockville only had one clothing store for girls. They all wore plaid skirts of different hues and color combinations topped with white blouses. They wore bobby socks, usually white, with thick uppers that were folded down creating a soft cuff around their ankles. Pre-teen girls in Stockville had a choice in shoes. The girls wore saddle shoes, mostly white trimmed in dark blue or black, or penny loafers, all brown, with actual pennies slid into the slits on the shoe fronts.

"Let's sit in the balcony," said Rudy.

John followed him. They stopped at the concession stand. Rudy and John each got a red and white cardboard box of popcorn and a Coca-Cola. They climbed the side staircase up to the top floor. The pre-show lights were still on in the theater so they had no trouble finding their way.

"Front row?" said Rudy.

"Sure," John replied.

John immediately recognized Jack and Jimmy, who had claimed two of the eight front row seats on the right side of the center aisle. Seeing them made John feel queasy again about the snub he got from the Jacks.

"Let's sit in the front row over there," John said, pointing to the empty seats on the other side of the center aisle.

"Can't sit there," said Rudy.

"No?" said John.

"That's for the Coloreds," said Rudy.

"Huh?"

"That section over there. That's where the Negroes sit."

On second glance John noticed the sign across the back of that section that read "Coloreds" and the three boys and two girls sitting in that section were Negro. Their seats were hardwood and cushion-less. The white section seats were plush and upholstered in gold velvet.

"I didn't see any of them in the lobby," John said.

"The Coloreds have their own box office down the alley by the fire escape."

The term "box office" was an overstatement. After entering through the side door, the Negroes handed their money to the ticket-taker, often a different Hill family member who was sitting in a chair on the musty landing between the first floor and balcony. If another Hill family employee was unavailable then the Negroes had to wait until all the white customers went through the front entrance and Mrs. Hill would then move from the box office to the landing and let the Negroes past the ropes, hung wall-to-wall on hooks, sometimes after the movie had started.

"They like it that way," said Jimmy.

John took the seat on the center aisle with Rudy next to him on his right, followed by Jack and Jimmy farther down the row. A few minutes later John heard a familiar voice coming from the opposite entrance. There was no mistaking the chatter. It was Harry. He, Victor and Doug were at the top of their staircase and had just come around the corner, Harry prattling the entire time. John waved and they immediately took the seats just across the center aisle.

"Hey guys," John said.

"Hi, John," said Harry, getting the attention of Rudy, Jack and Jimmy.

"You know those three?" asked Jimmy.

Before John could answer, Jimmy and Jack moved down a seat and Rudy's "hi" wasn't his warmest.

John decided against an introduction. Harry didn't mind, or didn't show it and probably didn't expect it.

"Have you seen this movie? I have," said Harry. "This is my second time. It's great. Lots of car chases and shooting guns and stuff."

"I saw *Dr. No* last year," John said. "That was great, too."

"I saw that one four times," said Harry.

"What are you guys doing after the show?" John asked.

The question was met with non-verbal awkward facial expressions, expected since no white person had ever asked them that question before. After three weeks living in Stockville, John was starting to understand the basics of how segregation worked, but still it didn't come to him naturally. Here he was with white friends on his right and Negro friends on his left, but they weren't allowed to interact with each other. He couldn't go sit four feet to the left and Harry couldn't come sit four feet to the right. Kind of stupid, he thought, but he didn't say anything. He had learned that much. The lights dimmed and the show started with a Daffy Duck cartoon, and then *Bond, James Bond*. John loved that line. He stared at 007, on the screen, big as a building.

Sean Connery was just too cool for words and he held the rapt attention of every kid in the place. About 15 minutes into the movie Rudy gave John a nudge and gestured for him to look over at Jimmy.

"What's he doing?" whispered John.

"Dunno," said Rudy.

It looked like Jimmy was tying something, maybe string, in his lap, but John couldn't make it out. A brighter scene came on the screen and John looked over again and saw that Jimmy had a ball of string and he was tying one end around the body of a large rubber spider. Rudy and John looked at each other and tried to ignore it. Then Jimmy shifted to the front edge of his seat and John could see out of the corner of his eye that Jimmy was lowering the spider down over the railing of the balcony to the seats below. John tried to watch the movie as Jimmy was tilting his head over the guardrail and guiding the spider down.

With 007 preparing to battle the Soviet SPECTRE agent, a huge girl-scream, coming from the audience down below, interrupted the movie and filled the Hill Theatre. A few seconds later there was another from the same vicinity. John hadn't heard a scream like that since he snuck into the movies back home to see *The Birds* by Alfred Hitchcock. These screams weren't a reaction to the movie. Jimmy had danced the spider onto Stacy Vincent's head and then he let go of the string so it fell in her lap.

On the screen, 007 ground to a halt, and old man Hill turned up the house lights. He followed the screams to the orchestra section. The boys looked over the balcony railing where they saw Mr. Hill with the fake spider in his hand. He glared up and took off for the stairs, commercial grade flashlight in hand. He took a left and then a right and bounded down the center aisle of the balcony, immediately shining the light in Harry's face.

"You pickaninny troublemakers get out," he said.

Harry was stunned. Victor and Doug didn't even know what happened.

"We didn't do anything," Harry said, careful not to look Mr. Hill in the eye.

"I'm no fool boy. We shouldn't let your kind in here at all."

"It wasn't us, Mister," said Harry, softly so as not to appear accusatory. Harry looked at John for help. "Tell him we didn't do anything," he pleaded.

John was confused. He couldn't think more than one sentence ahead. Old man Hill shined the light in his face.

"Okay smart boy, who did it?"

John froze. He knew about doing the right thing and he knew about ratting out his friends, even if Jimmy Cooper, Jr., wasn't really his friend. John couldn't come up with the right thing to say, so he said nothing. His face went blank and he looked down at the stained balcony carpet.

"I thought so," said Mr. Hill. "You three coons get the hell out of my theater. You're lucky I don't call the sheriff."

John looked up at Harry. His stomach cramped at the humiliation he saw flash across Harry's face. Victor, Doug and Harry stood up and headed down the row toward the fire escape, silently, with their heads bowed over their shoulders. Harry had tears in his eyes. Victor was angry, looking like he was about to explode at being falsely accused, but he just kept walking. As Harry crossed the balcony threshold, without turning back, he said, "I thought you were different." John watched the rest of the movie in silence. His face was red hot.

After the movie, John and Rudy walked down the block to

get a milkshake at Kreigel's. The fountain stools were filled so they sat in one of the wooden booths along the west wall.

"That was unfair," said John.

"What?" said Rudy.

"That Jimmy pulled that prank and the Negro kids got blamed."

"Why do you care?" asked Rudy.

"They're nice guys," said John.

"How do you know them?"

"When the Jacks wouldn't let me try out, my dad took me over to their side of town. We've got a basketball team for the PBC tournament," said John.

"You're playing on a team with niggers?"

"I don't think they like that name."

"They any good?" asked Rudy.

"Harry, the kid I was talking to, he's really good. So fast."

"Do they know the rules?"

"Of course they know the rules," said John.

"My grandpa says niggers are dumb," said Rudy.

"Does he know any?"

"Don't think so."

"Do you know any?"

"Nope."

"Take it from me then. These guys are as smart as anybody and they can play ball," said John.

"What's the team name?"

"Greyhounds."

"Well Greyhounds, prepare to lose to the Jacks by 20."

John smiled, ran his fingers through his puff of sandy brown hair and sat up straight as backboard. Even at 12 years old, revenge was an excellent motivator. He was confident that he and his new teammates were going to be good, really good.

"We'll see about that," he said.

❦

John arrived for Greyhound practice at the agreed time of 5 p.m. at Carver High. Carl dropped him off, hoping he'd run into Lenore. He didn't, so he drove to an appointment he had with the mayor to discuss the logistics of the upcoming March on Stockville in support of Negro voter rights.

John arrived at practice to find Harry and a few others taking layups. As players in front of him ran for the pass that led to their shot, John moved up to the front of the line. As it turned out, Harry was at the head of the rebounding line and got the ball. John ran in, expecting a pass from Harry, but Harry went right past him and passed the ball to Phil, who was next in line. John was surprised, but ignored it and went to the end of the rebounding line.

Harry stopped the drill and split the guys up into two teams to scrimmage. They began play with Harry, Victor, Doug, Ken and John on the same team. They brought the ball up against the others. Harry passed to Victor, who passed to Phil. Phil dribbled to his left and passed back to Victor. Victor passed to Doug, who shot, but missed. Back on defense, John covered Wesley. Harry picked up Phil. Victor on Larry. Doug played against Alvin. Ken on Greg. The other team passed the ball around and Wesley came off a pick set by Larry. Normally Victor would clear some space so John could slip past the pick or Victor would yell "switch" and pick up Wesley. On this play Victor did neither, and

John ran right into Victor, who not only seemed ready for the crash, but appeared to have orchestrated it, complete with a forearm shiver to John's chest. John went down, the wind knocked out of him. Nobody stopped play and Wesley scored an easy bucket.

As Harry brought the ball up the court, John got up off the gym floor and ran to the other end. He was wide open under the basket and called for the ball. Harry passed to Doug, who passed to Victor. John again yelled that he was wide open. Doug passed back to Harry. John moved from under the basket out to the wing. When he ran past Larry, Larry planted his elbow firmly in John's back and Ken pushed John out of his way.

John was getting more frustrated but ran back into the middle of the game. Then he pushed Victor. That's the moment they all stopped pretending they were playing basketball. Victor tackled John and the two of them wrestled to the floor. Their arms were flying, punches were thrown. The rest of the Greyhounds stood around in a circle, yelling for Victor. Nobody else joined in the fight.

The school janitor, a slight man in his early 30s, who had been sweeping the hallway outside the gym heard the commotion. He dropped his broom and came running. This wasn't the first fight he'd broken up, but he was shocked to find that it was between a Negro and a white boy. He pushed Victor away. His normal reaction was not to touch a white boy for fear of repercussions later. Victor's eye was swelling up. John's lip was bleeding. All the boys stopped and were silent. John picked himself off the floor, wiped his lip with his sleeve and recoiled in pain. Saying nothing, he sprinted up the terrazzo gym steps into the hallway and out the school's front door. Once outside he threw himself on the ground and started sobbing. He covered his head with his arms and continued crying uncontrollably, but not from the pain. Once again, he had no basketball team.

Lenore dropped her pen and stood up when she heard the front doors of the school slam against their door frames and ricochet back. School wasn't in session. She took three steps from her desk and looked down from her second-floor window. Lying face down on the school's front lawn was a young boy, a white boy, not moving. She ran out of her office, around the corner, down the steps and out the front door. As she approached she could hear the boy weeping.

"Are you okay?" she asked.

The boy's sobs slowed to whimpers. He rolled over. It was John Gordon. His chin and the top of his shirt were covered in blood. She moved closer, bent down and took his hand in hers, to help him up.

"Let's get you cleaned up," she said. "Where's your father?"

Breathing hard and having a difficult time getting the words out, John was able to tell her that his father had dropped him off for basketball practice and left. Lenore escorted John back into the school and took him to the infirmary, where she cleaned him up.

"What happened to you?" she asked when the situation had stabilized.

John thought for a moment about his answer. He shifted his weight and looked away from Lenore.

"Well?" asked Lenore.

"I ran into the wall," he lied.

Lenore shook her head empathetically, not believing him.

"Let's go back to the gym together. What time is practice over?" she asked.

"6:30."

"It's almost that now. Maybe your dad will be there," she said.

She certainly hoped so. Lenore took John's hand and they walked down the darkened Carver corridors, which were lined with grey lockers, student art projects and government public service posters. When they reached the gym, John pulled his hand back.

Lenore's vice-principal skills were working overtime, and the first thing she noticed was that her nephew Victor's eye was swollen. That's really all she needed to see. She walked right into the middle of their game and stole the ball from Harry as he dribbled past her. The gym was silent.

"Gather round, right here," she said in her best authoritative, vice-principal voice.

All the boys stopped and made a semi-circle in front of her.

"You too," she said to John.

Lenore held up her hand and ordered him into the group with the curl of her index finger. She knew right where to start.

"Harry? Explain," she said.

Harry looked right at John.

"Why didn't you stand up for us?" he asked.

"You saw that other kid lower the spider. Why didn't you tell Mr. Hall?" said Doug.

John was breathing heavily again and on the verge of tears.

"Hold on," interrupted Lenore. "What are you talking about?"

"At the picture show. We got thrown out for something a white kid did and *he* saw the whole thing and didn't say a word," said Harry.

John couldn't speak. He started crying so hard his chest heaved in and out. Lenore took a chance and put her arm around John's shoulder. She bent down to his level, got close to his face and spoke softly.

"Settle down. It's going to be all right. Do you still want to play on this team?" she asked.

John sniffled in and pushed out some words.

"More than anything," he said.

Lenore straightened back up and addressed the players.

"We're going to get past this. This is a team."

"Yeah, but—" said Harry.

"Don't give me the yeah but," interrupted Lenore. "This is the Greyhounds. Right?

"Yes, ma'am," said Harry.

"It's a team. You only accomplish your goals when you play together. Unlike the rest of our world, on this team you're all equal. Maybe the rest of the world can take some lessons from you guys," she said.

"Can I say something?" asked John. He scanned the group and took a deep breath. "I'm sorry," he said, through tears. "I don't know the rules around here. I don't know how I'm supposed to act or what I'm supposed to do." John took another deep breath.

Lenore looked right into Harry's eyes. "You have a better chance of winning if John is on the team?"

"I guess so," said Harry, looking over to Victor.

Lenore had skillfully put the team back together but there was one more piece to the pre-teen boy puzzle. She turned and aimed her sights at her other nephew.

"Victor, John told me he cut his lip and bloodied his nose running into that wall over there," she said. "How'd you get that shiner?"

All the boys looked at Victor, who looked at John.

"I ran into the wall, too," he said.

Lenore nodded her head and smiled.

"Be more careful. Okay then, carry on," she said, and she flipped the basketball off her hip back to Harry and turned toward the exit.

All the boys stood around, looking around, wondering what to do next. Harry broke the silence.

"Okay, Greyhounds. You heard the lady. Let's play ball."

❧

CHAPTER 17

Carl arrived at the church to find Pastor Williams tending the small garden on the south side of the building. There were ripening tomatoes, fuzzy okra, green peppers and yellow squash growing in neat rows.

"Garden of Eden?" he asked.

"Garden of good eatin,'" the pastor replied, without looking up. "Welcome, Mr. Gordon."

"Thank you."

"In the mood to pull weeds?"

"Why not," answered Carl.

Carl got down on all fours next to the pastor.

"I wonder if I can ask a favor," said Carl.

"You can always ask."

The reverend put down his shovel and rolled over so he was sitting on the ground facing Carl. He pulled off his gardening gloves, revealing again the catcher's mitts he had for hands. He crossed his legs and Carl squinted as the sun was setting behind him, creating a silhouette. The sky behind him looked like red ribbons with streaks of lavender, gold and burnt orange, on an ancient tapestry.

"You've made quite an impression in this town," he said.

"It doesn't feel that way," said Carl, pulling a weed from between two plants.

"People are talking."

"Good things?"

"Depends who's talking."

"How about your parishioners?"

"Mostly good. They like that you're here to help, but trust has to be earned and that takes time."

"I suppose."

"I heard about your diversionary tactics with the sheriff."

"Lost a tail-light on that one."

"I think you better watch out with him. White folks in Stockville aren't going to change to your way of thinking easily, you know."

"I know."

"They're going to fight you."

"I hope that's metaphorical?"

"I don't think the Klan knows that word," said the pastor, "and that weed you just pulled *was* a tomato plant."

"Sorry," said Carl, trying to push it back in the ground. Carl took a deep breath to steady himself and prepare for what he was about to ask. Pastor Williams, sensing Carl hadn't come to talk about local politics, peered at him from over the top of his bifocals. He had an unsettling ability to look inside a person, like he could take an x-ray of Carl's character just by looking at him.

"I'm 35 years old," he said.

"Happy Birthday. You want to talk to me about your birthday?" asked the pastor.

Carl knew from his prior encounters that the pastor teasing him in a good-natured way was not necessarily bad, maybe even positive. Carl let out his nervous laugh and spun around to face Pastor Williams.

"No sir, it's about Lenore. Lenore Geary."

The pastor said nothing. There was no change in his facial expression. There was no acknowledgement that they were having a conversation at all. Although Carl had counseled hundreds of witnesses that just because nobody's talking, it doesn't mean you should, Carl couldn't heed his own advice and babbled on.

"I like her."

"Beautiful girl," said the pastor.

"I'd like to ask her out on a date and in New York I think I could muster up the courage. Here in Stockville, I am so completely lost on this. There are probably six laws against it."

"Seven. Most people here would include the laws of nature."

"Right. And I don't want to screw up all the good things I think we can do."

"I'm pretty sure you've already pissed off all the white people here. Why not piss off all the colored ones too?"

"I was just thinking of dinner and a movie," said Carl.

"Right. Maybe someday. Maybe some place. If you think Lenore's brothers, and yes, I mean Thomas and Micah, are going to be pleased if she's seeing a white man, you better think again."

"So it's impossible," said Carl.

"Just because it's not going to happen doesn't make it impossible. You're different. People around here think you're some high-flying, hot shot lawyer from New York City."

"I'm really not," Carl said.

"Nothing wrong with it."

"I grew up the son of some guy who sold paint," said Carl.

"You didn't know his name?"

Carl lost his concentration and his mouth opened. Then the pastor started laughing so hard Carl thought he'd fall over.

"Help me to my feet," said the pastor.

Carl stood up and put his hand out for Pastor Williams to grab hold. He leaned back and pulled. Like a playground seesaw, the pastor rose up and Carl sunk back down. When the pastor began walking toward the church's front door, Carl scrambled to his feet again and followed.

"Might be time to make some changes around here. Isn't that what you're all about? Change," said the pastor.

"So *you'd* be okay if I asked Lenore out on a date?"

"You want my blessing?"

"Sure."

"Damn, son. Go ask her what *she* thinks."

"Just like that?"

"Just like that. And I'll visit you at Valley Hospital when Micah finds out."

Pastor Williams poured two glasses of tea and handed one to Carl.

"What else do you have in store for us?" asked the pastor.

"The Woolworth's sit-in on Thursday."

"Do you need any help?"

"A strategically placed prayer couldn't hurt."

"I'll do my part. Felt any push back yet?"

"Not yet. I've heard some things."

"Like?"

"Like a bomb threat. Just talk I think."

"Son, don't underestimate your enemy."

"Are those words of encouragement?"

"Reality."

The pastor handed Carl a small basket of ripe tomatoes. "Take them home for dinner with your boy," said the pastor.

"Thanks. I will."

"And be careful. People around here don't think much of the federal government and people who stick their noses where they don't belong."

Carl slipped back behind the wheel of the Mustang, and headed home. By now the sun sat firmly below the horizon and the countryside looked like an old photo postcard in shades of grey. About two miles out of town Carl pulled up close behind a slow-moving wheat thresher that took up more than its share of the road, and wasn't moving off to the dirt shoulder. There was nothing to do but wait until the driver pulled off the road or reached a wider stretch so Carl could pass.

Carl thought there must be something wrong with the tractor, because it seemed to be going slower and slower. He didn't think even a good-mannered tap on the horn was advisable from a car with New York license plates. So Carl followed and turned on the radio. Actually enjoying country music, Carl recognized the song. Loretta Lynn, *Before I'm Over You.* Carl glanced in his rearview mirror and saw the bright headlights of a pickup truck coming up from behind, fast. Before long the car was uncomfortably close, and then the tractor stopped completely and he could see the driver dismount on the passenger side and disappear into a field of corn. The truck bumped the back of Carl's car, wedging it against the thresher. The bright beams of the headlights made it impossible to see who was behind him.

"Get out of the car."

It was a southern male voice at Carl's driver's-side window, blinding him with a powerful flashlight in his eyes.

"Who are you?" he asked.

"Not important," said the drawl.

He let the flashlight drop a little and Carl could see the man, draped in a white gown, his face concealed by a pointed white hood. Carl thought of his options. He could jam down the gas pedal and try to move the tractor, but its back wheels were taller than the Mustang and he concluded that hitting the tractor would destroy his car and not provide an escape. He could throw the car into reverse and smash the truck that had pinned him in. Or he could try and talk his way out. He got out of his car, believing that would place him in a position of strength.

"Why did you stop me?" Carl asked.

"Go fuck yourself," responded the robed Klansman.

Another fully robed man appeared behind the first.

Carl cleared his throat and tried to sound authoritative.

"I'm an Assistant U.S. Attorney," he said.

"You got no fucking business here," said the second Klansman.

When the men moved closer, Carl smelled the alcohol on their breath even from behind their hoods. He could not make out any faces and the voices were unfamiliar. He thought he might have a chance of running away if they were truly drunk, but he would need an opening, since their truck pinned him in and the two of them were blocking the only escape route.

"We don't usually string up white boys, but we're going make an exception for your nigger-loving ass," said the taller of the two men.

"I got the rope," said the other. "Let's tie him to the truck bumper and see how he takes to that."

"If he loves niggers so much let's show him how it feels to be one," said the other.

"Hurt me and the entire FBI will be here tomorrow," said Carl, who didn't know if that statement was true.

"You don't know shit about what you're getting into," said the tall one.

"Goddamn nigger-lover. We should just shoot you now and dump you in this field."

Both men had iron pipes in their hands and one of them had a pistol.

"Tie his hands," said the tall one.

"Can you wait just a minute," said Carl, inching his way toward the hood of his car. He figured if he could jump onto the hood and over the other side they wouldn't be able to catch him. He had no way of knowing if the guy with the pistol could, or would, shoot him in the back if he tried running.

"Shut the fuck up, Yankee asshole."

The taller one raised the tire iron and smashed it down on the top of the Mustang, narrowly missing Carl. Carl instinctively ducked and covered.

"What's the matter shitface? Afraid I might muss up your fancy hair?"

With that comment, the shorter man raised his arm again and ran at Carl. Carl tried the car maneuver but the robed assailant grabbed his leg and pulled him back.

"Nice try, dick-weed," he said.

Then he raised his Billy club. Carl braced for the attack and hoped that if the club didn't find its mark, then maybe the Klansman would be off balance and Carl could get in a fierce kick to his balls.

Carl saw the club moving at him. He closed his eyes. He heard a solid thwack, but felt no pain. He opened his eyes as the Klansman went down in a heap on top of him. Out cold. The attacker's hood fell off as he collapsed and his sweaty, alcoholic tongue smeared Carl's face as he was hitting the ground. Another jolting thud followed right after. Carl pushed the first attacker's body off him and looked up to see the other Klansman on the ground too, face down, also out cold.

"You ought to be more careful," said a voice from out of the dark.

It was a soft voice but Carl couldn't see anyone. He was still shaken and sweating. He was pretty sure they were two young Negro men, but they were silhouetted by the truck lights that were still glaring from behind.

"Are you okay?" said another voice with no discernible body that Carl could see.

"I guess so. Who are you?" Carl tried to maneuver to a spot where he might be able to make out their faces.

"Stay where you are. The less you know now the better off you'll be later," said the first man.

"Let's just say after you left the church, Pastor Williams wanted to make sure you got home healthy," said the second voice.

"What happens now?" Carl asked.

"You get in your car and go home."

"What about these two?"

The men talked with a calm and easy-going confidence

that told Carl they had been in this kind of situation before.

"We're going to move the tractor and the truck. Drag these two off to the side. They're going to have some powerful headaches in the morning," said the first voice.

"Probably shouldn't drink so much," said the other.

"Also going to take their robes and hoods, douse them with gasoline and burn them. Send a message."

"Your car okay to drive?" asked one of the men.

"I think so. It looks like there's just a big dent in the roof," said Carl.

"Then you go on your way. Probably ought to forget this whole thing, okay?"

"I guess. Thank you. Can't you tell me who I'm thanking?" said Carl.

"Best not. Think of it this way. You know how Dr. King is?"

"Yes."

"We're not like him."

CHAPTER 18

Shirley's abrupt departure left a void in the kitchen, among other places, and all of the cooking duties had fallen to Carl and his cookbooks. John trended on the picky side as an eater, so at least three days a week dinner was hamburgers, a meal that worked for both of them. Carl had been preoccupied all day with a problem he never anticipated when taking the Stockville assignment—whether to report the attack against him and ask Justice to send down some national guardsmen or federal marshals. He wanted protection, but if he reported the KKK attack, the Attorney General might just pull the plug on his entire assignment.

Carl was meticulously slicing the reddest, most beautiful tomatoes he had ever seen, courtesy of Pastor Williams. Carl had only known New York tomatoes, which were a pale red, oblong and thick-skinned. These were redder and rounder. Tomato juice and seeds squirted in all directions when he bit into one. Carl had to wipe down his suit and the kitchen counter.

Carl was placing the uniform tomato slices on a serving dish with the hamburger buns, two on the plate for each one in his mouth, when the phone rang. He wiped his hands on the avocado green chambray dishtowel he had hung from his pant waist and picked up the receiver.

"Hello," said Carl.

"Carl? It's Travis."

Carl thought he might confide in his good friend and immediate supervisor. "Hi Travis. I'm glad you called. Can I ask—"

"Do you get *The New Yorker* there?" Travis interrupted.

"Real funny. The general store only sells *Field & Stream*," said Carl. "But—"

"This week's issue came out today. I'm putting a copy in an envelope and mailing it to you tonight."

"What's the big deal?" asked Carl.

"There's a story in it."

"Probably too long like the rest of them," said Carl.

"This one's different."

"It's short?"

"No. It's called *Accessory to Murder*."

"So?"

"It's about an Assistant U.S. Attorney named Carl Grayburn who kills his sick wife by smothering her with a pillow on their anniversary," said Travis.

Carl sat down on one of the kitchen chairs, stretching the spiraled telephone cord to its eight-foot limit. He hesitated.

"Carl?"

"So?" said Carl.

"It's written by Emily Harlowe."

"Are you in the office right now?" asked Carl, suddenly concerned about who else might be privy to this conversation.

"Yes," said Travis.

"Send the magazine. It's ridiculous. I'll call you back after I read it. I have to go now."

Carl felt dizzy as he walked back to hang up the phone in its wall cradle, missing the first time and steadying himself by putting his other hand flat on the yellow-flowered wallpaper before trying again. He was sure he had never mentioned any of it to anybody. He didn't write anything down. Was it possible he talked in his sleep, he wondered. Just a coincidence? Still, too close for comfort. *And what the hell is wrong with Emily*, he thought.

John's arrival at the kitchen door jolted Carl back to dinner reality.

"What are we having?"

"Hamburgers."

"Are those them, out on the grill?" asked John.

Carl looked out the back screen door to see four oblong balls of fire, like tiny flaming meteors from outer space had landed on his grill.

"Oh damn it," he said, running outside, spatula readied in his right hand, a glass of water in his left.

He moved the patties away from the flames and patted them until the fire went out.

"Might be a little crispy. You want cheese?" asked Carl, with no thought that these molten rocks might not be edible.

"American. And ketchup, no onions," said John.

"Would you get the ketchup from the refrigerator?"

"It's called an ice box here," said John.

"Yeah," said Carl, absentmindedly. "Get the ice box out of the coleslaw too, okay?" said Carl.

"Uh...sure thing, dad," said John, shooting his father a peculiar look.

John ate dinner while Carl had a few bites, but mostly pushed his burger and Tater-Tots around on his plate. After dinner John went outside to shoot baskets and asked his father if he'd rebound for him.

"I'll be out in a minute," said Carl, who went upstairs to the bathroom, closed the door behind him and opened the medicine cabinet. Behind the package of razor blades he found the plastic container he was looking for. He filled a Dixie Cup from the faucet and swallowed two Valium.

CHAPTER 19

When John arrived at practice, Harry and a few others were shooting baskets. John ran off to join them and Carl found a seat on a lacquered wooden bench at the far end of the gym. He pulled out his copy of *Cat's Cradle*, the latest novel by Kurt Vonnegut, his favorite author. Carl laughed out loud twice as he shifted the book a little to the left to catch a ray of sunlight sneaking through the torn window shade behind him. He liked that the book's protagonist was named John.

On the court Harry was talking and taking the team through warm-ups and all the boys were clapping their hands in unison. Carl had a good feeling about the team, and he tried to convince himself that the attack on him was just a test of his determination and resolve. The Emily thing just had to be a coincidence, he thought. He popped a couple more Valium to relax. He returned to his book when Lenore walked into the gym. She stood in the doorway, arms folded over her chest. She looked in every direction, except Carl's.

He pretended not to notice her. Carl's mind flashed Lena Horne in *Stormy Weather*. She walked right through the basketball players, heading toward Carl.

"May I sit down?" she asked.

"Sure," Carl said, pointing to the ten feet of bench he wasn't using. She sat down right next to him, looking straight ahead.

Immediately, Carl noticed her perfume. Citrus. Lime maybe? He couldn't tell, but it was delicious.

"I owe you an apology," she said, still looking straight ahead.

"I think I owe you one," said Carl, turning to face her profile.

"Okay, you win. You owe me an apology." Lenore made a quarter turn to face Carl.

"I guess I came on a little too strong. It won't happen again," he said.

"Not even if I say please?" Her tone was light.

Carl smiled. "If you insist. I can be offensive on request."

Lenore smiled back, and flipped her hair back, revealing silver hoop earrings.

"Do you really think I'm charming and witty?"

"I believe I said witty and charming...and beautiful."

"You do know we're in Alabama."

Carl smacked the side of his head with his open hand. "Really? I thought they said Albania when they gave me this assignment."

Lenore laughed and a smile curled up around her lips.

"So if we have this date, where do you propose to take me?" Lenore asked.

"The balcony at the Hill Theatre is out," he said.

"Definitely. Your arms are too short to reach across the aisle."

"I know a quaint, anonymous place," Carl said.

"Where's that?"

"Chicago."

Lenore laughed again and her perfect lips quivered slightly.

"What's plan B?" she chuckled.

Carl thought for a moment. "I'll cook you dinner," he said, hoping Lenore liked hamburgers.

"You'll cook me dinner?"

"How about Friday?"

"How about we cook together?"

"My place or yours?" Carl asked.

"Mine. I think I'm safer on my home turf."

"I'll bring dessert."

"So you're going to drive to my house at say...6 p.m. We're going to cook dinner together. Probably talk. Definitely talk. Then you're going to drive yourself home?"

"You might be leaving something out, but that's basically it," said Carl.

"What have I left out?"

Carl thought for a moment. "Music," he said.

"Are you a musician?"

"I play the radio."

"Then it's a date, I think," said Lenore, drawing back demurely and placing one of her lovely brown hands over the other in her lap.

"Before you leave, you need to know, I'm missing something," Carl said.

"War injury?" she asked.

"No. Your address."

"Mr. U.S. Attorney. I thought you knew everything."

"Not yet, but I'm working on it," he said.

"63 Potters Lane. In the Grove. White shingles, brown shutters."

With that, Lenore stood up and Carl watched her long legs walk across the floor and out of the gym.

Carl turned his attention back to *Cat's Cradle*. When he read the next sentence his headache returned and his hands went numb. It read, "What will John think?"

❦

Travis Frankel's voice on the other end of the line was firm.

"Absolutely not," he insisted.

"Nobody here will take her case," said Carl.

"That includes you," said Travis.

Carl continued to press. "This is why I was sent here. To prevent racial discrimination," said Carl.

"No Carl. Repeat after me. Monitor and report. You're an Assistant United States Attorney. You represent the federal government. You may not represent a private individual in a lawsuit."

"Can you take this higher up?" asked Carl.

"Are you kidding? If I ran it by Katzenbach he'd look at me like I was Fidel Castro."

"Kennedy?"

"You're joking, right? Carl, did you already tell this woman that you'd represent her?"

"Would I do something that stupid?"

There was silence on the line, while both Carl and his colleague pondered the proper response to that question.

"Carl. It's this simple—the moment you enter your appearance in a lawsuit for a private citizen is the moment you've tendered your resignation with the Justice Department. Is that clear?"

"Yes sir."

"Then go undo whatever you've already done."

"Yes sir. Bye."

Carl hung up the phone. He sat at the kitchen table, listening to the thump of the basketball hitting the driveway outside. He decided he'd do what he often did when he needed to think. He'd go rebound basketballs for John and figure out how he was going to disappoint Oleatha, embarrass Lenore and prove Micah right about him.

❧

Franklin Benshire, an architect from Opelika, had been hired by Frost County after an extensive search to build a new Stockville Courthouse in 1864, replacing the original, which had burned to the ground after being struck by lightning. Ultimately it came to light that Benshire was neither a licensed architect in Maryland, as he claimed, nor experienced in building any structure of note. He had, in fact, stolen the plans for his building from Benjamin Henry Latrobe, the British born American architect best known for his design of the United States Capitol in Washington. This also explained why the County Courthouse was an exact duplicate of the Lincoln County Courthouse in Southern Illinois, designed by Latrobe in 1815. Although Benshire couldn't legitimately claim originality of design, he apparently had construction skills and the building had fared remarkably well in its 100 years, with its six majestic white pillars still perfectly aligned, the roof leak-free and the clock in the tower still keeping time with minimal maintenance. Inside the building, the ornate plaster walls remained crackless, even after the earthquake of 1916 that was reportedly felt in seven states and knocked down chimneys, broke windows and left many of Stockville's wooden frame buildings tilted and unstable.

Shortly after Benshire's lack of credentials was made public by the *Times-Gazette*, he disappeared, rumored to have lived out his life south of the border in San Miguel de Allende. His courthouse was so sturdy that the anniversary of the earthquake, October 18th, had been celebrated as Franklin Benshire Day in Stockville for decades.

Carl was the first arrival at the courthouse when it opened at 9 a.m. and he headed straight for the law library on the second floor. Although dressed in his best lawyer uniform, grey suit, white shirt, striped tie, he endured scrutiny by the librarian, a portly woman of about 50 with a small-town personality, a penny-sized mole on her cheek and a twang the consistency of maple syrup. She cross-examined him on exactly why he was in need of the library. Carl assured her he was a lawyer, presenting his identification from the U.S. Attorney's Office and his membership card in the New York State Bar Association. He realized his credentials may have actually diminished his credibility with her.

"Respectfully, ma'am. If you could just point me in the direction of the Supreme Court Reporters, I'd be much obliged," said Carl, his Brooklyn accent surrounding a new down-homey kind of twang that made him sound ridiculous.

"What's your hurry? You'd think you were working by the hour," said the librarian, who was stamping new books with the court's name and address, as she looked up and chuckled at her joke. Finally, she pointed Carl to a room at the southwest corner of the library.

Carl made four piles on the oak table in front of him. One pile was law books, opened to the first page of the case he would be relying on. The second pile was a stack of white legal pads with blue lines down the middle. Third, the Northwoods Petition with the other legal documents attached to it, and fourth, an ample supply of blue pens. Carl reached for the Petition and read it again, taking notes in long-hand of the precedent-setting cases on restrictive covenants, both in Alabama and under federal law, including the 14th Amendment to the United States Constitution. He stood and paced and stood again over the project, like a shaman in a ritual trance. He shed his suit coat and loosened his tie as the temperature in the building rose. Later he removed his tie altogether and mopped his brow with a handkerchief from his back pocket. At 3 p.m. he was cutting and pasting his work into a seamless persuasion lawyers called a Memorandum to the Court. When he was finished, he returned the Scotch Tape to the librarian, and with his Frankenstein paper creation stuffed into his briefcase, he set off for his 3:30 appointment with Barry Beckley.

Carl hadn't ever met Beckley, but he spoke with him on the phone right after his meeting with the Gearys and his phone call with the New York AG's office. Beckley, an independently-minded liberal thinker, was more than happy to provide assistance for Carl, who had asked to use a desk and a secretary to type the memorandum. Carl hadn't yet asked Beckley if he'd also put his name on the memo and argue the case to the court. If Beckley declined, Carl had no other ideas. Carl walked the six blocks from the courthouse to Beckley & Callahan and met Beckley in the waiting room. He was bigger than he sounded on the phone.

"So Northwoods wants to fight," said Beckley. "Ted knew they would go crazy. More than anything, I think that's why he did it."

"Sounds like a guy I'd like," said Carl.

"A wonderful character," Barry answered.

Carl handed Barry the conglomeration of paper and Barry walked it over to his secretary and asked her if she would type it up.

"I've done all the research and I think the Memorandum is good and ready to go," said Carl.

"I'm happy to help in any way," said Barry.

"Do you really mean that?" asked Carl, his charming New York grin overtaking his face.

"Maybe, maybe not, judging from your expression," said Barry.

"My bosses have said that I can't be the lawyer of record on the case. I'm a *U.S. Attorney,* they've reminded me several times," said Carl.

"I write wills and trusts," said Beckley.

"I've done all the research."

"The last time I was in a courtroom was when I was sworn in 26 years ago."

"It's still in the same place," said Carl, his intonation heading directly toward begging.

"I get stage fright talking in front of people."

"Those bastards will win if Oleatha Geary doesn't have a lawyer," said Carl, pulling out the guilt gun.

"What about the NAACP or the Congress of Racial Equality?"

"I called both, and the Southern Christian Leadership Conference," said Carl. "The NAACP can get a lawyer involved in about two months, but they can't get one here for the hearing. They said they have bigger fish to fry right now."

"When's the hearing?" asked Barry.

🌿

Barry and Carl arrived in the courtroom a full three minutes ahead of Judge William T. Karr, the longest serving judge in all of central Alabama. His thinning grey hair and crow's feet wrinkles, extending from his eyes clear around to his ears, attested to his judicial endurance. Appointed to the bench in 1931, he contributed just enough money to the campaigns of local and statewide candidates to ensure his longevity but not enough to ascend the Alabama judicial hierarchy, which was just fine with him. He fished for bass and bream. He hunted quail and doves. Lawyers making passionate closing arguments in murder trials were interrupted in mid-sentence if necessary for Judge Karr to make his 1:12 p.m. tee-time every Friday at the Stockville Country Club.

"What have you got this morning Ezra?" Judge Karr asked Ezra Turner of Turner, Brink, Matthews & Turner, Stockville's largest law firm.

"Temporary Restraining Order, your honor," said Turner.

Ezra Turner was the second of the two Turners on his law firm letterhead. At 42 years old, he proudly followed in his daddy's footsteps, attending the University of Alabama as an undergraduate and earning his law degree at Vanderbilt, class of '48, after spending two years as a U.S. Navy Seabee.

"Bring it on up," said Judge Karr.

Hearing that comment, Carl nudged Beckley and put a copy of the memorandum in his hands.

"Go," he said, and Beckley shuffled around the table to where Turner and the judge were standing.

"Mr. Beckley?"

"Yes, Judge."

"The probate department is down the hall."

"I'm representing the defendant, your honor."

"No kidding? What have you got in your hot little hands?" asked the judge.

Beckley was sweating from every crease in his big body. *This is worse than a fish out of water*, thought Carl. *This is a beached whale.* Turner chuckled and looked back at Mrs. Spinz who was sitting in the gallery. Beckley handed the judge his stack of papers.

"Your honor, this is the Memorandum in Opposition to the Temporary Restraining Order."

There was silence. Beckley looked back at Carl.

"Go on," said the judge.

"The TRO should be denied for several reasons," said Beckley. "First, the Northwoods Neighborhood Association cannot show that there is a likelihood of suc—"

The judge interrupted and looked past Beckley to Turner.

"Ezra. Is this that Nigress inheritance case?"

"Yes, your honor," said Turner, stepping to the foreground and planting himself squarely in front of the judge.

"Mr. Beckley. You telling me you think a Nigress ought to be allowed to live in Northwoods?"

Beckley took a deep breath, stretching the buttons on his white shirt to their limit. Carl reached over and pointed to a paragraph in the memo and nudged Beckley.

"I would direct the court to the United States Supreme Court cases of Shelley versus Kraemer and McGhee versus Sipes," said Beckley.

"Northwoods. Mr. Beckley, you know we're talking about Northwoods here," said the judge.

The judge turned toward Turner.

"Ezra, you got an Order all written up?"

"Yes I do, your honor."

One of Turner's associates handed him the previously drafted proposed Court Order.

"Sign right here, Judge," said Turner, flipping to the last page of the four-page Order and showing the judge the line reserved for his signature.

Judge Karr signed the papers and then looked up.

"Anything else, Mr. Beckley?"

Beckley looked back at Carl, who shook his head "no."

"I guess that's it," said Beckley.

Carl and Barry loaded up their box of documents and walked to the back of the courtroom where Oleatha and Lenore were waiting.

"That didn't go too well, did it?" said Lenore.

Beckley again looked at Carl because while it didn't feel too good, he really wasn't sure.

"That did not go well," said Carl. "But that's not the end of it. Come on Barry. We've got some work to do drafting the appeal."

"Appeal? Me?" said Beckley.

"Us. We're going to the 5th Circuit Court of Appeals in Montgomery, my friend. I'll draft the appeal and requests for immediate relief tomorrow morning and my guess is we should be ready to re-argue the case next Monday morning," said Carl.

"Do we have a better shot there?" asked Lenore.

"I'm confident the federal court judge will have heard of the United States Supreme Court," said Carl.

"I'll pack my bags," said Oleatha.

CHAPTER 20

Oleatha gazed over her reading glasses at her son Thomas on the morning of the first day of the PBC Basketball Tournament.

"Honey, you look worse than the east end of a horse headed west," she said.

"I didn't sleep too well," said Thomas.

"This basketball thing?"

"Maybe you were right. It's one thing to put yourself out there at a rally or sit-in. It's different when it's your kid," said Thomas.

"Any whitey lays a hand on my grandsons and I'll knock him into the middle of next week," said Oleatha. Thomas smiled.

"It's just a basketball game," said Evie, from the kitchen.

"People are crazy. Just wait," said Thomas.

"I'm ready," said Harry, taking the stairs from his bedroom to the living room two at a time.

"You look fearsome," said Oleatha.

"Go Greyhounds," said Harry, who couldn't stand still normally and today was bouncing around the house like it had a trampoline for a floor.

Oleatha, Thomas, Evie and Harry left the house at 7:45 to meet the other six families at the Carver schoolyard at exactly 8 a.m. They set out in carpools with their 12-year-old sons to the Stockville Recreation Center, parking their cars and pickups at the lot on 14th Street where Carl and John were waiting. John moved right over to the cluster of his teammates.

Why can't life imitate basketball, thought Carl. Nobody on a sports team cared what color you were as long as you got the job done, won the game, and vanquished the opponent.

The boys chattered away in their homemade Greyhound uniforms, which were J.C. Penney t-shirts, created by spray-painting a cardboard cutout—that looked a lot like the bus company's logo—on the front of the shirt. Inside the cut-out, Lenore drew a uniform number with black Magic Marker, and the same number, only larger, on the back. From the waist down the Greyhounds sported a mishmash of dark colored shorts and sneakers. Harry's socks, white with two red stripes at the top, extended over his knees.

Unconsciously and instinctively, the fathers moved to the front of the pack. The closely knit group ventured toward the rec center, like a school of fish hoping that in shark-infested waters there is safety in numbers. Carl stood next to Thomas, feeling his whiteness and anxiety at having brought the group to this uncomfortable spot.

"What do you think?" Carl asked Thomas.

"I think we should have prepared the boys better," said Thomas.

The group rounded the corner to see Sheriff Bascomb standing at the top of the Rec Center stairs, flanked on each side by granite lions protecting the 1930s building. At the sight of the assemblage, he held out his left arm, pointing his authoritative palm at the group.

"Stop right there," he said.

The group stopped.

The sheriff's right hand was cocked by his side, an inch or so above his pistol. His holster was unstrapped, purposely, making the weapon more easily accessible, visible and intimidating. He wore his summer sheriff's regalia, complete with lapel buttons and badge reflecting the morning sun.

"Let's all be reasonable," he said.

He stared down at the group, nervously shifting his weight from one leg to the other.

"We're reasonable, Sheriff. No trouble. Just basketball," Thomas said.

"We've got rules," said the sheriff.

"We've got laws," said Carl, in a tone no Negro man would have dared.

"I can't let you past me," said the sheriff.

"Then please step aside so our boys can play," said Carl. "It's just a game."

"No can do," he said.

Sheriff Bascomb stared right at Thomas, who he knew as a Negro community organizer and probably the leader of this uprising. He tried to appear unyielding, but his left eye twitched nervously, betraying his lack of confidence.

Was he alone? Thomas wondered. Would he dare pull a gun on a group of kids?

"May I speak with you?" asked Carl.

The sheriff didn't answer. He kept staring, his hand gripping his patent leather belt, just above his pistol.

"Come up. Just you," said the sheriff.

Carl climbed the 11 stairs to the entrance, his knees crackling like dry twigs in a campfire. After the highway incident, he realized he couldn't trust anyone. When he accepted the Stockville assignment, he had no idea his life might be at stake. He had no desire to be a dead hero.

"You're messing with my town," said the sheriff, quietly so only Carl could hear.

"I'm just doing my job," said Carl, his back to the rest of the group at the bottom of the stairs.

"Since when does your job involve kids' basketball?"

"Sheriff, this would be a great beginning. You're right. It's just kids playing basketball," said Carl.

"I'm no racist," said the sheriff. "My constituency believes in segregation."

"This town is 57% Negro," said Carl. "Your constituency includes these adult folks behind me. Every one of them is going to be voting in the next election. You know that."

"Maybe."

"Absolutely. Why don't you be the guy who keeps Stockville from exploding?" said Carl.

The sheriff's jugular was chugging up and down in his neck. Rings of sweat had formed under the arms of his khaki uniform top. He moved his right hand and Carl could feel a shudder from the group behind him and a slight buckling in his own knees, but the sheriff just reached into his back pocket for his handkerchief.

Carl thought he was making his points. He thought he might be able to co-opt this discussion. He thought he could talk and reason their way into the rec center. Apparently he was wrong. This time he had a plan B, an ace in the hole he'd rather not have to play. But he did.

"Take a look over my left shoulder," Carl whispered. "Across the street, in front of the bank."

Carl drew the sheriff's attention to a U.S. Marshall standing at the northeast corner of the building. He was dressed in army drab green, his pant legs ballooning just above his calves where they were tucked into his black boots. The sides of his head were clean shaven, with a four-inch wide strip of buzz cut on top. His left hand held firmly onto a battle helmet by its sturdy leather chin strap. On his right side, he cradled a U.S. Army issue rifle.

"Now take a look to your left, down the alley," said Carl.

Carl directed Sheriff Bascomb's attention to two more U.S. Marshalls with stern faces, battle ready.

"Right now, you and I are the only people who know they're here. Can't we keep it that way?" asked Carl.

While Sheriff Bascomb was thinking, Jimmy Cooper opened the door from inside the rec center. He approached both men, standing on the side, between them. He put one arm over the shoulder of each and spoke softly so only they could hear.

"Sheriff, why don't we let the pickaninnies play?" Then he spoke louder. "Look at that sorry excuse for a basketball team," he said, loud enough for the boys to hear.

"You're okay with this?" the sheriff asked Cooper.

"Disappointment is the best teacher," said Cooper.

Bascomb and Cooper locked eyes so the sheriff could make sure Cooper was being sincere. Then the sheriff stepped back, turned around, and walked down the side stairs, avoiding the crowd, but leaving the scene. Cooper turned to the group.

"All right now. C'mon in. We're going to play some basketball," he announced.

The boys gave a yelp and ran up the stairs into the gym. The parents followed behind. Evie gave Thomas's hand an intimate squeeze. Lenore winked a "well done" at Carl, who breathed for what seemed like the first time in several minutes.

"Nicely played," she said.

Then she looked around to see that they were the only two left outside the building.

"Let me tell you a secret," she said, moving closer.

Carl leaned in to hear her, and when he turned his head slightly she gave him a tender kiss on his cheek, her soft hand on his bicep.

"Shall we go in?" she asked, as if nothing just happened.

"That was the second favorite secret of my life," he said.

"I guess I'll have to try harder," said Lenore, as they walked up the stairs and into the gym.

Lenore took a left to join the rest of the fans in the bleachers. Carl took a right, across the gym floor toward the team. At center court he crossed paths with Micah.

"I don't know what she sees in you," he said.

❦

The Montgomery, Alabama, Bulls looked impressive warming up in their Kelly green satin uniforms with white letters and trim. Their jersey had the name "Bulls" written across the front in white script, with the word "Montgomery" in smaller block letters painted in the flair below the team name. Their white socks extended above the knees of the smaller players and the trim on their tight-fitted shorts consisted of a black stripe, accented on top and bottom by a white one. In the bleachers, Thomas wondered if those white youngsters had any idea they were about to take part in Alabama PBC history, playing the first predominantly Negro team.

The Bulls formed two lines and took layups at the near end of the court, while their coach, a squat man, who looked like he'd be more comfortable on a wrestling mat than a basketball court, watched from the bench. Dressed in a matching green t-shirt and green satin sweatpants, his appearance conjured reminders of a fat leprechaun. Thomas's observation proved accurate when the referee called him.

"Stump. Coach's meeting."

Stump had thick eyebrows and a pointed nose that looked like it had been broken at least once. He jogged to the middle of the court where the referee was standing, whistle in his mouth and his hands on his hips. John and Harry headed to center court too. The referee took one look at the two homemade-uniformed youngsters, one white, one Negro and rolled his eyes, like a cop called out to break up a benign domestic squabble. The referee said something to John. John looked at Harry. Both of them, their faces filled with a "where's dad?" look, ran over to the bleachers.

"He won't let John and me be the coaches. He said we have to have an adult on the bench," said Harry.

"No problem," said Carl. He turned his attention to Thomas. "Coach Geary, I presume?" said Carl.

"Yes, Coach Gordon. Shall we go?"

Thomas and Carl walked to center court and introduced themselves.

"Problem?" asked Carl.

"Rules say there must be a grown-up coaching on the bench," said Stump.

Carl pulled the PBC basketball rule book out of the back pocket of his khakis.

"Didn't see that in here," Carl said.

The comment engendered only impatient, blank stares from the referee and Stump.

"Everybody knows that," said the ref.

"I guess so. Can we have two?" asked Carl.

"Sure," said the ref.

"Then here we are," said Thomas. The ref and Stump ignored Thomas completely.

The referee, a tall man with a crew cut and stomach paunch hanging over his belt, rattled through the rules and basics.

"We got four 12-minute running-time quarters. Five fouls and you're out of the game. When I call a foul, the player is to raise his hand so the scorekeeper knows who committed the foul," said the ref.

"Got it," said Stump, adjusting his green sweatpants, bobbing and weaving in place, and looking like the horrifying offspring of a Norwegian troll and the Jolly Green Giant.

"When your team scores a basket, tell your players not to touch the ball coming through the net. I give one warning on that one. After that, it's a technical foul."

Stump nodded his bald head in agreement.

"Any questions?" asked the ref.

"I think we're ready," Carl said, looking over to Thomas, who decided it would be better for the team to let this meeting finish as soon as possible. Carl went to shake the ref's hand and got no response. Thomas extended his hand toward Stump, who turned his back and walked away. The ref blew his whistle to alert everyone that the game was about to begin.

Back at the players' huddle, John and Harry swayed rhythmically from one foot to the other like nervous understudies about to get a shot at the big time. The Greyhound players clustered around them.

"Okay guys. We'll start with John, Wesley, Victor, Kenny and me. Let's play tight man-to-man on defense. On offense, just keep moving. Let's start with the tip play."

Thomas and Carl stood outside the huddle, listening. There was nothing for them to do. Nothing to say. Even at only 12 years old, John and Harry knew more basketball than either of them.

The Greyhounds gathered in a circle and put their hands in the middle. Harry yelled "one-two-three" and all the players yelled "Go Hounds" in unison, raising their hands over their heads as they cheered.

The Greyhound starters walked to center court. The two fathers sat down on the bench with Phil, Larry, Alvin, Greg and Doug.

"We have a tip play?" Thomas asked.

"Just watch," said Phil.

The Bulls came on the court after the Greyhounds and took their positions shoulder to shoulder with the Greyhound squad. John, who was the tallest player on the court, lined up in the center. He stood opposite the Bulls tallest player, ready to start the game with the opening jump ball. He extended his hand to shake the hand of the Bulls' center, but his counterpart looked him square in the eye and said, "nigger lover." John withdrew his hand and faced the basket where the Bulls warmed up. Outside the center circle Wesley stood on his front-right and Victor to the front-left. Flanked behind John were Kenny and Harry.

The ref moved into the spot between John and the kid wearing number 14 for the Bulls. He blew his whistle, got a nod of approval from the scorer's table, and tossed the ball high above the two tallest players. With the toss of the ball, John jumped. Victor set himself, ready to get the ball. Wesley took two quick steps to his left, his feet apart and firmly planted on the court. Harry took one step backwards, and then raced so close past Wesley that their shoulders touched and the boy covering Harry ran right into Wesley, who barely flinched. John tapped the ball to Victor who immediately threw a baseball pass to Harry streaking down the right side of the court toward the basket. Harry caught it, took two dribbles, and laid the ball high on the backboard and watched as it fell delicately through the hoop. Two – zip.

"Wow," said Carl.

He and Thomas looked at each other, shook their heads and smiled. They knew the boys had practiced twice, but that play was executed with a precision usually reserved for older, more experienced teams, like the St. Louis Hawks.

"Stop that little nigger," yelled a parent from the Bulls' cheering section.

An eerie silence fell over the gym.

"That's what I wish we had talked to the boys about," said Thomas.

The screech of the ref's whistle interrupted the moment.

"No basket. Traveling," he yelled, spinning his arms and waving off the basket.

The two points the scorekeeper had already put up for the Greyhounds was reversed on a call that was clearly wrong. Carl stood up, a sneer replacing his smile and he was about to scream at the ref passing by when Thomas pulled him by the back of his belt back down onto the bench.

"Don't do that," said Thomas, calmly shaking his head.

Carl hadn't considered that the Greyhounds might be playing against a team of six. He looked over to Thomas.

"Complaining now would be a big mistake," said Thomas.

When the Bulls brought the ball down the court, it was obvious to Carl that this was a good team, but not a great one. He saw hesitancy in their dribbling and a lack of confidence in the way they passed. Still, it was a team that had played together for longer than a week and in that way, the Bulls were more impressive than the Greyhounds.

The small Bulls guard who wore number 12 passed the ball to number 14 at the high post. Kenny, his stance wide and low, was between his man and the basket. Number 14 turned around to face the basket and Kenny. Kenny adeptly knocked the ball out of his opponent's hand and grabbed it cleanly.

Whistle.

"Foul on number 31," yelled the ref. "Raise it up."

"Wait a minute," said Carl, about to rise to his feet again. Thomas anticipated the outrage and put his arm on Carl's shoulder to keep him in place.

"No," was all he said. Carl's body tensed but he remained still.

Kenny raised his hand as instructed, shrugging his shoulders at the phantom call. The players lined up along the key. The Bulls player missed the foul shot and John got the rebound. John took a couple of dribbles and passed the ball to Harry. Harry brought the ball up over midcourt, dribbling effortlessly with his left hand and held up his right hand.

At the far end of the court, the older brother of one of the Bulls players unrolled a homemade sign that read, "Baboons should play in the jungle."

Thomas saw heads turn and whispers of concern in the Greyhound parents' section. Harry was too busy running the offense to notice the sign.

"Five," he yelled.

"Five?" said Thomas. "We have five plays?"

"Just watch," said Phil again.

Hearing "five" Victor ran from the right wing to the foul line. John ran from the left wing down toward the basket and then reversed his course out and around Victor. Harry passed the ball to John, who turned to face the basket. With his man lost in the shuffle of Greyhounds moving in every direction, John lofted a shot toward the hoop that went right in, swish.

No whistle. 2-0 Greyhounds.

"I guess he doesn't mind if the white kid scores," said Thomas softly to Carl.

The Bulls were a better team with the help of the referee. At the end of the first quarter they were winning 12-6. The ref had called seven violations and six fouls on the Greyhounds, to only two violations and one foul for the Bulls. Carl could see the frustration mounting in John. By halftime the Greyhounds had three more baskets disallowed by the referee and were called for walking, double-dribbling, palming and setting illegal screens. Thomas knew enough about basketball and Stockville to know the fix was in. *This was a big mistake*, thought Thomas.

At halftime the Greyhounds trailed 21-13.

As the Bulls players took turns at the water fountain, the Greyhound players drank cups of water from buckets the parents brought. There was no *Colored* water fountain. Evie Geary also brought a tray of orange slices for the boys. Thomas and Carl stood together near center court pondering the biased referee and the predicament they were in.

"Can I talk with you?"

It was Vernon, Phil's dad. He was a large man with big eyes like dark buttons. Dressed in overalls and a t-shirt, his scruffy steel-toed work boots squeaked on the polished gymnasium floor when he walked. He worked seven days a week at the John Deere factory, picking up extra shifts whenever he could, but took the day off to watch Phil play on the new team. Arriving from the bleachers, he asked Thomas if he could sit on the bench for a few minutes.

"I'm told each team can have three bench coaches," Thomas said. "Join us."

"Just for a minute," Vernon said.

Carl shrugged at Thomas who shrugged back.

Vernon sat there quietly staring into space until the referee came back in the gym after a halftime swill at the water fountain in the hall. Then Vernon stood up again and strolled toward the ref. Thomas and Carl watched from the bench.

Vernon and the ref talked for a minute or so, friendly but not warm, shaking heads but not hands. Vernon's hands, planted deeply in his pockets, stayed there. Then Vernon and the referee smiled and nodded. Thomas and Carl looked on, wondering. Vernon nodded his head goodbye and shuffled backwards a few feet so as not to turn his back on a white man. He returned to his seat in the bleachers, his gait easily taking two steps at a time.

"You got me," said Carl.

"I have no idea," echoed Thomas.

Both of them continued their *coaching* from the sideline, while Harry addressed the team.

"We've got to play tougher defense," he said to the other Greyhounds sitting on the bench getting ready for the second half.

The referee strolled to the scorer's table and checked the score in the book against the scoreboard on the wall.

"Let's go boys. Game time," he announced to both teams.

He blew his whistle and called for the center jump to start the second half. The Greyhounds used the same tip play again, but reversing the roles so that this time, Harry got the ball on the left side of the court and scored an easy layup from the left side. The small group of Negro parents sitting politely in the bleachers held their collective breaths and waited. No whistle. Basket good. 21-15.

"Way to go, Harry!" yelled Evie, who then looked around nervously to see if she had made a mistake in cheering. Oleatha backed her up.

"Great play, Victor!" she screamed.

As the second half unfolded, even the basketball novices in the crowd could sense something different about the game. No quick whistles. No contrived Greyhound violations. The referee was calling the game evenly, to the obvious benefit of the Greyhounds.

On offense John and Harry looked like lifetime teammates, with Harry making perfect bounce-passes to John's back-door cuts to the basket. Wesley pulled down seven rebounds and got the Greyhound fast break going. Phil made two fantastic defensive steals and passed to Harry for easy baskets. By the end of the third quarter the Greyhounds had tied the game 33-33.

The Bulls struggled against an unrestrained, faster Greyhound squad. Nobody on the Bulls could keep up with Harry at full speed. The Greyhounds' quick hands and tough defense forced the Bulls into turnovers all over the court. All the Greyhound players scored and the calls were extraordinarily different, which was to say, fair. The game ended Greyhounds 44, Bulls 41.

When the game was over, the Greyhounds lined up to shake hands with the Bulls, but Stump and the parents shuttled their children away, as if skin color was contagious.

"PBC rule 17.1 requires that the players shake hands at the end of the game," said Carl, smiling, opening his rule book and pointing out the section to Thomas.

"We stumped'em," said Thomas, snapping his fingers and a smile filling his face.

The Greyhound parents and friends ventured onto the court, hugging their children and cautiously shaking hands, trying not to call too much attention to themselves after the fine performance of the new team. Lenore stayed in the background to let the boys have their celebration. Carl noticed her standing by the bleachers.

"Good game," he said.

"Brilliant coaching," she said.

"Yes, Harry was spectacular."

"I meant you."

"I'm not the coach. But if it impresses you, I suppose you could consider me the team owner," he said.

"How's that?"

"I bankrolled this team. That's $4 for the uniform shirts, $10 entry fee and 75 cents for the spray paint. Stick with me baby and someday this dynasty could be yours," he said, spreading his arms over his imaginary empire.

"You are amusing," said Lenore.

"And you are lovely. Let's find someplace private and romantic."

"So amusing, and crazy," Lenore said.

The call of "hey Dad" interrupted their private flirtations. It was John calling from the other side of the gym.

"Can we get lunch?" yelled John, now running over to be hugged and congratulated by his father.

"Nice game, John," said Lenore.

"Thanks. Want to come with us?" he asked.

"Sure," said Lenore.

"Where should we go?" asked Carl.

Lenore rubbed her temples and shrugged her shoulders. She smiled. "I haven't been in this situation before," she said.

"Keep thinking," said Carl. "I'll be right back."

Carl ran over to where Vernon was standing, his muscular arm resting gently on his son's shoulder while he congratulated the team and the ceremonial coaches.

"Greyhounds. Team meeting over here," yelled Harry.

All the boys scooped up their stuff at the bench and followed Harry to the far corner of the gym. Thomas and Carl strolled over to Vernon, a sly smile sneaking its way across his face as they approached.

"What did you say to the referee?" Thomas asked.

"Oh, Horace Chambers isn't such a bad guy."

"You know him?" asked Thomas.

"I guess so."

"Yeah, so?"

"So I asked him if he recognized my son Phil in the game."

"And?"

"He said he didn't."

"That's all?"

"That's about it. Maybe we talked a little business," said Vernon, raising his bushy eyebrows, like Groucho Marx in *A Night at the Opera.*

"Business?" asked Thomas.

"I'm fixing his tractor."

"Okay."

"I told him I checked it out this morning and I wasn't sure if it just needed some timing adjustments, or if the engine block was cracked. I told him I was sure hoping it was just a timing thing, because a cracked engine block would need to be replaced. About $100 for a used one."

"That's it?"

"That's it," said Vernon. "I told him he could count on me to be fair. Just like I knew I could count on him."

"Nicely played," said Thomas, reaching out and shaking Vernon's hand.

Carl concurred and jogged back to where Lenore was standing. John ran back from the Greyhound meeting.

"We have a plan," said Lenore.

"We're going to pick up some sandwiches and drinks at a place called?—"

"Russo's," said Lenore.

"And Lenore's going to get a blanket and we're going to meet her behind the rec center in 20 minutes," said John.

"Sounds like a plan," said Carl.

As the three of them walked toward the front door of the rec center, John reached up and took Lenore's hand in his. Lenore flinched. Her cheeks flushed and a frightened countenance filled her face. She looked straight ahead. *Now what*, she thought. In six more steps taken in unison, the three of them exited the double doors, out into the bright Stockville sunshine. She gave John's hand a small squeeze, smiled at him and pulled her hand squarely back by her side.

Two hours later, with Horace Chambers the referee for the Greyhound's second game, the Greyhounds closed out the first day of the tournament, trouncing the hopelessly overmatched Selma Sparrows 52-19.

CHAPTER 21

Micah unbuttoned his green, grease-stained mechanic's shirt and tossed it into the hamper near the rear washroom. Once inside, he stripped down to his skivvies and began his end of the day ritual. He lathered his hands and wrists with a homemade mixture of Bar Keepers Friend, beef tallow and olive oil, having received the miracle recipe from an uncle who was a retired railroad mechanic.

Once his hands were clean, Micah took a horse-hair brush to his fingernails, scrubbing out the black arcs of grunge that embedded there during the day. If he was less than vigilant in closely clipping his fingernails, he used a sharp scraper tool he bought from a dental supply company, but with that, one slip of his hand and he wound up a bloody mess.

On most days Micah worked until 7 p.m., giving customers on their way home from work an opportunity to stop in for gas or to make an appointment for service. But on Tuesdays, Micah pulled shut the bay doors and flipped the sign on the office glass window from "open" to "closed" at precisely 5:30.

Micah finished by wiping an Ivory-soaped washcloth

over his face, his broad shoulders, neck, chest, and legs. Then he followed up with a plain, damp washcloth to remove the soap. The final pass was made up and down with a dry bath towel.

Micah pulled on a pair of khaki pants and buttoned a green and yellow plaid short-sleeved shirt around him, tucking it in, and encasing the whole outfit in a brown belt with a silver buckle. He brushed his short-cropped hair with front to back motions on the sides and then the top of his head. He slipped his feet into a pair of Thom McAn brown leather lace-ups, opened the washroom door and walked out into the hazy sunshine, locking the shop behind him.

On Tuesday evenings Micah attended the weekly meeting of the church brotherhood. After his family, there was nothing more important to Micah than the pastor's teachings and a chance to connect with the other like-minded Negro men of Stockville. It was Micah's library. Micah climbed into the spacious cab of his black Ford 100. Micah pulled the truck onto Primrose Road, sitting high and feeling mighty. Seven minutes later he arrived at the corner of Bellows Avenue and Bixby Street where, as always, Quincy Weston and Donald Jones were waiting. The two of them climbed into the truck cab, three across the bench.

Quincy was compact, a description he embraced over chunky or stout. He was the oldest of five, had a medium brown complexion and closely clipped black hair. He quit school in the 8th grade to help support his younger siblings after his father, a sharecropper, was crushed under a wheat thresher. The circumstances of the accident were never fully investigated, but the family was paid a small settlement from the owner of the farm. People who knew Quincy said his father's death turned him. Where he had been easygoing and loquacious, he was now sullen and angry for long stretches at a time. His anger at the farmer grew to anger at the South. Then anger at the world. The only time he seemed at peace was with the church brotherhood. Even then, there was something unsettling about him. He'd cultivated extraordinary defense mechanisms. High walls and a moat around his castle.

Micah's other passenger, Donald Jones, never went to school at all, but was on a first name basis with all the employees at the public library. At age 27, he was never without a book under his arm, and preferred biographies to fiction. Married with a set of twin girls, he worked as a renderer at Kohlson's Meat Packing plant on Stockville's eastside. He was shrewd, well-versed and opinionated, but suffered the insecurity of no formal education. He was perfect in small doses.

Quincy and Donald shared a love of music and an unwritten Tuesday night rule had emerged over the last year that the person sitting in the middle seat was king of the truck's radio. Tonight that was Quincy, who turned the dial to WLAV, the local blues, gospel, rock n' roll station.

"What's that playing?" Micah asked.

"You don't know?" answered Quincy.

"Do you think I'd be asking if I knew?"

"Everybody knows that song," said Donald.

"It's *Sh-Boom* by The Chords," said Quincy. Quincy puffed his chest just a little at knowing the tune, and sat back to listen with the coolness of Coltrane. At least until Donald spoke.

"Wrong," he said.

"Yes it is," said Quincy.

"I'll bet you a dollar it's not," said Donald.

"Why do you always want to bet me?"

"Easy money."

"My ass."

"So bet me," said Donald.

"I don't want to take your money."

"You're doing me a favor?"

"Look, my sister plays this 45 constantly. It's *Sh-boom* by the Chords."

"If you're so sure, then put up or shut up," said Donald. He reached into his shirt pocket and pulled out a dollar. "George Washington says this is not *Sh-Boom* by the Chords.

"You're on," said Quincy.

The three men sat silently, both Donald and Quincy holding their dollar bills in front of them. The song ended and all three waited to see if another song followed, or whether the D.J. would settle the score.

"Good, good evening everyone out there in central Alabama. This is Danny 'Moon Man' Derrick bringing you the best in Blues, Country and Rock n' Roll on WLAV, 1640 on the AM dial. Coming in at number eight on this week's oldies countdown, off the Mercury label, that was Sh-Boom *by the Crew Cuts."*

"Pay up time," said Donald, plucking the dollar out of Quincy's hand.

"Give me that back. I was right. It's *Sh-Boom*," said Quincy.

"No. You bet that the Chords were singing that song. You heard the man. That was the Crew Cuts."

"Who are the fucking Crew Cuts?" asked Quincy.

"The white group that ripped off the Chords."

"Give me my money back."

"No, it's my money," said Donald, putting both bills in his right trouser pocket where Quincy couldn't snatch them back.

As he drove, Micah avoided the dips and gullies of the dirt road leading to the church as best as he could, but the ride was often as bumpy as the conversation. He parked the truck on a patch of graveled ground, packed tightly and beaten down by oil leaks and green transmission fluid. The three men got out of the truck and entered the church.

Once inside, they joined the group of eight men in the first two rows of pews. Pastor Williams, standing at the pulpit took his Bible from the top of the lectern and placed it on a lower shelf.

"Welcome brothers," said the pastor.

"May God be with you," the men responded in unison.

"And with you as well."

Pastor Williams, dressed in a black suit, white shirt and simple red bow tie, reached into the pocket inside his jacket and pulled out some notes he'd made for tonight's talk. His eyes sparkled differently than on Sunday mornings. He nodded to Quincy and Uriah, who were sitting on the right and left outer seats, and they lowered the window shades of each of the four windows that ran down the church's side walls. The pastor pushed his bifocals up the bridge of his nose and began.

"A rich white man sits at a table laden with cookies along with a poor white man and a poor black man. The rich white man reaches to the center of the table and grabs all the cookies on the tray, leaving only one behind. He turns to the poor white man and says, 'Better watch that nigger. I think he wants to take your cookie.'"

There was a small laugh among the men.

"Tonight I want to talk to you about our community. I want to talk about controlling our community. First, someone tell me how you would define our community," said the pastor.

"Stockville," responded Donald.

"Brother Donald says Stockville is our community. Let me ask you Brother Donald, do you think you could open a store in Stockville? Do you think the white man would let *you* open a store in *his* neighborhood?"

"Our community is right here. A community of eleven," said Jonah.

The men laughed at the uncomfortable truth in the statement.

"Let's explore that," said the pastor. "The white man. The white man is too smart to let you have any control over his community. If you opened a clothing store, you think he'd come and shop in your store?"

"Hell no," said Donald.

"And yet every day, I bet your wives, your kids and you go shopping in his stores. What's the matter with us? Don't we have any sense at all?"

Pastor Williams, his voice increasing in volume and passion, answered his own questions.

"Don't talk to me about downtrodden Negroes and slave mentalities. We have let the white man control our community. We have invited the white man to control our housing, control our education, the businesses in our community and our jobs," he added, maintaining a steady and forceful voice. He paced three steps to his left before returning to the lectern.

"Dr. King, Abernathy and James Farmer tell us the way

out of this is to integrate. Integrate? Brothers, we live in Alabama."

"Ain't that the truth," said Micah.

"Amen," said two others in unison.

"You, Jonah, you shop at Hudson's?" asked the pastor.

"Yes sir."

"Ever wonder what happens to your money?"

Jonah shook his head. From the unknowing looks on all the men's faces, the pastor could see that none of the men had ever analyzed the economics of Jim Crow.

"I'll tell you. At the end of the day Mr. Hudson takes his basket full of your money and buys groceries in the white market, buys shoes at the white shoe store, pays local taxes to keep his all-white neighborhood sparkling and puts what's left in his white bank."

The pastor wiped his brow with the handkerchief he took from his back pocket.

"Gentlemen, we need to learn from the white man. We need to adopt the economics of Black Nationalism. When we spend our money in the white community, that community gets rich and our community gets shat upon."

"Right on," said Donald.

The pastor walked three choreographed paces to his right, turned and continued.

"Then we complain that our houses are run down, our schools are falling apart and our neighborhood is crumbling. Who are you complaining to? The white man isn't going to build our homes, our schools or our community. We have to create our own jobs. You need to spread the word. We need to support black businesses, go to black-owned movie houses and shop at black-owned general stores."

"You know any?" asked Uriah Jamison, a light-skinned Negro textile worker who walked with a limp since he was beaten by a group of white teenagers.

"We can build them," said Micah.

"We need employment in our community, not picketing. Picketing is stupid and disgraceful. Holding a sign, begging the man for a job or a vote. Gentlemen, this government has failed us. America has failed us. We live in 1964 and the singing of 'We Shall Overcome' is embarrassing. You can sing for what you want, but I'd rather *swing* my fist for what I need."

"Amen," said Micah.

Micah looked around the room. The pastor, as usual, was right. At the far end of his row sat the three Jackson brothers, Zeke, Danny and Ruben, who all worked as construction laborers and carpenters. During the week they worked for Tellson Construction, a white family-owned business that built warehouses and light industrial buildings. The Jacksons once rebuilt Micah's screened-in porch in a weekend in exchange for Micah replacing the engine in their pickup. They don't have to build for whitey, he thought. Micah's attention was brought back to Pastor Williams.

"Brothers. Another thing. Don't be fooled by those white, liberal Freedom Riders who come down here and say they're our friends. They are fooling us, too. Don't turn to them. Turn to yourselves. We need a self-help philosophy. We need a do-it-yourself manual. We need a do-it-right-now attitude. We need a do-it-at-any-cost approach," said Pastor Williams, reaching all the high notes. "I have listened to the lies and the trickery of the white man for too long. We are all the victims of white nationalism, white separatism and white racism."

Uriah, raised his fist and shouted, "Black Power!"

The pastor took off his jacket.

"We are 22 million Afro-Americans who have put up with slavery and Jim Crow and now we're supposed to believe that by laying down our guns, by marching peacefully through the streets of Birmingham and Selma and Montgomery, and yes, marching through the streets of Stockville on Sunday, we are going to change the white devils into white angels?"

Pastor Williams took a deep breath, small droplets of sweat beading down from his temples past his ears, and turning the top half of the collar of his light blue shirt a much darker blue.

"But, brothers, it is not the devils or the angels we need to be wary of. It is the whites, *all* the whites who are our nemesis."

The pastor couldn't help injecting some sarcasm into his remarks.

"Oh, and those same pastors, when they don't have us marching, they suggest we *sit-in* as a means to force change. Think about the concept of *sitting-in*. Old men and old women sit. Tired people sit. A chump sits. A coward sits. We need to start doing some standing, and fighting to back that up."

Two men jumped to their feet. Jonah slapped his left hand on his thigh and raised his fist high in the air. Micah pumped his chest with his fist and his blood pressure ticked up 10 points. He looked at the others, who stared straight ahead, intent on every word, as if the pastor's words were dripping intravenously into their bloodstreams.

"We have all heard George Wallace say he is not a racist. He says he is a segregationist and I take that white man at his word, because I too am a segregationist. I will continue to be a segregationist when we have every right to which all black men are entitled. I will meet violence with violence. I will fight fire with fire. Mr. Wallace hasn't seen the fury of 22 million Afro-Americans."

Micah thought about his brother Thomas and his naive, Svengali-like following of Dr. King. He wondered how his younger brother could be so foolish to think that the white southern power structure would open its arms, its wealth and its children to non-violent marching Negroes.

"Let's talk about politics. A bunch of lies," the pastor continued. "The first thing a white elected southern congressman does is invite a bunch of Negro pastors for coffee. Then he fills their heads with promises he has no intention of keeping. Those pastors leave and report to their congregations that the white Democrat, the Dixiecrat, can relate to the plight of the American Negro."

"Like hell," injected George Lamkin, a 29-year-old field worker.

"That's right. I say like hell he does. That's just lip service. That's what those Uncle Tom pastors got. Lip service. Lip service built on the sweat and blood of our fathers and our mothers. You can tell me we need integration. You can tell me we need segregation. Brothers, what we need, no, what we demand, is freedom."

The men stood up. Uriah slammed the back of the pew with his open hand, making a loud crack. A mix of rage and disenchantment, anxiety and frustration permeated the air around them. The pastor took it down a notch.

"You don't need to be a Muslim to embrace Black Nationalism. Malcolm's message is clear, and you can do it as a Christian. I will do it as a Christian. You can do it as an atheist if you damn please, but you must do it. Some of you have met Carl Gordon, the young U.S. Attorney in town. I've met with him twice. He's just a northern version of the southern white dog, but he can be a great help to us. He has connections we need. He can be useful. We had an incident last week. Mr. Gordon was here talking with me and I was pretty sure he was followed. I asked brothers Uriah and George to follow him home. Two Klansmen ambushed him at the four-mile marker. Kelvin Vittern and Sonny Davis. I didn't think they were stupid enough to kill him."

"I think you underestimate their stupidity," said Micah.

An uncomfortable laugh spread among the attendees.

"Thanks to Uriah and George, only Mr. Gordon's car was damaged a little and the two Klansmen were found the next morning by the side of the road with horrendous headaches."

"Right on brothers," said Jonah.

Uriah and George nodded in response to the recognition.

"Amen," said Micah.

"What about the march on Sunday?" asked Quincy.

"Support their movement. Let the non-violent protests continue with our active participation. Micah's brother Thomas will be leading a sit-in at Woolworth's tomorrow at lunchtime. I'll be there. By all means, appear to show support. For now, our movement is best clandestine. But our day will come."

"You know there'll be retaliation for what we did," said Uriah.

"A Klan show of strength," said Micah.

"They're trying to find out who we are," said George.

"We must not be detected," said the pastor. "Sunday, when we're marching, be vigilant my brothers. If revenge is what the Klan wants, that will be the time."

The pastor took one more look around the room. He stopped his preaching and walked down from the pulpit to stand among his small flock. He wiped the sweat from his forehead with the embroidered handkerchief he again fetched from his back pocket.

"May God be with you," he said. "Donald, Uriah, Micah and Quincy. Stay for a few minutes please."

The rest of the men filed out of the church's front door, still engaged and restless. When they closed the church door behind them, the pastor addressed the four men.

"We are ready for phase one. We'll meet here at 9 p.m. Micah and Uriah, you'll take Micah's truck. Donald and Quincy, you'll take Quincy's truck. We'll load them up with everything you'll need. Everything as we planned."

Pastor Williams lowered his voice and his face went stone solid.

"Klansman number one on our list goes to the VFW hall every night to play horseshoes and drink beer. By the time he leaves, almost always at 11:30, he's drunk and alone. He drives from Hastings Street, down Benning Road to Route 12. Micah and Uriah, you'll be parked at the entrance to the highway. Follow behind him from there. Stay back."

Pastor Williams looked each of his vigilantes in the eyes to make sure they were paying close attention.

"Then our Klansman takes the Winthrop cutoff as a shortcut home. About a mile in, at the far side of the one-lane bridge over Jackson Creek, that's where Quincy and Donald will block the road with their truck. Open the hood. Make it look like you've broken down. That's where the two of you will be waiting, in the brush."

The pastor nodded at Micah and Uriah. Uriah was

breathing heavily and the hair on his arms stood on end and itched. Micah was locked in on every word. He made eye contact with Donald and Quincy.

"Then?" asked Micah.

"You want to arrive and stop your truck at the near end of the bridge so he can't back up. Trap him. When he gets out of his truck to investigate, Donald and Quincy, you've got tire irons and Billy clubs, knock him out, put the burlap sack over his head and tie it around his neck. Tie his hands behind his back. Throw him in the truck bed. Then the two trucks drive in tandem to Given's Overlook. You know the huge oak tree that overhangs the cliff?"

All the men nodded affirmatively.

"That's where we inaugurate the black man's Maker Oak," said the pastor.

"A new beginning, my brothers," said Donald.

"Fighting fire with fire," added Quincy.

"An eye for an eye," said Uriah.

"A score settled," said Micah.

"The day after the peace march, there's going to be some bloodshed," said the pastor, slamming his Bible closed from both ends to the middle.

❦

CHAPTER 22

Carl, Oleatha and Lenore met as agreed outside the
5th Circuit Court of Appeals building in downtown
Montgomery. The five-story structure, a Second Renaissance
Revival, covered an entire city block in the shape of a U. The
first story exterior was constructed of rusticated 12-inch
square granite blocks, and the upper walls were matching
granite rectangles, polished to a smooth, seamless façade.
Together they provided the background for a variety of
ornate doorways and perfectly arched windows, lined up
like soldiers standing at attention. At the top of the building,
a heavy cornice made the low angled roof invisible from the
street. Although beautiful and a public building, to Oleatha
and Lenore, it looked anything but friendly.

Carl had spent a restless night at the Biltmore Hotel and
Oleatha and Lenore were up late into the night at the home of
Lester's second cousins. On short notice, Lenore and Oleatha
were unable to locate a hotel or motel in Montgomery that
would allow Coloreds. At 9:45 in the morning all of them
wondered where Barry Beckley could be.

"After breakfast this morning he said he needed a walk and he'd meet us here," said Carl.

"I'm sure he'll arrive any time," said Oleatha.

The three of them waited on the sandstone steps as Ezra Turner and his cadre of three identically dressed associates, each one carrying a banker's box, walked by with the precision of a halftime college marching band. They entered the courthouse in silence. Following them close behind was Edith Spinz, attired in an appropriate dark blue suit, with starched frills on her white cotton blouse and medium heels.

At 9:50 there was still no sign of Barry.

"Maybe he meant to meet him inside," said Lenore.

"Let's go in," said Carl.

The three of them walked together up the stairs, past the huge oak doors, and into the grand foyer.

"This is like in the movies," said Oleatha, looking up at the 22-foot ceilings adorned with crown moldings and filigreed brass light fixtures hanging from plaster ceiling medallions with carved *fleur de lis* designs.

At the center of the hallway, next to their courtroom number four, stood a greater-than-life-sized, imposing white marble statue of lady liberty, blindfolded and holding the scales of justice.

"That's quite a statue," whispered Carl to Lenore.

"I'd like one for my house, only in black," she said.

When he was sure no one was looking, Carl brushed his hand past Lenore's and gave it a gentle squeeze.

"This is our day," he said.

"You look handsome," she whispered back.

Carl smiled at her.

"Don't look at me like that," he said. "I have to concentrate."

"Where's Barry?" she asked.

At two minutes to 10 Carl said they should go into the courtroom. Appellate judges, as opposed to trial judges, tended to be prompt, Carl explained. With no Barry in sight, Carl could make appropriate excuses, but he couldn't think of any off the top of his head. Carl gestured for Oleatha and Lenore to sit on the benches outside the brass-hinged wooden gate that separated the attorneys' tables from the gallery. They looked to their right in time to see Edith Spinz turn up her nose and sniffle air into her nostrils. She crossed her legs so that her back faced the two women. Oleatha and Lenore sat down on the court pews to their left. Carl moved past the gate and took a seat at the empty table also on the left, the other table already filled with documents, folders, legal pads and pens and surrounded by Stockville's best team of recent law school graduates sitting at the spit-polished heals of Ezra Turner.

At precisely 10 a.m. a loud buzzer sounded, jolting everyone to attention.

"Please rise," said the bailiff, a stiff middle-aged man in a uniform that looked equal parts U.S. Marine and Boy Scout, with gold bars on his chest and sewn-on badges running up his khaki shirt sleeves from his elbows to his shoulders. His voice was loud and authoritative. "The 5th Circuit Court of Appeals is now in session. The Honorable Judge Gary T. Couples presiding."

Judge Couples, black-robed and bespectacled, entered the courtroom from behind a maroon, velvet curtain. His brown wavy hair was longer than current southern styles for men, curious for a former army lieutenant, thought Carl. Judge Couples had a reputation as a bourbon swilling southern gentleman after 5 p.m., but in court he intimidated with his wit, his tone and his gavel. Carl had heard that with Judge Couples it was "pick your poison, counselor."

"Be seated," Judge Couples growled, as he sat down on his high back, carved walnut chair and pulled himself up to his heightened perch, like a Roman emperor looking to be entertained by the lions or the Christians, he didn't care who won.

"Good morning counselors," said Judge Couples.

"Good morning your honor," the lawyers droned, like a congregate of hypnotized disciples.

"We are here this morning on the matter of Geary versus Northwoods Neighborhood Association, Cause Number 1964-AL-122. Make your announcements," said the judge.

Turner stood up. Mrs. Spinz uncrossed her legs and arched her back. She tilted her head so that her "good ear" pointed to the front of the courtroom.

"Ezra Turner on behalf of the respondent, Northwoods Neighborhood Association."

Carl looked around in one last futile hope that Barry was somewhere in the courtroom. Carl stood up to address Judge Couples.

"Your honor, I don't know where Mr. Beckley could be, but, I'm sure..."

"Is there a lawyer here on behalf of the Appellant?" interrupted the judge.

"As I was explaining..."

"Identify yourself. Who are you?" demanded the judge.

"I'm Carl Gordon."

"Are you a lawyer?"

"Yes sir, Assistant..."

"You're sitting at that table, do you represent Mrs. Geary?"

"I've been assisting Mr. Beckley throughout the case."

"Counselor, I'd appreciate it if you'd answer the question I ask," said the judge, his nostrils flaring and his eyes as big and black as checkers. "Listen carefully. Do you represent Mrs. Geary? If not, we can move on to the next case."

Carl looked around again for Barry. No luck.

"Your honor, I would like to enter my appearance on behalf of Mrs. Oleatha Geary," said Carl.

"Right now?" asked the judge, his disgust evident in having to deal with an unexpected procedural side issue. Judge Couples looked to the back of the courtroom.

"Is one of you Mrs. Oleatha Geary?" asked the judge.

With the spotlight all of a sudden on her, a nervous Oleatha raised her trembling hand.

"Stand up when you address the court," bellowed the bailiff.

Oleatha, with a small shove from Lenore, stood up.

"I am, your honor," she said.

"Is it okay with you if..." the impatient judge looked back at Carl and said, "What's your name again?"

"Carl Gordon."

The judge focused back on Oleatha.

"Is it okay with you, Mrs. Geary, if Carl Gordon represents you today?" asked the judge.

Oleatha looked down at Lenore for advice. She nodded her head and Oleatha stared right back at Judge Couples.

"Yes sir," said Oleatha and she sat back down.

"Nicely done, Mama," whispered Lenore in her ear.

Oleatha's face flushed with a mixture of pride and fear.

The judge looked at Ezra Turner and his cadre of Brooks Brothered assistants.

"Mr. Turner. Do you have any objection to Mr. Gordon making the oral argument on behalf of the Appellant?"

Turner stood.

"None whatsoever," he said, all smiles and smirking at his loving throng. He turned to Edith Spinz and gave her a big wink.

Judge Couples waved his hand nonchalantly and refocused his steely stare on Carl. He pulled up on the sleeves of his black pleated robe, revealing large cufflinks of gold guillotines. His lips curled, looking as if he was about to witness a train derailment and enjoy it.

"Mr. Gordon. Please begin," he said.

Carl opened his briefcase and pulled out his legal pad and a pen. He had none of the briefs that were filed with the court, no copies of the statutes or cases on which their argument was based. All those were in Barry's briefcase. Carl was flying solo without a map. He took a deep breath.

"We don't have all day, Mr. Gordon," said the judge.

"May it please the court," Carl began. "This case is on appeal from the 21st Judicial Circuit of Frost County in the State of Alabama. The facts are not in dispute. Mrs. Geary inherited real estate and a home on that real estate in the Northwoods section of Stockville, Alabama. My opponents have thus far successfully argued in the lower state court that Mrs. Geary, who, it is also not disputed, is a Negro, may not own property in Northwoods because all of the real estate there is subject to a 1902 restrictive covenant that purportedly reserves the land for Caucasians only. The case is here in federal court on our appeal because the controversy involves a federal constitutional question."

Carl hesitated a moment, figuring the judge would never let him speak for more than one sentence without interrupting with a question or comment. To Carl's surprise, Judge Couples just sat there, taking notes and looking amused. Carl continued.

"The 14th Amendment, adopted on July 9, 1864, states that all persons born or naturalized in the United States, and subject to the jurisdiction thereof, are citizens of the United States and of the state wherein they reside. No state shall make or enforce any law which shall abridge the privileges or immunities of citizens of the United States; nor shall any state deprive any person of life, liberty, or property, without due process of law; nor deny to any person within its jurisdiction the equal protection of the laws."

"What are you reading from?" asked the judge.

Carl held up his blank pad for the judge to see.

"I'm not reading from anything, your honor."

"I believe you have just quoted the 14th Amendment word for word. Mr. Gordon, please continue," said the judge, his raised eyebrows acknowledging for the first time that Carl might actually be competent legal counsel.

Carl led the judge through the cases of Shelley versus Kraemer and McGhee versus Sipes, reciting the facts of each case and reminding the judge that those cases were decided together by the United States Supreme Court in 1948. Carl explained that those cases, from Missouri and Michigan, were no different from this case, and both cases were decided in favor of citizens like Mrs. Geary. Carl explained that the Supreme Court invalidated all restrictive covenants based on race. Carl spoke smoothly and authoritatively for six minutes without interruption. Then he stopped to catch his breath, instinctively casting a glance at his still-blank pad on the table. He gazed up at Judge Couples, who had stopped taking notes and was just listening to Carl's logically crafted arguments.

"I can answer any questions the court might have," said Carl.

"I bet you could," said the judge, turning his attention to the other table. "Mr. Turner. You may begin."

Turner opened his black leather notebook, stood up, and smiled an old boy smile.

"May it please the court, my name is Ezra Turner and I represent the Northwoods Neighborhood Association," said Turner.

"Mr. Turner," interrupted the judge, "explain to me why *your* race restriction is different from the restrictions in the cases just discussed by Mr. Gordon."

"Northwoods is a unique place. It was planned and developed by renowned architect Harlan Bartholomew to create a park-like environment. Northwoods has no sidewalks and no public parks because each residence is a serene and elegant space in and of itself."

Turner looked up. The judge looked down. He turned his head quizzically, but said nothing. Turner continued.

"Our city's most important people live there. The Mayor of Stockville lives in Northwoods. The owners of our largest corporations live in Northwoods. Several doctors and lawyers live in Northwoods. Judge, I happen to live in Northwoods," said Turner.

"Is that your answer?" asked the judge, his voice trailing up for the first time.

"I think so. Yes, your honor," said Turner.

"I just want to be clear, Mr. Turner. That's your answer to the question of how this case is different than the ones already decided by the United States Supreme Court?"

"Yes sir. If I may continue," said Turner.

The judge's spine straightened like the stem of a rose. He rubbed the temples of his head and his eyebrows, looking down at his desk, before removing his glasses and focusing directly on Turner.

"No Mr. Turner, you may not. Instead, let me tell you a story," said the judge.

Turner backed up a few inches and unbuttoned and re-buttoned his grey gabardine suit. All the other lawyers in the courtroom came to attention. Judge Couples spoke, while his court reporter typed furiously.

"There was a man from Stockville, Alabama who had some beautiful fabric. He took this fabric to his tailor in Stockville and asked the tailor if he could make the man a suit from this fabric.

"The tailor replied that indeed the fabric was stunning and he could make the man a beautiful suit. But the man remembered he had a business trip planned to Montgomery and in Montgomery was a world-class tailor. So the man decided to take the bolt of fabric with him on the business trip. After arriving in Montgomery and attending his important meetings, the man drove to the small tailor shop. When the tailor came to greet him, the man presented the tailor with the bolt of fabric and asked him if he could make a suit.

"The tailor opened the bolt of fabric and examined it closely. Observing that the fabric truly was beautiful, the tailor told the man that, in fact, he could make him two suits from the fabric.

"How can that be?' asked the man. 'Just yesterday I took the fabric to my tailor in Stockville and he said there was only enough fabric for one suit.' And the tailor replied, "Perhaps you're not as big a man in Montgomery as you are in Stockville."'

As he finished, the judge glared down at Turner. Carl covered his mouth to prevent himself from laughing. Other lawyers in the courtroom were less restrained, and a wave of laughter filled the gallery. Lenore, who was gently holding her mother's hand, smiled and gave it a victory squeeze. Both of them, the only Negroes in the courtroom, were still too nervous to make any noise and call attention to themselves. Mrs. Spinz's jaw dropped and she cupped her hands against her chest.

"In light of the Supreme Court decisions in Shelley versus Kraemer and McGhee versus Sipes, why are you wasting my time with this bigotry and nonsense?" lectured the judge. "The lower court's decision is reversed and your case is dismissed. We'll take a 10-minute recess."

The judge hammered his gavel down hard on his desk, stood up and stormed out of the courtroom. Carl looked over his shoulder at Oleatha and Lenore, who were hugging. Carl put his pen and pad in his briefcase and walked back past the swinging gate where they were sitting.

"Ain't that the berries?" said Oleatha while pressing the sides of her dress in place. "Is it okay to hug your lawyer?" she asked.

"Throw caution to the wind," said Carl.

Oleatha gave Carl a big hug, while Carl looked over her shoulder and winked at Lenore. Carl was a little embarrassed, but clearly enjoying the victory and the attention. Oleatha stepped back.

"Thank you," she said.

Lenore stepped up and hugged him too, a not-too-tight one with Oleatha's stern gaze carefully chaperoning.

"You're brilliant," Lenore said.

And possibly unemployed, he thought.

The three of them walked back to the hotel where they found Barry Beckley in the lobby bar, his wobbly right hand gripping a Johnny Walker Red on the rocks.

"How'd we do?" he asked.

Beckley snored in the backseat all the way back to Stockville, while Carl, Oleatha and Lenore smiled, talked and delighted in victory. Beckley, barely awake when they dropped him off at his house, made them all promise to be available the next morning.

"I'm going to make it up to you," he said. "Mrs. Geary, be ready outside your home. I'll pick you up at 9 a.m. sharp."

The next morning, Oleatha, Lenore, and Carl stood curbside in front of Oleatha's home as Barry Beckley's Cadillac Sedan DeVille glided to a stop in front of them. Beckley, sober and well-slept, was shoehorned between the steering wheel and the plush white leather seats. Carl opened the rear door for Lenore, who slipped into the spacious back seat behind Beckley. Her mother joined Lenore in the back, running her fingers along the leather seam where the armrest cradled the stainless steel door handle. Carl let himself into the front passenger seat.

"No hard feelings?" asked Beckley, his face flush with embarrassment over his no-show in Montgomery.

"No harm done," said Lenore. "The backup quarterback scored a touchdown."

"This is a lovely car," said Oleatha.

"This morning, I'm going to make your head spin," Beckley said.

"Like his, yesterday," whispered Oleatha to Lenore.

"Mama?" said Lenore, as she gave her mother's shoulder a little push and smiled at her.

Beckley drove through the Grove and past downtown Stockville. He continued west about two miles until they reached an immaculately paved road that continued between two granite balustrades, a greater than life-sized statue of a lion perched on each one. The grand homes of Northwoods which covered 114 acres, were framed by wide cobblestone sidewalks and stone walls. Prior to the Civil War it had been an antebellum estate belonging to Colonel Colson Henshaw, an old line cotton plantation owner with strong ties to the African slave trade and no evidence that he ever attained any actual military rank. His grandson, Colson Henshaw III, president of the Crimson Tide Trust Company, lived in the pillared mansion which wasn't burned to the ground by Union troops as an oversight. It was common knowledge among Stockville's upper class that Governor George Wallace's famous quote said in the doorway of University of Alabama, that he was for "segregation today, segregation tomorrow and segregation forever," was stolen from a marble engraving that hung above the stone fireplace at Colson Henshaw III's private hunting club, although Wallace's speechwriter Asa Earl Carter took historical credit for it.

Beckley's Cadillac coasted to a stop in front of a Georgian Revival brick, with black shutters surrounding white window frames, copper gutters, leaded glass windows and a four-pillared portico guarding the front door like the Queen's Guards at Buckingham Palace.

"Welcome home!" chuckled Beckley.

The four of them exited the car and followed Beckley up the brick walkway. He removed a set of keys from his suit pocket, opened the front door and handed the keys to Oleatha, who clenched her fist tightly around them. When Beckley flipped a wall switch, a crystal chandelier, suspended overhead like a shimmering white cloud, lit up the foyer. Below their feet was an Oriental rug that sat centered on pine floors, polished to a satin patina. Oleatha noticed the scent of cinnamon and roses that was emanating from a sachet on the mahogany staircase handrail. The beige walls were framed by white semi-glossed baseboards, crown moldings and casement windows.

"It's a museum," said Oleatha, her palms damp and her breathing labored and erratic.

"Do you want to sit down a moment?" asked Lenore.

"Yes, please," said Oleatha, who, with Lenore on one arm and Carl steadying the other, lowered herself onto a rattan loveseat covered with blue and white patterned pillows. Lenore sat down next to her and put her arm around her mother's shoulder.

"The house includes all the furniture," said Beckley. "But if you don't like it, it's yours to sell, or give away, and move in your own things."

"My stuff couldn't fill this one room," said Oleatha.

"I don't mean to be a killjoy, here," said Carl. "But how are you going to afford the real estate taxes, electric bills—"

"Not a problem. There's a codicil to the will that I didn't read at our meeting. Ted funded a $100,000.00 account at First Southern Bank. Here's the check book," said Beckley, walking to the fireplace hearth, picking up the black leather-bound checks and handing them to Lenore. "If you ever did run out of money in the account, you could always sell the artwork."

"I get the pictures too?" asked Oleatha.

"That painting behind you...it's a Thomas Hart Benton."

"A what?" asked Oleatha.

"Thomas Hart Benton is the artist, Mama," said Lenore. "He paints scenes of America, mostly. He's pretty famous."

"There's three or four of his in the house, and some Grant Wood's, some Ben Curry's and three Max Beckmann's in the living room."

Oleatha took a deep breath and announced she was feeling better. Beckley guided them to the living room, where they found velvet floor-to-ceiling drapes and a gold-leaf pier mirror between two leaded windows at the far end.

"Here they are," announced Beckley, presenting a triptych of Beckmann's work, like the proud father of triplets.

"Look at that," said Carl, admiring the vivid colors and layers of people, objects and shadows intertwined on the canvases.

"Those are mesmerizing," said Lenore.

"Those are disgusting," replied Oleatha. "Half the people are naked. Won't have no orgy going on in *my* living room."

"So you're going to take the house?" asked Lenore.

"We'll see," said Oleatha, breathing in deeply through her nose and allowing her chest to expand and relax.

Beckley continued the tour, showing Oleatha her new kitchen, the five upstairs bedrooms and three renovated bathrooms. At the rear of the house was a rectangular swimming pool surrounded by irregularly shaped grey slate tiles. A waterfall at the far end spilled streams of cool water into the pool like hair ribbons in the breeze. Oleatha, Lenore, Carl and Beckley sat under a red, white and blue awning which shielded them from the morning sun, as they admired the backyard.

"What'd ya think?" asked Beckley to Oleatha.

"It's big," said Oleatha. "and I'm just fine where I am...but Mr. Beckley, you've got me thinking," she said.

❦

Lenore set off to the sink to wash the dishes after dinner, and Carl volunteered to dry them. With her hands wrist-deep in soapy water, she sensed that he was close behind her. She felt him touch her shoulder with his fingertips.

"You know I'm holding a knife," she said.

"Don't let me distract you."

He put his hand on her waist and she closed her eyes for just a moment. Then she felt his lips gently kiss her neck. Carl put both his arms around her and she could feel the heat of his body all the way up and down her back. She put the silverware down and turned to face him. His hands were still wrapped around her and hers were wet and soapy. She pulled back a little.

"I'm dripping all over the kitchen floor," she said.

"I can fix that," he said, and proceeded to meticulously massage each of her fingers with the towel he had slung over his shoulder. He took both his hands and placed them behind her head and gently pulled her closer, until their lips were only a few inches apart.

"I've never kissed a white man," she said.

"See, another thing we have in common."

"I haven't been this close to any man in a long time."

"I forgot my instruction manual. Now shhh," he said.

Carl and Lenore moved closer and their lips met softly at first and then harder. She could feel his tongue touching her lips. She opened her mouth slightly. They kissed again and Lenore felt her back pressing against the kitchen counter.

"Wait a minute," she said. "It's not like I haven't thought about this, but I need to slow down."

She slid away sideways, stepped back and took a deep breath, her heart pounding in her ears and her blood rushing to her face.

"Not good?" he asked.

"Very good," she said. "Too good. Way too good."

He moved closer again and pulled her toward him. This time she put her arms around him too. They stood there locked. They didn't speak. Just eyes in eyes. Between deep kisses she managed some halting breaths. She wasn't expecting him to smell delicious. He did. Kind of spicy. Unlike any other man she had ever been close to.

Suddenly, she was moving him toward the bedroom and it was as if someone else inside her had taken over. On the bed they were kissing again and garments were finding their way to the floor. She put her cold hands on his bare chest. He was jolted for just a beat and then took her hands in his and moved them down his torso. His tongue flickered up and down her neck. They were lying next to each other, her lips, chest and hips pressing against his. She wanted to close her eyes, but for some reason she couldn't stop staring into his.

"Are you okay?" he whispered.

"I think so," she said.

"Talk to me."

She just couldn't put anything into words. He could see the tears forming in her eyes. She wanted to ask him who they were, where they were heading, but for the first time in ages she couldn't speak and didn't care.

"Wait here, I'll be back in two minutes," he said, and he rolled off the bed, completely naked and apparently right at home in her home. He wrapped one of Lenore's scarves around him, strangely bringing to mind a burlesque queen, and went back to the kitchen. Lenore pulled the bed sheet over her, and tried to calm down. A few minutes later he returned with a small plate in each hand.

"My contribution to dinner," he said. "The best cake ever."

With the sheet wrapped around her, she sat up against the bed's headboard and he handed her one of the plates, a slice of chocolate cake with white butter-cream frosting.

"Is this a metaphor?" she asked.

"A metaphor?"

"Black cake covered in white butter-cream."

"My dear. Sometimes chocolate cake is just chocolate cake."

Then he proved the opposite.

He dipped his finger into the butter-cream that covered his cake and placed it to her lips.

"Try this," he said.

She licked the cream from his finger.

"Delightful," she said.

Then he placed some more on her lips, leaned in and this time he licked it off.

"More delightful," she said. She looked into his eyes, which sparkled like blue agates.

"Hold this," he said and placed his plate in her other hand.

He dipped his finger again, this time in her plate of frosting and spread a small amount on her chest, just above the sheet that she was still holding up under her arms. He moved himself down to the top of her breasts and gently licked and kissed her. There she was, thinking she was powerless but not anxious, and at the same time marveling at the ingenuity of being handcuffed by the two desserts. More of the cream found its way to her breasts and the space between them as he folded down the sheet and she stared at the far wall and the top of his brown-haired head.

He looked up only long enough to dip his long finger into the cream again and placed it gently below her navel and on the insides of her thighs. She was breathing harder now and she could no longer hold the plates steady. She put them down on either side of her. All her attention was being drawn to his tongue and fingers that were sending internal pulses down to her toes and back up again to her brain. This had never happened to her before. She couldn't keep track of how long it lasted, but she felt breathless and warm. Her mind was flashing and her body was quivering and she could feel her muscles contracting and overpowering her and then relaxing and contracting again.

When she caught her breath, she felt an overwhelming sense of safety, belonging and amazement and she thought she looked a little embarrassed. Just like that he was again lying next to her, having placed the plates on the edge of her night table. He held her gently in his sturdy arms, as she regained a measure of her composure.

"How was dessert?" he asked.

"Sometimes chocolate cake is more than just chocolate cake," she said.

Lenore lay with her head on Carl's shoulder and the rest of her body warmly aligned with his. She pressed her lips into his neck and kissed him just below his ear. She slipped her legs over his and sat down on his thighs facing him. She took his chin in her hands, tilted his head up, kissed him deeply and looked into his eyes.

"Now it's your turn."

CHAPTER 23

Carl returned home from a meeting of the Student Nonviolent Coordinating Committee, and opened the corrugated aluminum mailbox to find an electric bill, a letter from his mother to John, and a large manila envelope secured at both ends with cellophane packing tape and a return address of the New York division of the U.S. Attorney's office. There it was. Carl was both anxious and relieved. His blood pressure ticked up a notch and he felt cold and nauseous all over again.

He carried all the mail into the kitchen and placed the package on the countertop near the sink. He paced around the kitchen, looking at the package from all different angles, like a tiger eyeing its prey from a safe distance, not knowing if what was moving out there was a doe or a rattlesnake. Carl opened the refrigerator and stood there, not hungry, and not thirsty either. He looked at his watch. It was 4:30 and John would be arriving home any minute. *Time to slay the dragon,* he thought. He sliced into the package with a brass letter opener he received as a gift for his small donation to the Columbia Law School Alumni Association.

Carl slid the magazine out of the opened end of the envelope. He held it up to the light, like he was holding a vital piece of evidence that needed to stay fingerprint free, especially his. The cover was typical for the edgy magazine, an illustration showing a clash of cultures as two fishermen in overalls arrived at their dockside fishing boat, only to find well-dressed socialites engaging in what appeared to be an all-night game of roulette, a white-jacketed croupier tending to them.

Carl gently opened the cover, paged through the advertisements to the table of contents and located *Accessory to Murder* by Emily Harlowe on page 62. He realized that Travis had already dog-eared the page for him. Carl started reading. He had decided he'd read the entire article, not stopping to make notes or comments. He could do that on the second read, or preferably not at all. Carl found some details that were eerily accurate and that Carl was sure nobody but he knew. The damned pillow. The thoughts that crossed his mind before the mercy killing. There were also a lot of generalities that fit his misadventure, like his love for Beth and his strained relationship with a son who was named Billy in the short story. He discounted the entire story line about the character's affair with the beautiful "actress" as Emily's vanity and self-centered reality. Every one of her novels had a mysterious, or sexy, or enticing, or intelligent heroine, easily traceable to whatever Emily thought were her most attractive attributes at the particular time.

Other scenes and storylines in *Accessory to Murder* were completely wrong. The story's "Carl" was from a small town, attended college and law school in Chicago and then moved to New York. All of the self-doubts and guilt were missing, and instead of a breakup after the affair, there was an engagement. Wishful thinking, thought Carl. Still, there was enough accurate information for his bosses to believe that *Accessory to Murder* was not all fiction, brought to life by the overactive imagination of Emily Harlowe, and that worried him.

Carl decided to phone Emily after John went to sleep. At 9:30 Stockville time, he dialed her number. After three rings she picked up the phone.

"Hello."

"Why did you do this?" asked Carl.

"Who is this?"

"Stop it, Emily."

"Carl? Is that you? How's life in East Bumble-fuck?" said Emily, the lilt in her voice followed by a smug chuckle.

There was no doubt about it, Emily was back in top form, Carl thought.

"What are you trying to accomplish?"

"Honey, I miss you."

"Why, Emily?"

"I don't know why, after you walking out on me, but I'm willing to forget the whole thing. Come on home."

Carl needed to know how much Emily knew and how much she just made up and got lucky. If nothing else, working at the U.S. Attorney's office had taught Carl to always talk like the other person was wearing a wire. He knew J. Edgar Hoover was everywhere.

"Your story is going to make people think I had something to do with Beth's death," said Carl.

"Oh, darling. We know better than that. I write fiction,

right?" said Emily. "And that's exactly what I told Nick Katzenbach when he called."

"He called you?"

"Actually, his secretary called and then he got on the line after. We hardly talked though. I told him I had an appointment but I'd call him back in a few days. I'm so lonely without you. When are you coming home, love?" she said.

Carl had no interest in reigniting his relationship with Emily, but couldn't risk her talking to the U.S. Attorney about him. He needed time.

"I think I'm going to fly up there this weekend," he said.

"I knew you felt that way too."

"Don't talk to anyone until you've talked to me. Okay?" asked Carl.

"As long as I'm talking to you, there's nobody else I ever want to talk to," Emily purred into the telephone receiver.

"I'll call you back when I know the plans."

"Hurry home, sweetheart."

"Bye," said Carl.

Carl hung up the phone. He bent over, placing his hands on his knees to keep from fainting, as waves of nausea rolled over him. Sweat dripped down his cheeks.

"Now what?" he said to nobody.

❦

Three Klan members drove three separate trucks six miles up a winding dirt road north of Stockville. Just before midnight, they arrived at the White Citizens' Council headquarters, formerly a hunting lodge. On this moonless Saturday night, the southern country humidity pushed hard against their easiest movements. Their headlights lit the way to a clearing between the lodge and a small marina, with two wood-slatted docks jutting out 20 yards from the shore.

The men gathered next to a flagpole flying both the American and the Confederate flags. Large rocks had been placed in a ring around a barbecue pit where Klan VIPs and their families enjoyed campfires, roasted marshmallows, told ghost stories and preached the efficacy of segregation.

The men exchanged greetings and the handshake of the Sons of the White Camellia, a splinter group of exceptional men who had worked together for God and white supremacy. The largest of the three opened the back of his truck and dragged an eight-foot length of rough-hewn poplar out of the truck bed and set it on the ground where the headlights of their vehicles provided construction light. Another Klansman, a stout man with hulking shoulders and a noticeable limp, pulled a three-foot piece of lumber from the same truck and set it across the long piece. He hammered three-inch steel nails through the shorter plank, attaching it to the larger one. The third Klansman, much younger than the others, wrapped twine in a crisscross pattern around the intersection of the two wooden planks, creating a sturdy eight-foot by three-foot cross.

The large man, the leader, returned to his truck and pulled out five alfalfa seed burlap bags which had been sliced from top to bottom along the seams. While the young man wrapped the burlap around the cross, the stout Klansman followed close behind with the twine, looping it around the burlapped poles to hold the material in place. Once they had wrapped both the vertical and horizontal, the three of them loaded the cross back into the pickup, threw a sturdy pointed shovel in the back and tucked a five-gallon can of gasoline in the right rear corner. Packed up and ready, the three men fastened their white robes around them, over their street clothes. They carried their KKK hoods in their hands so as not to be obvious and for better visibility while driving. They climbed into the truck cabin and drove back to Stockville, headed for the Grove.

At 1:15 in the morning, the Grove was as quiet as bare trees. Occasionally a Negro foundry worker or Ford assembly plant employee arrived home from the second shift, but mostly it was still and dark. There were no operational streetlights and most homes had their interior lights off to save money.

As the pickup truck made its way past the courthouse and city hall, past the downtown businesses and banks, the driver slowed down to make less noise and not jostle the cargo. He turned the radio off. Conversation was kept at a minimum on instructions from the Grand Wizard himself. The driver had driven this route earlier in the daylight to make sure of the destination address and to map out an efficient strategy.

The truck turned on Briar Street and continued down Holly Hock Drive. It made a left on Potters Lane and a right on Benton Park Court. The driver turned off the headlights and coasted to a quiet stop, grazing a broken curb with his front left tire. The three men put their white hoods over their heads, adjusting the fit so that the round eye holes matched up with their eyes underneath. They looked at each other and the driver nodded.

"Let's go," he said to the others.

The three robed Klansmen bolted from the truck, looking like white mice after cheese. They left the truck doors open for fast and easy re-entry. The stout one grabbed the shovel and jammed it into the lawn about six feet left of the mailbox. Four vigorous stabs into the ground produced a deep, narrow hole. The other two hoisted the cross up over the truck bed and, holding the middle of the eight-foot length, together jammed it directly into the hole, while the stout Klansman pounded some of the displaced dirt back around the base of the cross to hold it in place. The young one, standing by and ready for the signal from the leader, doused the burlap liberally with gas from the can. The leader grabbed his silver lighter from the back pocket of his dungarees under his robe, flipped the flint and touched the small flame to the base of the cross. It erupted into flames.

"Let's get out of here," said the leader.

Two of the men ran back to the truck. The stout one looked up and down the block to make sure there were no witnesses. Then, veering off script, he reached one more time into the truck bed and pulled out a dark red construction brick, rough to the touch with two rows of five holes drilled through it. Running past the burning cross, he cocked his arm back and heaved the brick through the home's front picture window, like a pitcher throwing a fastball high and tight. It shattered the plate glass and sounded like an explosion. The stout man let out a whoop, then retreated to the truck, climbing in. They drove away. Three champions of the night, their adrenalin pumping.

"Nice touch," said the driver.

❧

Oleatha bolted to a sitting position. Dressed in a gown, with spongy blue curlers in her hair, she reached for the yellow cotton housecoat she had laid across the end of her bed before she went to sleep. She looked at her alarm clock, 1:20 a.m. Her first thought was that someone had broken into her home so she grabbed her only available weapon, a broom that was propped up against the doorframe in her bedroom. Her one telephone was in the kitchen. Oleatha felt her heart pumping and the muscles in her neck contracting around her vocal chords. Drawing in a deep breath, she cracked open her bedroom door and peeked into the living room. Thousands of glass chards covered the furniture and the floor. Oleatha didn't dare venture out. Crime in the Grove was unusual, but not impossible, and she was still unsure if a thief, or a murderer, was in her house.

"Anyone there?" she yelled. "I got a shotgun," she bluffed.

There was no answer. The boundary between inside and outside had been shattered along with the window. The chirping of cicadas was overpowering. She looked down and saw the brick that had come to rest against one of the legs of her velour couch. An orange glow bled through the hemlock trees that shaded her southern-exposed front window and she knew immediately that it wasn't a full moon kind of glow. That light was pale, calming and familiar. This glow behind the trees was orange and cracking, like the static between stations on the radio. Reasonably sure she was alone, Oleatha put on her slippers and walked slowly and carefully through the living room, pieces of glass scraping the floor under her slippers. She thought about picking up the brick, but decided to leave everything where it was. That's what detectives did on TV shows, she remembered. Oleatha opened the front door and looked into her yard. The heat from the burning cross hit her like a slap across her cheeks. The flames lit up her dark brown face and tears formed at the corners of her eyes. A quick breeze pushed the smell of burning gas in her mouth and she gagged, moving back inside just in time to avoid vomiting. Fearing that the Klan might still be outside, Oleatha slammed the door shut. She ran back to the kitchen, picked up the phone and dialed Micah's number. The phone rang several times with no answer. After the sixth ring, Micah, startled and sleepy, picked up the receiver.

"Hello?"

"Hello," she nearly whimpered.

Micah snapped to attention.

"What's the matter?" he said, knowing his mother didn't make social calls in the middle of the night and that Thomas would have gotten the call in a non-emergency.

"Can you come over right now?" Oleatha asked, her voice raspy and her hands shaking so much she was having trouble holding the phone to her ear.

"What happened?" Micah asked.

"Someone threw a brick through my window," she said.

"Okay."

"And there's a cross burning on my front lawn."

"Lock yourself in your bedroom. I'll be right there."

❧

Oleatha, Evie, Roslyn and Lenore worked together vacuuming the braided area rugs and sweeping the glass off the floors and furniture into large metal dust pans. Micah broke off the remaining jagged edges of the damaged window with a baseball bat before cutting and nailing plywood into the window frame. Thomas toppled the charred remains of the cross onto the scorched patch of front lawn beneath it, then carted it away in Micah's truck. Throughout the morning, neighbors and friends stopped by with baskets of food and gentle, supportive comments, as if a member of the family had died. Pastor Williams arrived at 8 a.m. before heading out to the church for Sunday services. Thomas, Lenore and Micah were concerned that although their mother was not physically injured, her trauma might have lasting, ghastly effects. Cross burnings were power plays, the calling cards of white supremacy. More than any other statement of segregation, except a lynching, they left Negroes feeling helpless and vulnerable, defenseless and weak. Cross burnings sapped the Negro soul. Lenore suggested that Sunday dinner be held at her house.

"We'll have it here at 3 p.m. like we always do," said Oleatha, in a tone that invited no argument.

When the cleanup was complete, Oleatha hugged her children, thanked them for their help and sent them on their way.

"I've got work to do. I'll see ya'll back here this afternoon," she said.

Just before 3 p.m., Thomas, Evie, Harry, Denise and Cara arrived. The grandchildren had been told of the events at grandma's house in age-appropriate detail. Harry knew that the KKK was angry at being beaten in court over a house grandma now owned, and Denise and Cara knew there had been an accident, but grandma was alright. When they arrived, Harry couldn't contain himself when he spotted the lavish array of food on the expanded dining room table. The aroma of freshly fried hushpuppies just about knocked him over.

"Today I've got a real choice," he said to his grandmother, as he surveyed the banquet.

Evie looked up and down the table.

"You've been busy, Oleatha," she said.

"Busy as a stump-tailed cow in fly time," said Oleatha. "I am on a mission."

At the far end of the rectangular table was a napkin-lined, cross-weaved basket piled high with skillet-baked cornbread. Next to it was a full platter of fried chicken, large bowls of black-eyed peas, stewed okra, mustard greens and candied yams. Harry spied desserts on the buffet, next to the fireplace. Peach cobbler, pumpkin pie and apple fritters.

Lenore arrived next, followed by Micah's family.

"What's all this?" asked Lenore.

"Sunday dinner," said Oleatha.

"Are we expecting the 7th Cavalry?" asked Micah.

Oleatha herded everyone to the table. All the Gearys, except Micah, bowed their heads as Thomas thanked the Lord for the bounty they were about to receive and for his mother's safety. After the prayer, serving spoons went flying in every direction. Plates were filled and happy chatter from the children made the day seem normal again. Harry and Victor, to nobody's surprise, ate like teenage boys. So did their fathers. The food was over the top, even for Oleatha.

As Evie, Roslyn and Lenore cleared the plates between the main courses and dessert, Oleatha tapped her spoon to her water glass to get everyone's attention. She waited for Victor and Harry to stop talking about basketball, and for the ladies to return from the kitchen. When she had everyone's attention, she stood up at the head of the table.

"It has been a difficult day," she said. "I have never been one for fighting. I prefer to be like the old lady who fell out of the wagon," she said.

"What's that mean?" said Harry to his mother.

"It means quiet when your Grandma's talking," Evie whispered.

Oleatha answered him.

"Harry, darling. It means if it ain't none of my business, then I ain't getting involved," said Oleatha. "Now mind your mother." Oleatha continued. "I believe these days your sociologists are calling that being *non-confrontational*. Isn't that right, Thomas?"

"That's a good word, Mama," said Thomas.

"I never cottoned much to Thomas's civil rights movement. I figured it's not my fight. And I did not approve of Micah's way, who's that young, handsome Malcolm fellow with the bow ties and funny last name?"

"Malcolm X, Mama," said Micah, rolling his eyes.

"That's right. Malcolm X. I didn't like what he was selling either. *The Ballot or the Bullet.*"

"How do you know that?" asked Micah.

"In case you forgot, *I'm* the one who taught *you* to read," said Oleatha, causing both Thomas and Lenore to smile and chuckle. "Last night those bastards, pardon my French, those dogs barked up the wrong tree if they think they can shut me up," said Oleatha, her oratory gaining speed and volume.

"We've got some history in this family that we don't talk about. Maybe we didn't fight back the way that the Lester Geary family ought to have. Thomas is right. We should have. But we did okay. Times were different then. That's what I keep hearing and today I believe it. I am living in your new world. It's my grandchildren's new world too, and I can help. By God, I am fighting mad."

"Amen, Mama," said Thomas, a proud smile filling his face.

"As of right now, I'm fighting for what's mine. I'm fighting for what's right. Move over Thomas, I am joining the front line and fighting Dr. Martin Luther King, Jr.'s battle for equality. And if God sees fit to take me into his army, so be it. The Geary family will not back down again."

"You tell it like it is," said Roslyn.

"Go Mama," said Lenore.

"So Mr. and Mrs. Northwoods, move over cause I'm movin' in. Thomas, I'll be marching on Stockville with you on Sunday. I want to vote in the next election. I am *going* to vote in the next election. Most important, I am marching for my grandchildren because they should not, they will not, know a time when they couldn't vote because of the color of their skin."

Oleatha looked at each of her five grandchildren, as they stared in rapt attention, mesmerized by a side of Grandma they had never seen before. Oleatha talked right to them.

"I want this world to be a better place for you and I've decided it isn't going to happen without all of us sacrificing. I am putting it on the line. Better lives aren't going to happen unless we make them happen."

Lenore jumped to her feet and applauded Oleatha. All the other Gearys joined in. Rugged Micah wiped a tear from his eye and hugged his mother and Roslyn. Lenore hugged her nephews and nieces. Thomas gazed proudly at his mother, shook his head in grand approval, and kissed her on her cheek.

"We're going to win this thing," he said.

"I believe you and I believe *in* you," said Oleatha.

CHAPTER 24

Thomas Geary paced up and down the sidewalk outside the Stockville Woolworth's, glancing at his wristwatch every few seconds. At precisely 11:30 a.m. on Monday, August 10th three young Negro college students and one white Freedom Rider from Wisconsin converged on the sidewalk next to him. Thomas spoke first.

"Above all else, there can be no violence from you," he explained.

Lunch counter protests had popped up sporadically across the South since the summer of 1962. First in North Carolina, where a small group of Negro college students refused to accept that they could purchase their school text books, but not get a meal, at the local Woolworth's. For the past six months Thomas had worked with CORE, training Stockville-area college students in non-violent protest and passive resistance. The lunch counter movement was about to claim Stockville.

Greg and Walter, the two young men, were dressed as instructed. Each wore a dark suit, white collared shirt wrapped by a solid tie. Their shoes were freshly polished. Each had his hair closely cropped and neatly combed. Greg had a moustache and Walter had a pair of black glasses which sat securely on his nose. They looked like they had stepped out of the pages of *Ebony Magazine*. Purposely so.

The women were attractive and well-dressed too. Julie, the white Freedom Rider, wore a blue and white striped skirt which ended just below her knees and a white blouse tucked neatly into a wide, brown leather belt. She wore white leather sandals, tied with a bow at her ankles. Beverly, who was Negro, wore a sleeveless white cotton blouse with a wide collar which flowed over her shoulders. Her skirt was appropriately conservative in solid robin's egg blue with pleats all around. Her shoes were brand new closed-toe flats, also white leather.

"Passive resistance," reminded Thomas, as the four walked toward the entrance.

Greg led the way, followed by Julie and Beverly. Walter guarded the flank. None of them had ever done this before. Nobody had dared try this in Sheriff Bascomb's Stockville, and the image of blood streaming out the temple and down the neck of the North Carolina A&T student who led a similar protest in Greensboro a year earlier was prominent in their minds.

Greg knew where to go. He had actually walked the store a few days earlier, and in the guise of shopping for school supplies, he had mapped out in his head which lunch counter stool to sit at and how to engage the soda fountain waiter in conversation.

In Stockville, the Woolworth's lunch counter was a favorite of most of the town's white population. The grey

Formica countertop stretched on for 30 feet, with 15 swivel chairs lining the row. Each seat, permanently bolted to the white tile floor, was covered with dark red vinyl stretched over silver steel tubing. Behind the counter, the Coca-Cola Company supplied a state of the art, bright red Coke dispensing machine. It sat next to a cardboard ice cream cone holder and a Jet Spray bubbler, pushing beautiful limeade around and around, often, it seemed, in time to the music playing on the juke box in the store's back corner. Hand-made signs touting ham salad sandwiches for 30 cents and 10-cent coffee were pasted on the white ceramic tile wall behind the counter. A large mirror hung in the middle, giving the lunch counter a feeling of being twice its size.

The four protestors sat down in predetermined order. Greg at the far end, then Beverly and Julie, then Walter. Greg reached for the laminated menu. Behind the counter a slightly built, middle-aged white man, whose nameplate read "Stuart" looked confused. He had considered that someday a lunch counter sit-in might reach the Stockville Woolworth's, but his manager was a man with an unmistakable ability to avoid confrontation and unpleasantness, and had never told him what to do if it happened.

"I'd like a cup of coffee and an egg salad sandwich," said Greg, a line he had practiced innumerable times at CORE.

Stuart, dressed in his short order whites and a white disposable paper cap shaped like a rowboat, pretended not to hear. Julie, Beverly and Walter sat nervously, shifting on their counter stools, carefully avoiding eye contact with others at the lunch counter and the small group of shoppers who had come over to see the commotion.

"Pardon me, sir," said Greg.

This time Stuart looked up and walked closer to the group.

"You know I can't serve you. If it was up to me...I'll lose my job," said Stuart.

"I understand perfectly," said Greg. "I'd still like that coffee and sandwich," he said, in the most matter-of-fact voice he could muster.

At the far end of the lunch counter, two middle-aged women stopped eating halfway through their meal.

"Wrap these up and we'll take them to go," said one of them. In a voice loud enough for everyone to hear, she added, "I've never dined with niggers and I don't plan to start now."

Stuart tore a large piece of brown wrapping paper from a roll under the counter and slid what was left of the grilled cheese sandwiches off their plates and onto the paper. The store manager, alerted by another customer, arrived at the counter.

"You'll have to leave," he said to Walter.

"We'd just like to eat lunch," Walter said.

"I'll have Stuart prepare a sack for you to take," he said.

"We prefer to eat right here," said Beverly.

"I can't do that. I don't want any trouble," said the manager, turning rapidly back and forth from them to his white customers. "I'm so sorry," he said to them.

"I can assure you, sir, you won't get any trouble from us," said Greg on cue.

The sit-in was proceeding exactly as rehearsed.

"We're staying right here," said Julie, with just a hint of insolence in her voice. She surprised herself by talking at all.

Sit-in to standoff, it was 11:45 with no food or resolution in sight. The four protestors were the only people sitting at the lunch counter, the white customers having fled. The four students weren't going to be served and they weren't going to leave.

Two blocks away, Jimmy Cooper handed his customers the shoebox containing a pair of size six black leather Buster Browns and wished them well. He grabbed his keys from behind the cash register, closed the Juniper Tree door behind him, deadbolt locked it, and headed for lunch. By the time he turned onto State Street, there was already a small crowd gathered outside Woolworth's front door. Many white regulars heard about the Negroes sitting at the counter inside and refused to enter. There were whispers of the sheriff's impending arrival and the Negro offensive on one of the town's hallowed institutions. Cooper arrived like he owned the place, walked right in and back to the lunch counter.

"What do you all think you're doing," said Cooper to the group.

Greg responded without looking up from his seat. "We're just trying to order lunch, sir."

"Don't you talk back to me you coon bastard," Cooper whispered in Greg's ear, so close Greg could feel Cooper's hot breath.

Greg stayed focused, like it had been rehearsed earlier in the day and so many days before. He and the others stared at their menus and looked across the counter at the soda fountain or at nothing in particular.

"Y'all are disturbing the peace," Cooper said.

Again the group said nothing. They sat silently for at least three minutes, when Sheriff Bascomb arrived with two of his uniformed deputies.

"What's going on, Jimmy?" asked the sheriff.

"We got a party right here, Sheriff. These four think they're going eat lunch here."

"That right?" the sheriff asked Greg.

"We just want lunch, no trouble," said Greg.

"Don't you darkies know enough to stay out of a place where you're not wanted?" yelled Brett Sharp, a white 19-year-old who had made his way from the other side of the store. Dressed in a white t-shirt and blue dungarees, Sharp was a regular in police line-ups, a troublemaker with a big mouth. "Hey jungle bunny, how 'bout I shove my boot down your nigger throat for lunch?" said Sharp.

Cooper stepped back, always happy to let someone else do the dirty work, but he nodded his approval.

"We just want lunch," said Greg again, softly.

"I'd like you to leave now," said the sheriff.

"I'm sorry, sir, but we are not going to leave," said Greg.

Beverly and Walter sat, unable to move. Walter's hands were shaking and he tried to calm himself by holding tight onto the ledge of the counter. Beverly was having it a little easier, still putting up a confident front to mask her trembling insides. Walter's legs went numb, the product of the adrenaline that was hammering through his body and the force with which he was crossing his legs in fear under the counter. He saw Julie shaking and tears forming in the corners of her eyes. He put his hand over hers to comfort her and reassure her that this was her struggle too.

"Take the white girl first," said the sheriff to his deputies.

The two uniformed deputies stepped up behind Julie.

"Please come with us," said the taller, more muscular of the two.

"I can't do that," said Julie.

"Then, Miss, please excuse our intrusion."

Each one of the deputies put one hand under Julie's arm and another under her knee and lifted her off her bar stool like she was a 10-pound ham. Her hand slid out from under Walter's. As she had been schooled to do, she let her body go completely limp, but that was little distraction for the brawny deputies. They simply carried her down the cosmetics aisle and out the front door, and placed her in one of the two waiting patrol cars. Then they went back in.

"This is the nigger who was sassing me," said Cooper to Sheriff Bascomb, pointing to Greg.

"We'll take care of it, Jimmy."

"I want to file charges against this one," Cooper said.

"I want to bash that one upside his head," said Sharp.

"That's fine. Just step back for now," said the sheriff.

When the deputies returned they were instructed to remove Beverly next and they did so, much in the same manner and with the same minimum effort needed. Beverly was placed in the same patrol car as Julie and a third deputy immediately drove them to the sheriff's department. When the deputies returned to the lunch counter they found Greg and Walter, still sitting quietly, now separated by two empty bar stools.

"Is it going to be the same for you two?" asked the sheriff.

"I'm afraid so," said Greg, in a calm, serene voice.

"Let's beat the shit outta these two," said Sharp.

"Take this one next," said the sheriff, and the two deputies moved toward Walter.

Walter knew he was supposed to let his body go limp, but he was so nervous he tensed even more and his right calf muscle cramped. He instinctively reached down to grab it.

"Nigger's got a gun!" yelled Sharp.

Sharp ran at Walter, who had his head down and back to the crowd and didn't see him coming. Sharp smashed Walter's head with a forearm shiver that sent Walter's face pounding into the hard Formica and back up before he collapsed like a pheasant full of buckshot. His eyeglasses flew off his face and broke into pieces. Blood poured out of his nose and a gash above his eye.

The rest of the crowd ducked and dispersed and all three of the deputies drew their pistols. Greg covered his head with his arms, afraid he was going to be shot. One of the two deputies pounced on Sharp.

"Be cool. No problems here," said Sharp, holding up his hands in retreat. "We're on the same side."

Walter collapsed on the floor. He was dazed and choking on his own blood. He had no gun. The sheriff grabbed Sharp's shirt, while his deputies held back Sharp's arms.

"What the fuck's the matter with you? Get him out of here," he said to the deputy who now had Sharp in a full-nelson.

The deputy shoved Sharp out the front door, pushed him down the sidewalk and told him to go home. At the lunch counter, Sheriff Bascomb was barking out orders.

"Get this guy to Mercy Emergency," said the sheriff.

Walter was still lying on the floor with Greg cradling his head, redirecting the blood and trying to stop the bleeding with his handkerchief.

"I think we've had enough for today," said the sheriff to Greg.

"I guess so," said Greg, looking up. "Others will follow."

The sheriff spoke softly to his two deputies.

"When the ambulance arrives, put this one in and take that one to the department for booking. Charge them both with a peace disturbance and resisting arrest," said the sheriff. "I'll be back at my office."

Sheriff Bascomb then addressed the crowd.

"Everybody get on with it. Show's over. Go home. Clean this mess up."

Jimmy Cooper hung back until only the deputies, Greg and Walter were left at the scene. When Cooper saw the deputies in conversation with the store manager, he tapped Greg on his shoulder. Greg looked up. Cooper smiled at him and spat in his face.

❦

Thomas Geary held the banister and walked up and down the left side of the eight wooden stairs that led from his home to the sidewalk. The right side of the stairway had two loose boards, which didn't pose a danger so much as a reminder that he still hadn't hammered them solidly back down. He would get to it, he told himself, as soon as fundraising for the United Negro College Fund and serving as volunteer executive director of the local Southern Christian Leadership Conference slowed down a bit. With more Negroes going to college and the civil rights movement gaining momentum in the South, slowing down wasn't likely any time soon.

His responsibilities pulled him in all directions, each one away from his family. He traveled from Montgomery for political meetings to Winston-Salem and Kentucky State for college visits and fundraising. When Dr. Martin Luther King, Jr. or Reverend Fred Shuttlesworth called, it was impossible not to respond to those men who, it seemed, worked 24 hours a day on the most important campaign in American Negro history. Memories of the assassination of Medgar Evers drove Thomas to exhaustion.

Thomas's wife Evie, a strong, modern Negro woman, had different ideas. She wasn't shy about letting him know when he wasn't home enough for her and their three children, which lately was just about always. Twice in the last six months she'd threatened to leave him and take the kids with her to Tidewater, Virginia, to live with her parents. The threats worked and Thomas cut back on his schedule, only to feel he was failing at everything. In those moments he couldn't shake the feeling he was letting everyone down. Evie suggested marriage counseling, which Thomas viewed as an invasion of their privacy and another demand on his time. Instead, Thomas and Evie argued a lot, sometimes in front of Harry, Denise, and Cara.

There were days when the only thing Thomas looked forward to was walking the family dog, a four-year-old collie mix named Rascal, who delighted in herding ducks at Planters Pond and chasing after sticks. But this morning Thomas wasn't even looking forward to that. He and Rascal took a left past the front gate, heading three blocks north and one block east to Potters Lane. Thomas walked past the house owned by Dora Billings, a life-long friend of his grandmother, who was at least 96 years old and rumored to be 101. Thomas used to sit with her on her porch listening to her stories of slavery and Reconstruction and drinking lemonade that Miss Billings laced with rum. Thomas hadn't seen Miss Billings in several months, and he had no time this morning to knock on her door because he was on a family mission to see Lenore.

He stood in front of his sister's home, took a deep breath, tied Rascal's leash to a fence post and knocked on the door. In a few moments it opened.

"It's Thomas Geary, community organizer extraordinaire," said Lenore.

"I'm in no mood," said Thomas.

"I heard about the sit-in."

"That's the way we have to play it."

"But those poor college-aged children-"

"They're trained and ready. Non-violent civil disobedience has its price," said Thomas. "But I'm here to talk about you."

Lenore, startled just a bit, put on her stern face.

"What's on your mind?"

"Are you out of yours?" asked Thomas.

Realizing something was deeply bothering her brother, she ushered him inside and closed the front door.

"Carl Gordon and you? It's all over the neighborhood," he said.

"What is it Mama says? Bad news always beats you home," said Lenore, smiling a little.

"This is no laughing matter," said Thomas.

"He makes me laugh," said Lenore.

"He's taking advantage of you."

"What makes you think I'm not taking advantage of him?" said Lenore, frowning and annoyed at being addressed like a teenager.

"You think he's going to marry you?"

"Are you saying I'm not worthy?"

"Oh sure, he'll give up New York and live the rest of his days as the new sheriff of Frost County?"

"I haven't thought that far."

"Well think, Lenore."

"Stop lecturing me, Thomas. Did someone forget to tell you you're my *younger* brother?"

"I don't want to be you when Micah finds out."

"I can handle him."

"You're being played. Carl Gordon is a carpetbagger with a briefcase. Here for three months, maybe four. Then he's back up North and his sophisticated white girls."

"And what if he is?"

"I don't want you hurt. And nobody wants used merchandise."

Lenore *was* hurt by Thomas's comment. A look of great disappointment covered her face and she turned away.

"I didn't mean *that*," said Thomas.

Lenore gathered her composure.

"Listen to you, Mr. High and Mighty. I'm 33 years old. Single. There's nothing for me in Stockville. Thanks to Mama and Papa, I have educated myself right out of the Stockville eligible husband pool."

"You're a snob," said Thomas, as he reached for the pitcher of iced tea sitting on the counter.

"You're a jerk," said Lenore, taking the pitcher from him and putting it in the refrigerator.

"What about Gerald Haney?"

"Gerald Haney is a kind, gentle imbecile."

"What ever happened to Lonnie Henson?"

"Five to 15 in Leavenworth."

"Probably learning a valuable trade," said Thomas. They both started laughing. Thomas straightened himself. "Promise me you'll be careful," said Thomas, opening the refrigerator, taking the tea back out and pouring himself a glass.

"I promise. I'm a big girl."

"You know he has a kid."

"Is that what they call that smaller version that follows him around? We have some of those at school."

"You're impossible."

"Yes, I am," said Lenore. "Impossible and possible at the same time."

Thomas downed the tea in one long gulp.

"You're such a...guy," said Lenore.

Thomas walked toward the front door. His business was finished, even if he didn't want to go home. Anything else was just idle talk, something no man in Stockville prized or appreciated. He certainly wasn't going to share his marital problems with Lenore, after lecturing her two minutes earlier. Lenore walked him to the door.

"Just be careful," Thomas warned. "And be discreet. I mean really, inviting the guy for dinner at your place?"

"Next date we'll just hold hands and stroll down Main Street," said Lenore, mimicking an evening stroll. "And then we'll dodge the bullets."

"So funny."

"Besides, dinner was the tame part."

"I don't want to know."

Lenore, stood in her doorway as Thomas untied Rascal.

"Bye, little brother. And thanks for caring," she called out.

CHAPTER 25

Micah arrived at his Sunoco station, inhaling the lingering scents of spent motor oil, gasoline, turpentine and car exhaust which rushed out into the Alabama morning. He hoisted up the sliding glass bay doors as a signal to the community that he was open for business. He checked the level of the underground gas tank, reviewed the repairs for the day, checked his parts inventory and hosed down the area around the gas pumps to wash away any left-over oil drippings. By 6 a.m. the sun cracked the space between two brick buildings across the street, like an open doorway to heaven. It was still early and serene as Micah studied his appointment notebook. The stillness was interrupted when a Ford Mustang with New York license plates pulled into the driveway. Micah closed his book and walked outside toward the unexpected early visitor.

"Good morning, Mr. Geary," said Carl, upbeat and trying not to look like he was suffering from escalating anxiety and insomnia.

"Kind of early for a lawyer," said Micah.

"I'm not here as a lawyer."

"I didn't know that's something you can leave behind."

"I'm here as a customer."

Micah didn't trust anything Carl Gordon said.

"Car problem?" he asked.

"It's making noise."

"Most cars do that. Especially when you turn them on."

"Is that your professional opinion?"

"Educated guess."

"This noise is kind of a screeching sound."

"In my car that's usually my kids," said Micah, a comment that would have made Carl laugh, but he didn't dare because Micah's tone was always deadly serious and his delivery was anything but funny.

"John usually rides in the back and this screeching is from the front," said Carl.

Micah walked confidently to the front of the car, flipped a lever and opened the Mustang's hood, still waiting for the real reason for the visit. The motor ran smoothly and there was no screeching, no scratching and no squealing.

"Get into the car and turn the steering wheel to the left," said Micah.

When Carl turned the wheel, the screeching noise started.

"That's it," said Carl.

"You can turn it off," said Micah.

Carl obliged.

Micah walked into the bay of the garage, grabbed a two-foot square red vinyl tarp, several hand tools and a tin can filled with a greasy substance. He spread the tarp over the car's front right quarter panel. He laid out his three wrenches, two large screwdrivers and rubber mallet on top of the tarp with the exactitude of a doctor organizing his sterile instruments for the surgery ahead. Micah grabbed the largest screwdriver in his right hand and a wrench in his left. He levered the screwdriver into the engine innards, pushed slightly and notched the wrench a half turn clockwise. Then he picked up the can of grease, and placed a quarter-sized dollop on a gear attached to a rubber belt.

"Start the car," he said.

Carl got back in the car and started it up.

"Now turn the wheel to the left again," said Micah.

No screech.

"Turn it all the way to the right."

No screech. Micah removed his tools and tarp, closed the hood of the car, a little harder than necessary, walked back into the office and opened his appointment book. Carl stood alone, shifting from side to side, waiting for Micah to return. He didn't, so Carl walked into the station's office.

"What do I owe you," asked Carl.

"No charge," said Micah, not even looking up from his paperwork.

"You don't like me, do you?" asked Carl.

Micah looked up. *Now we're getting somewhere*, he thought.

"I just fixed your car for free," he said.

"If you don't like me, I understand," said Carl.

Micah stood up from behind his desk, deciding exactly how to respond to that statement. The tension was obvious from the contractions of his shoulder muscles and vein twitching on his bicep. Holding back, he purposely spoke in a constrained, deliberate voice.

"No, you don't. If there is one thing I'm sure of, it's that you don't understand. You don't understand what it is to be black. You don't understand Alabama. You don't understand racism or segregation. You don't understand the emasculation of Negro men or the disrespect of Negro women. Whatever you have to say to me, don't ever tell me again that you understand."

Carl swallowed hard. He brushed back his hair, something he habitually did to waste time and think. He was reluctant to speak for fear of saying the wrong thing again.

"Your car is fixed. Go back to your side of town," said Micah.

"My side of town is the east side of Manhattan," said Carl.

"Then go there," said Micah, leaving the office and walking back to the garage bay, where a Nash Rambler was sitting atop the hydraulic lift.

Carl followed Micah around the elevated Rambler. He decided he might as well confront Micah now as much as later.

"Do you hate me because I'm white?" asked Carl.

Micah turned. He looked at Carl like an annoying fly he wished he could swat to stop the buzzing in his ear.

"I hate you, *and* you're white," said Micah.

"So it's racism when a white person hates you without knowing you, but it's okay for you to hate me. Is that it?" said Carl.

"I've got a hundred years of experience on my side," said Micah, pushing past Carl to his large red tool box.

"A hundred years ago my people lived in Odessa and

spoke Ukrainian."

"I bet they didn't arrive here in chains," said Micah.

"No, you're right. No chains. Just starving."

"When you walk down the street, people can't *see* that you're a Ukrainian American. I don't recall ever seeing a sign that says *No Ukrainians or Dogs Allowed*, or inferior hospitals and schools for Ukrainians, or laws that prevent Ukrainian Americans from voting. Should I go on?" asked Micah.

"I didn't do any of that. All I can do is try to change it," said Carl.

"You? You can't even take care of yourself and you're going to help me?"

Micah picked up a tire iron, shook his head and put it back down.

"I know the law. What do you know?" asked Carl, feeling courageous as the accusatory words came out of his mouth.

"You want to get personal?" asked Micah.

Carl decided to go on the offensive.

"Sure, how'd you get that scar?" asked Carl.

"None of your fucking business."

"Too personal for you?"

"All right, counselor. When I was 15, three older white boys held me down. Then one took out a switchblade. He said he was going to cut off my dick. Personal enough?"

Carl just listened.

"They started pulling on my pants when a car drove up, so instead, he put the knife up in my cheek and pulled it through my lip. They said they wanted to give me something to remember them by."

"I'm sorry," said Carl.

"Don't be sorry. I'm not sorry. Just don't tell me how

you're going to make everything better because you know the law. Your *laws* saw to it that there were no arrests and no charges filed. The sheriff came by. He did. He said I was one lucky nigger."

"You know who did it?"

"Of course I know who did it."

"If I file federal charges will you testify?"

"I'm not buying your bullshit. You're nothing to me. You've apparently conned everyone else in my family. My brother thinks having you here helps his non-violent, passive resistance, bend over and get fucked civil rights movement. My mother thinks you walk on water. You've got my son all excited about a basketball team that's going nowhere. How long will it be until you pack up your now screechless Mustang and head back to New York City, leaving us to pick up the pieces?"

"It doesn't have to be that way," said Carl.

"It's always that way."

"Times change."

"Alabama doesn't."

"It does. Last summer George Wallace stepped aside and let James Hood and Vivian Malone enroll at the University of Alabama. The Montgomery bus boycott worked. The busses are still integrated," said Carl.

"Again, you don't understand," said Micah. "I'm not interested in *successful* integration. I'm just fine with segregation. I don't want your kind around me any more than Jimmy Cooper wants us darkies around him. But I'll be damned if what I have is inferior to what you have. I'm *taking* what's equal and nothing is going to be non-violent about it."

Micah looked down into Carl's guarded expression.

"That's not any more realistic than thinking the whites

are going to keep themselves separate. Segregation is ending," said Carl.

"Yes I know. Tomorrow. We need to be patient," said a sarcastic Micah.

"I want to find some common ground for us," said Carl.

"I like hush puppies and chitlins, you?" asked Micah.

"I don't know what that is," said Carl.

"See, we tried. We failed. Now I've got work to do."

Micah turned to leave and was halfway back to his office when Carl called out to him.

"Micah. Can't we at least keep the lines of communication open?" he asked.

Micah turned back to face Carl.

"Sure. I'd like to communicate one more thing," said Micah.

Carl took his hands out of his pockets. He was exhausted, but trying to look calm and hopeful.

"What's that?" he asked.

"Keep your goddamn hands off my sister or I'll break your neck."

❧

Jimmy Cooper bounded through the front door of the Frost County Sheriff's department as if he owned the place. The department, located 14 miles east of Stockville, was a one-story cinder block building constructed in 1938 with federal funds from President Roosevelt's WPA program. The building had been painted white, with a navy blue eight-inch horizontal stripe, waist high, around the entire perimeter. Near the door was a bright red Coca-Cola machine that dispensed 7-ounce bottles and the machine, according to the sign hand-painted on it, was for "whites only." There was no corresponding "Coloreds" machine. Inside was a main room for bookings and fraternizing among the sheriff's deputies, with a TV in the southwest corner and stolid portraits of past county sheriffs lining the interior walls. There were two private offices, one for Sheriff Bascomb and one for interrogations—a total of four in the last year. Attached at the rear of the building were three holding cells, each with a sink and a toilet and a thin mattress on top of a World War II surplus military cot.

The department remained most active between shifts, from six to seven in the morning and five to six in the evening. It was late in the day when Jimmy Cooper came bounding through the front door, strutting around the front room, a man on a mission. He looked like the happiest man in America.

"Hey Roger," said Jimmy to the on-duty intake deputy. "How's the baby?'

"Wish he'd sleep through the night. Rough on the missus," said the deputy.

"In no time at all, he'll be running you ragged, and you know, we give 10% off on shoes to all law enforcement families," said Jimmy.

"When he's ready," said the deputy. "You here to see the sheriff?"

"Yep."

"Expecting you?"

"Yep."

"He's in back," said the deputy, his uniformed arm pointing the way.

Jimmy walked past another two young sheriff's deputies, both with kids who were Juniper Tree customers.

"Howdy fellas," said Jimmy.

"Afternoon, Mr. Cooper," they said in unison.

"Boys. Good afternoon. Great days ahead," Cooper said, smiling and patting backs.

"We're glad to be of service," said the larger deputy. "We're here to serve," said the other.

"Is he home?" asked Jimmy.

"Yes sir. Go right in."

Jimmy knocked on the sheriff's door, more a courtesy than necessity. He was a regular, and one of Frost County's largest donors to the sheriff's benevolent foundation, which provided scholarships for the children of deputies killed in the line of duty. Jimmy poked his head around the frosted glass door.

"Sheriff?"

"Jimmy. C'mon in and shut the door. What can I do for you my friend?" asked Sheriff Bascomb.

On the wall behind the sheriff was a framed collection of the sheriff's commendations from three different governors, and his picture with various famous Alabama politicians including Senator John Sparkman, Adlai Stevenson's vice-presidential running mate in 1952. On the opposite wall hung a 1964 calendar, courtesy of Atlantis Automotive, which had a different picture of a pretty white girl in a bathing suit for each month.

"Howdy Pete," said Jimmy, moving toward one of the two red cushioned chairs on his side of the sheriff's desk. "First things first. I brought this pair of Buster Browns for your grandson."

Jimmy held out the Juniper Tree bag and handed it to the sheriff, who smiled and put the bag inside his desk drawer.

"Thanks, Jimmy. Right nice of you."

"If the fit's not right, you have Betty bring them in and we'll exchange them. Kids' feet grow faster than the rest of their bodies." Jimmy settled into the chair, slapped his hands on the armrests and looked pensively at the sheriff. "You know, Pete, outside agitators have got our niggers all riled up," said Jimmy.

"Shouldn't start what they can't finish," the sheriff mused.

"I hear a lot of them are coming here to Stockville on Sunday for a protest march."

"I cannot guarantee the safety of a fool. That's what these people are, fools," the sheriff replied.

"Maybe 300 of them. In busses. Maybe even Martin Luther Coon himself is coming."

"I don't like it when people get hurt, but they're asking for it."

"You got enough men?"

"Probably not."

"Well I've got an idea. You give us 15 minutes. That's all. Just 15 minutes. Then your men can step in and be the heroes and we'll never have to worry about the Negro problem again."

Jimmy Cooper, flush with the success of his visit with Sheriff Bascomb, made his next stop the downtown office of the *Stockville Times-Gazette*. He parked his '63 white Thunderbird convertible directly across Main Street from the newspaper office, gathered the papers he kept in a shoebox and tucked it under his arm.

"Darling, where's Paul?" he asked the receptionist at the front desk.

"He's back in advertising," she said.

Looking at the newsroom invariably led to the conclusion that it was a miracle that a newspaper was published there every day. Columns of old newspapers rose like stalagmites from floor to ceiling. Row after row of dented, aging file cabinets snaked their way around the flecked linoleum floors. Desks were covered with files and books and mounds of blank white paper so high that the black Royal typewriters barely poked their cartridges out of the mess. Government issued oak benches were strategically placed where no one would think of sitting. All of this catastrophe of an office was illuminated by banks of florescent tubes that dangled from the ceiling, which was a sickening shade of tan from years of reporters' floating cigarette smoke.

"Paul," yelled Jimmy.

Owens turned his attention from fixing a typo in a full-page ad to his energetic lunch-mate.

"Hey, Jimmy. What's shaking?"

Jimmy put down his shoebox, opened the lid and pulled out a flyer that he had folded in half. He handed it to Owens, who looked it over.

"What's a Solemn Summons of the Fiery Cross?" Owens asked.

"It's a call to arms. Serious shit going down here Sunday and I'm pulling out all the stops," said Jimmy.

Owens read the flyer out loud:

By the Solemn Summons of the Fiery

Cross you are hereby summoned

to appear armed and ready at an

EXTRAORDINARY gathering to be

held this Sunday promptly at 2 p.m.

in the Stockville town square. The call

is IMPERATIVE, by mandate of his

Lordship the Imperial Wizard. Read

this carefully. Note the place, day and

hour and then completely destroy this.

Your Exalted Cyclops – JC

"Can you print me a thousand of these?" Jimmy asked.

"I guess. Why?"

"We're having a party. A nigger ass-kicking party."

"If the Negroes walk to City Hall, wave American flags, make speeches and go home, nobody notices. Nobody cares. If you do this, the whole country will be watching it on the *The Huntley-Brinkley Report* the next night," said Owens.

"The whole country should watch. Niggers have no business trying to mix themselves with us. Most of these marching fools on Sunday are outside agitators who should mind their own business. Our Negroes know the southern white man is their best friend. We're all happy here," said Jimmy.

Owens raised his eyebrows and stared at Jimmy over his reading glasses right into Jimmy's eyes.

"They don't look happy to me. Times are changing, Jimmy. The South is changing. Governor Wallace stood down at the university when federal marshals allowed those two Negroes to register for classes. Same in Mississippi. It's going to happen. Every court has ruled Jim Crow unconstitutional."

"Fuck the courts. They don't know jack about the South. The federal government should build highways and leave running Alabama to Alabama."

"I'll print them. But you're making a big mistake," said Owens.

"Just print them."

"And a warning, Jimmy. On Sunday, I'm sending reporters and photographers."

CHAPTER 26

Oleatha arrived unannounced, straightening her green and yellow flower print dress, before knocking twice on Lenore's front door. She had a wicker basket steadied on her left arm, the top covered with a white linen napkin. Oleatha knew that Saturday morning was the best time to find Lenore at home and available to talk.

Even at 9:30 on a summer morning, Lenore looked put-together, her black tapered pants hugging her thighs and calves. A yellow and white striped button-down blouse, open at the neck and untucked, completed the casual outfit. She allowed herself the informality of going barefoot in her home. She walked over and opened the door.

"Hi, Mama, I was just making a fresh pot of coffee. Come on in."

No matter how many times Lenore had hinted to her mother that she preferred Oleatha telephoning before dropping by, Oleatha persisted in what Lenore called her *surprise attacks*, justifying them by inventing collateral excuses.

"Sorry to bother you honey. I was just at Delores Tyree's house down the block and she gave me these beautiful tomatoes from her garden. I thought you might like some."

"It's fine, Mama. Thank you."

Lenore led her mother to the kitchen, lit a fire under the coffee pot, set the creamer and sugar bowl down on the kitchen table and waited for the real reason her mother decided to visit. Lenore had a private chuckle, thinking it might be that oil had been discovered under Edwin Paterson's 50 acres.

"It smells delicious. Have you been baking?" asked Oleatha.

Oleatha knew that Lenore loathed baking and the sweet smelling biscuits that were sitting on the kitchen counter in plain view were store bought. Lenore knew that asking for a biscuit was way too direct an approach for her mother, and Oleatha's seemingly innocuous comments on the outside edges of conversation was number 12 on Lenore's top 20 of her mother's habits that drove her crazy.

"They're from Backwater Bakery. Would you like some strawberry jam with yours?" asked Lenore.

"Thank you, dear."

Lenore poured hot coffee into the cup sitting on the placemat in front of Oleatha.

"Help yourself to cream and sugar," she said.

Oleatha took one teaspoon of sugar, stirred it in her coffee, and then took another spoonful from the jar with the wet spoon, ensuring that the next person wanting sugar would find it lumpy. *Annoying habit number eight*, Lenore thought, but said nothing.

Oleatha then added too much cream for Lenore's taste,

and stirred again. Without looking up, she said, "This morning I was thinking about how lonely it is for me growing older without a husband."

Standing at the refrigerator, Lenore silently clenched her fists and locked her jaw. *Annoying habit number three. Say something about yourself that's really meant for me*, thought Lenore. *Two can play at that game*, she decided.

"Interesting you say that. Just this morning *I* was thinking that you and Earl Carson would make a great couple," Lenore said.

"Oh please, Lenore. He's seen the other side of yesterday. He must be 70 years old."

Oleatha was stopped dead in her verbal tracks and Lenore turned toward her mother with a confident smirk and an eyebrow rise.

"Lenore one, Mama zero," she said, smiling.

"I didn't come here to talk about Edwin Paterson," said Oleatha.

"Then come clean, Mama. What's on your mind other than an emergency tomato delivery?"

"This is difficult," said Oleatha.

"Give it a try," said Lenore.

Oleatha took a deep breath, a sip of coffee and pinched off a small piece of the biscuit. Then she took another sip of coffee.

"Is this a new brand of coffee?"

Translation. I don't like this coffee, thought Lenore.

"Mama?" said Lenore.

"Okay."

Oleatha hesitated again.

"Whatever it is, just say it," said Lenore.

"I've seen the way that white New York lawyer looks at you," said Oleatha.

"Don't tell me how to run my life," Lenore interrupted. "Did Thomas put you up to this?"

"When he asks, I think you should marry him," said Oleatha.

Lenore sat down directly across from her mother. She wasn't sure she had heard correctly, since they were both talking at the same time.

"What did you say?" she asked.

"I said, I've always been a good observer of people and that boy is head-over-heels for you, and unless I've lost my God-given sixth sense of matchmaking, you're smitten right back."

"This is—"

"Never in a million years did I think I'd be saying this about a white boy, but this Carl Gordon fella just may be the right man for you."

"But Mama—"

"Don't interrupt me honey, you got me going and I'm on a roll."

Lenore couldn't feel her fingertips wrapped around her coffee cup. She leaned in, dazed, but attentive and interested too.

"I don't always show it, or say the right things, but baby, you are my proudest accomplishment. You came back to Stockville for two weeks to go to your father's funeral, and you've been stuck here ten years because of me and my tuberculosis. I'm sorry."

Oleatha clutched the cross around her neck to gain back her composure.

"When I look at you I see the best parts of me and your father."

"Mama, you don't need—"

Oleatha put up a gentle but persuasive hand telling Lenore that she wasn't finished.

"I wanted you with me so bad that I haven't ever told you what I really think. I guess I was hoping that if I never said it, it would never happen. Now I'm going to say it. You don't belong here. You're too smart and too talented for this rat-hole of a town. And you know what I think of Alabama."

"One whistle stop from hell," said Lenore. She felt dizzy from the heartfelt speech, but also wondered when her mother would ruin the moment.

"If this Carl loves you like it looks like he does, don't let the opportunity pass you by. It makes me scared, but I hear people are more open to those sorts of things in New York City," said Oleatha.

Lenore sat quietly for a moment, her eyes fixed on the table. "I don't know what's going to happen," she said. "You're right though, whenever I'm with him, I get the feeling I can be who I am, not who Stockville demands I be."

"What happened to the wife?" asked Oleatha.

"She died in February of Lou Gehrig's disease."

"And the boy?"

"John. I think he likes me. I think he's adorable."

"Honey, they're all adorable at 12, but take it from me, at 14 they're just a lot of laundry."

Lenore stood up and walked to the other side of the table. Oleatha stood up too and reached out for her daughter, holding her tightly in her arms.

"Mama, you're beautiful."

"I love you, baby."

"I love you too, Mama."

❧

Carl, who couldn't get a good night's sleep after his telephone call with Emily, was beginning to appreciate Alabama's August sunrise, a silent time of day most often shared by farmers and bakers. It happened in stages, with red streaks peeking through the lavender ink of low flying clouds, followed by ribbons of yellow silhouetting the long leaf pines that framed Stockville's cotton and corn fields. When even the Valium couldn't reduce his stress to a manageable level, he paced all night around the house, imagining a life sentence for a former U.S. Attorney in Attica. He had to fix the Emily problem. He had to find out what she knew and who she was talking to. With *Accessory to Murder* hanging over his head, he couldn't think straight. As he had explained it to Lenore, he had been called back to New York for a high level meeting and would have to leave early Sunday morning and miss the voting rights march on Stockville.

"Several of the Assistant U.S. Attorneys are being flown in," he lied.

With Shirley back in the relative safety of New York's five boroughs, Carl asked if Lenore would be willing to watch John while he was gone. He'd be flying out of Birmingham Sunday morning and back on Tuesday night.

When Carl looked at Lenore, his stomach clenched and his arms and legs tingled the same way as when he had been with Beth. Lenore's chest filled with air and she got short of breath just looking at Carl. She had babysat her nephews overnight in the past, and also thought staying with John might be just the opportunity for her to get to know him better. They decided John would stay at Lenore's place. Having Lenore stay at Maiden Lane would certainly cause an upheaval in the neighborhood, and adding to the rumor mill seemed unwise. Carl and Lenore also decided it would be best if John didn't march without Carl around. Lenore reluctantly agreed that she wouldn't be missed either. A short-term sacrifice for a long-term gain, she reasoned.

John's bicycle poked out of the Mustang's half-opened trunk, which Carl tied in place with yellow twine. As the car pulled curbside, Lenore walked outside to greet them.

"Got time for a cup of coffee, sailor?" she asked.

Lenore was dressed in a silk bathrobe in pastel pinks and purples that draped over her shoulders and down to her knees. Her hair was gathered on top of her head, giving Carl a beautiful view of her tempting neck, his first target of amour a few nights earlier.

"Sure. Let me get John out of the backseat and into the house," he said.

Carl slowly opened the passenger side door, where John's head was propped up on a pillow. Carl caught the pillow and gently pulled at John's shoulders, coaching him up. He walked the half-sleeping John past Lenore, who was holding the front screen door open. Lenore had made up her living room couch with a feather pillow at one end, a white sheet over the cushions and a double wedding ring patterned patch-work quilt on top.

"Lay him down right here," she whispered.

John adopted the fetal position and promptly fell back asleep. Carl, who was dressed to travel in his blue suit, white dress shirt and solid blue tie, went back outside to the car. He untied the trunk, lifted the bike and set it down against the side of the house. Then he grabbed John's suitcase out of the back seat and brought it inside.

"This is so nice of you," he said.

"I'm actually looking forward to it."

Lenore poured Carl a cup of coffee. Smiling his irresistible smile, he led her to a spot in the kitchen, out of view from the couch. He drew her close and kissed her. She pulled back just a little.

"Dangerous," she said.

"Extremely dangerous," he agreed.

"What time is your flight?"

"11:15."

Lenore glanced at the clock sitting on the kitchen countertop.

"Don't start what you can't finish," she said.

"Oh, I could finish, but *you* might be disappointed."

They kissed again.

"I had an interesting conversation with your brother," Carl said, lifting the cup of hot, black coffee to his lips.

"Thomas?"

"No, Micah. I brought my car in for service and we had a valuable exchange of ideas."

"Your jaw doesn't appear to be broken. No sling on your arm," she said.

Carl proceeded to relate the story, beginning with the screeching fan belt and ending with the threat that Carl should keep his goddamn hands off Lenore.

"I think that episode with the white teenagers slicing open his lip explains a lot," said Carl.

"He told you about that?"

"How they held him down and were threatening to castrate him. Then told him he was lucky they just cut his lip open," said Carl.

"That's it?"

"Pretty much," said Carl.

"Micah didn't tell you the whole story," said Lenore. Lenore's face turned serious and solid. She bit her lower lip, trying to distance herself as much as she could from what she was about to say. "I was there, too," she said.

Lenore crossed her arms in front of her chest, like a cold front had just come in from the North. She took a step back from Carl. She stared into his eyes trying to anticipate the consequences of this conversation.

"While the three boys held him down, two of their friends raped me."

Lenore refused to cry, but Carl could see the walls of her time-tested defense mechanisms going up. Her eyes stared ahead, emotionless. She crossed her arms tighter in front of her, a self-imposed strait jacket. The skin around her jaw stiffened. Carl shivered and he felt a stabbing pain in the side of his head. He reached out, inviting her to take his hand. She did.

"My God, Lenore. I'm so sorry," he said. Carl couldn't stop himself from falling back into law enforcement mode. "Were they prosecuted?" he asked.

"Of course not," she said.

"It's not too late. Do you know them?"

"One of them was killed in Korea. The other one is still around."

"We can—"

"No we can't," Lenore interrupted. "I've moved on. Probably better than Micah has. Just leave it alone, counselor."

"Are you okay?"

"I'm 33 years old and I've been told by at least two men that I'm emotionally bankrupt. With you, I feel different. Unless I'm reading things all wrong, I may be in the first serious relationship in my life," she said. "Does that make me okay or damaged goods?"

Carl took a step closer to Lenore and put his arms around her. She embraced him back and squeezed as hard as she could.

"You're much more than okay. You're magnificent," said Carl, remembering that the last time he used that word it was to say goodbye to Beth.

Should I tell her? he thought. He didn't.

Their embrace continued beyond a normal hug. For the first time their touching wasn't sexual. It was tender and friendly, supportive and assuring. Lenore looked up demurely, as if she'd found an oasis in a desert she'd been wandering around for years. She pulled herself back a few inches.

"You're going to miss your flight," she said, tears forming in her eyes.

"What can I bring you from New York?" he asked.

"Bring me the World's Fair."

"The whole thing?"

"How about that Unisphere globe thing?"

"That's all?"

"And the fountains around it," she said.

"Done," he said.

They kissed again. This time deeply and for a long time.

"You have to go now," she said, exhaling.

Lenore took Carl's hand and walked him to the front door.

"Now go. But do come back," she said.

Their eyes met. He gave her hand a gentle squeeze, looked to see if any neighbors were spying, and kissed her one more time.

"I love you," he said.

Lenore exhaled. She steadied herself on the screen door handle with her left hand. She needed more to believe it was real.

"Just the way I am?" she asked.

"Exactly that way."

Carl let go of Lenore's right hand and jogged to the Mustang. He opened the driver's side door and blew her a kiss. She smiled and waved as Carl drove away. Lenore walked back to the kitchen where a full cup of lukewarm coffee was still sitting on the counter. She took a sip and walked to a spot where she could stare at John, who was breathing deeply and asleep.

❧

Emily Harlowe sat alone in her regular corner booth at Atwell's Restaurant on 57th and Broadway, drinking coffee and eating French toast smothered in powdered sugar and Vermont maple syrup. Novelists weren't everyday celebrities like movie stars and professional athletes and Emily could be anonymous behind large white plastic sunglasses. Anonymous is not the same as understated, and Emily, even on Sunday morning, drew attention to herself with red hot lipstick and an unbuttoned blouse, clearly announcing to the world that she didn't attend church that morning.

She looked up from reading the Sunday *New York Times Book Review* to see a slightly built, cleanly shaven man with a crew-cut and a crooked nose. Dressed in a brown suit, he was checking her out. He clutched a copy of *Double Trouble*, her most recent novel, in front of him and he appeared to be comparing the picture of Emily on the inside back dust jacket with the real thing sitting in the booth. She tried to ignore him. When he seemed convinced the picture was Emily Harlowe, he walked up to her table, less timidly than her usual autograph-seeking fan.

"You're Emily Harlowe, right?"

"You've found her. The Alfred Hitchcock of novelists," Emily said, putting down her fork, but keeping the knife in her hand, just in case.

"Excuse me?" said the man.

"Hitchcock has never won an Oscar for best director. Can you believe that?" Emily said.

"I didn't know," said the man.

"And me? Four books on *The New York Times* best-seller list. Three made it to number two. Not one has ever reached number one," she said.

The man, with a noticeable hair lip when viewed at close proximity, shrugged his shoulders in response. Having four books on *The New York Times* best seller list seemed pretty successful to him. He tried to say something flattering.

"I love your books. Read every one of them," he said.

"Have you also read *The Spy Who Came in From the Cold?*" she countered.

"I have. It's terrific."

"Fucking le Carre. Twenty-seven weeks at number one."

Emily flipped the book review section around and smacked her finger down at the top of the list.

"Can I sit down?" asked the man.

"Why?" asked Emily.

"I'm actually more than a fan. I'm here on business."

"Business?"

"Can I sit down?" he asked again.

"Sure. But if you're some kind of weirdo, I know the people who own this place."

"Nothing like that," he said.

The man sat down on the bench seat across from Emily. He set his brown straw hat on the seat next to him and he put his copy of *Double Trouble* on the table facing Emily.

"My name is Tony Mercurio. FBI."

Tony reached into the inside breast pocket of his jacket and pulled out a worn, leather billfold. He flipped it open revealing his gold badge.

"Just like in the movies, Mr. Mercurio," said Emily, feigning disinterest, but her body language clearly showed her increasing apprehension, as she shifted her body weight and crossed her knees under the table.

"Thank you. I practice at home, with my wife," he said, the edges of his lips turning upwards into a fleeting, confident smile.

"You haven't asked me to autograph your book," said Emily.

Mercurio ignored her statement.

"We at the Bureau take *coincidences* seriously, and by we, I mean, Mr. Hoover. If we've got a bad apple he wants to know about it, stay ahead of the curve, and nip it in the bud."

With her elbows resting on the table, one on each side of her plate, she opened both palms to the sky. Even having spent countless hours at police stations to bring authenticity to her crime novel characters, Agent Mercurio's stirring string of clichés left her confused.

"You've lost me, Mr. Mercurio."

"*Accessory to Murder*, Miss Harlowe. You don't have to be a brain surgeon to know, you know? And the fact that you and Mr. Gordon have been...friends. Do you follow?"

Emily understood, but decided to play coy and let Agent Mercurio continue. He pulled out a small notebook from the other breast pocket of his jacket. *This guy is a classic,* thought Emily.

"Mr. Gordon had a sick wife. Your protagonist has a sick wife."

"Good word Mr. Mercurio, protagonist," said Emily.

"Thank you. I read a lot of stuff," he said. "Sometimes on a stake-out you wait all day. Got to pass the time. That's when I read *Double Trouble,* in a motel room in Jamaica Estates. I liked your main character, excuse me, protagonist. Good cop that Alton Remington, right?"

"Except for the opium addiction," said Emily.

"And the wife beating shit," he said.

"And the shake-downs," she said.

"You do cops really well," said Mercurio, rattling on. "Anyway, Carl Gordon and Carl Grayburn. Both got sons. Both got pillows. Both got anniversaries. Both got dead wives on their anniversaries. You get my drift? Is there something Mr. Hoover should know about Carl Gordon? You know what they say, 'truth is stranger than fiction.'"

"That's not true," said Emily.

"What's not?" said Mercurio.

"Truth is not stranger than fiction," said Emily, lifting her napkin from her lap and wiping powdered sugar from the corners of her mouth.

"No?"

"No. I'll tell you what, you tell me any true story and I'll make one up that's better," said Emily.

"What about Carl Gordon?"

"You obviously know about us," said Emily.

"At the Bureau, let's just say we're good listeners," said Mercurio.

"Carl jilted me. I was pissed. Still am. But it's not real, it's fiction," said Emily.

"You're sure?"

"I'm still in love with that bastard. I'm a writer. That's how writers exact revenge. Kind of like when a psychiatrist has a patient punch a stuffed animal instead of his wife."

"Projection," said Mercurio.

"Impressive, Agent Mercurio. Are you a Freudian?" asked Emily.

"Sagittarius," he said.

Emily laughed. *This Fed is actually entertaining*, she thought.

"Carl once told me he didn't think Beth would live to see their anniversary. I wrote that down, because that's the kind of sentence you can build a story around. Then, right after the bastard left for Alabama, *The New Yorker* called with an offer I couldn't refuse. It was a natural. Hate is real easy to write. Sorry to disappoint you, but that's it," said Emily.

"Miss Harlowe. If I prepared an affidavit recounting what you just said, would you be willing to sign it?" asked Mercurio.

"If you prepare an affidavit, you can send it to my lawyer."

Mercurio flipped through pages in his notebook.

"You're a lawyer, New York University, 1952," he said.

"I hardly call having a 12-year-old, unused law degree being a lawyer," said Emily.

"I don't even know that we need to do that affidavit thing," he said. "I'll get back to you if we do."

"If you want to reach me, call my agent. Paul Reynolds."

Mercurio wrote the name in his notebook, flipped it closed and put it back in his breast pocket. He grabbed his hat and sidestepped out of the wooden booth. Once he was standing where they'd started talking five minutes earlier, Agent Mercurio nodded at Emily and thanked her for her time. He put *Double Trouble* back under his arm and took one step toward the door. Then he turned back with a slightly quizzical look.

Just like in the movies, Emily thought again.

"By the way, I loved the title of the story. *Accessory to Murder*, Miss Harlowe. That's a great play on words. The pillow is a bedroom accessory. Whereas usually in my, let's say our, business, the accessory to murder is the person who knows that a crime has been committed, but doesn't come forward."

Emily smiled and a small chuckle came out of her mouth. Agent Mercurio would be stored in her memory in the file called "Everything is copy."

"Very smooth, Agent Mercurio. I catch your drift," she said, accentuating each syllable, trying to sound like his New York accent. "Thank you for warning me, but I have nothing to worry about. You have nothing to worry about. Mr. Hoover has nothing to worry about and Carl Gordon has nothing to worry about. Until I see him again," she said, shaking her fist.

"Have a good day Miss Harlowe," he said, putting on his hat and stepping confidently into the Manhattan morning.

🌿

Carl couldn't stop his mind from looping his conversation with Emily, during the drive from Stockville to Birmingham. *The New Yorker* short story and the showdown looming with her distracted him so much he missed the airport exit and, like an airplane, had to circle around to try a proper landing again. Finally, he parked his car in the airport lot, grabbed his suitcase and the brown paper bag he had filled with nickels, dimes and quarters and walked toward the terminal. Carl looked at his watch. It was 10:40, almost an hour before his flight. He found a bank of phone booths. He opened the door to one of them, sat down and set his bag of coins on the shelf under the phone. He put a dime in the slot to get a dial tone. He dialed zero for the operator.

"What number please?" asked the voice at the other end.

"I'd like to place a long distance call to 212-JU4-0998," Carl replied.

"Please deposit $3.25 for the first three minutes," said the operator.

Carl started feeding his quarters into the slot, hoping Anthony was home. Carl dropped one of his quarters. It landed somewhere near his feet, but he didn't have time to waste and the tall, narrow confines of the phone booth made bending down without opening the door impossible. He kept feeding quarters into the phone, with the quick repetitive movements of an assembly line worker. When he counted to 13 quarters, he stopped. He waited. One ring. Then a second.

Carl waited, the phone pressed into his ear.

"Come on, pick-up," he said.

A third ring. No answer. A fourth ring.

"Hello."

Carl could hear Anthony on the other end, but there was a delay while the phone company registered Carl's stream of quarters inside the pay phone and the quarters slid from inside the main section of the phone to the locked coin slot beneath. It sounded like a jackpot in Vegas.

"Hello?" Anthony said again.

"Anthony? It's Carl. Can you hear me?"

"Loud and clear, my friend. I just got back. Mission accomplished," Anthony said. "More fun than bedding a bridesmaid."

"Tell me," said Carl.

"She was right where you said she'd be at Atwell's. Carl, she doesn't know anything."

"Details," said Carl.

"Wow. She's hot," said Anthony.

"Not those details. What happened?"

"She bought it hook, line and sinker. FBI agent Tony Mercurio at your service. She said you once told her you didn't think Beth would live past your anniversary, and her criminal mind made up all the rest."

Anthony proceeded to reenact the entire restaurant scene, his brilliant acting, Emily's nervous flirting and the *Accessory to Murder* big finish, while Carl fed more quarters into the phone.

"Best of all, I got the whole thing on tape. I had the recorder stashed inside my pants," said Anthony.

"I owe you big time," Carl replied.

"With all you've done for me? Doing this for you just gets me a little closer to equal," said Anthony.

"Thanks pal. When I get home, we're celebrating on me. I've got to go cancel my flight. I'll call you later," said Carl.

Carl hung up the phone, pulled on the louvered phone booth door, pumped his fist in the air and yelled "yes" loud enough for everyone in the terminal to hear. Carl jogged up to the TWA counter and got a refund for his plane ticket. He checked his watch. It was 11:00. If he hurried, he might be able to make it back to Stockville in time to hear some of the speeches outside City Hall.

❧

CHAPTER 27

Pastor Williams climbed the four makeshift steps up to the wooden podium placed in the back of Chester Hollister's truck bed and looked over the gathering crowd of marchers. Dressed in a charcoal grey suit and white shirt, the pastor reached into his jacket pocket and pulled out the notes for his sermon. He looked out over the gathering of about 500 people. Word had spread quickly throughout the Grove that Sunday's Thankful Baptist Church service would take place outside, adjacent to the Hamden Lumber Yard, the starting point for the March on Stockville in support of Negro voter registration.

"Brothers and sisters. Children of God. Good morning all you glorious citizens of Stockville and supporters of our march for voter registration. One hundred years ago the Negro in the South wore the manacles of slavery. I'm sorry to report that we still wear them. Today we wear the chains of Jim Crow. The shackles of segregation."

The pastor paused as the crowd moved gradually into a semi-circle around the truck. At the front stood Thomas and

Evie Geary, Harry, Denise and Cara, all of them wearing their Sunday best church clothes and feeling the delightfulness of hope. Standing next to her grandchildren was Oleatha, by her own words, "champing at the bit" to get the march started.

The pastor continued his sermon, playing to the flock before him.

"Segregation is an insidious slavery and there is only one way out. It doesn't take a shrewd politician to know that the way to keep Negroes subservient is to deny us the right to vote. With no vote, we are prevented from a meaningful education. With no vote, segregationists keep us in menial jobs, prevent us from moving up.

"For the last 10 years our struggle has been focused on registering Negro voters, and the white establishment has battled our effort on every front with overt obstinacy. Fifty years ago the all-white Alabama legislature created a poll tax. In order to vote, just to vote in this free country of ours, all Alabamans had to pay a fee most of us could not afford."

Pastor Williams paused again, both for effect and to catch his breath. He looked to his left, where two older parishioners were holding hands and looking as if their entire lives were being rewritten that day.

"When poll taxes weren't working well enough, the Alabama legislature passed a law requiring citizens to take a literacy test to vote. The white lawmen created all kinds of exceptions so the whites didn't have to take the test. They were exempt if their father was a voter or if they could show that they could read a child's text book.

"Negroes on the other hand, we were given obscure sections of the U.S. Constitution to read and interpret and if we could do that, then we got a written test with questions only the most learned of historians could pass. Not only were the questions impossible, they were carefully designed to intimidate us too."

"Amen," shouted a young freedom rider who carried a sign that read "Give us the Vote."

"We march. Yes, today we march through the streets of Stockville to let everyone know that we will take part in the election process. We will be first-class citizens. Our children and our children's children will look back on this glorious day as the beginning of the end of Negro oppression. Men, women, and children, join me today in non-violent expression. Let us march to freedom together. God bless you all and God bless America."

The march began at 11 a.m., from south of town and finishing at City Hall, about eight miles. The organizing committee of the Southern Christian Leadership Council lent its experience and expertise and at least 150 supporters. People continued to arrive by car, bus and truck. The lumber yard was chosen as the starting point because Scott Hamden, a white supporter of the civil rights movement, volunteered the use of his parking lot. The outside supporters, both white and Negro, readied themselves to march side by side with the citizens. Many of them brought signs, enough for most in the march to carry one. Others carried small American flags stapled at one end to wooden dowels.

"The people keep arriving," said Thomas Geary.

"I suspect there are more than 500," said Pastor Williams. "Where's your friend, the Assistant U.S. Attorney?"

"I don't know," said Thomas, surveying the crowd, looking for Carl.

"Do we have the national guard?"

"Carl offered. I declined," said Thomas. "What kind of message would that send?"

"That we're safe?" asked the pastor, his eyebrows raised and his voice low and crusty.

"This is all peaceful, Rev. I'm going to start," said Thomas.

Thomas hopped up in the truck bed, breathed deeply the aroma of crushed pine needles and pressed the button on the back of his yellow bullhorn to address the crowd.

"Hello. Can I have your attention?"

The marchers grew silent, standing still and ready, like Olympic sprinters waiting for the starter's pistol. Oleatha wiped a tear from her cheek as she watched Thomas standing above the crowd and leading the march. She squeezed Evie's hand and put her arm around Harry's shoulder.

"Thank you all for being here today. Your support is overwhelming. We are going to start our march in a few minutes."

As often as Thomas had addressed groups of people while raising money and awareness for the United Negro College Fund, his legs still felt wobbly every time and he nervously shifted his weight from one leg to the other. This was easily the largest crowd he had ever addressed. He cleared his throat and stroked his forehead with his free hand.

"I will be at the front and there will be SCLC volunteers throughout. They are wearing blue armbands. If you have a question or a problem, ask one of us."

A camera crew from the National Broadcasting Company had started filming earlier in the morning, and were recording both the pastor's remarks and Thomas's directions. They'd pack up and drive to a position on the march route about half-way to town for additional background footage before setting up again at City Hall.

Thomas continued: "We will end the march at City Hall. We have busses and cars to bring you back here if you need a ride," he said.

Thomas surveyed the crowd, which continued to grow, even as the front of the line was forming. He spotted Bennie Elsberry holding a placard that read, "*We Demand Equal Rights Now.*" The slogan, written in black, appeared on both sides of the white sign, which had a wooden stake stapled up the middle as a handle. Bennie stood determined and strong and immaculately attired in a dark grey suit and freshly starched white shirt, open at the top, revealing a white undershirt. His shoes, as always, were glistening soldiers in the war against the dusty roads ahead. Bennie's wife Annell stood by his side, herding their two excited daughters who didn't know they were about to make history. Annell, marching in a paisley print dress, had a silk scarf folded into a triangle and tied around her head with a bow under her chin. Each of the girls waved a small American flag. It seemed that every child under age 15 was carrying a flag, creating a splendid spectacle within the gathering Stockville flock.

Micah Geary stood among the marchers, skeptical but appearing supportive. Roslyn, Victor and even Martha were eager participants. Martha was too young to understand the significance of a voters' rights march, but knew something big was happening and her excitement revealed itself as she gripped her small American flag in one hand and the waistband of her mother's skirt with the other. A group of teenagers gathered near the gate leading to the lumber yard, their faces revealing an impatience fueled by puberty. Several elderly Negro citizens were making the march in wheelchairs, pushed by strong, younger men.

Thomas and Pastor Williams took the lead.

"Let's begin," shouted Thomas into the bullhorn.

Many of the Stockville Negroes didn't expect so many white men and women marching with them. They were mostly, but not all, college students turned summer Freedom Riders. The showing of solidarity buoyed the already energized but anxious locals, and their participation also fueled the national news coverage. Tiny Stockville might get the nation's attention. There were rumors that the *Times-Gazette* might actually cover the march after completely ignoring the civil rights movement up until now.

Gathering near a chain-link fence, a group of Carver High School teachers were marching together in a statement of solidarity. Some held signs that said *We March for Integrated Schools*, an interesting choice since integrating Stockville's schools might put some of them out of a job. The prospect of teaching white children certainly made them nervous. Others in the group held signs that read, *We Demand Voting Rights Now*.

Marching two and three across, the group began its trek up Route 27. Unseasonably low humidity made a normal morning temperature of 83 degrees feel comfortable. There was a slight breeze from the west.

About a mile into the march, Oleatha, standing at the front of the crowd, started singing a song that worked its way back.

This little light of mine/I'm gonna let it shine
This little light of mine/I'm gonna let it shine
This little light of mine/I'm gonna let it shine
Let it shine/Let it shine/Let it shine.

With the first part of the journey up a slight hill, Thomas couldn't resist walking backwards to marvel at the sight and sound of 500 civil rights marchers in harmony, many with their arms linked in colorful rows. He stood a bit straighter than usual and kissed Evie on the lips.

"This is beautiful," she said, smiling at him.

"You're beautiful," he said.

"This is the peaches and cream," added Oleatha, her red tuliped dress riding a small breeze from the north. She wore her "best Sunday walking shoes," black flats with open toes and a worn leather sole.

Most of the Stockville residents exuded a confidence not nurtured by segregation. Where Negroes lowering their heads was the Southern social norm, today heads were held higher. Thomas looked back at the marchers again, who spread back at least a quarter mile. He had worked tirelessly to create this moment. He put his arm around Harry, who was singing.

Everywhere I go/I'm gonna let it shine
Everywhere I go/I'm gonna let it shine
Everywhere I go/I'm gonna let it shine
Let it shine/Let it shine/Let it shine

An hour into the march, when they had walked about three miles, the first tier reached Paxton, the other one of Stockville's two Negro neighborhoods. Men and women along the route, even those who chose not to march, lent support in their own ways. Families lingered on front porches and steps, waving and encouraging the smiling passersby. One older, stout woman with an embroidered apron tied snugly around her waist poured water into paper cups while her grandsons carried the cups to the marchers.

Thomas estimated that 15 percent of Stockville's Negroes were participating in the march, a number which at first disappointed him. Now, seeing whole families smiling and assisting bolstered his spirit and his feeling that changes were coming. It made the march, for him, seem 10,000 strong.

As the marchers headed into downtown Stockville, still singing, still holding hands and waving flags, they encountered their first white residents. Reaching the white neighborhood meant the street was paved and pothole free. The whites who were scattered along the sidewalks appeared more curious than fearful, as if a band of gypsies had made its way to Stockville. The whites wanted to both see them and keep their distance at the same time. Four white high school teenage girls, standing on the sidewalk in front of the Givens & Banks law office, chattered away, occasionally pointing with a youthful fluidity that kept them nervously changing places every few seconds. Their freshly starched white blouses made them look like *American Bandstand* contestants.

Farther down Central Avenue, Thomas saw a white middle-aged man who was slightly built with deep set dark eyes. He wore a black suit, white dress shirt and thin black tie. His face was expressionless, his demeanor stiff and disconcerting. He held a Confederate flag about a foot long at the end of a wooden dowel, and waved it in a figure eight motion, up and down, back and forth, hypnotized by his rhythm. No doubt he meant to be an affront to the cause. The Confederate flag, even as it flew over the Alabama State

Capitol, sent a clear message of oppression and slavery to southern Negroes. Thomas turned to Evie.

"I guess the right to peaceful assembly flows in both directions," he said.

On the other side of the road Thomas saw a Buick that looked like it could be a float in the Thanksgiving Day Racist Parade. Fastened to the roof was a three-foot cross, flanked on one side by an American Flag and on the other by a larger Confederate flag. A loudspeaker bolted to the front hood spewed phrases at the marchers.

"Go back to Africa." "Don't start a fight you can't finish." "Segregated we stand, integrated we fall."

Oleatha clenched her teeth and both her hands curled into fists. She stood up straighter, looked the other way, and kept marching.

❧

John woke up like a 12-year-old boy—hungry. Lenore cooked him a 4-stack of pancakes and a half pound of bacon. John washed the whole thing down with a large glass of fresh-from-the-dairy milk. She would need a significant increase in salary if she were ever to raise one of these, Lenore thought, looking at him from across the kitchen table.

Lenore couldn't help noticing that John had a certain boy-smell about him. Not terrible, just kind of moldy, like a wool blanket that's been left in the rain. She had smelled this odor before, on Harry and Victor, she thought, but neither of them had slept at her house for a long time. She thought it was probably a first-thing in the morning smell. John didn't talk while he was shoveling the food down his gullet.

Conversation was going to have to be initiated by her.

"What do you want to do today?" Lenore asked.

"What time is it?"

"It's noon," she said.

"Do you like basketball?" he asked.

"Not really," she said. "We could go to the library. Do you like reading?"

"Not really," he said.

That answer was okay with Lenore since she hadn't considered which library she would take John to, the one for whites where she might not get in, or the one for Negroes, which would get the entire Grove population gossiping.

Lenore noticed a gold chain hanging around John's neck, visible because of the low cut of John's V-neck pajama top.

"What's that around your neck?" asked Lenore.

"That's what I got from my mom before she died," said John.

"I bet you got more than that," said Lenore. "I think you probably got her smile, her nose, or maybe her personality?"

"I never thought about that. I don't look like my dad, do I?" he asked.

"Not really. Do you have a picture of your mom?"

"Back at the house we have a whole book of pictures from before she got sick," said John.

"Would you show them to me sometime?"

"Yeah. Sure."

John normally changed the subject whenever anyone inquired about his mother, but with Lenore he didn't. With Lenore it felt comfortable. To John she was the first person who seemed genuinely interested rather than nosy.

"I tell you what. You can watch TV for a while and think

about what you'd like to do. I'm going to take a bath, get dressed and we'll figure out our day," Lenore proposed.

"Fine," John agreed.

John walked into the living room and pulled the knob to start the Zenith television, looking for a new cartoon or at least a rerun of Quick Draw McGraw. John sped back and forth through the four channels, whirling the dial with a hint of the male testosterone to come. His ferocity made Lenore cringe in the background, hoping John didn't break the knobs right off. She excused herself to her bedroom.

Twenty minutes later Lenore emerged, dressed and groomed for the day. The TV was still on, but John wasn't watching.

"John?" she called, but there was no response. She walked into the living room. He wasn't there. She looked outside. His bike was missing.

"John?" she called loudly into the front yard.

"John!" she called into the back yard.

Still no response. She went back inside and walked over to turn off the television. Taped to the front of the screen was a note.

"Lenore. I went downtown to meet up with Harry at the March."

Lenore ran back to her bedroom and slipped her feet into her black leather flats. She sprinted to the kitchen, grabbing her purse off the countertop, sending her car keys flying across the wood floor and under the couch on the other side of the room. On all fours, stretching the full length of her torso and arms, she reached her keys, the right side of her white cotton blouse and skirt now covered with the grey dust that had collected there. Breathing heavily, Lenore pushed open the front screen door with her shoulder and ran to her car, praying she would catch up to John before he got to the March.

❦

Sheriff's deputies yanked the small American flags out of the hands of Negro children as they walked by, as if the children were less American without the tiny stars and stripes. The children were told to ignore what happened and to keep walking. A few blocks from City Hall, the front of the group, more compact now on the wider, paved streets, turned onto State Street. As they rounded the corner, staring at them from a block away was a wide line of state troopers and Klan members in full white robes and pointed hoods. They stood shoulder to shoulder blocking the entire street, with white fire fighters, in uniform, poised on the far right side of the blockade and deputies with police dogs flanking the left. Mayor Lockhart and Sheriff Bascomb stood center stage.

The NBC crew scrambled to find a suitable spot. Two of them hoisted their camera, mounted on a tripod, up the side of a parked bus to the third member of their crew, who quickly set up and began filming.

Thomas turned to the marchers and signaled them to stop. They were 50 yards from the blockade when Thomas asked Pastor Williams to accompany him. Together they walked toward the mayor and sheriff.

"May I have a word, mayor?" the pastor asked.

The sheriff answered, "You've got two minutes to disperse."

The deputies stood perfectly still. A row of fully-armed and nervous neophytes, their pistols parked in unstrapped holsters, and their tear gas canisters in full view, stood at the ready. All of the Klan members had Billy clubs clenched between their hands, gripped in front of them, waist high. Under their riot helmets the sheriff's deputies wore gas masks. The official seal of the state of Alabama was patched to their uniform shoulders, next to the gold stars they had earned in the line of duty.

"We are simply walking to City Hall, then leaving," Thomas said.

"Minute and a half," said the sheriff.

"We have no weapons. Look around, Mr. Mayor. Don't you see the women and children?" said Thomas.

"I don't see your U.S. Attorney or his pals today," said the sheriff.

"We don't want any trouble," said Thomas.

"Then tell your niggers and your nigger lovers to start marching in the other direction," said the mayor.

"We have the right to peaceably assemble."

"Then today's the day we dis-assemble," said the sheriff, lifting his right arm over his head. Thomas looked back at the hoard of men, women and children, all unarmed and apprehensive.

"Give me a moment, Sheriff," said Thomas.

Thomas turned to Pastor Williams.

"Have we made our point?" asked Thomas.

"There are a lot of women and children here," said the pastor.

There hadn't been any SCLC training for this standoff, thought Thomas. He tried to think what Dr. King would do.

He looked back at his courageous marchers, locked in arm-in-arm solidarity, but helpless compared to the fortified militia the sheriff had assembled.

"You win, Sheriff. We're leaving," said Thomas.

Sheriff Bascomb looked right back at Thomas.

"You bet I win," he said.

The sheriff cocked his wrist back and then forward, motioning toward the protestors with a predetermined signal to attack. The mayor and sheriff took a step back and the Klansmen in the blockade started walking forward. The marchers stood dumbfounded, faced with the reality that significant harm might come to some of them. In a few steps the Klan broke rank in order to stride past Thomas and Pastor Williams.

"March back to fucking Africa," said one robed Klansman as he walked past Thomas and then quickly turned and whipped his Billy club into Thomas's midsection. Thomas crumbled like a marionette with its strings cut. Pastor Williams bent over by his side, afraid that he would be next, but the KKK marched past him and headed right for the center of the group.

Their leaders down, the marchers turned to walk or run away, but another line of Klansmen had formed behind them and cut off all roads and other possible escape routes.

Two white firemen, lugging the heavy metal nozzle of a fire hose connected to a yellow-topped fire hydrant, aimed it directly at Pastor Williams. One of them flipped a switch and water exploded out like pay-dirt crude from an oil rig. The blast knocked the pastor to the ground in a heap, at least six feet from Thomas. Next the firemen took aim at a group of three Carver High School students, who had fled for the safety of a building, a few strides too late. The pressurized spray hit the smaller of the two boys, drenching his black trousers and then directly hitting him in the chest of his blue polo shirt. The force of the water knocked him into the plate glass window of the Dominion Savings & Loan and the window shattered, sending glass shards flying all around and cutting the three students, one critically.

After several minutes of mayhem and confusion, the deputies moved in, walking tightly, shoulder to shoulder, filling the entire street. At first the marchers thought they were going to stop the Klan, but then, on orders, they lowered their gas masks. Five deputies tossed tear gas canisters at Negro groups that had huddled together. Drawing their clubs above their heads, the deputies, now surrounding many of the marchers, began pushing. With the area tightening around them, some of the protestors tripped or fell over each other onto the ground. Marchers started screaming in pain from the clubbing and the sting of tear gas burning their eyes. One Klansman hit a Negro Freedom Rider so violently that he collapsed to the ground, as if his internal electricity was cut off.

The firefighters discounted the vanquished and bleeding teens and moved to their next victims. They shifted the nozzle at a young white Freedom Rider, driving her head-first into a parking meter, splitting open a gash on her forehead. Aimed in another direction, the water pinned two children against a brick wall. They screamed, which set more people into a panic.

Lenore arrived at the south end of the town square just as the sheriff's deputies were joining the melee. The dust on her blouse had turned darker and caked from perspiration. Her hair, without the stretchy headband she normally wore on weekends, was napped and disheveled. She climbed up on a cement bench to scan the crowd looking for John. She had no idea where he might be, whether he and Harry had discussed a meeting place or John mistakenly thought he'd be able to find him. She called out his name even though she could hardly hear herself with tear-gas canisters exploding and unintelligible phrases being shouted out of bullhorns. Lenore searched for familiar faces. She spotted Bennie Elsberry, who had been separated from his family, instructing them to run away while he diverted two deputies with German Shepherds. She ran toward Bennie hoping he might have seen John. Focused and frightened, Lenore didn't realize she and Bennie were trapped against a building, the dogs barking and snarling and coming at them. One of the dogs bit Bennie in his leg and blood splattered over the dog. The deputy pulled furiously at the dog's leash, trying to regain control, but one of the dogs had Bennie's pant leg tethered between its locked jaws. When the deputy pulled the dog away, Lenore bent down and tied her scarf around Bennie's leg to stop the bleeding. One of the dogs snapped at her, tearing her skirt, but missing her leg. Lenore helped Bennie get out of the street to a spot of relative safety as the deputies moved toward another group.

Lenore hoisted herself onto a mailbox near the bus stop to look over the crowd again. Looking to her left, she saw a boy lying on the ground next to a bicycle, but her direct view was clouded by smoke and streams of tear gas. She jumped down from her perch and ran toward the boy. It was John, lying on the ground, unconscious. She checked his pulse and could see that he was still breathing. She bent down and cradled his head in the bend of her arm, unable to lift him and take him somewhere safer, out of the fray.

A Klansman threw a rock into the crowd that hit Victor Geary in the side of his head. He collapsed. Had Micah not scooped him up, Victor would have been trampled by three more frenzied Klansmen. Micah lifted Victor onto his chest and instructed Roslyn to pick up Martha and follow him.

"There's an alley over here," he yelled.

Micah and Roslyn ran together. Blood poured down Victor's face turning Micah's shirt a morbid dark red. Martha cried. Roslyn barely kept up with her husband, who was pumped with adrenalin, anger and fear. Nearly out of trouble and headed toward safety in the alley, Micah heard Lenore screaming. He looked to his right and saw his sister, cradling the limp body of John Gordon.

"Micah, help!" she yelled.

Micah stopped running long enough to stare at his sister. He looked again at his own family and then back at the white boy lying motionless on the pavement. His expression was stone cold. Lenore could see Micah was unmoved.

"Micah, he's a child," yelled Lenore.

Again, Micah stared down at them without moving. He had to get his family to safety and Victor to the hospital. Micah took another step toward the alley before he stopped, shifted Victor into his left arm, changed directions and ran back toward Lenore. While still cradling Victor and with Lenore's assistance, Micah picked up John with his powerful right arm and set John's head on his right shoulder.

"Let's go," he instructed Lenore.

The two of them ran back to where Roslyn was holding Martha and they all ran down the alley between the Old South Title Company and Confederate Realtors. Fifty feet in they found themselves face to face with a hooded Klansman, holding a club high in his right hand. With Victor cradled in his left arm and John in his right, Micah stopped and stared directly into the eye holes of the hood. Micah was easily a head taller than the diminutive, robed Klansman who stopped, too, and they looked at each other for what seemed like several seconds.

Micah's entire body steamed with sweat. Had he not had his arms full of children, he likely would have disarmed the Klansman and beat him to death right there in the alley. He glared at the man until he lowered the club, looked away and ran past them to find easier prey. Micah started running again and didn't stop until they were more than a block away. He laid Victor and John down on a grassy hill and inspected Victor's wound.

"This is going to need stitches," he said.

Lenore ripped off a piece of her skirt that had already been torn by the police dog, dunked it into a nearby fountain and put a cold compress on John's forehead. John reacted. He was woozy, but he moved his arms and legs slightly, and put his hand over his eyes to shield them from the sun. Martha cried into her mother's shoulder. Micah turned toward the street to flag down a passing car, his shirt stained with Victor's blood. The first car that passed was a red Chevrolet pickup driven by an elderly white man with his wife next to him. Micah didn't bother to wave at them. About 50 yards past, the truck stopped and backed up. The man lowered his window.

"Do you need help?" the driver asked.

"My son is injured. Would you take us to Mercy General?"

The driver hesitated. He looked at his wife. She nodded her head.

"Climb in," the driver said.

Roslyn got in the truck bed first and Micah carried Martha and placed her on her mother's lap. Lenore opened the back of the truck and helped John climb in. He was alert, but his eyes stung from direct contact with the tear gas. Micah took off his dress shirt and placed it against Victor's wound.

"Keep this pressed tightly against your forehead," Micah told Victor.

Micah lifted Victor and placed him in the truck. Then he closed the truck bed and looked past Victor to Roslyn.

"Please don't go back," she said, her eyes pleading.

"Has anyone seen Mama?" asked Micah, his chest pumping and his breathing fast and deep.

"No," said Lenore.

"The last time I saw her was when Thomas and the pastor went to the front to talk to the sheriff," said Roslyn.

Micah ran over to the driver's side window.

"Thank you," said Micah to the couple in the front seat. They drove off to the hospital.

Micah, his undershirt and pants stained with dirt and blood, scrambled back toward the alley. He grabbed a two-by-four that was stuck in a metal garbage can. He arrived back at the town square to see a police dog bite off a chunk of Delores Hasting's calf muscle. She cried for help, falling to the ground, trying to shield herself when the dog bit her again, breaking skin near her neck and ripping open her blouse before the deputy pulled the dog away.

Two adrenalized deputies heaved their tear gas canisters into a small group that had huddled together for safety. The gas blinded and immobilized several of the marchers, who lay down on the pavement in passive response. The deputies

BLACK HEARTS WHITE MINDS

beat them with Billy clubs, cracking open the skulls of two college students and shattering the kneecap of another. Only small children, who were crying and screaming and shielded by their parents, were spared beatings. A group of older women, including Oleatha, escaped the melee when the owner of Harris' Pharmacy opened his store from the inside and waved them in.

Out in the town square, some of the Negro men, still passively resisting, were grabbed and handcuffed and placed into police vehicles. Pastor Williams, who was pushed into the back of a wagon with seven others, looked out through the bars. He saw three deputies grab Thomas and Bennie, both of whom had been gassed and beaten. They handed them off to two Klansmen who pointed pistols at their heads, stuffed them into the back seat of a white car and drove off. A few minutes later, Micah, sneaking in from behind the wagon, smashed the sheriff's deputy over the head with his two by four, but he couldn't find the key to open the padlocked door.

"They got Thomas and Bennie," the pastor yelled through the bars.

"The sheriff?" asked Micah.

"The Klan. Two guys. They drove north in a white Plymouth."

Pastor Williams pushed past the others inside the police wagon up against the bars on the back windows.

Don't worry about us," said the pastor. "You need to find your brother. Here."

The pastor jammed his arm through the bars and slammed a set of keys into Micah's hand.

"My car is up Craig Street, at the corner near Renshaw," said the pastor. "Take the blanket in the trunk."

Micah squeezed the keys in his right hand and took off running, grinding the heel of his steel-toed boot into the solar plexus of the unconscious sheriff's deputy.

❦

Two white men had broken the glass door on the rear patio of Oleatha Geary's home ten minutes earlier. The last thing they did before leaving the Northwoods home was spray-paint a five-foot tall *KKK* across the front lawn. Ten minutes earlier, the two white men had broken the glass door on the rear patio to get inside. Then they made their way down to the basement and poured gasoline from their five-gallon plastic containers over the floor. Upstairs they left a bottle of gas, with gas-soaked rags stuffed into the mouth of each bottle, in each of the seven rooms on the first floor.

"We'll teach that bitch," said the shorter, squatter of the two.

"There ought to be laws against moving into a neighborhood where you're not wanted," said the other.

They timed their attack to coincide with the arrival of the civil rights marchers at city hall, insuring that the fire department was not available. One of the two men lit the rags of one of the Molotov cocktails and threw it down the basement stairs. Immediately they heard the whoosh of gasoline catching fire. They ran out the front door, did their KKK painting, and drove off to a safe distance to watch their handiwork.

Within a minute, clouds of lead colored smoke pushed out of the home's foundation windows. A minute later flames flickered inside the windows on the first floor. One window blew out from the force of the Molotov cocktail exploding in the living room. Within six minutes black smoke was pouring out of the roof and flames were darting out broken windows and licking at all four sides of the house. The roof collapsed, making a thunderous sound.

A neighbor across the street called the fire department, but the entire volunteer department was, at that moment, standing erect, shoulder to shoulder, about to unleash powerful jets of water at the civil rights marchers.

It was just about then that a small warm-front moved in from the southwest, pushing the blaze to the east. Ten-foot high flames from the second floor of the house, bent by the wind, lapped up against the east wall of the Fitzgeralds' house next door. That house, a white two-story Greek Revival with a low pitched triangular gable at the top and a heavy wooden cornice all around, burst in flames like dry kindling at a campfire. The fire, once inside, pushed out the front door and over the entry porch, then climbed back up the home's five squared wooden columns.

Earlier in the morning, the Fitzgerald family left home and was picnicking on the banks of Garrison Creek, celebrating 9-year-old Jason's birthday—except for Nancy, an awkward and pouting 13-year-old, who said she'd be totally bored and who stayed behind to do her homework. The fire department finally arrived at 3:00 to find both homes completely burned to the ground.

Carl rolled down all the car windows and turned the radio full blast, singing along to *Nadine* and *No Particular*

Place to Go by Chuck Berry. He loosened his tie and then took it off and tossed it into the back seat. He was a carefree man again. He made a pledge. No more Valium. From now on, Lenore was his new drug of choice. He was falling deeply for her, no matter what the obstacles, like her brothers, society, and the laws of the state of Alabama.

Carl reached the Stockville outskirts at 3:15 p.m. He parked the Mustang and began walking the two blocks south to City Hall. He thought for sure the loud speakers would carry this far, but it was eerily quiet. The closer he got, the stranger things looked. Everything seemed jolted, out of place. There were wooden police barricades overturned. The streets were wet, but it hadn't rained. The air smelled like formaldehyde. The Brooklyn morgue in August came to mind. Carl noticed two smashed store windows and a mailbox tipped on its side and smoldering. He realized he wasn't looking at the aftermath of a rally. He was looking at a battlefield after a war. Carl bent down and dipped his finger into a small pool of what he thought was brackish water and turned out to be blood. He quickly wiped it off with his handkerchief.

Carl sprinted back to his car and drove to Lenore's house. Along the way he heard ambulance sirens but stopped for no one. He knocked on the door. Lenore didn't answer. John's bike was missing. He knocked again. This time harder. Carl looked through one of the small, square windows that framed Lenore's front entryway. Finally, he saw Lenore coming toward him. Thank goodness, he thought. Lenore pulled the door open.

"John's fine, he's sleeping in my room," she said. "But why aren't you in New York?"

"I missed my flight. What happened today?"
"Oh my god, Carl. It was awful."

CHAPTER 28

The editorial staff of the *Times-Gazette* agreed to meet back at the newspaper's office at 3 p.m. Sunday afternoon. The four reporters gathered around the conference room table swapping observations of the protest march and riot, while the three photographers, including one who was talked out of retirement just for the day, were developing their photographs in the darkroom. Owens entered the conference room, instantly commanding the attention of his small but pumped-up troop.

"Somewhere, this paper lost..." Owens stopped, looked around, swallowed hard and started again.

"Somewhere, I lost my way. As an editor-in-chief, I've embarrassed myself, I've embarrassed all of you, and I've embarrassed the Fourth Estate as a source of accurate information in our democracy. I've ignored the single biggest story to hit the South since Reconstruction."

Owens paused and the reporters shifted uncomfortably in their seats, hopeful looks on their faces.

"That's over today," said Owens. "We are going to report the news of the day as it happened. I'm moving our deadline back to 1 a.m. We're going to be here all night, ladies and gents. Get used to it."

Owens looked first at Sally Breakstone, 37, a veteran reporter of Stockville Garden Club flower shows and highway dedications. She flipped open her reporter's notebook with renewed enthusiasm and a smile and a half.

"What do you got?" asked Owens.

"I've got the sheriff's department. They didn't do anything. The marchers followed an order to disperse. That's when all the cops stepped back, crossed their arms and let the Klan beat the crap out of the marchers. I tried to interview Deputy Sheriff Akers, but he said only Sheriff Bascomb was authorized to speak."

Sally turned the pages of her cardboard covered, spiral notebook as she spoke.

"I've got some quotes from two Klansmen, but they refused to identify themselves. One said, 'Niggers have been asking for this for a long time. It's their own fault. They brought this day of reckoning on themselves.'"

"Try to get someone on record with that. We need a name even if we don't have a face."

"Call the Klan?"

"Yeah. Call Jimmy Cooper. Then get Bascomb on the phone. Find out what he says and take it with a grain of salt. Then head over to Mercy and interview some of the victims. Take a photog with you."

Sally closed her notebook and grabbed the handles of her oversized black leather purse, practically diving out of the conference room and heading for the phone sitting on her desk at the far end of the newsroom.

"Wendell, how about you?" said Owens to Wendell

Jackson, a 40-year-old, self-made reporter, whose tenure at the *Times-Gazette* predated Owens' arrival in Stockville. Wendell, all five-foot-three of him, with a pointed nose and a swirling bald spot on the back of his head, started at the paper when he was 16 as a copy boy. Wendell mostly covered college and high school sports. He flipped through the pages of his notebook.

"I heard a rumor that Thomas Geary, the SCLC executive director, is missing. I spoke with Pastor Bertram Williams at the jail. He told me he saw sheriff's deputies hand him over to two white civilians, Klan. He said they knocked him out and dragged him into a white car," said Wendell.

"Follow up with the White Citizens' Council. Ask them if they're taking credit for a kidnapping. Go visit their headquarters if they'll talk to you, and see if you can find a phone number for Geary's family. Get an interview," said Owens.

Jackson grabbed his pad and pen and dashed for the door.

"Wendell. One more thing. When you speak to the Council, ask them to explain this," said Owens, stuffing one of Jimmy Cooper's fliers into his hand.

Wendell looked quizzically at the creased piece of paper. He read the first few sentences.

"What's a Solemn Summons of the Fiery Cross?" he asked.

"That's what I want to know. I found that crumpled up in the gutter," said Owens. "Okay? Go."

Owens turned his attention to Seth Abrams, a current Journalism student at Wake Forest, interning at the *Times-Gazette* for the summer.

"Abrams?"

"Yes sir," said the intern, who looked so young, Owens was sure he wasn't even shaving yet. Owens stared right at the brown button eyes that topped the intern's smooth cheeks.

"You heard Sally say that Pastor Williams was arrested. Go find him and any other prominent Negroes who are locked up. Take notice of how many people they've got in the cell. The jail doesn't hold more than 10. Where's everyone else?"

"Yes sir," said Abrams.

"Knock off the sir stuff," said Owens.

"Yes sir. Yes chief," said the intern.

"Get going."

Larry Clawson, the paper's most senior photographer, walked into the conference room holding an 8x10.

"I think we've got our page one," said Clawson, handing the photo to Owens.

Owens examined the black and white glossy. It was shot from behind two uniformed firemen, but the focus of the shot showed a blast of water from their hose driving a young black teenager completely off his feet and through a storefront plate-glass window. Owens handed the photo to his last reporter, Allen Oliver, a brittle veteran of three bigger city papers and another small-town daily, working his way down the journalistic ladder to retirement on the installment plan.

"Find this kid, if he's alive. If not, find his family. We want to know everything," said Owens.

"Oh yeah, the four w's," said Oliver, sarcastically. "Who, what—"

"I don't have time for this, Allen," Owens interrupted. "Find the firemen in the photo. Why were they there? Who gave the orders? Do this right, Allen. It's our lead story, big headline, big photo, all above the crease," said Owens.

"Right on it, *chief*," said Oliver, imitating the intern.

Making his way slowly out the door, Oliver turned back to Owens.

"Didn't we print those fliers?"

"So?"

"So you said you found it," said Oliver.

"That one I handed Jackson? I crumpled it up, threw it in the gutter and then found it."

Oliver glanced at Owens with a look that screamed *bullshit*.

"You got a problem, Allen?" asked Owens.

"It's about fucking time we took a stand on something important," said Oliver.

When all the reporters had gone on their assignments, Owens returned to his office and sat down, hands poised over his typewriter ready to write a page one editorial. He considered his station in life, his family's journalistic history and his country club membership. He contemplated his one-acre lot in Northwoods, his spot on the board of curators at the Stockville Art Museum and all the advertising revenue his paper would lose by tomorrow afternoon. He pulled out the lowest drawer on the right side of his desk and stared at the three-quarter's empty bottle of Jim Beam and the shot glass sitting next to it. He poured himself a full one and swallowed it whole.

Fuck it, he thought, and began typing.

❦

Thomas felt his eyes burning the moment he came to, and an attempt at a deep breath yielded a mouth full of dust and piercing pain in his ribs. He tried to move his legs but they were wrenched between two immovable objects he couldn't identify. He reached his left arm down to his knee and felt hard rubber with ruts and creases. He wondered how long he had been in the trunk of a car. In the dark, he couldn't tell if the liquid dripping from his forehead was sweat or blood. Leaning back caused extreme pain again in his ribs. Broken by the blow from the Billy club, he thought. He couldn't remember how many times he had been hit. A blow to his forehead by a deputy on horseback was the last he could remember. It felt like a fireplace poker was lodged against the back of his skull. Whatever car he was in, it wasn't moving now and he could hear muffled voices outside.

The voices drew closer, having heard Thomas shifting inside the trunk. Thomas heard a key being inserted into the trunk's lock. A latch scraped and the trunk sprung open. The sunlight, high in the afternoon sky, and the residual effects of the tear gas, blinded him.

"Hey nigger boy finally woke up," said one of the men.

Thomas shielded his eyes as best he could with his hands, but every move involving his right side brought a rush of pain from his ribs, like an ice pick prying one rib away from the others.

"We're going to have some fun with you, agitator," said the other man.

As Thomas's eyes adjusted he could see them, he realized,

only out of his left eye because his right one was swollen shut. He knew one of the men by name, Nathan Perkins, a former sheriff's deputy who was on every Stockville Negro's list of white men to avoid. He was big Klan. Thomas didn't recognize the other man.

The two men pulled Thomas out of the car and propped him up. Thomas's legs hadn't returned to working after he lay unconscious in the trunk.

"Hey, Danny. This college coon and his uppity nigger friends are going to change the southern way of life. What do you think of that?" said Perkins.

Thomas realized who the other man was. Danny Rutledge, 38-year-old family man, grain elevator operator and one of the two men who raped Lenore 20 years earlier. Thomas struggled to stay conscious.

"I think his jigaboo friends are going to have to continue their crusade without him," said Rutledge.

While Perkins continued propping Thomas up, Rutledge slapped Thomas across his face. The blow landed so hard that he spun around and fell to the ground. Grass stains scarred the left side of his swollen, misshapen face.

Despite the fall, Thomas stayed alert.

"I wish you no harm," he said.

"How do'ya like those fancy words," said Rutledge. "Must be all that teaching at the nigger college."

Rutledge bent down and pulled Thomas back up by the back of his shirt. He pulled a two-foot long length of rope from his pocket and tied Thomas's hands behind his back.

"Okay, Martin Luther Coon's nigger. You got a date with destiny," said Perkins.

"Beg us not to kill you," said Rutledge.

"I'm ready when my time comes," said Thomas. He wasn't going to play their game. He knew it wouldn't change anything and would just delight them.

"Smart ass," said Rutledge.

"Kill me and five will take my place," said Thomas.

That comment met with a Rutledge-delivered, brass-knuckled punch to Thomas's already damaged ribcage.

"Let's go," said Perkins.

Rutledge pushed Thomas in the back and he stumbled, nearly falling again. He smelled pine. They must be in the woods. Thomas tilted his head and squinted, trying to see out of his only working eye. His body jerked and his mind locked when he realized they were at Garrison Creek, heading down Prior Lane. Rutledge pushed Thomas again, down the wooded path that Thomas knew dead-ended at the Maker Oak tree.

"I think what's nice about living in a small town like Stockville, is you never know who you're going to run into," said Perkins.

Thomas' hands were shaking. They rounded a corner, approaching the clearing.

"Well look who's here," said Perkins.

"If it ain't good ole Bennie Elsberry," said Rutledge.

Thomas looked in all directions. He couldn't see him, just a 10-foot wooden ladder lying sideways on the ground.

"Not there. Look up, nigger," said the delighted Perkins.

Thomas had to move his entire body to tilt his head up. He did. There was Bennie, hanging at the noosed-end of a rope tied to the massive branch of the Maker Oak, his head slumped on his shoulder at an unnatural angle, the product of a brutally broken neck. Perkins and Rutledge had stuck

Bennie's pork-pie hat backwards on his head.

"Still stylish," said Perkins, admiring his work.

"Won't be parading around in that fancy new car no more," said Rutledge.

Thomas looked again at Bennie. His eyes were distended and crusted with dirt. His tongue rolled up in his throat. His bare feet pointed straight down, six feet off the ground. Bennie's clothes were in tatters, a sure sign they had dragged him before hanging him.

Rutledge pushed Thomas again. That's when Thomas saw that hanging next to Bennie was another rope.

❧

Micah sprinted to the pastor's car. He unlocked the driver's door, jammed the key in the ignition and peeled out, heading north.

Micah reminded himself of what the pastor had said. A white Plymouth. Micah assumed that Thomas and Bennie were going to be taken to one of two places, the headquarters of the White Citizens' Counsel or Garrison Creek. Either way it wasn't good, and Micah already was 30 minutes behind. He also had little idea what he'd do if he did find them. He thought about rounding up Quincy or Donald or Uriah, but decided against it. No time, he thought.

Micah decided on the cabin, figuring the two Klansmen would be looking for reinforcements or accolades from like-minded compatriots. He turned onto Highway H, flooring the gas pedal for much of the four-mile ride. There was little chance he'd be pulled over for speeding because all the sheriff's deputies were downtown cracking Negro skulls.

As Micah arrived at the long dirt road that ran from the highway to the cabin, he concluded that they hadn't been there. It had rained overnight and there were no fresh tire marks in the dirt. No sign of anyone in or out. To be completely certain, Micah would have to drive down the one-mile dirt road to the lake. He didn't think he had that time to waste, and if any Klansmen arrived while Micah was searching, it would be difficult for him to get away unnoticed. He turned the car around, tires screeching, and headed for Garrison Creek.

Micah started planning. If they had clubs or knives, he figured he could take them both. He didn't think there were two men in Stockville who could outmaneuver him or out muscle him. Especially not white ones. If they had guns, he'd figure out something else.

Ten minutes later Micah arrived at the Garrison Creek parking area, the closest place anyone could park for a hike to the Maker Oak tree. As he rounded the clearing he saw the white car, its trunk open, but nobody around. He pulled into a secluded, wooded area and parked the pastor's car where it wouldn't be noticed.

Now what? Micah thought. He checked the glove compartment. Three maps of Alabama and one of Florida. A pen-sized tire pressure gauge that wouldn't be much of a weapon. A Pontiac Bonneville Owner's Manual.

"Shit," said Micah out loud, throwing the maps to the floor.

Micah hoped there was a least a tire iron with the spare tire in the trunk. He took the keys out of the ignition and plied the trunk key into the lock. The trunk jumped up. No spare tire. No tools. Just a big brown blanket. Micah remembered the pastor said to take it, but that didn't make much sense now. Out of frustration and desperation, Micah grabbed for it anyway. Underneath, pressed against the back of the trunk, was the pastor's Winchester 70, a bolt action rifle with a five-round magazine. Tucked neatly behind the Winchester, Micah found a 20-round box of .30-caliber bullets. Micah grabbed both, slammed the trunk shut and ran up into the woods toward the bluff above the creek. He stopped once to get his bearings and load the rifle with five of the 150-grain soft point bullets. Then he continued running, drenched in sweat and adrenaline, the movement of the water in the creek covering the sound of breaking branches as Micah dipped and deked through the woods.

Micah arrived at a clearing where he stood on an overhanging granite boulder 100 yards from the Maker Oak. Looking down he could see three figures, two standing, one on the ground. Then he refocused quietly to his left a few feet and he saw Bennie's limp body hanging from the tree branch. Micah swallowed deeply to keep his composure and avoid vomiting.

Micah couldn't make out Thomas's features on the ground, but he knew his light blue shirt and brown pants, even caked with dirt and blood. Standing still, Micah could feel his heart thumping like a stereo speaker with the subwoofer pumped up too high. He lay down on his stomach for stability, placed the rifle butt into his sturdy shoulder, wiped the sweat off his face with his palm and gazed steely-eyed into the rifle's scope, offering six-times magnification.

Two white men were hovering over his blindfolded brother. One of them bent down and grabbed Thomas by his shirt front and pulled him up to his feet. The back of

Thomas's shirt was soaked in blood, an indicator that he already had been whipped by the two Klansmen. Thomas couldn't keep his balance. Through the scope, Micah could see that Thomas's face had been battered too. One of the two Klansmen reached over to the noose that was hanging empty next to Bennie's body, the rest of the long white rope thrown over the huge Maker Oak branch and tied loosely on a tree limb several yards away. The smaller of the two white men grabbed the noose and loosened it enough to easily fit over a man's head. Micah steadied himself, took a deep breath and held it.

The bigger man turned sideways and slipped the rope over Thomas's head and onto his neck. Then he re-tightened the noose and, while he held Thomas up on his feet, the smaller man walked toward the tree-limb at the rope's other end. He would pull on that end, pulling Thomas up off the ground, at which time the noose would strangle him under the weight of his own body. As the smaller man arrived at the tree-limb, Micah had a shot. This was no time to aim at anything but the center of his torso. Micah smoothly, methodically, squeezed back the trigger. The rifle fired and kicked back hard against Micah's shoulder. The smaller man gaped, dropped the rope and lived long enough to see his blood pour out of a baseball-sized hole in his chest, the bullet having gone right through him from front to back, shattering his entire rib cage in the process.

The bigger man, realizing where the shot had come from dashed behind Thomas, but without the rope taut at the other end, Thomas collapsed to the ground and in that moment Micah looked through the scope directly as the bigger man's face came into focus.

Rutledge.

With no hesitation Micah stroked the trigger again and put a bullet through Rutledge's nose, splattering his cranium all over the ground as the bullet left the back of his brain. Rutledge was dead before he hit the ground. Micah jumped, slung the rifle over his shoulder and sprinted down the serpentine path to where Thomas, still blindfolded, was laying on the ground, badly beaten, but alive.

"Who is it?" Thomas mumbled.

"It's Micah."

"Thank God," said Thomas.

Then he passed out.

Micah opened the noose and slipped it off his brother's neck, then lifted Thomas in his arms and carried his limp body the half-mile back to the pastor's car. He laid Thomas in a fetal position across the backseat, and carefully closed the car door. Thomas was breathing, but barely. Micah unstrapped the rifle from his back, keeping it at arms-length in the front passenger seat in case the sheriff's department or the Klan had set up road blocks. He wouldn't hesitate to shoot first and answer questions later.

In 15 minutes Micah pulled the car up to the Mercy Hospital Emergency Room entrance. He could hear the noise and see the chaos of more than 100 marchers waiting their turn to be bandaged, mended and stitched by the one doctor and three nurses. Micah opened the car's back door again and cradled Thomas in his arms. Thomas's external injuries were obvious and frightening. Blood still leaked from a gash under his hairline, administered by a foot-long piece of lead pipe wrapped in masking tape. His right ankle hung limp at an abnormal angle to his leg. Thomas's shirt was caked with a combination of sweat, dirt and blood, and his back was serrated with several bleeding horizontal stripes, a result of the bull whipping Micah was too late to prevent. It would take an x-ray machine to determine Thomas's internal injuries, including three broken ribs and a shattered eye socket, but Mercy's Negro patients were allowed access to the white hospital's x-ray machine only on Wednesday mornings.

At the sight of Micah carrying Thomas into the emergency room, the other patients, with bumps, bruises and sprains, quieted their children and drew back, creating a direct path for Micah and Thomas to the doctor. As Micah walked quickly but carefully through the ER, women cried and men cursed under their breath. One patient started clapping, then another, a few more, and in a few seconds everyone was standing and applauding Thomas. Micah laid Thomas down on a gurney and all three nurses stopped attending others and moved over to help the doctor try to keep Thomas alive.

CHAPTER 29

Jimmy Cooper screamed into the telephone.

"What the hell does he think he's doing?"

"This ain't good," said Sheriff Bascomb on the other end.

"Isn't it enough we have to deal with 30 minutes of Cronkite with his nose in our business? But the *Times-Gazette*? I'm pulling my ad right now," said Jimmy.

"What's going on, what's the racket?" asked Patty, as she came downstairs in her terrycloth robe and slippers.

"This!"

Jimmy slammed the *Times-Gazette* on the kitchen table.

She looked at the pictures and the stories.

"Oh my Lord," she said.

Under the masthead, four columns wide and three deep was the picture of the Negro teen being propelled through the Stockville Bank and Trust's front window, with a caption:

"On orders from County Sheriff Peter Bascomb, firemen Hugh Trask and Vincent Berazzo turn their hose on unarmed Negro teenager Alton Surrey, 14, sending him crashing through the window of the Stockville Bank and

Trust yesterday. Surrey is in critical condition at Mercy Hospital with severe cuts all over his body."

The story which accompanied the picture was equally graphic.

Stockville Riot Sends Over 100 to Mercy Hospital as Sheriffs Watch

By Sally Breakstone and Allen Oliver

More than 400 Negro non-violent Civil Rights marchers and their supporters were attacked yesterday by white civilians as the Frost County Sheriff's Department watched and did nothing to stop it. When finally the law did get involved, sheriff's deputies and local firemen joined in beating defenseless men, women and children who did not resist or fight back.

"The outside agitators were asking for it by refusing my order to go home," said Sheriff Peter Bascomb, at the Sheriff's Department after the riot finally broke up at about 2 p.m.

Other eye-witnesses described a completely different series of events.

"We walked for five miles with not a single incident," said Millie Renfro, who has lived in the Grove neighborhood in Stockville her entire life.

"Out of nowhere, men with nightsticks started attacking everyone."

The story continued for several inches to the bottom of

page one and continued on page three.

On the other side of the page-one picture was another startling story:

Negro Hanged, Two Klansmen Shot Dead in Aftermath of Stockville Riot

By Wendell Jackson

Following the lynching of Stockville's Benjamin Elsberry at Garrison Creek yesterday, two Ku Klux Klan members, Nathan Perkins and Danny Rutledge, were shot dead in circumstances that remain unexplained. All three bodies were found early last evening under the Maker Oak tree.

It is believed that Thomas Geary, local chapter director of the Southern Christian Leadership Congress was also targeted for lynching, but survived and is in critical condition at Mercy Hospital. According to police, they have no suspects, but an investigation has begun. A source close to the situation said that the United States Attorney's Office has intervened and will conduct the investigation itself.

On the left-hand side of page one, below the fold was another gruesome story:

Teen Dies in Northwoods Home Fire Investigators Suspect Arson

Stockville Junior High School student Nancy

Fitzgerald, 13, was killed yesterday when a fire that started in the Northwoods house next door, spread to her family's home. Investigators suspect arson. Both homes were burned to the ground when the Stockville fire department was hosing down protesting Negro peace marchers downtown and was unable to arrive on the scene fast enough to put out the fires.

The fire started at 55 Watkins Road, the home formerly owned by recently deceased millionaire Theodore Tatum. The home has been the subject of a recent court battle to keep Negro Oleatha Geary from moving into the home she inherited from Tatum. Mrs. Geary's right to own and live in the home was upheld by the federal court of appeals in Montgomery last week after the Northwoods Neighborhood Association filed suit to keep her out.

The Fitzgerald family has not yet announced the funeral arrangements.

At the bottom of page one was Owens's editorial.

Our Apology: Civil Rights Changes are Inevitable and Overdue

By Editor Paul Owens

It has come to my attention that for the past 10 years this newspaper has neglected to cover the civil rights movement. We regret the omission.

Starting today, the *Times-Gazette* will strive to be your eyes, ears and, I hope, your conscience on matters of integration and the constitutional guarantees of life, liberty and justice for all American citizens. The time to redefine "the southern way of life" is now. In fact, the redefinition is long overdue.

As the Reverend Martin Luther King, Jr. said last year, "I look to a day when people will not be judged by the color of their skin, but by the content of their character."

The *Times-Gazette* embraces that philosophy and will strive to do better.

❦

Lenore and Micah huddled around the table in the hospital's visitor lounge, reading the front page stories and the *Times-Gazette* editorial.

"I don't know who's in more danger, me or Paul Owens," said Micah.

"What are you going to do?"

"I'm not sure."

"Do you want to speak with Carl?"

"Don't tell me you've got him waiting in the hallway."

"How can you joke at a time like this?" said Lenore.

"It's joke or run."

"You should probably leave the hospital. After your home, they're sure to come looking for you here."

"Are there still two federal marshals outside Thomas's room? Your friend arranged round-the-clock protection for him."

"I think you need it too."

"Okay. Call him and I'll call you at home later," said Micah. "And Lenore?"

"Yes, Micah."

"I don't want to wind up dead. Please hurry." Micah bolted down the hospital hall, out the front door, and sped off in his truck.

❧

The *Times-Gazette* continued to publish stories critical of the White Citizens' Council and Ku Klux Klan in the days following the riot, referring to the members as "mobs of cold-blooded, out-of-touch hoodlums" and "hell-bent racists."

The local sheriff's department and federal marshals, brought in from Washington, patrolled the streets, intent on keeping the peace as tensions mounted at the funerals of Danny Rutledge, Nathan Perkins, and Bennie Elsberry.

At the First Thankful Baptist Church of Stockville, 200 folding chairs were set up in the shape of a fan outside the church and powerful round loudspeakers were bolted to the electric poles to broadcast Bennie's funeral, anticipating a considerable turnout of the Stockville Negro community. To the shock of the undertaker, Bennie's widow, Annell, demanded an open casket so that all could see what the Klan had done to her husband. Two hours prior to the service, photographers from *The New York Times* and *Associated Press* arrived at the church, at Pastor Williams' furtive invitation, to photograph Bennie's pummeled and misshapen face. The pastor opened Bennie's blue suit jacket, loosened his tie and unbuttoned his gleaming white shirt so they could take photographs of his mutilated torso and broken ribs jutting through his skin. The pastor loosened Bennie's belt and trousers so the whole world could see his castration. The pastor prayed that Bennie was already dead when the Klan did that to him. When the photographers were finished, Pastor Williams redressed Bennie exactly as the mortician had, went into the rectory and threw up.

For the service, the casket was draped in white gardenias and sat below the pastor's lectern. At 9:30 a.m., mourners began arriving and a line formed for the viewing. Parents were warned that the viewing was not suitable for children, but some parents opted to have their children see for themselves. It took 45 minutes for the crowd to be seated. Annell and her two girls sat in the front pew, surrounded by friends and relatives, including Lenore and Oleatha, Roslyn, Denise, Cara, Martha, Victor and Harry, representing the Geary family. The Grove community knew from experience the healing power of children at a funeral. At 10:15 a.m. Pastor Williams, wearing a black flowing robe with a red, green and black embroidered shawl around his neck, walked up the three stairs to the pulpit and approached the lectern and microphone.

"This morning we are gathered here in this church and out over the landscape to pay tribute to Benjamin Aaron Elsberry, who died at the hands of brutality and vindictiveness. Bennie was killed in a way that has become synonymous with hatred and the claim of white supremacy. Lynching a Negro man has become an evil ritual of the white oppressors to not just take his life, but to intimidate us all."

Pastor Williams paused and glanced at the two fatherless children in the front row. He slammed his fist on the podium and his voice changed from reflective to enraged.

"We shall not be intimidated. Bennie's murderers were struck down and have met their maker. We do not gloat, and in fact we mourn with those families, but let all our white brothers know that we will not sit idly by and allow our citizens to be slaughtered anymore."

"Amen," shouted several mourners sitting inside and outside the church.

"An eye for an eye is one of the most deliberated sections of the Hebrew Bible. Some say it is a statement of the vengeful nature of man. Today I say it is a parable with a legitimate warning that people can be oppressed for only so long. We, the Negroes of the South, have reached our farthest bounds of oppression."

Pastor Williams wiped sweat from his forehead and continued.

"Am I angry? I am beyond angry. As much as I want to forgive, and know I will forgive tomorrow, today I am consumed with rage and hate. As much as I blame the murderers who battered, dragged and lynched Bennie Elsberry, I blame the white sheriff who looked the other way. I blame the white governor who turned his back on his Negro citizens again. And I blame the President and all those senators in Washington, D.C., to whom we appealed for protection and who left us to be victimized again."

Experienced in eulogies, the pastor knew that after expressing his personal views of reprisal and reprimand, he could not ignore hope and healing.

"A word to the family."

Pastor Williams looked intently at Annell and the two girls.

"Your cherished Bennie is in the hands of God. It is not

the end for your beautiful husband. It is not over for your beloved father. He is on his next journey. Death is not the end of a passageway. Death is a door to a more exalted existence. Death does not play favorites. It is universal that rich and poor, educated and uneducated, pious and vicious, all die. I can tell you with complete assurance that Bennie did not die in vain. His death is going to be remembered as a catalyst for the time when everything changed. When democracy replaced hypocrisy. When courage replaced caution. When 'soon' no longer meant 'never.'

"Starting tomorrow we will look back and know that Bennie is still with us as we proceed and succeed in our quest for justice. In spite of this darkest of days, we must believe that even the worst of the white racists will see the light and understand the sanctity of life and the pursuit of freedom. We will march again. And each time we march, Bennie will be marching with us. Amen."

Six pallbearers, Bennie's two older brothers, two cousins and two friends, approached the casket and Pastor Williams closed the lid. They lifted the casket and carried it out the church's center aisle, through the double front doors, down the steps, between two sections of mourners unable to fit inside the church, to the waiting hearse. The Elsberry family followed. Lenore and Oleatha decided they would forgo the burial, opting instead to return to the hospital and visit Thomas.

Thomas' forehead was still bandaged and the bridge of his nose was a discolored reddish brown, where the nurse had applied Mercurochrome to several small lacerations. He had black rings around both of his eyes, the right one still purple-red and swollen shut. His neck was lathered with a white salve, used to treat burn victims, but also soothing to the raw splotches of skin created by the rope burn of the noose around his neck.

Lenore and Oleatha were greeted at the door by two armed federal agents and inside by Evie and Dr. Harold Pollard, who was checking on his patient.

"He's a fast healer," said Dr. Pollard.

"Doesn't feel that way to me," said Thomas, who was propped up to an almost sitting position by the strategic placement of three pillows behind him. His lower lip was stitched and still swollen but he was able to speak clearly and use his left arm to lift a cup of water close enough to his mouth for him to sip through a straw. His right arm, a plaster cast from his armpit to his wrist and immobilized across his chest, protected his broken ribs.

"When can I go home?" asked Thomas.

"See, he's feeling better," noted Lenore.

"A few more days," said Dr. Pollard.

Arriving at the hospital room door, nodding to the Marshals outside, Carl entered, holding a bouquet of roses.

"What is it with you always arriving with flowers?" said Lenore.

"It was either flowers or cake," said Carl, making eye contact with Lenore, then nodding to Evie and handing the flowers to Oleatha. "Hi, Mrs. Geary. Your lawyer is back."

When Oleatha took the bouquet in her left hand, Carl took her right hand in his and covered them both with his left hand.

Oleatha was enthralled again. No white man had ever looked at her eye to eye, called her Mrs. Geary, or even approached charming in demeanor. She got all three at once from Carl. She smiled and winked at Lenore.

"How's the patient today?" Carl inquired of Thomas.

"Impatient. I want to go home."

Thomas stuck out his good arm and the two men shook left-handed.

"I've been thinking," said Carl.

"Uh-oh," said Lenore.

Carl shot her an amused smile that he hoped wouldn't be correctly interpreted as lovesickness.

"I've been thinking that in light of everything, we should withdraw from the basketball tournament," Carl continued.

Thomas didn't miss a beat.

"Absolutely not," he said.

"It seems insignificant, silly," said Carl.

"I think it's ten times more significant now."

"What about safety?"

"Are those guys standing outside basketball fans?" asked Thomas.

"I guess so."

"I tell you what. Let's do whatever the parents want."

"Hey, we're finally getting the vote," said Lenore.

Thomas and Carl both shook their heads and smiled.

"Well it's a start," said Lenore.

❦

Carl followed the directions Lenore had written to campground number eight. The mid-August sun and drought had left the southern-exposed hillsides singed and parched. What had been lush green grass at Benton State Park in April was now dry, mushroom brown and straw-like, crunching under Carl's feet. He parked the Mustang in the shade of a tall pine tree, got out of his car and waited.

He thought about Rudyard Kipling's poem that "only mad dogs and Englishmen go out in the noonday sun." *I must be mad*, Carl thought, *to have agreed to this meeting.* With further introspection Carl might have come to the conclusion that most of his decision-making was being affected by Lenore. In his quiet moments he imagined life with her, a fantasy seen through his usual rose-colored lenses. What he couldn't imagine was life without her. He wondered how he could have fallen so deeply so fast. He had always thought the term *soul-mates* was pathetic, for high school infatuations, but now it seemed to fit him and Lenore.

Carl's daydreaming was interrupted by the growl of a pickup truck bounding its way through the bumps and valleys of the half-mile, circular dirt road of the campground. Even to Carl's untrained and ignorant automotive mind, the engine sounded perfectly tuned. It had to be him, Carl thought.

In a few moments, Micah's Ford appeared, rounding the curve that separated campgrounds seven and eight. Carl didn't wave. Micah, without acknowledging Carl's existence, shut down the Ford and exited the truck. The two men stood looking at each other without speaking.

Finally, Micah ventured a word.

"Well?"

"Well, what?" said Carl, a hint of disgust in his tone.

"Lenore said you wanted to speak with me."

"Go fuck yourself," said Micah.

Carl forced a laugh. He had been taught since childhood not to walk away from a conversation, no matter how heated or obnoxious, but he was thinking this might be the first time.

"I drove 15 miles out here to nowhere state park as a favor to Lenore so her hothead brother, who just killed two Ku Klux Klan imperial pooh-bahs, could tell me to go fuck myself?" Carl said. "On top of that, I could get fired just for being here with you."

Carl wasn't even sure if he was still an Assistant U.S. Attorney. He had defied the Justice Department when he entered his appearance for Oleatha in Montgomery, but there was a decent chance nobody in New York would ever find that out, and he wasn't one to broadcast his indiscretions.

"Why should I trust you?" asked Micah.

"Fine. Go back to Stockville and tell your story to the KKK crew of racist lunatics who want you dead yesterday. Better yet, tell it to Sheriff Bascomb or the county judge. You'll be strung up by this time tomorrow."

Micah flinched noticeably at a white man's mention of a lynching. It was the first time he had ever let his guard down in front of Carl. Micah's chest expanded with his need to get fresh air into his lungs. For the first time Carl saw real fear in Micah's eyes. The man needed help and it wasn't like Carl to make it so difficult. He took a breath.

"Sorry," said Carl, defensively.

"We are who we are," said Micah.

"Let's try it this way. I'll tell you what happened," suggested Carl. "The first thing we know is that at all times prior to arriving at the creek you were operating under the belief that the kidnappers were going to kill your friend Bennie and your brother Thomas. So far, correct?"

"Correct."

"You saw the white Plymouth the pastor told you the Klansmen were driving. When you found the car, you were just a quarter mile from the Maker Oak tree, where many Negroes have been lynched by the Klan. That's the reason you took the pastor's hunting rifle with you. Correct?"

"Sure."

"When you arrived on the bluff above the river, one of the first things you saw was that the two men had already killed Bennie, correct?"

"Correct."

"You probably couldn't make out for sure any faces from your perch on the bluff, but you believed it was Bennie hanging because you knew the clothes Thomas was wearing, and he was still alive with the two Klansmen around him."

"Well..."

"Wait. Let me finish," said Carl. "The two Klansmen were preparing to hang Thomas."

"I saw them put a noose around his neck."

"Right. And pull it tight. Then one of them moved in the direction of where the rope was loosely tied to a tree limb."

"Correct."

"To save your brother's life, you shot the first kidnapper as soon as you had an open shot."

"Yes."

"The law states that if you kill someone to prevent that person from killing someone else, that's justifiable homicide. That's not a crime. If, however, you kill a person when he is no longer a threat to do further harm, that's not justifiable.

That's called using excessive force, and that's a felony," said Carl.

The two men continued staring at each other. Micah clasped his hands in front of his waist, like he might if he were praying. Carl continued his story.

"In spite of the fact that the first Klansman was dead, the second one appeared to be trying to finish the job. So as soon as he made a move toward the end of the rope, you fired again and killed him to save your brother's life."

Micah stood stone-faced, his angular muscles expanding and contracting in time to his increased anxiety.

"One more thing. I don't believe you knew who either of these men were, even looking through the rifle's scope."

Micah's eyes narrowed and his teeth clenched together in response to the inaccuracy.

"An overzealous prosecutor might misconstrue that fact to claim that you used excessive force to kill the second Klansmen, because you had some past, unfortunate experience with him."

Micah listened with no palpable change in his demeanor.

"Once you shot him in the face, he was completely unrecognizable, even when you ran down to rescue Thomas. You paid little attention to the two killers, anyway, because you needed every bit of your energy and concentration to save your brother, who was covered in blood, barely conscious and near death."

"Actually..."

"I'm not finished. Listen carefully. The first time you realized the identities of the killers was when you telephoned your sister the next morning. You had both read the names in the *Times-Gazette*. You talked about the second man being

Danny Rutledge, one of the men who raped Lenore. It didn't make you gleeful or happy that you killed him, like you figured it would. Basically, you felt nothing. You stopped him from killing your brother and that made you happy. You're not in the revenge business. You're a Christian."

"Why are you doing this?" asked Micah.

"Aside from everything else your sister told me, she also told me how you picked John up off the ground with one arm and carried him out of danger last Sunday. I think I forgot to thank you for that."

"I made her swear she wouldn't tell you," said Micah.

"She told me that, too. That sister of yours is not a good listener."

"So is that it?" asked Micah.

"No, there's more. This meeting never happened and you and I have never talked about this in any detail."

"No?"

"We had a phone call and the only thing I told you was to get in your truck and drive to Atlanta where you should turn yourself in to the U.S. Attorney's office. Ask to see Assistant U.S. Attorney Leonard Lieberman. He will know that I sent you. That's it. Any questions?"

"I don't think so," said Micah.

Carl turned, walked to his car and got in. He started the engine and edged it up to where Micah was standing.

"Your tail light is broken," said Micah.

"Yeah, but my car's running great," said Carl.

"Actually, I think you should bring it in for a tune up."

Carl smiled.

"I didn't expect we'd agree on that either," he said, pressing down on the gas pedal, heading back to town.

Micah sat down on the campground picnic table weighing his alternatives. Return to his family in Stockville. Flee the state. Follow the advice of a white man he despised, although a little bit less than before.

CHAPTER 30

The Greyhound players walked single file up the stairs of the Stockville Recreation Center, resolute and right between the three federal marshals who purposely positioned themselves to block the *No Coloreds, No Dogs* sign on the wall. Each player had a black ribbon safety-pinned to the sleeve of his Greyhound uniform t-shirt, a gesture suggested by Thomas in remembrance of Bennie Elsberry. By a vote of the players, Victor, his temple stitched and still patched with a small white piece of gauze taped to his forehead, led the team into the gym. The parents had decided unanimously to let their boys play. The Jacks had already arrived and were going through layup drills, their coach, Jimmy Cooper staring wildly at his clipboard and looking up periodically to bark at one of his players.

"Got to want it more than that," he yelled at Hack or Jack. Cooper never could tell them apart.

The Greyhounds burst through the gym doorway at the Jacks' end of the court. As Victor approached the end-line under the Jacks' basket, he took a hard left and jogged out to the sideline, dribbling the team basketball down to the other end of the court, his teammates close behind. Harry was second, followed by Wes, Kenny, Phil, Doug, Craig, Alvin, Larry and John. The boys had coordinated their uniforms so they all had their spray-painted greyhound jerseys tucked into blue shorts.

Next into the gym was Thomas. The doctor had ordered him to stay home and rest, and use a wheelchair to get around the house. Thomas refused. He walked into the gym, a cane in his left hand assisting his uncertain gait. He limped noticeably, favoring his right leg. His right arm was still in a sling, shielding his four broken ribs that were being supported by layers of adhesive tape under his blue shirt. His right eye socket was still purple but the swelling had receded enough that he could see out of it again. The unbandaged gash on his cheek that took 20 stitches to close remained noticeable and a dark red crust had collected around it. Where the Greyhound players took a left turn at the end of the court, Thomas turned right, a route that led him past the Jacks' bench. He stood taller than was comfortable, passing silently in front of Jimmy Cooper, who refused to look up, pretending not to notice him. The Jacks' parents were shocked at Thomas' appearance. Two women covered their eyes with handkerchiefs.

The tournament referees, huddled in the far corner of the gym, stopped talking and watched Thomas's painful entrance. He arrived at the Greyhounds' bench, carefully pivoted on his cane and began the slow, excruciating process of sitting down. The other Greyhound parents had followed slowly behind him before moving up to the bleachers.

There was no denying that the Jacks were a polished,

experienced team. They warmed up with eight players and eight basketballs. When they practiced shooting before the game started, Coach Cooper positioned himself under their basket to rebound and pass the balls back to the players. At the other end of the court, the Greyhound 10 shared three basketballs, taking turns.

The referee blew his whistle, calling the coaches to center court. Cooper jogged out. Carl helped Thomas to his feet. They walked slowly together the 20 feet to the meeting.

"You've been here before, you know the rules," said the referee. "Any questions?"

"You going to let those boys play with safety-pins on their shirts?" asked Cooper.

"Problem?" asked the ref.

"Dangerous. They could open and cut one of my players," said Cooper.

"It's a memorial," explained Carl.

"Remove them," said the ref. "Let's have a good game."

The coaches started back to their benches when Cooper turned back, facing Thomas.

"Had a rough week?" asked Cooper.

"Buried your friends yet?" asked Thomas.

Carl helped Thomas back to the Greyhound bench.

When the players lined up at center court for the beginning jump-ball, John could see that the Jacks had Mickey off the center circle, lined up at the foul line of the Greyhounds' basket.

They know our jump play, he thought. John looked behind his right shoulder at Harry and gave him the sign that he was going to tap the ball back to him. Harry nodded his approval.

The referee tossed the ball in the air and John reached

it first, easily, and tapped it right to Harry, who raced up the court, little Jimmy Cooper trying desperately to stay with him.

"Four," yelled Harry, signaling his teammates to take their positions for play number four.

John ran from the top of the key to the baseline under the basket. Victor and Doug set a double screen on the left side of the key, and Harry dribbled from the center of the court to the right wing. As Harry dribbled, John went in the opposite direction, taking his man, Mickey, around Victor and Doug, and then cutting back through the key facing Harry, who threw him a perfect pass. Mickey got tangled up with Victor and Doug, and neither Jack nor Ben, who were covering them, switched to pick up John. Two dribbles by John and a layup. Greyhounds 2-0.

Jimmy, Jr. passed the ball in for the Jacks, who were wearing their red satin uniforms with white trim and numbers. Hack dribbled past midcourt and passed back to Jimmy on the left wing.

"Bama," shouted Coach Cooper, and his players ran their first play of the day, a high screen that resulted in a pass to Rudy, who shot a nice left-handed layup. 2-2.

The teams traded baskets and looked to be evenly matched. Neither team led by more than three points the entire first half, which ended Greyhounds 22, Jacks 21.

"We've got to play tougher on Rudy, number 12," said Harry to his teammates, who were gathered around the Greyhound bench, sucking on orange slices provided by Doug's mother. Harry wiped his face and hands with a towel and passed it to John, who did the same.

At the other bench, Coach Cooper was unhappy with

his squad. He had believed his Jacks would roll right over the Greyhounds. His boys were more experienced, more talented, smarter and had a better coach, he thought.

"Can't anyone here guard number 11," he yelled, referring to Harry.

"He's really fast," said Mickey.

"Outsmart the little nigger. Move in, then back. Keep the ball out of his hands," said Cooper. "Rudy, you have to cover the white kid. He's their best player."

Rudy nodded his approval, and when Coach Cooper turned around, Rudy and Hack looked at each other as if to say, *yes coach, that's why we brought him to practice.* John and Harry had combined for 16 of the Greyhounds' 22 points. Rudy led the Jacks in scoring with 10.

The referee blew his whistle to start the second half. Again, John easily won the tip, flipping the ball to Harry behind him. The Greyhounds started the second half cold. Harry missed an outside shot and threw a pass that sailed over Phil's head out of bounds. John missed an easy layup, and thought he was fouled, but there was no call from the referee, who, nevertheless, appeared to be calling the game fairly. Rudy and Jimmy Jr. each made two baskets and five minutes into the third quarter the Jacks led 33-28.

Victor scored four points in a row, each time muscling his way next to the basket, rebounding a Greyhound miss and putting it back up for an easy two points. 33-32 Jacks.

With Jimmy Jr. bringing the ball up with 15 seconds left in the third quarter, Coach Cooper called out "Kentucky." Jimmy looked up to make his next pass, but Harry's fast hands swiped the ball out of Jimmy's. Harry took five dribbles in the other direction and laid the ball up softly on the backboard and into the hoop as the buzzer sounded, ending the third quarter with the Greyhounds leading 36-35. Coach Cooper slammed his clipboard on the bench and it ricocheted into the first row of bleachers. One of the Jacks' parents retrieved the clipboard from under her seat and handed it back to Cooper as his team came off the floor.

"Are you kidding?" he screamed at his son.

Jimmy Jr. was on the verge of tears, but held them back. Crying had always just made the verbal lashing worse.

"Dammit. C'mon. You're not going to let this rag-tag nigger team beat you?" yelled Cooper.

The Jacks' players stood silently. Coach Cooper had lost his temper many times, but this tirade was bigger and different. Coach Cooper's eyes darted from one player to the next. He waved his arms over his head and smacked his fist into his open hand.

Both teams had their best five on the court for the fourth quarter. Victor set a rock-solid screen for Doug, who scored on a backdoor play when Harry made another perfect pass. Mickey made a nice shot from the left corner and Jimmy Jr. made a terrific bounce pass to Rudy, who made the shot and was fouled by Doug. Rudy made the free throw and with 30 seconds left in the game, the Jacks were up 44-42. The Greyhounds had the ball and they had it where they wanted it. In Harry's hands. Harry dribbled left, then crossed over to his right and drove to the basket. Hack moved over to help Jimmy Jr. as Harry raced right by him, something Harry could do anytime he wanted. When Harry jumped, so did Hack, and when he tried to block Harry's shot, Hack smashed right into Harry, sending him flying out of bounds.

The shot bounded off the rim and there was no foul called. Rudy got the rebound and started racing down the court in the other direction. Harry leapt back up and ran after Rudy. He caught up to him at the Jacks' foul line, where Rudy made a nice move on the much shorter Harry, took a short jump shot that went in and now the referee blew his whistle, calling a foul on Harry, who hadn't touched Rudy at all. Harry couldn't believe it, but said nothing, for fear of a technical foul that the referee most certainly would call against a protesting Negro player.

Rudy calmly stepped to the foul line and made the foul shot, putting the Jacks up 47-42. The Greyhounds tried moving the ball up the court quickly, but they ran out of time and the game ended 47-42. Jimmy Cooper raised his fist over his head in victory. The Greyhound players walked slowly off the court. Harry was especially disappointed, feeling like he was the one to blame for the defeat.

"Nonsense," said Thomas to his son. "You all played a great game."

"That team's been playing together for three years," said Carl. "You guys have had four practices."

The Greyhounds lined up to shake hands, but Jimmy Cooper was shuttling his players out the gym door.

"Great game boys," he told his players. "Get some rest, some water and get ready to play again."

The final game of the District Boy's 12-and-Under was scheduled to start in 20 minutes. The Jacks versus the Bulls. The Greyhound players said they wanted to come back and watch the game. As the team and parents walked past the Jacks' players sitting on the stairs outside the rec center, Harry yelled, "Let's go Jacks."

Some of the Greyhound parents were visibly upset by Harry's remark, coming on the heels of such a tough loss. But of course, Harry was right.

❧

Thomas and Carl sat in the front row of bleachers on the opposite side of the court from the team benches.

"Pretty strange, I mean, sitting here about to root for the Jacks," said Thomas.

"I know what you mean," said Carl.

Other Greyhound parents and the 10 players filled in the seats behind them. Doug's dad Vernon leaned in from behind them.

"Where are we?" he asked.

"This is how Harry explained it to me. The Sparrows lost to the Bulls, the Greyhounds and the Jacks. They're out. We beat the Bulls 43-40 and lost to the Jacks 47-42," said Thomas.

"That's two wins and one loss for us," said Carl.

"Right. Going into this last game, the Jacks have two wins and no losses and the Bulls have one win and one loss," said Thomas.

"So we're rooting for the Jacks?" said Vernon.

"Yep. It's strange, but if the Jacks win, their record is 3-0, we're 2-1 and the Bulls are 1-2," said Carl.

"The Jacks get first place and we get second. Both teams move on to the state tournament," said Thomas.

"What if the Bulls win?" asked Vernon.

"If the Bulls win, the Bulls, the Jacks and the Greyhounds all have two wins and one loss," said Thomas.

"Which two move on?" asked Vernon.

"There's a tie-breaker. It's the point differential among the three teams in games against each other," said Carl.

"John and Harry have it figured out. We'll ask them at halftime," said Thomas.

The game began. The Jacks won the opening tip and moved the ball up the court where Rudy made an easy lay-up to put the Jacks ahead 2-0.

"Go Rudy," yelled John from the upper bleachers, where he sat between Harry and Victor.

"Yeah, go Jacks," yelled Harry, again collecting some awkward looks from both the uninformed white and Negro parents.

In the first half the Bulls showed that despite the loss to the Greyhounds, they were a good team. Not too big, but well organized. They ran lots of pick and rolls. They played tough defense, causing the Jacks to make mistakes. Hack Watson double-dribbled twice and Jimmy Jr. bounced the ball off his foot and out of bounds. Coach Jimmy Sr. shook his head and stared him down.

"You're not helping us out there," he yelled.

Jimmy Jr. swiped his brow with his sleeve so it would look like he was wiping away sweat and not tears.

"Get back on defense, damn-it," Cooper yelled again.

Cooper was always hardest on his own son, but none of the Jacks players escaped his vocal criticism and demeaning stares, except maybe Rudy, who got kid glove, star treatment.

Mickey Riley made a nice pass to Hack, who hit a shot from the left side. Hack gave a little flick of his fingers, signaling his pleasure at the ball going in the basket and Coach Cooper immediately took him out of the game for grandstanding.

"Sit there and shut up," he barked at Hack.

The Bulls' best player, a kid named Charlie Bruer, dribbled well with either hand. It took the Jacks some time to figure out that Charlie was left-handed, something their coach missed when he scouted the Greyhounds game with the Bulls earlier in the tournament. Bruer dribbled right around Mike Johnson for an easy layup to put the Bulls ahead 23-22 at halftime.

"Somebody out there stop number 14," Cooper yelled at his kids as they gathered at their bench for the three-minute rest.

"Come on, Rudy, don't go nigger lazy on me," demanded Cooper. "You guys are playing like crap. Jimmy and Jack, I want you to get the ball to Rudy under the basket. He's five inches taller than any Bulls player. Let's take advantage. Okay?"

"Yes sir," said Jack.

"Yep," said Jimmy.

Cooper pushed his way into the middle of his players, got down on one knee and started diagramming a play on his chalkboard.

"Jack. You bring the ball down and pass it to Mike on the wing. Take one or two steps toward the foul line and then zip down the lane."

Cooper drew the play frantically.

"Mike, you pass it back if he's open, if not, you go set a pick for Rudy on the other side. Rudy, you take your man off the pick and cut across the middle."

Coach Cooper glared at Mike.

"Get Rudy the damn ball," he said.

Starting the second half, the Bulls and Jacks traded early

baskets. The Bulls continued their great defense and their smoothest player, a boy named Chester Nally, hit two foul shots. Charlie Bruer was hot too, making four baskets in the third quarter. The score see-sawed back and forth, with neither team leading in the second half by more than five points. Andrew Boynton made a short shot from the left side near the baseline to put the Bulls up 38-36 with two minutes left in the game.

Jacks ball, down two. Cooper called time out. He gathered the players around him and seemed genuinely calm. No yelling at his players. No frantic diagramming of plays.

"Here's what we're going to do," he said.

He calmly mapped out a stall offense on his chalkboard. The players listened. Rudy looked confused. The Jacks broke their time-out huddle and ran back out onto the court, where the referee blew his whistle and handed Jimmy the ball. He passed it to Hack, who dribbled past midcourt and then passed it to Mike far out on the wing. He passed it back to Hack.

"No shots," yelled Cooper from the sidelines, crossing his arms confidently over the red Jacks' logo on his polo shirt.

While the Jacks tossed the ball around the perimeter, the Bulls, ahead by two points, were content to let the Jacks waste time.

"Hands up boys," counseled Stump, the Bulls coach. "Be ready."

The Jacks continued passing the ball around the outside, until it got to Rudy on the left wing. He faked a long shot and then dribbled toward the basket and launched a high-arcing shot that hit the front rim, then the backboard and then rolled around the rim again, before falling off to the left.

Rudy charged in between three Bulls' players, and got his own rebound.

"Time out," yelled Cooper from the sidelines and the referee blew his whistle again, stopping play just before Rudy was about to shoot an easy layup. The Bulls players ran back to their bench and the Jacks hustled toward Coach Cooper.

"Are you deaf?" Cooper screamed at Rudy. "I said no shots."

"Coach, we can win this game. We're only down two. There's a minute to go," said Rudy.

"Shut up, boy. Do as you're told. No shots means *no* shots. You got that? No shots."

Cooper stood face to face with his young star, who was completely baffled. The same confusion spread around the gym, including the Jacks' parents, the Greyhound parents and the referee, who also didn't understand what was happening.

The Jacks players sat silently waiting for the timeout to end. John and Harry came running up to their fathers.

"Do you see what they're doing?" said John.

"They're losing on purpose," said Harry.

"What?" asked Thomas.

Harry, tearing, took a deep breath to maintain his composure.

"See, if the Bulls win, it's a three-way tie," said Harry.

"We know," said Vernon.

Harry continued, "We beat the Bulls by three and lost to the Jacks by five. That means our point differential is minus 2."

Harry's voice cracked, and he held back tears.

"So if the Bulls win, but only by two points, then the

Jacks, who beat us by five, have a point differential of plus 3 and the Bulls, who lost to us by three, but will beat the Jacks by two, will have a point differential of minus 1."

Harry, now crying, was using his uniform top as a handkerchief. John, who was much more angry than sad, continued the explanation because Harry couldn't.

"By losing on purpose by two points, the Jacks not only win the district tournament and move on to the state tournament, they keep us out," John said.

The referee blew his whistle for the last minute of play to begin. All the Greyhound players and parents clustered together, feeling powerless and numb. The Jacks broke their huddle and jogged back out on the court. Carl, as the only Greyhound parent who would dare, yelled, "You're really gonna make those boys lose on purpose?"

Coach Cooper looked up and stared at the Greyhound group. First he smiled and when he was sure he had everyone's attention, he saluted like a midshipman, his middle finger leading the way.

Mike passed the ball into Jimmy Jr., who stood between mid-court and the foul line. He dribbled the ball as the clock ran down. 45 seconds left. He passed the ball to Hack, who just stood there holding it. 30 seconds. The Bulls, as instructed by their coach, packed the lane in a two-three zone defense and let the Jacks pass and dribble as much as they wanted as long as they were far from the basket.

Hack dribbled three times and passed it back to Jimmy Jr., who made no effort to advance the ball.

"Good job," yelled Coach Cooper.

10 seconds left. Then five. Then the final buzzer. The Bulls ran off the court triumphant. They won the game. They

were going to Birmingham.

Coach Cooper had the Jacks celebrating as well. They were the tournament champions. The tournament director handed Coach Cooper the 12-and-Under District Champion trophy, which he pumped up and down over his head. Harry laid his head onto his father's polo shirt and continued crying. Thomas grimaced from the pain, shifting Harry to the other side of his chest, away from his broken ribs. John looked like he did when he was told they were moving to Stockville. The other Greyhounds wiped away tears too. Carl explained to the players and parents that they wouldn't be going to the state tournament.

"I told you some things never change," Vernon said.

"It was stupid to think we had a fair shot," said Nora, Doug's mom.

"There is a consolation tournament next weekend in Montgomery that all the losing teams can play in," said Thomas.

"Lots of teams, single elimination, and only the winner gets an invitation to the state tournament that begins the week after," said Carl. "It's a longshot, but it's still a shot."

"I don't think we should bother," said Nora.

"I vote no," said Evie. Thomas looked at his wife, surprised.

"Whitey will figure out some way to screw us there, too," said Vernon, looking right at Carl.

The only way out of the gym for the Greyhounds was to cross the basketball court, where the Jacks and their parents were still celebrating. The Bulls, already out the door, were heading home. The Greyhound group was silent and moved deliberately as if in a funeral procession. They avoided eye contact, just as the South had demanded of them. Their heads were bowed. It was impossible not to feel the Jacks' celebration going on at midcourt.

"Hey," yelled Jimmy Cooper, stopping everyone in the gym. "Sorry it didn't work out for you. Y'all ought to try the losers' tournament," he said.

Nobody spoke. Ignore him and move on, Carl thought. Then Cooper spoke again.

"John Gordon. The rules say any team can add one player to their roster after the Districts. Son, let's let bygones be bygones. What do you say? How about joining the Jacks for that state tournament?"

All eyes, brown and blue, stared at John. Under other circumstances Carl would have answered for him, telling Cooper that he could shove his offer where the sun don't shine. He decided John would ask for help if he needed it and let the question linger. Carl looked down at John. John looked up at his dad. Everybody in the gym was staring at John, who two months ago had never heard of Stockville, Alabama.

John looked at Harry. He remained steely-eyed and still. Harry looked away. Visions of his fight with Victor dashed though John's mind, right along with thoughts of winning a state championship. Out of the corner of his eye, John spotted Rudy whispering to his father. There was a nod of approval and an upturn at the corners of Rudy's father's lips. While everyone waited for John to speak, John watched Rudy step forward.

"Before you answer that, I'd like you to answer a question for me," said Rudy.

All attention turned to him.

"Would the Greyhounds consider taking me?" he asked.

Attention shifted again to Coach Cooper. His jaw clenched

and his eyes went wide, then narrowed. His face turned red.

"Team meeting," yelled Harry, and all the Greyhounds gathered around him like a rugby scrum, their arms entwined around each other in a circle. None of the adults could hear what they were saying. Jimmy Cooper took a step toward Rudy's father, who held up his hand and said only one word.

"Stop."

Everyone remained silent. With the Greyhound team in a closed ring around the center of the court, all the white parents were on one side and the black parents on the other. There was some eye contact and uncomfortable stares back and forth. A few moments later the circle opened with Harry in the center, all the other boys in a line now, still with their arms linked around each other. Harry stared at Rudy and Rudy stared back.

"Welcome to the Greyhounds!" Harry shouted as the rest of the team started jumping up and down. Rudy tore off his Jacks uniform top and flung it in the air. He raced over to his new teammates who quickly remade their circle, this time around him.

All the Greyhounds, and even the Greyhound parents, were jumping around and dancing as if some invisible orchestra were playing an up-tempo Count Basie arrangement. The Jacks players and parents stood silent. Cooper kicked over a folding chair. Rudy's parents joined the Greyhound celebration as they spilled out of the gym and onto the street. Only then did they stop to catch their breath and reflect on what just happened. Rudy's parents were introduced to people they could have known their entire lives, shaking hands down a row, like meeting the other side of the family at a wedding. They might have stood there all day, just because they could. Just because it felt so good. When the introductions were done, adrenaline retreating to normal, their high spirits were interrupted again by Harry, beaming and gently hugging his father around his waist. Harry raised both arms in the air as if to quiet the crowd.

"Greyhounds. Practice tomorrow at 5 p.m. We've got a tournament to finish."

THE END

EPILOGUE

"When I'm standing at the Pearly Gates, I pray that Saint Peter will consider my entire body of work."

Those were the words my father used to explain to me how he killed Beth, his first wife and first love. He also told me the only other person who knew about the mercy killing was my mother, Lenore. He told her in the fall of 1964, in Stockville, Alabama, when he flew from New York to Stockville to ask her to marry him. First, he asked permission from Grandma Oleatha. My parents were secretly married on the afternoon of November 24, 1964, Pastor Martin Luther King, Jr. presiding over the ceremony as a personal favor to my Uncle, Thomas Geary. The wedding was attended only by my grandmother, my Uncle Thomas, his wife Evie and my half-brother John. My parents got married again by a New York judge a few weeks later, since interracial marriage was illegal in Alabama. The Supreme Court struck down all state laws prohibiting interracial marriage in 1967, but Alabama didn't repeal its law until 2000.

On December 22, 1964, four days after George Washington Carver High School began its Christmas break, my parents and John hitched a U-Haul trailer to their 1965

Mustang, loaded it with all things precious, and drove to New York City to start a life together. 16 months after they arrived in New York, I was born. My name is Martin Malcolm Gordon.

Through the years, as I labored through the obstacles of growing up with a white father and a black mother or questioned the limitations my parents placed on me, the response I got was always the same.

"You want to know obstacles? We could have stayed in Stockville," said my mother, who rarely spoke about the town, as if she had stuffed Alabama in the closet and brought it out only when necessary to frighten me.

My first visit to Stockville was for my grandmother's funeral in 1978. I was 12, the age John and my cousins Harry and Victor were when they met in 1964. We flew from Kennedy Airport to Birmingham by way of Atlanta. John met us there, flying in from Portland, Oregon, where he worked for a new athletic shoe company named Nike. That week I met several family members on my mother's side for the first time. All stories told that weekend led to the summer of '64.

I knew the part about how my parents met, but as it turned out, I knew only the versions of history provided by my parents, whose rose-colored recollection was influenced by their falling in love. I knew my Uncle Micah disapproved of my parents' marriage and refused to attend the Stockville ceremony. Time must change people, because Uncle Micah was a most gracious host to my mother and father and me, and he delivered a beautiful and emotional eulogy about grandma Oleatha.

Grandma never moved into Northwoods. She collected the insurance and sold the land. With the money, and the help of attorney Barry Beckley, she set up trust funds for every one of her six grandchildren to attend college and still have some money left over. She also contributed $10,000 to the Nancy Fitzgerald scholarship fund at Samford University in Birmingham.

After the funeral, we all gathered at Grandma's house and I sat on the maroon velour couch next to the fireplace, eyes as big as silver dollars, as Uncle Thomas told the story of how Uncle Micah saved his life and killed two men in the process. Uncle Thomas cried at the part when the Klansmen pulled the noose tightly around his neck and he felt the sharp stick of the rope's twisted strands. He said he remembered hearing a loud noise, but the next thing he recalled was being carried out of the woods in Micah's arms.

Uncle Micah told how after the shooting he lived under federal protection in Washington, D.C., for 60 days, until he was exonerated for killing those two Klansmen in defense of his brother. My mother said a special prayer for a man named Bennie Elsberry, who died that day, lynched earlier by the same Klansmen who were going to kill Uncle Thomas.

Uncle Micah told us there had been a proposal to cut down the Maker Oak tree, but Bennie's widow Annell and other Stockville African Americans worked with a new, more progressive and integrated city council to build a memorial instead. Now, surrounding the tree is a black granite semi-circle, inscribed with the names of every Negro citizen who was killed there, including the date of the hanging. *Bernard Elsberry, August 16, 1964*, is the final name. The entire Geary family went to visit the site during our visit and every adult, even Uncle Micah, stood silently and wiped away tears with Kleenex my mother fetched from her purse. Victor and Harry took me up the hill to show me the place where Uncle Micah pulled the trigger that saved Uncle Thomas.

I found out that weekend that seven other Klansmen were arrested and later tried and convicted on charges ranging from murder and rape, to assault and income tax evasion. I learned that Uncle Micah converted to Islam in 1968 and tried Buddhism in the 70s. He swore off all religion by 1981.

My Uncle Thomas was the Alabama NAACP Man of the Year in 1973 for his work in state education reform and school busing. After college, my cousins Harry and Victor used the rest of their inheritance to open a sporting goods store in Stockville in 1974. Today they are the co-owners of Geary's, the largest minority-owned chain of sporting goods stores in the South, every one of the 22 stores located inside a black community.

That night my aunts cooked up a feast of all grandma's favorite Sunday foods and we sat around grandma's table like, I was told, in the old days. My mother and uncles talked until 2 a.m., reminiscing about grandma and grandpa, Carver High School, the Grove and of course their children, of which I'm the youngest.

The best night, though, was when John, Harry, and Victor invited me to tag along with them to Hugo's Bar & Grill in downtown Stockville, where they met Phil, Doug, and Rudy. They drank pitchers of Budweiser while I drank something called sarsaparilla. John's favorite stories had always been about the 1964 Stockville Greyhounds, and tonight they all talked and laughed, and I listened, for three hours straight.

With Rudy on the team, the Greyhounds steamrolled right through the losers' bracket tournament, winning every game by double figures, and gaining the final spot in the PBC State Tournament. With federal marshals watching over them, they won the state tournament too, beating a team from Selma in the finals. As I listened to the five of them reliving the games, it was apparent that their only regret was that they didn't get to play the Jacks again. The *Rudy-less* Jacks were beaten in the first round by the Mobile Mustangs.

Doug pulled out his scrap book to show everyone the *Times-Gazette* front-page article about their victory. The Headline read:

Stockville Greyhounds Take State PBC Crown; First Integrated Basketball Team to Play

Below the banner headline was a huge picture of Harry jumping into John's arms as the final buzzer sounded. The final score was Greyhounds 53, Selma Stingrays 46.

"What ever happened to coach Jimmy Cooper?" I asked.

They were all stunned that the little mixed-race kid at the table knew the story and all the characters.

"He's still around," said Harry. "He was never prosecuted and he still owns the Juniper Tree. I don't think the store is doing so well because they've got some serious competition from..."

Harry looked at Victor.

"Geary's!" said Victor, and they high-fived each other.

"And you want to know one of the most amazing things, Martin?" asked Harry.

"Sure," I said.

"One of the most amazing things is that the Juniper Tree can't seem to get any of the hottest new athletic shoes," said Harry, who winked at John.

🌰

Reading Group Topics for Discussion

1. How do you relate topics covered in this book to what is happening in terms of race and class in today's society?

2. Who is the hero of *Black Hearts White Minds?* Why did you choose that character?

3. Is Carl Gordon courageous or a fool? Did you agree with his decision to take John and move to Stockville, Alabama?

4. Did you admire or dislike Micah Geary? Is he arrogant or astute?

5. If you were living in Stockville, Alabama in 1964, which character do you think you would have been most like? Which character do you wish you were most like?

6. Do you think you could have sat at the Woolworth's lunch counter and absorbed the insults, punches and racial slurs and not struck back? Why does passive resistance work in our society?

7. *Black Hearts White Minds* is all about the cause of Civil Rights in the United States. Would you have been part of the Civil Rights movement in 1964? Is there any cause today that you would risk your life for?

8. Martin Luther King, Jr. was a leader of the non-violent Civil Rights movement in the 1960s. Malcom X led a group promoting violence and aggression to take the freedoms guaranteed to all Americans. Who do you agree with? Would Martin Luther King, Jr.'s non-violent movement have been successful without Malcolm X?

9. Mitch Margo is a lawyer from New York who is practices law in St. Louis, Missouri. To what extent is his book based on his personal experience?

10. Do you feel a novel needs to be based upon fact and research in order to be interesting and valid? Do you think this book is more powerful because it's fiction, rather than a non-fiction memoire?

Invite Mitch to Speak

Mitch Margo, a seasoned lawyer, accomplished speaker, and author, is available to speak for your organization. Following is a brief list of suggestions. Mr. Margo is also available to join others on Discussion Panels at Writers Conferences, Educational Seminars, etc.

For Community Organizations:
- Overcoming Polarity
- Moral Courage in Community
- Act Local, Think Global

For Sports Organizations:
- What Makes a Good Team?
- How Team Sports Transforms a Young Person's Life
- For Writers' Conferences & Author Panels:
- Adapting Current Events in Fictional Narrative
- Fact or Fiction? The Author's Process
- Can Fiction Go Deeper than Non-Fiction?

Contact: AuthorMitchMargo@gmail.com
Facebook: Mitch Margo
Website: MitchMargo.com

About the Author

A former reporter for *The Detroit News* and *Los Angeles Herald Examiner* and a syndicated columnist for 14 years, Mitch Margo is a native New Yorker and St. Louis trial lawyer. He's witnessed the clash of cultures which are woven into his first novel, *Black Hearts White Minds*. Much of the story is drawn from his personal experiences, interviews, and hundreds of hours of research. He credits his eclectic law practice for a new storyline every few days.

One of Mitch's defining moments came when a *Herald Examiner* editor assigned him to drive to San Fernando Valley so the paper could be the first to report a brushfire, should one start. Aware that San Fernando Valley spans 260 square miles, he interpreted the request as one to *start* a brushfire, so he drove to the Lakers game instead and applied to law school the next morning.

As general counsel to the Missouri Valley Conference, and a former youth coach, Mitch has an insider's view of basketball that enables him to write about it authentically. He's also a member of the Washington University Sports Hall of Fame, at one time holding the school record in just about every baseball statistic. He's proud of his days as a student/athlete, but hasn't lost sight of the fact that you can't get too much farther from Cooperstown and still be in a hall of fame.

CPSIA information can be obtained
at www.ICGtesting.com
Printed in the USA
FFOW03n1738170118
44348416-44066FF